Unreliable Narrator

ALSO BY ARAMINTA HALL

Everything and Nothing

Dot

Our Kind of Cruelty

Imperfect Women

Hidden Depths

One of the Good Guys

Unreliable Narrator

Araminta Hall

MACMILLAN

First published 2026 by Macmillan
an imprint of Pan Macmillan
The Smithson, 6 Briset Street, London EC1M 5NR
EU representative: Macmillan Publishers Ireland Ltd, 1st Floor,
The Liffey Trust Centre, 117–126 Sheriff Street Upper,
Dublin 1 D01 YC43
Associated companies throughout the world

ISBN 978-1-0350-1831-4 HB
ISBN 978-1-0350-1832-1 TPB

Copyright © Araminta Hall 2026

The right of Araminta Hall to be identified as the
author of this work has been asserted in accordance with
the Copyright, Designs and Patents Act 1988.

All rights reserved. No part of this publication may be reproduced,
stored in a retrieval system, or transmitted, in any form, or by any means
(including, without limitation, electronic, mechanical, photocopying, recording
or otherwise) without the prior written permission of the publisher.

Pan Macmillan does not have any control over, or any responsibility for,
any author or third-party websites (including, without limitation, URLs,
emails and QR codes) referred to in or on this book.

1 3 5 7 9 8 6 4 2

A CIP catalogue record for this book is available from the British Library.

Typeset in Goudy Oldstyle Std by Palimpsest Book Production Limited,
Falkirk, Stirlingshire

Printed and bound in the UK using 100% Renewable Electricity by CPI Group (UK) Ltd

This book is sold subject to the condition that it shall not, by way of
trade or otherwise, be lent, hired out, or otherwise circulated without
the publisher's prior consent in any form of binding or cover other than
that in which it is published and without a similar condition including this
condition being imposed on the subsequent purchaser. The publisher does not
authorize the use or reproduction of any part of this book in any manner
for the purpose of training artificial intelligence technologies or systems.
The publisher expressly reserves this book from the Text and Data Mining
exception in accordance with Article 4(3) of the European Union
Digital Single Market Directive 2019/790.

Visit **www.panmacmillan.com** to read more about all our books
and to buy them.

To Jamie, reliably

Part One

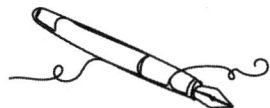

'I suppose I've been wondering what it's like to be damned by the story of your own life.'

The words pulled Hope from sleep in that way where, as she struggled to consciousness, she wasn't entirely sure where she was. The room was dark, apart from the flicker of the television, but she realized quickly that she was lying awkwardly on her own couch in her own lounge. It was, after all, the only place she could have been, considering she never went anywhere else, apart from work. Her neck cricked as she sat up, her mouth already dry and beginning to taste of the familiar decay that came from having drunk too much, too fast.

'Considering the huge, worldwide success of *The Ruined Girl*, did you always plan to write a sequel?' Hope focused her bleary attention on the television, vaguely aware that something consequential was happening, when usually nothing of consequence ever did.

'No, not at all.' Her heart leapt as she registered the second voice, a voice she knew so well it felt almost impossible for it to be outside herself.

'Has it surprised you that it's taken a decade for the story to emerge?'

'Not really. You can't write a sequel, or anything, simply to satisfy the market, however much everyone wants it. You have to wait for a story worth telling.'

Hope dropped to the floor and crawled on her hands and knees, right up to the television. She had avoided him for so long, but how could she be expected to resist when he had appeared, like magic, or maybe a sign, right there in her flat. Rosie crossed his legs loosely and she drank him in. He was still slim and dressed in his favoured cords – a crinkled jacket matching his trousers, an open-necked linen shirt, beaten-up brogues and mismatched socks on his feet. But his hair had greyed and there were many more lines on his face. Lines which felt like arrows, because she hadn't watched them form and they spoke too loudly of experiences she hadn't been part of.

'Nothing really surprises me about story-telling,' he said, smiling so his eyes twinkled and Hope could almost feel the surge of female hormones in the audience.

'Can you tell us what this one's about?'

Rosie ruffled his hair in that abstracted way he had. 'Oh, I guess memory and perspective. You know, versions of the truth, which is all life is, after all.' He paused as Hope held her breath, her heart fast against her ribs. 'The central question I've been pondering in this book is what does it mean to have murdered someone you love? You know, what Teresa did wasn't a mistake; she meant to pull that trigger. But what does that do to a person? How do you live with that knowledge about yourself?'

The bottle of wine she'd drunk that evening rose up Hope's gullet. She slapped her face, but she was awake. Rosie was laughing at something the interviewer had said, but she couldn't hear anything because the blood was thumping too loudly in her ears.

'No!' she shouted at the TV. 'Stop it.' Because how could he be so stupid as to ask that question, like that, out in the open, for everyone to hear? In their final conversation he had begged her not to say anything about what had happened that summer. And she'd kept to her word, wrapping her misery around her like a shroud, driving her mother away, shutting out the world, existing in only the smallest, most fragmentary way. And now here he was, just *saying* it. All to, what, promote a book?

Except that didn't make sense. Rosie's new book appeared to be addressing her life's central question. Her plot.

What does it mean to have murdered someone you love?

But how could that be right if it was a sequel? And what the fuck did that mean *The Ruined Girl* was about?

Hope stood, swaying slightly, and stumbled to her bedroom. The noise of laughter from the television followed her as she knelt by her bed, having to lie on her stomach to reach the box she'd pushed into the furthest corner. The dust tickled her nose as she pulled it out, making her eyes water. She sat back on her heels and lifted the lid, which made her stomach contract again as she looked at the contents: a delicate china bowl with a swirling pattern of roses winding down its interior, *The Ruined Girl* and a battered black hardbacked notebook. She selected the bowl first, but even after all these years it was still charged with memories of Shadowlands, so the place rushed through her, weakening every muscle. But she forced herself on, picking up *The Ruined Girl* and flicking through the pages. Perhaps the time had come to read to it? The thought was scary, although not as terrifying as the words contained in the notebook.

Hope let *The Ruined Girl* slide to the floor as she reached for her journal, laying it on her lap for a moment before daring to turn the first page. It wasn't a book she had ever intended to open again. In fact, the whole box was not something she would have imagined revisiting. But Rosie had ambushed her and what was she supposed to do?

She cracked the cover and saw on the first page, in her own rounded handwriting: *Shadowlands, June 2016*. She tried to focus on the curlicues she'd drawn around the letters, little childlike flowers sprouting from the large S. But it was all too late; already she could feel herself being pulled backwards as if there was a rope around her waist. She shut her eyes and immediately they were all there, her and Tom and Rosie and Delia, sitting round the terrace table, the long lawn stretching away in front, the house rising majestically behind and the heat of the sun beating into their bones. A little cry escaped as she opened her eyes again, because she had been so careful, doing everything she could to banish the memories. She'd locked away anything that led back to Shadowlands – been careful with the news, banned music, films and novels from her life, discarded friends and driven away her own mother. While always keeping enough wine on hand to blot away anything sticky.

Hope looked back down at the book in her hand. It felt suddenly very foolish to have ever imagined that she could outrun the past. And besides, maybe it didn't even make sense. Pretending something hadn't happened didn't make it go away. Maybe she had always been who she was and, one way or another, with or without Rosie and Shadowlands, she would have always been someone capable of murder. She turned to the first entry and, like a cannibal, began to feed on her own words.

8 June

It's been only three days since I arrived at Shadowlands and it already feels almost unbelievable that I haven't lived here my whole life. How did I not know this place existed? I have begun again – ta-da! – reborn like a religious experience. When I duck my head under the water in the swimming pool it is a baptism. I am becoming my true self.

It's too simple to say that I've never been anywhere that comes close to Shadowlands before, because that would be true for most people – one of those places most of us will only ever see on TV. It reminds me of a giant's crown, built from honey-coloured stone that shines like gold, long and sumptuous, with a row of urn-like structures running along the top. I like what they call the back of the house best, although to me it's the front as it's what you see when you first drive up. It's covered by a magnificently twisted plant, with thousands of elegant, almond-shaped leaves, and these incredible dripping purple flowers that look almost decadent, or not real somehow (I thought it was a type of vine but apparently it's called a wisteria). Anyway, whatever its name, it's managed to extend itself impressively, only leaving gaps for the windows and three massive sets of

French doors. These doors open onto a stone terrace, where you can step down to a long lawn that runs down to the woods. Romantically planted borders wider than our lounge at home are dotted everywhere and neatly trimmed hedges hide a vegetable garden and even a swimming pool. But this place is more than a definition of beauty. I can't put my finger on it yet, but there's something in the air, a sense of promise or abandon that feels as dangerous as it is exhilarating.

On the train here I felt overcome by a strange sense of newness; it felt a bit like a premonition, as if I realized that Shadowlands is going to be where I can clear my mistakes and launch myself afresh. I am twenty-three years old and that means I have so much in front of me, so much time to be a different, better person than I am now. Life doesn't come looking for us: we have to find our moment, and this has to be mine.

I'm done with waiting tables, holding my breath for some man (why do I always think it's going to be a man?) to thrust his business card at me and say that I have the exact star quality he's been looking for. Done, for that matter, with men who wouldn't know the truth if it hit them square in the face. Done with doing nothing about my dreams.

Which isn't to say that I don't also feel scared. My mind keeps flashing back to the way Mum cried as I walked through the barriers at the station. How her face collapsed in on itself like a piece of paper being scrunched. It made everything feel unreal, like I was enacting a scene from a film. Because in some ways the situation was, maybe still is, absurd. I am here by chance – an advert seen just over a fortnight ago in a magazine that Mum brought home from work – *Live-in secretary wanted for novelist. Generous salary. Based in Somerset.*

She had shown it to me before she even took off her jacket, tripping over her words as she told me it was a wonderful opportunity, which of course it is, but I think her real motive was to get me out of London and away from all the mistakes of the past few years. I know Mum has aspirations for me – college, a faithful boyfriend, a good job with prospects. But all those traditional things have always felt too constricting, so sometimes I can't catch my breath with the thought of a steady life like that. When I told my careers tutor at school that I wanted to write novels she actually laughed, countering by asking if I'd thought of nursing, or maybe working with children, perhaps office work. And in a way she was right: I have no idea how to actually become a writer. I once read an interview with a very successful novelist in which she said all that mattered was the story. But I don't even have a good one of those. Which is maybe why I bought this notebook before I left and why I'm writing in it now. Perhaps I'm looking for my story?

'And you're so pretty,' Delia said at one point in our strange phone interview, which made me laugh sharply. 'Sorry,' she said, 'I hope you don't mind. I made a special trip to the village to stalk your Instagram before I called. I always think seeing someone is so important, it gives you such a sense of who they are.'

I blushed at the thought of her looking at my usually blurry photos of neon-lit nights out and sweaty faces pressed too close together. God, that one of me in a T-shirt and pants in my bedroom mirror. And all the travelling clichés of sunsets and cocktails and nearly naked boys.

'You simply have to say yes,' Delia said in her languidly posh voice that almost works like a trance. 'We've been looking for ages and ages and you are too perfect to let slip through our fingers.'

And then she started talking about Rosie. Rosie this, Rosie that, until my mind spun with the thought of her writing away and making a living from it. Idiot! I can't believe I thought Rosie was a woman.

I meant to find Rosie's novels in the library, but the week before leaving was so busy, what with my last shifts and saying goodbye to everyone. And then that awful scene with Dexter's wife. I still can't wrap my head around the fact that he's married. Oh God, thinking about our mortifying slanging match, in front of all the customers, makes me want to hide under a bed for a year. It wasn't even me and her who should have been fighting... I wish I'd been calmer, and pointed out how I couldn't be a home-wrecker when I hadn't known he had a home to wreck. Moving forward I need to summon those lines quicker, not think them up after the opportunity to say them has passed.

Delia met my train and, as there was only one person on the tiny platform, I knew she had to be the woman shielding her eyes from the sun as she peered into the slowing carriages. Everyone in my carriage, probably on the whole train, turned to look at her. Three days of constant Delia hasn't reduced her impact. I'm not sure I've ever seen anyone up close who is both as pretty and sexy as she is. Her features are so fine, her cheekbones so high, her eyes so green, her attitude so bloody nonchalant. She always looks like she should be walking down a Parisian catwalk because her clothes are stylish in a very relaxed way. Genuinely, I'd say she's as gorgeous as any film star.

That first day she was dressed in a loose white cotton shirt with rolled-up sleeves, tucked into a long red skirt printed with little birds. A brown suede belt was wrapped around her trim waist and lots of silver bracelets jangled up her arm. Her blonde hair was piled up under a battered straw hat and she had flip-flops on her feet revealing chipped red nail varnish. As I wheeled my suitcase towards her I was filled with a bursting sense of pride that she was there for me, while also feeling foolish in the smart white dress and sandals Mum and I had spent hours deciding would be the best outfit to arrive in.

She led me out to the car park, where we got into a very surprising car. A battered Ford Escort with half the back number plate missing and the inside festooned with rubbish – food packets and paint brushes, old newspapers, broken CDs, even two china mugs. Delia crammed my case into the boot, brimming with wellington boots, more newspapers and an oil painting with a huge gash across it.

We left the village, Willerton Banks, behind quickly, soon on country lanes bordered by lush hedges and towering cow parsley, with thick white heads like wide lace petticoats. We both wound down our windows and hot air flooded the car. I kept sneaking glances at Delia as she drove, one arm dangling out of the window and the other barely touching the steering wheel. She wasn't wearing a scrap of make-up and had a line of reddened skin across the bridge of her nose. And she drove with an exhilarating abandon, too fast and too near the middle of the road. She must be about the same age as Mum, who I've always thought of as a very youthful forty-four, but Delia's youthfulness is more than that. It isn't simply her appearance, she also speaks like my friends, jumping from one topic to the next, as if she's interested in and eager to know everything, as if everything could be exciting if you just give it a chance.

After about twenty minutes we turned off the road and drove between two crumbling pillars holding up rusty-looking iron gates. The car jolted against the pot holes Delia refused to slow down for and branches from the overhanging trees brushed the roof. But then we turned a corner and the house came into view, and nothing else seemed relevant.

I must have made a sound of appreciation because Delia laughed and said, 'Yes, Shadowlands does have that effect on most people.'

'It's so beautiful, Mrs Glencourt,' I said, as we climbed out of the car, although the words were inadequate. The air struck me immediately – soft and fragrant, so sometimes just breathing here feels like drinking some sort of health elixir. Two large Labradors bounded out of the already-open front door and jumped up at me, their big paws heavy against my stomach.

'Down, Sheba. Down, Clem,' Delia shouted and they obeyed immediately.

Delia went to the boot and hauled out my suitcase, which made me so embarrassed I tried to take it from her, but she waved me away.

As I followed I saw she'd left the keys in the ignition, but when I pointed it out she just laughed and said, 'Oh no, don't worry. I always leave them in the ignition. I'm a terrible scatterbrain and I'd lose them if I didn't.' I barely had time to process that before she said, 'Also, for God's sake, call me Delia and Rosie, Rosie. Mr and Mrs Glencourt were his parents and, quite frankly, shoot me if I ever become one of them.'

'Mr Glencourt?' I said, as I followed her through the door.

'He's working,' she said, not noticing my confusion. 'You'll meet him later at supper.'

(Can't believe I didn't work it out then. Life has taught me a fair amount of street smarts, but Shadowlands immediately knocked them out of me, so I have spent the past few days feeling like a wide-eyed innocent, blindly feeling my way through situations without my usual bearings.)

The hall at Shadowlands would take up half our flat: huge, generous stones on the floor and a round table in the centre, on which there's a large green stone vase which is always filled with tall wild flowers from the garden. Delia kicked her flip-flops into a corner, underneath a row of hooks, off which were hanging silk scarves, battered straw baskets and stiff mackintoshes. That first day I didn't know if I was meant to remove my shoes as well, but it felt too personal, so I kept them on, although for the past couple of days I haven't even put them on in the morning. Delia never has shoes on her feet, the only concession the flip-flops for driving. The soles of my feet have already hardened and the cracks filled with a dark dirt that I doubt I will ever be able to fully wash away. I wonder if hers are the same or if her skin magically cleans itself – I suspect the latter.

An elderly woman appeared from behind the large stone staircase which dominates the hall, fanning out at the top like there are so many places to go.

'Mrs A,' Delia cried, as if she was welcoming a long-lost relative. 'This is Hope.'

The very round woman was holding a duster and bottle of cleaner, which she put on the table. 'Let me get your suitcase,' she said.

'Oh no,' I spluttered. 'I can manage.'

A tense silence filled the air and the woman narrowed her eyes at me. I now suspect that Mrs A isn't my biggest fan, and I wonder if that first moment was when she decided to dislike me? Not that I know what I did wrong. Although, what just three days here has taught me is that this life has a lot of unspoken rules. Rosie and Delia act like everything is always fine and inconsequential, a breeziness to all their interactions that lulls you into thinking everything is completely relaxed. But actually I can see that there are numerous complex rules – it's just that they know exactly the right words to say, exactly how to hold their bodies, exactly what's important or not. But it's fine, I'm a quick study.

Delia broke the atmosphere by picking up my suitcase herself and making for the stairs, saying over her shoulder, 'Hope is Rosie's new secretary.'

Mrs A bobbed her head. 'I gathered as much.' I rushed after Delia, trying to take my case from her, but she batted me away, even though I could see the strain on her face. We went all the way to the top floor, where eight doors lead off a bright landing wallpapered in a busy green pattern. She opened the door at the furthest end and we walked into a large room with sloping ceilings and wonky beams. I am writing this in that room now, sat on the cane chair pulled up to the old-fashioned desk, with one of those pull-down tops and lots of little compartments for letters and pens and secrets – a Jane Austen desk as I've come to think of it. When I look up I can glance out of one of the three windows, each one revealing breath-taking views of woods and rolling hills and even a glinting river. It feels impossible that I will fail to write something worthwhile here.

'The bathroom is just across the landing,' Delia said. 'And

we've turned the next-door bedroom into a sort of sitting room for you. We even got Pete to rig up a TV, although I'm not sure what the reception's like. Rosie hates the television, you see, so we don't have one downstairs.' When I didn't answer she went on, 'It's just you up here. Well, usually it's just Rosie and me in the whole house. Tom's staying with us at the moment, but he's on the floor below so you won't be disturbed.'

She was talking like I'd booked a room in a hotel, or was a guest who already knew who everyone was. I couldn't think of an adequate response, just stammering out something inane about how beautiful it was.

She looked round the room like she was only seeing it properly for the first time, before she laughed lightly. 'Anyway, you must be exhausted after that journey. Why don't you settle in and then come join us for a swim? Come and find me when you're ready and I'll show you the pool.' She made for the door, but stopped as she reached it. 'Oh, and if you hear buzzing from the cupboard in the sitting room, don't open it. I don't think it's their time right now, but there's been a hornet's nest in there for years.'

Once she'd gone I lay on the bed, which feels like what I imagine it would if you slept on a cloud. It's dressed in gorgeous pale yellow linen with a blue quilt along the bottom, embroidered with tiny flowers. I tried to call Mum, but could only get one bar of service, wherever I stood in the room. I gave up after a while and unpacked, ladling my clothes into a tall chest of drawers, on which someone had placed a small vase of the same flowers as were in the hall and a beautiful mirror inlaid with a mosaic of broken tiles. The floor is stripped bare and tilts down to the left, which makes me feel quite off-balance, but I'm sure I'll get used to it.

After that I investigated the bathroom, where I immediately fell for the wonky tiles and old-fashioned bath, a line of rust running along the enamel underneath each tap. The sitting room is just as stunning – the walls covered in dreamy paintings and all the furniture comfy and relaxed-looking, as if the chairs are longing for you to lounge on them. But it was the two books on a low table in front of the sofa that immediately drew my attention, *Unforgiven* and *The Last Day of Autumn*, both by Ambrose Glencourt. I worked it out then – Ambrose, Rosie. I don't know if it's embarrassing that I haven't heard of him, but I'm pretty sure I would have done if he's well-known. I flicked the book over and took a first look at him – a black and white photo of a striking man, his face cast in deep shadows. Even then, I realized it made the situation much more interesting.

Of course I also opened the hornet cupboard. I held my ear up against it, listening for buzzing, and then opened it very slowly, my breath coming fast, images of large, winged beasts rushing out and digging their stingers into me. But it was impossible to imagine that I wouldn't have, that I'd have left the possibility there. The cupboard is shallow and smells dusty, but there were no buzzing hornets. Although the floor is littered with their dead bodies in various states of decay. I prodded the mound with my foot, emboldened by the thought of the damage they could do if they were alive. They were even bigger than I thought they would be, their bodies curled into commas, their perfect stripes, the mean ends of their tails. Some of them had turned almost entirely white, ghostly shells of themselves on the very verge of disintegrating. I shut the door and pushed a chair up against it.

After I put away my clothes and arranged my cosmetics, I dug out my swimming costume and put it on, trying to work out what I looked like in the mosaic mirror. I bought it online just a few weeks ago, so pleased with its bright colouring and fancy straps, but even on that first day I could sense how wrong it was for Shadowlands. I slipped a sundress over it and found the straw sandals I bought in a market in Greece – thank God I packed them.

When I got downstairs the house was still and quiet and I had no sense of where to go. The safest bet seemed to be to look where Mrs A had come from, so I followed the passage behind the stairs that leads to a large open kitchen. The same stones on the floor, a mismatch of cupboards with checked material instead of doors, a large old wooden dresser groaning under the weight of china, an AGA puffing away and a large wooden table in the middle surrounded by an assortment of chairs.

Mrs A came in carrying a basket of washing and we both jumped slightly.

'Oh, hello, Mrs A . . .' I hesitated as it seemed like an intimate nickname.

'Mrs Allard,' she said, 'but call me Mrs A, everyone does. It's because of Mrs B.'

'Mrs B?'

'Yes, Mrs Buckle. She does the cooking and I do the cleaning. So Mrs Glencourt likes to call us Mrs A and B.'

I can't work out why they call Delia Mrs Glencourt, but she's asked me to call her Delia? And why she calls them by their surnames, well, sort-of surnames, but me by my first name? I hope it's because she's seen something in me that means I'm not simply going to be an employee. Already I want to be more integral to the life here than that.

I gave a little laugh, unsure whether or not it was funny, and asked where Delia was.

Mrs A motioned with her eyes to the back door.

I went through the door as Mrs A started to get out the ironing board. Sure enough, I could see Delia on the lawn throwing a ball for a selection of dogs. The two Labradors were there, along with a whippet, a small spaniel of some type and a terrier that wouldn't stop barking. I walked out to join her.

'Hope,' Delia trilled as soon as she saw me. 'You must meet the pack.'

The closer I got the more excited the dogs became, the terrier jumping so high he often had no feet at all on the ground. 'So you've met Sheba and Clem,' Delia said, pointing at the Labradors. 'This is Willow, Daisy and Jack.' She clapped her hands, which set them all off barking in a way that made me too aware that they were nothing more than animals. 'So now, to swim.'

She started walking towards a tall hedge over to the left of the garden and the dogs rushed after her, so I did the same. We slipped through an artfully cut out opening, emerging into a picture-perfect scene – a glittering turquoise pool surrounded by the same honey-coloured slabs of stone as have built the house, with huge urns filled with brightly coloured flowers on each corner and wooden loungers running along the edge. Of course it's incredible, but I know now that the pool doesn't quite live up to its first impression. It's always covered in bugs, so swimming in it involves negotiating lots of little corpses. And no one ever takes in the towels that are draped over the loungers, which means they're stiff and scrape your skin. Also, at the far end, hidden in the hedge, is a moss-mottled statue of a woman weeping, which seems like an odd choice for somewhere designed for relaxation; I try not to look at her too closely.

'Now, I swim in the morning, before breakfast,' Delia said. 'And Rosie can't stand water, either inside or outside of him, so never comes here. Really you must swim whenever you feel like it. Sometimes I can't bear to think of the pool going unused. I almost feel sorry for it.'

I couldn't find the words to answer, couldn't even drag my eyes away from the sight. Delia clapped her hands again, making me jump. 'Come on, dogs, let's leave Hope to swim in peace.' She turned just before she went through the gap in the hedge. 'God knows when dinner will be. Rosie writes in the afternoon, so we just wait and see when he finishes. I'll give you a shout when we're going to have a drink and then you can finally meet him.'

The whole pool scenario was too good not to share, and I knew some of my friends would get a kick out of a FaceTime from somewhere that bougie, so asked for the Wi-Fi code. But the request made her frown and she shook her head as if I'd said something rude.

'Oh no, we don't have Wi-Fi.' She took a step back towards me. 'Rosie thinks the internet is the end of civilization, even though it's 2016 and the internet has been around for years and I'm yet to see any sort of societal collapse. Although I do also see his point. I mean, wouldn't it be boring to know everything about everyone. And I certainly don't want anyone to know everything about me.' She laughed. 'None of us have mobiles here, although I've been told by friends that you can get a good signal by the gate. But feel free to use the house phone any time, no need to ask.'

I mumbled some inanity about how a detox would be good for me, while really wondering what I will do without access to everything my friends are doing. I felt suddenly very cut off, unsettlingly so.

9 June

I presume because I wrote all that before going to sleep, I dreamt about that first supper last night. We were eating a still-beating heart and Rosie and Delia had a horrible row, screaming at each other across the table.

Mum has a book of dreams at home, and I don't think you need to be Freud to interpret that as an anxiety one. Which I guess isn't totally surprising because, despite my joy at being here, I don't yet feel entirely at home. Rosie makes me nervous – I can feel my heart clench in his presence and I'm always desperate to think of exactly the right thing to say (not that I've come close yet).

I want to please him so much. Even more than that I want him to see something special in me.

Is there something special in me?

In the end, it was after nine when I met Rosie on the first evening. I'd swum and lain by the pool for a bit, taking a few photos for a time when I have service again, then went in and showered, which was more challenging than it sounds. There are no showers here and instead all the baths have these odd plastic sort of hoses that you attach to the taps, mostly unsuccessfully, and not one of them is long enough. But, for some reason, it doesn't irritate me like it would at home. After that I spent an agonizing twenty minutes trying to find a suitable outfit. Mum and I had spent ages discussing what people like the Glencourts might wear, we even wondered if they could dress for dinner, like they do in *Downton Abbey*. In the end I opted for a slightly smarter sundress than the one I'd worn to the pool and tamed my curls into a bun at the nape of my neck. I longed to call Mum to ask her advice, but I wasn't going to walk all the way to the gate, and I felt too shy to go downstairs and find a telephone. Thinking of Mum alone in our little flat, maybe settling down for a bit of TV on her own, made my throat feel sore and tight.

I was ready by seven and then sat on my bed reading Rosie's novel, *Unforgiven*. I've finished it now, and it's unlike anything I've ever read before. His words snake across the page like a work of art, and I still feel shocked by his genius. If I could have one wish, it would be to make language work in that way, as if it belongs to me and I can bend it to my will. It makes me want to make a real effort with this journal, to not just find a story here, but to make it sing.

At eight I wondered if they'd forgotten about me. I went to listen on the landing, but the house was so quiet I didn't dare go downstairs, so went back to my room. And then I must have fallen asleep, because I was woken by Delia shouting that it was supper time. Everything about the day, combined with being pulled out of sleep, made the descent through the wide, portrait-lined stairways of Shadowlands feel dreamy and unreal, as if my feet might sink through the polished floors and take me on to the other side.

I could hear them in the kitchen when I reached the hall, Rosie's loud, languid voice saying, 'Oh God, not another of Mrs B's pies.'

And Delia replying, 'You always say how much you like them.'

'Yes, but not every bloody night.'

'It's hardly every night. And I've made a salad.'

I hesitated at the end of the passage, not wanting to interrupt an argument, but then Rosie laughed and said, 'Well, at least we can count on Pete for nutrition.'

I stood in the doorway for a moment before anyone noticed me. Delia was struggling with getting the pie out of the AGA and a man I assumed to be Rosie was sitting at the table with his back to the door, smoking a cigarette. Delia turned with the hot pie and I was relieved to see she hadn't changed into different clothes – if anything, she looked even more dishevelled than earlier. Her belt had been discarded, her hair had escaped its band so it was wild around her face and a streak of something which could have been dirt was smudged across one cheek.

'Hope!' she exclaimed as she set the pie on the table, as if my presence was a complete surprise, so I momentarily wondered if I was actually meant to be there. But then she waved me forward, as she said, 'Please, come and sit down.'

Rosie turned as I made my way to a chair opposite him. He made me blush instantly because he's as striking as the photograph on his book suggested. The same high, wide cheekbones as Delia, bright eyes and a mass of thick, scruffy black hair that he has a habit of constantly ruffling. His skin is pale and his eyes deep-set, but his smile is wide and generous. He also dresses in the same way as Delia – natural fabrics that look like they've never seen an iron, sleeves rolled up, fraying cuffs on his trousers. Although, in contrast to Delia's bare feet, he was wearing socks and battered lace-up brogues. In fact, I've not yet seen him out of his shoes and socks, even though the weather is very warm. 'The wondrous Hope,' he said. 'Would you like a glass of wine?'

I was unsure how I was supposed to respond, but accepted because I really did want one.

'Good girl,' he said as he stood, which allowed me to see how tall and thin he is, his limbs extending from him like string. He went to a wooden cupboard painted a bright green, with glass panels in the door, where hundreds of glasses glinted, a type for every occasion. I scanned the room quickly, but it made me feel a little dizzy. Things are piled everywhere in the kitchen, all over the dresser and on every surface. Stacks of magazines, a strange pile of woollen hats, boxes of paint, a vase filled with hairbrushes. Keys and ribbons and even strings of beads dangle off the dresser hooks and photographs and postcards (not holiday ones, but works of art) are wedged into every picture frame or balanced against mugs and plates propped up on shelves. It's not even especially clean – dust on the shelves, cobwebs in corners and the china on the dresser is slightly greasy to the touch.

Rosie sat back down and folded his legs over each other in a strangely feminine way as he placed a normal wine glass in front of me and poured a red wine so luxuriously thick it left a mark as it ran down the side.

'Sorry we're eating late,' he said in the same way Delia had spoken to me earlier, as if I was a guest. 'You must have thought we'd forgotten all about you. Mea culpa. I got totally carried away this afternoon.'

Delia started to ladle the pie onto plates. They were mismatched, mine was even chipped, which would have made Mum blanch. 'Rosie is terrible with time. He doesn't like clocks.'

'It is so bloody tedious, though, isn't it,' Rosie said as he began to fork the steaming pie into his mouth in large, ungainly gulps. 'Makes you too damn aware of your mortality.'

I instinctively looked down at Rosie and Delia's wrists, then glanced round the room. I have since checked and there are indeed no clocks in the whole house, and no one wears a watch. And of course, no one carries a phone around with them – I've even taken to leaving mine in my bedroom, which felt very strange at first, but now I can really see the appeal. Maybe this is actually just what I need – a break from constant useless information and messy nights out and hours lost to social media. Maybe my imagination will fire?

'So, it's just us three this evening,' Delia said, 'which is lovely, because it gives us a proper chance to get to know you, Hope.'

'Where's Tom?' Rosie asked.

'He didn't bring enough medication, so's had to go back to Ridgeview. But just for a day or so.' She turned to me. 'You'll meet him soon.'

It was the second time she'd mentioned Tom, so I asked if he was their son.

She shrieked with laughter. 'Oh goodness, no, I don't have any children.'

'Although you could almost call him our honorary son, he's here so much,' Rosie said.

'I volunteer at a drugs rehabilitation centre,' Delia said, leaning across the table. 'And I met Tom there, goodness, ten years ago now, when he was just fifteen. He's had a hard life, poor lamb, but he's absolutely brilliant. So kind and funny and warm. And he has no family to speak of. Like Rosie said, we sort of took him under our wing and he does stay with us quite a bit.'

'My wife is a bona fide saint,' Rosie said, winking at me. I looked over at Delia and she did look like someone good, serenity pouring from her as she smiled down at her plate.

Rosie pointed his fork at me. 'Now, Hope, tonight you are being treated to a Mrs B speciality. Rabbit pie. Which, by the way, you'd better get used to, as she is a woman of the fifties.'

'Oh, Rosie,' Delia said. 'She's an angel.'

Mum and I had also speculated on the food I might eat here. We'd fantasized about caviar and smoked salmon, champagne and roasted pheasant, but a few days here has felt like reverting to childhood. The Glencourts like bland, comforting food – baked potatoes and cold meats, fish fingers and white bread, cream and jam.

'It's delicious,' I said.

Rosie laughed. 'So, Hope, apart from being a terrible liar, tell us all about yourself.' The request was so frightening, my mind went completely blank in that way where you can barely remember your own name. 'Well,' I stammered. 'I live in Kilburn in London with my mum.'

'Just your mother?' Rosie asked. 'No dad? No siblings?'

Delia had asked me all of that in my phone interview, but I repeated myself. 'No, just the two of us.'

'And what do you like to do?'

My body heated. 'Um, well, I like reading, obviously. And travelling.'

'Oh God,' Rosie said in a way that made my stomach clench. 'Don't tell me you're one of those people who likes to lie on a beach for two weeks.'

I do, or at least I did, like to lie on beaches. The thought of doing that now already seems a bit pointless. But that evening I made do with lying. 'Well, no, I more meant, you know, seeing a place a bit.'

'Where have you been?'

'Nowhere far, it's too expensive, although I'd like to. One day I'd love to go to Japan. I got back from a month in Greece a while ago.'

'So you do that backpacking stuff.' Rosie mimed hitching a lift with his thumb. He pushed his finished plate away and immediately lit a cigarette.

'Yes.' I tried to force a bit more pie down. Delia, I noticed, had only eaten salad and was sitting back in her chair sipping at her wine. We never have salad at home, but at Shadowlands it's the one healthy food they eat and it's served at every meal, the dressing always potent, laced with garlic and sharp vinegar.

Rosie pointed his cigarette at me. 'Jolly good. If you have to go abroad, it's the only way to travel, to actually see the damn place.'

He smiled in a way that made me feel like I'd said exactly the right thing, which spun my head slightly. I took a sip of wine and tasted blackberries and headaches.

'Holidays are one of modern life's more terrible inventions,' he said. 'Now, if I could do a grand tour like Shelley I might be up for it, but all that two weeks on the Costa fucking Brava is insane. They say it's relaxing but that's bollocks because it's impossible for anywhere to be as relaxing as home.' He turned to Delia. 'Anyway, why would we want to go anywhere. Nowhere's as beautiful as Shadowlands, is it, darling?'

She smiled. 'No, nowhere in the world.' Which is a totally correct statement. I already know that if I were to go anywhere ever again it would never match up.

'Was the clay good to you this afternoon?' Rosie said, addressing his wife now.

Delia nodded. 'It's coming along.'

'Has Delly told you about her hobby?' he asked, turning back to me.

I glanced at Delia again, but she was looking at Rosie. 'No, I don't think so.'

'I dabble in pottery,' she said, finally looking at me. 'Just for fun.'

The mark on her cheek made sense then.

'Anyway,' Delia said, 'you must be exhausted, Hope. We've kept you up far too late.'

'Now,' Rosie said, 'we'll start work next Monday, so don't worry about getting up early tomorrow. Give you a chance to settle in to the place.'

In fact, it's had the opposite effect. I really don't like all this loitering around, doing nothing.

I started to clear the plates, but Delia put a hand on my arm. 'No, no, please don't worry about that. Just get yourself some rest.'

It felt very odd to walk away from a messy table. Mum and I always clean our kitchen straight after eating because she says it's too depressing to be faced with dirty dishes before work. I thought of Mum washing up alone and it made me desperate to speak to her, except I didn't know if the invitation to use the phone extended to all times of the day and night. As I walked back to the stairs I did peer into a couple of rooms to see if I could see one, but they intimidated me too much to go in. But yesterday I forced myself to be braver and did a bit of exploring. They have an actual library and a formal dining room where you could sit fifty people, I reckon. Delia has a bloody letter-writing room! And, at the back of the house, behind the kitchen there are a series of pantries with these ridiculously tall cupboards that hold acres of silverware and glass jugs and dinner services so large they could feed hundreds of people.

And the gardens are huge. They don't just have the terrace and the lawn and the swimming pool and the vegetable garden; there's also a wood with a stream in it, which Delia has a studio at the edge of, and there's a huge stone wall which runs around the whole place and near the gate is a sort of derelict barn/mini house which is apparently called a gatehouse.

But that night I simply climbed the stairs back to my room. As I crossed to the bathroom I heard David Bowie downstairs invoking Major Tom and the bark of Rosie's laughter. The sound thrilled me because Mum and I can't play music late at night and always have to turn the TV down because our walls are thin and our neighbour bangs if he hears even the slightest sound. I got into bed and looked at the moonlight shimmering on the ceiling in thick strips. An owl hooted outside and my body felt light. Geographically speaking I have been much further away, but that first night I don't think I've ever felt as far from home.

10 June

Managed to find a phone and call Mum, who annoyed me by asking a million questions that felt intrusive. How crazy that I should feel like that. Wouldn't I be more annoyed if she wasn't interested? I guess it's just that Shadowlands already feels a little like a secret world. It's not that I couldn't describe it – I mean, hello notebook – more that I don't want to give any of it away until I'm ready.

11 June

Met Tom at supper last night. He seems nice, around my age, very tall and dark, with skin that has taken on an almost reddish-brown colour from the sun. He speaks with one of those musical Bristol accents, and I'm impressed by how well he keeps up with Rosie's conversation, which is often provocative or esoteric. I'm not sure Rosie means everything he says; I think it's more that he entertains himself by making people feel uncomfortable. Last night we hadn't been sat down for more than five minutes before he squirted salad cream over his cold ham and caught my eye, saying, 'Don't judge. I have a terrible weakness for things I shouldn't like.'

'It's because of your upbringing,' Delia said. 'If you're denied affection at a young age, it makes you reckless.'

Rosie laughed. 'Or it's all predetermined. It is simply who I am.'

'I think I have an addictive personality,' Tom said. 'I would have been who I am however I'd been brought up.'

'Oh no,' Delia said. 'That's awful to think that we're all born who we are. No hope of redemption.'

'Born bad, that's me,' Tom said. He smiled, but it didn't reach his eyes.

Rosie forked a huge piece of ham into his mouth and spoke before he'd finished it. 'I hate how humans always want to explain themselves. The truth is none of us have the first fucking clue who we are. Everything we do is just a series of steps in our lives, informed by what's gone before, the things we've seen and heard, the quality of our education, the views of our parents, the laws of our land, etcetera, et-bloody-cetera. We like to think we're special, but we're not.'

'Well, I like to believe you can be more than your collection of cells or the things that happen to you,' Delia said, her eyes on her plate.

'That's because you're a fundamentally good person,' Rosie replied. 'Whereas I'm not.'

Conversations here often make me feel heady, as if my brain has suddenly become hungry, aware of all the knowledge that exists out there, all the things I don't know. I couldn't even decide if it was better to be like Delia and fundamentally good, or like Rosie, and fundamentally not. I suppose I would plump for whichever made you more interesting and, in truth, aren't the devils more exciting than the angels?

But then Rosie turned to me. 'What say you, Hope? Do you come down on the side of nature or nurture?'

The idea of expressing, or even forming, an opinion in their presence felt insane. I would have happily agreed with anything any of them said, but they were all looking expectantly in my direction. 'Of course I think we're products of our environment,' I said in the end, just before the silence became uncomfortable. 'But also, who we are has to mean something. I mean, I've certainly done things outside what might have been expected of me.'

Rosie nodded and Tom smiled at me. 'Good point,' he said, 'although for me, some might say I've done exactly what was expected.'

He was wearing a T-shirt, which meant I could easily see the red scars on the inside of his arms. Delia said she met him at a drug rehabilitation centre, so it doesn't take a genius to work it all out. Of course, my friends and I have dabbled with soft drugs, but I've never met anyone who had taken heroin. I've always thought of people who do as addicts, dangerous and sordid. But I can see now what a simplistic and judgemental way that is to think. Rosie's right, surely none of us knows exactly who we are, which also must mean it's stupid to judge anyone on anything they've done unless you know everything about them, which in turn is impossible. I want to shake my brain clear of itself. To scrub it clean and start again.

12 June

Delia wandered in when I was reading by the swimming pool this afternoon. She did it in a casual way, but I had the sense that she'd wanted to find me. She sat on a lounger next to mine and the dogs flopped on the hot stones by her feet.

'So, you're starting work tomorrow,' she said, leaning back and tilting her face to the sun.

When I said I was looking forward to it, she tipped her face towards me. 'Goodness, you really are very pretty, aren't you? And your body is fantastic. Photos don't do you justice.'

I half laughed, wanting to cover myself with a towel or put my sundress back on. I didn't know if I should thank her, even though I didn't actually want to.

'Rosie hates ugliness,' she said. 'He finds it affronting, says it gives him a headache. So, obviously, I have to make sure anyone who works for him is up to par, so to speak. Which was why I checked your Instagram before we spoke. But, honestly, you're much better in the flesh. I mean, you're almost irresistible.'

I sat forward and drew my legs up to my chest, embarrassed to be in my swimming costume, lounging by her pool. Embarrassed by my whole physicality and the attention it was receiving.

I'm often confused by remarks like that – do I like them or don't I? The male waiters at work were always commenting on what they'd like to do to various celebrities, sometimes even the female waiting staff. Part of me knew it was wrong and part of me was almost flattered. And Delia obviously wasn't saying it in a lewd way or meaning to make me feel uneasy. It's almost refreshing to have a woman notice me in that way – I don't think it's ever happened before and there was something thrilling about it.

'Rosie is a funny fish. He can be very . . .' Her gaze vaulted over my head, as if she was looking for the right word. 'Well, confusing, I suppose.' She looked back at me. 'I wouldn't want you to take anything he says too seriously.'

I genuinely couldn't think of the right thing to say and every option felt wrong, so I just made a strange spluttering noise.

But she carried on. 'That's the thing about geniuses. Their brains work in a different way to ours. So much faster. They understand things that you and I never will. Which is of course totally fantastic, but can be difficult for the rest of us mere mortals.' She laughed. 'It's obviously very important that you do what he says, but also, well, you must remember to keep doing the right thing. And then you won't go wrong.'

I wanted to ask what the hell she meant, but was, once more, terrified of sounding stupid.

'We're putting a lot of faith in you,' she said, smiling, as if we were two friends having a casual chat. 'This is such a great opportunity and I wouldn't want anything to jeopardize that for you.'

It felt like I had already disappointed her in some way. 'Nor would I.'

'Well, that's excellent then.' Delia stood, but stayed looking down at me for a moment in a way that made me want to cover the top of my head. 'I have this feeling that you're going to work out just wonderfully, Hope.'

13 June

The conversation I had with Delia woke me early, so I lay in bed fretting for two hours before I had to get up, and then felt so jittery as I was getting dressed, I whacked my hip on an open drawer. I bruise easily, and when I came up here after lunch a greying discolouration was already forming on my skin. Rosie told me he's going to write this afternoon, but does that mean we've finished work? It's only two thirty and we've already had lunch, which means they're paying me quite a good salary for about three hours' work. Not entirely sure what to do with myself. Would it be rude to go to the pool?

I actually wish I was going back to Rosie's study, even though Delia is right and he is confusing. But I have to get used to it; like cold water, I have the feeling that immersing myself is the only answer.

He was sitting at his desk when I went in this morning, his feet propped up on it and crossed at the ankles. I felt immediately claustrophobic, but I think that was more to do with the fact that every wall is lined with floor-to-ceiling shelves stuffed with more books than most book shops, no order to anything, the books haphazard, many on their sides or resting on top of others.

The floor around Rosie's desk is also covered with stacks of books, yellowing newspapers and magazines. Even the desk itself is a mess of papers broken only by an ancient typewriter, a brass lamp with a green glass shade, an old dial telephone and a chipped vase stuffed with pens.

The first thing he said, still in his nonchalant position, was, 'So tell me, Hope, why are you doing this?' He must have seen my confusion because he swung his feet off the desk and sat forward. 'I mean, what brings you here? We all have reasons for everything we do and I'm just wondering what yours are in this instance.'

I obviously didn't want to tell him about Dexter and his wife, or the way I've found it hard to settle on anything in the past few years. Besides, I do have a legitimate reason, and standing in front of him I couldn't think of a reason not to tell him. What better opportunity am I going to get? I am finally in a place where saying you want to write isn't laughable. I can see the smallest chink of light, when before the door has always been closed tight.

When I confessed to my own writerly ambitions, his face split into a wide grin. 'Ah, a fellow fantasist. How fantastic. Well, well, I do predict we're going to get along famously. Because stories are how we make sense of life. Which, of course, makes being a writer the best job in the world because that means we get to decide what happens.'

I longed for something witty or clever to say in return, but it didn't matter because he went on, 'Now, my best advice is to keep your wits about you. And to absolutely banish guilt. If you're really up for this strange profession, then you're going to have to become a burglar of life. Take everything you can.'

I laughed, not sure if he was serious. Being a burglar of life sounds illicit and immoral, but I suppose there has to be some alchemy to writing that I'm unaware of, and there's no reason that it has to be good. I think, as well, that I know what he means. Since I can remember I've been able to occupy myself for hours watching and remembering – filing away moments, storing them up for future use. My favourite game has always been to tell myself stories about people, to make up a whole life for someone sitting next to me on the bus or standing in front of me in a queue. I've not thought of it as stealing before, but maybe it is? Maybe every time a writer records something they're stealing a little piece of that person?

'Also, you obviously have to read as much as you can,' Rosie said. 'What do you like to read, Hope?'

No one has ever asked me a question like that before, and I felt a tingling excitement at the thought that I am now part of a life Mum and I have fantasized about. 'I really like Virginia Woolf.'

Rosie made a noise somewhere between a laugh and a grunt. 'Yes, of course you do. I find her a bit too . . . well, much. I mean, you can't write without going into feelings, obviously, but also I think you can feel too much. In the end how much navel-gazing can any of us bear? I'm a firm believer that you have to get on with the hand life deals you.'

I'd been so pleased with my answer, but his reaction made me think it was stupid, so I said that I like Sylvia Plath and Iris Murdoch as well.

Rosie frowned. 'Also, something should happen in books. It can't all just be I did the shopping, I love so and so who doesn't love me, I'm in emotional pain, blah, blah.' He stood and plucked a couple of books off a shelf, which he handed to me. 'Now Hardy, there's a man who knows how to write story and emotion. And Conrad if you want to see how to write conflict. You could even do worse than Dickens, although his stuff is a little saccharine. Also, you are absolutely only allowed one coincidence in a book. In fact, you are duty bound to have one coincidence in every book because of course life is strewn with them, although they feel clichéd if you have too many in novels. All of which is unfair on Dickens, but still, he has one per page, which is just lazy writing.'

I looked down at the books in my hands and felt a disbelief that I'm still feeling now – not only is all this available to me, but I also have my own private tutor in Rosie, however intimidating he might be.

'So, Sara, how this works,' Rosie said, as he sat back down, not seeming at all aware that he'd called me by the wrong name and I felt too embarrassed to correct him, 'is that in the mornings we answer letters and things like that. I might get you to make a few phone calls, or look something up if I need a bit of research doing. Often I'll get you to transcribe my mad ramblings.' He picked a Dictaphone off the desk and waved it at me. 'I carry this with me everywhere and whenever I have an idea or come up with a sentence I record it. All you have to do is type up what I've said word for word. That's very important that you write down every little thing I say into this thing.' He was looking very serious, so I nodded in what I hoped was a definite manner. 'Also, the other hard and fast rule is that every single piece of research or letter or note from my editor or anything about my book gets filed in one of these.' He pointed at three huge box files on the shelf next to his desk, covered in a beautiful, fussy pattern that reminded me of the wallpaper on the landing outside my bedroom. The titles of Rosie's novels are written along the spines: *Unforgiven*, *The Last Day of Autumn* and *The Ruined Girl*. 'Obviously most of what we're doing will go in *The Ruined Girl* file, as that's what I'm working on now. Got it?'

'Yes, absolutely.'

'Good. And then in the afternoon I write. Which you will also eventually transcribe as I do it all longhand. But I'm not at that stage yet, unfortunately.'

'And what should I do then?'

'When?'

'When you're writing.'

He blinked as if he'd never considered such a question before. 'I don't know. Read, swim, walk, get drunk, take part in a Satanic ceremony, whatever floats your boat. Unless Delly can think of something.'

I'm sure he was joking, but I can never tell with him. And I hate how I can't ever think of something witty to say back. I looked over his head in my confusion and noticed a large rectangular painting suspended in a cut-out of the bookshelves. It was a striking image of a fully nude woman lying on the impression of a bed, her legs splayed so you could see her pubic hair and the intricate redness of her vagina.

Rosie followed my gaze. 'Recognize anyone?'

I peered closer at the young woman looking at me through heavily lidded eyes, her body dripping with desire and longing.

Rosie laughed. 'My lovely wife was Seigal's muse. Clever bastard gave that one to us as a wedding present.'

I'm pretty sure my mouth actually fell open. I definitely felt the heat of a blush washing across my face. Knowing it was Delia changed everything about it. It felt suddenly ten times more shocking that it had moments before. Is it strange that Rosie should be displaying an image like that of his wife? Or even that she posed for it? Which doesn't even take into account the fact that they have a genuine Robert Seigal – Mum and I went to his bloody retrospective at the Tate last year – calmly hanging on the walls of their own house. It must be worth a fortune! I looked back at Rosie and he was chuckling quietly at my response in a way that gave me an odd dipping feeling, like water rushing through my stomach.

'Delly hates it,' he said.

'Because of the . . . well, I mean because she's naked?' I'd started speaking before I'd fully formulated what I wanted to say.

He roared with laughter. 'God, no. Nothing to do with that.' He turned in his chair, twisting his neck so he could look at it. 'But I rather like everything about it.'

God, this world is opaque. As I watched Rosie looking at his naked wife I realized that nothing and nobody here is willing to easily give up their secrets. Becoming truly part of their lives will take hard work and dedication. I'm going to need to be always alert, always learning, always recording. And I think I had just learnt my first big lesson: never be shocked.

I held Rosie's stare. 'She looks amazing.'

His laugh faded, and he almost pouted, as if I'd surprised him. It felt like the greatest achievement and I am determined to make it happen again.

15 June

Things I've noticed after ten days:

The dogs shit wherever they like in the house and garden. Mrs A is in a constant war with them, the steaming, stinking piles replaced by wet chemical circles that smell almost as bad.

Could not tell you how old Pete the gardener is. Honestly could be anywhere between thirty and fifty. Also he blushes as bright as the roses if you try to speak to him.

Thinking about Mum still makes me want to cry. When I speak to her on the phone she sounds plaintive and says heartbreaking things like 'don't be a stranger'.

If you lie on the stones by the pool the heat actually penetrates your body, right through to the bones. It makes me feel almost perfectly contented, like an internal warming.

Delia oozes this crazy, effortless style that makes me want to change everything about myself. She doesn't appear to make any effort in her appearance, but I don't think it's so much to do with how she dresses or her beauty anyway. I think it lies in the confidence that wafts off her like most women wear perfume. I'm starting to wonder if confidence is the most intoxicating of all qualities, and also the hardest to fake.

Nothing here works properly. There are damp patches on walls and doors stick and the pipes clang every time hot water is run. I've never seen anything like their dishwasher, a totally bizarre contraption, literally held together by a piece of thick string with a wooden spoon wound into it to get it to close. And when Mrs A puts it on it makes a noise like it's going to explode. Could they be short of money? Although that has to be impossible when you take into account the house and the presence of Mrs A and B, Pete and now me.

Rosie only drinks real coffee, which I have to take to him at the start of the day – well, the start of his day, which is 10 a.m. I measure out four tablespoons of richly scented grounds into a glass pot with a strange silver top that he pushes into the liquid. He doesn't take milk or sugar and when I set it in front of him every morning he says the same thing, 'lifesaver'.

They never lock and sometimes don't even shut the three massive sets of French doors that lead from the drawing room (as I've learnt to call it) onto the terrace. Delia claims they lost the keys years ago and no one seems at all bothered by it. But sometimes I hear creaks on the stairs late at night and worry that I'm about to be attacked in my bed.

Speaking of the drawing room, it is my favourite. Everything about it is epic. Some days it feels like my own private gallery, the mustard-coloured walls covered with hundreds of paintings in ornate frames. The gaping fireplace, with its confusion of flowers in the grate, and the intricately carved wooden mantelpiece, each dent and curve like an expression of intimacy. I am already attached to the stream of mismatched objects running along it – little tin figures, some shells and beads, a bright blue feather in a tall green bottle, and postcards of beautiful artworks wedged into the frame of the age-spotted gilt mirror that reveals a hazy version of myself.

I like to fall into the sagging sofas covered in fraying floral linens, leaning back against the feather cushions, dented from frequent sitting, or the feel against my feet of the stripped floorboards and woven rugs in deep reds, blues and yellows. I run my hand through the tassels of the billowing silk scarf that covers the huge black piano and then inspect each of the silver-framed photos sitting on top, scanning over all the children and feasting on the one of Delia and Rosie on their wedding day, looking impossibly young and beautiful, Delia especially, in her white silk shift, a garland of flowers in her hair and absolutely nothing else.

But Rosie's study is the room I feel most happy in. He is confusing and you do have to be constantly alert, but I love being in there alone with him and the sense of promise that each day brings, the feeling that I'm part of something brilliant, that the perfect words are just a thought away.

16 June

I'm so embarrassed! Just went back to Rosie's study after lunch to check that nothing more was needed of me and Delia was there. He was standing, leaning back against his desk and she was wedged tight between his legs, his hands digging into her bottom, his mouth on her neck. I turned away immediately, but he must have seen me because he called me back. Delia twisted around, but stayed between Rosie's legs, leaning back into him, his hands now casually resting against her stomach. Her mouth looked red and swollen and my whole body heated so dramatically I knew I would be glowing red.

Rosie smoothed a lock of hair against Delia's neck and she pushed herself forward, moving away from him slightly, so I couldn't help looking at the swell in the front of his trousers.

'Actually, Hope,' Delia said, 'some friends are coming for supper tonight. Why don't you join us?'

She said it in such a casual way, but shit! What should I wear and, more terrifyingly, what will I have to speak about? After I left the room I managed to give Mum a quick call, but she wasn't any help. She suggested my red silk dress with the ruffles, but I can't wear that and when I snorted at the idea I could tell I'd irritated her. I couldn't even articulate why I knew it would be wrong because she wouldn't understand. But it's another of those strange, unwritten lessons that I'm starting to learn: this one being that you should never appear to have tried too hard in anything. And all my clothes are trying too hard. I hate myself for having always been drawn to a loud pattern or bright colour. Oh, how I long for a soft cotton shirt, an unstructured sundress, a pair of linen trousers that nip in at the waist.

Later –

The moon is hanging huge over the hills out of my window and the breeze blowing in is still warm so it feels like being on holiday, when the heat coats your body like a layer of clothing. My belly is full and my head is light with the conversation that was as intoxicating as the wine.

The guests were a novelist who lives locally called Antonia and her daughter, Grace, plus a composer called Roger and his boyfriend, Jonty, who have what they called 'a weekend house' nearby. We ate outside on the long terrace table, covered over by a white tablecloth, with candles flickering all down the middle. A smart young woman did the cooking – much nicer food than Mrs B's – and there was champagne before supper and then bottles and bottles of wine. The novelist drank too much and her daughter didn't even look at me once. They were, in truth, quite boring, but amazing to look at. Antonia was dressed in a long flowing multi-coloured dress, with huge sparkling rings on each finger, while Grace was in jeans cut so short they revealed the crease between her bottom and legs, a green sequinned boob tube, and huge garish trainers on her feet. She also had slashes of green across both her eyelids, her hair was scrunched into a bun on either side of her head and she had three gold rings through her nose. They've made me wonder if there's a subset to the 'never try too hard' rule. Can't quite work that one out though – maybe something to do with it's okay if you make a mockery of yourself while trying too hard? Delia was easily the most attractive person there and she didn't look like she'd spent more than a few minutes getting ready. She was naturally bare-footed and -faced and wearing a very simple silver silk shift dress. She had also plaited her hair and wrapped it round her head, the whole effect turning her into a Greek goddess. 'Athena,' Jonty exclaimed when he saw her, but Roger knocked his arm and said, 'Please be kind to our beautiful hostess. Surely, Irene.'

Delia laughed and said, 'Oh, please, always Athena over bloody Irene. Who wants peace when you can have war?' (Something to look up.)

Must tell Mum, I did wear the red silk in the end. I've noticed that Delia alters many of her clothes by hacking away at them; dungarees cut to mid-thigh, T-shirts made into vests, skirts shortened. And when I looked at my dress in despair I realized that the ruffles were the most offensive thing about it. Once I got rid of them and shortened the sleeves it looked quite nice, I even liked the frayed edges.

Interestingly Tom was as quiet as I was during dinner. He caught my eye a few times and smiled with just the corners of his mouth, like he wanted to keep it private. He especially did that when either Antonia or Grace were speaking, which I was very thankful for because it gave me a warm feeling of inclusion.

'I'm losing friends,' Antonia said towards the end of the evening, her eyes glassy with wine.

'How so?' Rosie asked.

'They keep accusing me of putting them in my books. Unfavourably, of course.'

Grace was sitting next to Rosie and all night he'd been whispering in her ear, making her giggle. He leant towards her as her mother was speaking, his lips touching her face, and she hit him playfully on the knee before saying, 'Because you do, Mummy.'

Her mother waved a hand in front of her face. 'Well, maybe a smidge.'

Rosie circled an arm around the back of Grace's shoulder, his fingertip tracing a pattern against her shoulder. I couldn't help glancing at Delia, but she was staring at Rosie, her smile set. 'It was quite obvious that Davina was the murderer in your last novel,' Grace said, rolling her eyes and dragging violently on the end of a cigarette.

'Touché,' Rosie said, cupping his hand around Grace's head and drawing her into him. 'That is a brilliant observation, brilliant, Grace.'

He let her go and Grace almost bounced away from him, recovering herself by lifting an arm onto the table and cupping her head in her hand, staring up at him, in a move that looked so perfectly languorous I felt a mean stab of envy.

'And I would love to be cast as anything in your incredible books,' Rosie said.

'Darling Rosie, you're too kind,' Antonia said, reaching into the air for his hand, which never came.

'It's all bollocks anyway,' Rosie said. 'Honestly, don't be friends with a novelist if you don't want to end up in a book.'

After they'd gone Delia said she had a headache and went to bed. Tom and I began to carry plates through to the kitchen, but Rosie stopped us, insisting that we join him in a final glass. He already seemed quite drunk, his eyes not entirely focusing, but he's not a man you say no to. 'Oh Mummy, Mummy, you are terrible,' he said as he poured out the wine, in an almost perfect imitation of Grace's high-pitched voice.

Tom laughed. 'Christ, she's vile, that one. Looks at you like you're shit on her shoe. Well, not you obviously, Rosie, just the rest of us.'

'Well, at least I didn't have to speak to Roger all night like poor Delly,' he said. 'No wonder she has a headache. That man could bore for Britain.' He leant forward, lighting a cigarette from a candle. 'And I tell you what. If Antonia does put me in one of her books I will hunt down every copy and burn them. Half of them are fucking sequels – the pathetic fallback of the washed-up writer. I've never read such tripe as the shit she writes.'

It's confusing because Rosie had been such a perfect host all evening; I'd even go as far as to say that he was flirting with Grace. But then he sounded like he couldn't stand them. And if that's true, then how much of what he says and does is real? Although I also love that he clearly trusts me enough to speak like that in front of me. It's like he's inviting me to step behind the curtain of this life. I know things other visitors don't – we have secrets. And anyway, he's right, Grace was awful. Although I liked that move she did – it made her look confident and grown-up. I've just practised it in my mosaic mirror and can see it's a good trick to have at your disposal.

18 June

The days have begun to merge in a delicious way, as if everything is made of wax melted by the heat, and we've re-formed intertwined in a beautiful, languid routine. Rosie and I are shut up in his study in the morning, then we all have lunch, Delia goes to her studio, Rosie back to his study, and Tom and I to the pool. In the evenings we eat outside in a Mediterranean warmth, sitting around the terrace table, staying on for hours after the food is finished, chatting or playing cards. The night draws down around us, as insects rustle in the plants and the dogs bark at passing foxes.

The more time I spend with Tom the more I like him. He has that rare quality of really listening to what you say and then asking relevant questions. Mum has always said that men don't do that, and that's been true in my experience, too, but now I wonder if that's just the men we've met. I nearly told her about Tom when we spoke earlier, but I couldn't think of a way of introducing him into the conversation that didn't sound contrived. I'm not even sure what I'd say about him, because Mum knows me too well to let me get away with casually mentioning a young man who is also living here. Not that I know yet if my mentioning him would be casual or not. And even if something is there between Tom and I, it would probably be very stupid to act on it. This is meant to be about my career, not another ill-advised romance.

And things are going well on that front. I really think Rosie is starting to value me. Just this morning he asked if I know anyone called Tessa. He has a particular expression when he's thinking, a cross between a scowl and a smile which looks almost painful, as if he's physically exerting himself, and it makes me desperate to help him.

I said I didn't so he suggested Tamsin, then Tansy.

'Is that even a name?' I asked, which made him laugh. God, I love making him laugh – it feels like being given a present you've forgotten you wanted.

'You're right,' he said, 'it's stupid. But I've become fixated by her name beginning with a T. I like the hardness of the beginning, followed by a dissolution. What are girls in their twenties called? Apart from Hope, of course.'

How amazing that we've slipped into this way of talking about his characters with no preamble, as if we both know them intimately. With every bit of research he gives me I feel a little more connected to them, especially the female protagonist, who at the moment he just refers to as T. I'm still not entirely sure of the plot though. When he gives me tapes to transcribe it's not sections of the book like I'd imagined it would be. It's more abstract thoughts or reminders to himself, sometimes lines, and occasionally whole paragraphs. The most he's told me is that it's about a man and a woman in their twenties and their tortured love, to use his phrase.

'I know someone called Teresa,' I said.

'Teresa,' Rosie repeated. 'Teresa.' It sounded like he was tasting the word. 'You know what, Sara, I like that.'

(Who is this Sara?)

20 June

Tom was hauling himself out of the pool yesterday when he said, 'You can ask me about them, you know.'

His words made me blush because he was right – I had been staring at his scars and I mumbled an apology.

He sat on the lounger next to mine and lit a cigarette, shaking the water out of his eyes in a way that tightened my stomach. There's no denying that he's objectively attractive, but over the past week or so he's become better-looking than the sum of his parts, in the way some people do when you get to know them. Almost as if you can see past their physicality, to the essence of them.

'Okay, how did you get into it?' I asked.

He shrugged. 'The usual way. Thought I was a big deal at thirteen. And the only lads on my estate who had any money were dealing. At first I just ran errands for them, but it wasn't long before I was using. And then, once you've started, you have to find a way to pay for it, so you get in deeper every day.'

The words felt wrong for the setting we were in. 'How did you get in the rehabilitation programme?'

'After Mum kicked me out, which I don't blame her for by

the way, as I stole anything that wasn't screwed down, things got ugly. Long story short, I ended up on the streets and overdosed one night. The hospital referred me to Ridgeview.'

It feels crazy to try to marry the Tom I know with the person he was describing. That person sounds wild and dangerous and makes me wonder at all the things he must have seen and done. I'm obviously glad I've met him now he's clean, but there's also something intriguing about the person he was describing. Almost like the roughness and trauma of his past made him more attractive, which has to be my own bullshit, always pathetically drawn to the bad boy.

'And you met Delia there?' I asked.

He ground his cigarette into the stones. 'That woman is a proper angel. She's incredible, everyone at Ridgeview loves her.'

'But how come she, well, has you to stay and stuff?'

A faint blush washed over his cheeks. 'Well, we always got on. I was a bit of joker at Ridgeview and she found me funny. But then, one of the other lads, who I was quite friendly with, overdosed, and I went through a rough patch. Delia was the only person who I felt able to properly speak to about it. You know, there was no judgement at all. And, even though she comes from this mega-fancy world, she understood about disappointment and not feeling safe. Anyway she asked me to stay here one weekend and I got on with Rosie as well and, well, we sort of got into a habit. She once said that if she'd had a kid she'd have liked him to be me.' I saw the pride in Tom's eyes when he said that and felt a weird stab of jealousy. Of course I wouldn't swap Mum for anyone, but I can imagine how good it would be to hear Delia say those words. I want to matter to her that much.

'You're lucky to have met her,' I said and then wished I hadn't, because it made it sound like everything good about him was to do with her.

He frowned. 'I'm scared that I won't be able to stay clean. I really want to. And I hate letting Delia down. But sometimes it feels like I'm just not capable of sustaining it. Mum always said I was a born wrong'un. Apparently I cried all night, every night until I was two, and by then I was running away from her in the street and getting into trouble.'

The assessment sounded bleak and made me feel protective of Tom. All the stories I have of my childhood from my mother are bright and sparkling. 'I'm sure you were a lovely kid,' I said.

Tom laughed and lay back on the lounger. We lapsed into a comfortable silence, just the noise of birds and the water lapping at the edge of the pool. 'Do you know anyone called Sara?' I asked eventually.

Tom turned his head to me. 'Do you mean Rosie's assistant before you?'

'Oh right, that makes sense.'

'What does?'

'He's called me Sara a couple of times.'

Tom propped his head up with his hand. 'Shit, don't tell Delia.'

'Why not?'

'Promise you won't say anything.'

I nodded, but my chest had tightened and I could feel my heart in my throat.

'Look, I don't know anything for sure, but she left very suddenly, about a month before you came. I was staying here at the time, and I'd only met her once before, but, well, she seemed very different from the first time I met her. She'd lost a crazy amount of weight and always looked like she'd been crying. And she and Delia avoided each other and didn't speak, if they were ever in the same room, that is. Then one day she wasn't there and when I asked Delia where she was, she just said she'd left. No explanation.'

I sat up. 'Are you saying something bad happened between her and Delia?'

Tom shrugged. 'More like between her and Rosie.'

It took me a minute to get my head round what Tom was saying. 'You mean, you think he had an affair?'

Tom shrugged. 'I mean, I don't know for sure, but it would hardly be out of character for him, would it.'

I thought of how he'd acted with Grace. 'But he adores Delia.'

'Yeah, but I'd say he adores himself even more.'

The air appeared to have thinned around us, so my head felt light. It was strange how much I didn't, still don't, want that to be true about Rosie.

'Nothing's, I mean, he hasn't . . .' Tom coughed like something was stuck in his throat. 'He hasn't tried anything with you, has he?'

'God, no.' Should I feel offended that he hasn't? I wonder if I can find a photograph of Sara. Except also, WTF, that is a ridiculous thought. Obviously I don't want to have an affair with Rosie. But also I don't want him to have liked another assistant more than me. I don't even want him to have had an assistant he liked more than Delia. I don't want him to have had another assistant, full stop! I'd like to preserve us all in amber, no one else allowed inside.

'What do you do then, locked in that study with him every day?' Tom said, breaking into my thoughts.

'Oh, various things. Answer his letters, research things, transcribe anything he says into that Dictaphone.'

'So you know what his book's about then?'

'Not really.'

'Oh, come on. I won't tell anyone.'

'No, really. The things he says on tape aren't a story as such. It's definitely about love. You know, how intense it can get. But I couldn't tell you what actually happens.'

Tom lit two cigarettes and handed one to me, which relaxed the atmosphere enough for us both to lie back down. I had an odd, tingling sensation when I put my lips around the filter and it was still wet from his mouth.

'I know,' he said, 'he's writing about a princess who leaves her prince for the lady-in-waiting. Or aliens who invade earth and drink each other's blood.'

I laughed. 'Yeah, right. I reckon he'd rather die than write that.'

'Oh no, I've got it. He's writing about the ghosts of Shadowlands.'

I flicked some ash by the side of the lounger. 'Do you know, that's something I've been wondering about; I can't think why anyone would call this house Shadowlands. I mean, it's one of the brightest, friendliest places I've ever been.'

Tom peered at me over his dark glasses. 'You're kidding, right?'

It was amazing how quickly the fear encircled me that I'd said something stupid. 'No, what?'

He turned his head back towards the sky. 'You must know what Shadowlands means?'

'No.'

He blew smoke rings into the air above his head. 'It's a place of imagination. You know, like that place between reality and fantasy. A place of spirits and thought and allowing free rein to your darkest fantasies.'

'But that's so weird.'

'What is?'

'That Rosie's a novelist and his house is called Shadowlands.'

Tom let out a huge guffaw. 'No, no. Rosie named the place Shadowlands. It's been in his family for generations. His parents died in a car crash when he was about our age and he was given it.' Tom lowered his voice. 'People like them don't have to give their homes back when they die, you know.'

I snorted. 'Of course I know that.'

'Anyway. It was called Something Grange. After Rosie got hold of it, he changed the name and moved the front door.'

'He moved the front door?'

'Yeah, Delia told me about it when I was here a few summers ago. It used to be on the river side of the house, but that was where Rosie wanted his study to be, so he had the old front door bricked up. You can sort of see it in the wall, if you know where to look, between the windows in his study.'

I looked more closely at the space between the windows this morning and found a faint indentation in the plaster that's doorshaped, a small, shadowed outline of a little secret I am now privy to. I ran my fingers over the line and was filled with a sense of exhilaration, but also strangeness. It's made me too aware of the history of the house and all the lives that must have occupied the rooms that already feel so familiar to me. I looked back into the room and imagined Sara standing between Rosie's legs instead of Delia. An odd sense of impermanence flooded over me, like I'm an actor on a stage, no real tether to life here. But I don't want to drift away. I'm not sure I ever even want to leave.

22 June

Fucking hate myself. I shouldn't be finding situations like dinner tonight shocking. And what if I've messed up? Shit, what would that mean?

The party felt different from the beginning, the guests much louder, more boisterous. They were the same age as Rosie and Delia, but it felt like being with my friends at home when they've drunk way too much and things have got a little out of control.

We'd finished eating when one of the men shouted down the table that we should play wine breath. There were shrieks when he said that and thumping on the table. I glanced at Tom, but he was looking at his plate.

'Bloody hell, Drew,' Rosie laughed. 'You're incorrigible.'

The man blew a kiss at Rosie. 'Pass a bottle this way, love.'

As I watched the bottle make its way to him, I became aware of how many other empty bottles were on the table, the green of the glass glittering in the candlelight. When it reached Drew he held it aloft, like he'd won a prize, which made everyone cheer. My whole body felt tense but also alive, my skin more sensitive than usual. Drew took a giant gulp, a red dribble leaking out of the corners of his mouth, his cheeks bulging. Then he leant to his left, towards the woman sitting there. She tipped her head back and opened her mouth, pressing her arms onto the chair behind her so everything jutted from her. Drew stayed standing, but he bent right over her, lowering his face to about an inch above hers. For a moment everything stilled, the whole table enthralled. And then he started to release the wine into her mouth, slowly and delicately, like a minute turn of a tap. She took it for as long as she could before snapping forward, holding her hand over her mouth, as he let the rest of the wine dribble on to her head and down her face, so it looked like he'd taken a heavy object and slammed it into the top of her skull. She slapped at his legs, but she was trying not to laugh as she moved towards the woman on her left, who leant into her, snaking a hand around the back of her head. Their lips came together and more of the wine dripped out of another mouth as the new woman turned to the next person.

The rules of the game were obvious. But then I understood, in a hot rush, that because I was sitting next to Rosie it meant that he would be passing the wine to me. He accepted the wine from the woman on the other side of him, theatrically laying his head on the table as she spat it into his mouth, so I could see bubbles of spit mixed with the now only pinkish liquid.

Rosie pushed himself upright, his eyes fixed on me, and all sound dropped away. I wanted to think of some funny way of presenting my mouth to him, but nothing came and so I sat frozen, too aware of everyone looking at us, of Delia and Tom directly across the table. Rosie swept a look around, waving his arms like a conductor, which made everyone start a rhythmic clapping, the noise filling all the space in my head. He took my face in both his hands and pulled me towards him, until our lips were touching and I could feel the strain in his lips. I opened my mouth because there was nothing else I could have done and let him transfer the warm, rich liquid to me, his tongue slithering into my mouth in a way that was impossible to determine. He pulled away but kept his hot hands on my face for a few seconds too long. He laughed as he let go, turning forward and taking the beam of his attention off me, and I felt strangely winded. But then I had to turn as well, to the man on the other side of me, who made a stupid play of opening his mouth too wide and all the wine spilt out, so then people were banging the table and chanting his name until another bottle was passed to him and he stood and downed it in one triumphant, sucking gulp.

I felt dizzy when he'd finished, as if it was me who'd drunk the wine. I wanted to leave, but it felt too exposing. I looked across the table instead, hoping that Tom might shoot me one of his smiles, but his chair was empty, pushed back as if he'd left in a rush. Delia was looking at me, though, her eyes narrow, and then I just wanted to cry because I didn't know what had happened or what I was meant to do. I stood, mumbling something incoherent, and went straight to my room.

And now the night is hot and heavy outside, and I feel out of breath. I can hear screams and shouts from the wood, even the splash of bodies jumping into the pool. I thought I'd figured out most things here, but now I feel all at sea again. I want to cry.

23 June

Lay awake half the night, worried that I would be asked to leave this morning. The things Delia said about Rosie by the pool the first week I was here nagged at me and I couldn't decide if I'd done what he wanted, which she said I had to, or if I'd taken him too seriously, which she'd said I shouldn't. I kept feeling his tongue in my mouth, which embarrassed me so much I could barely look at him this morning. And I still don't know how he meant it – if it was accidental or a type of kiss. But now it's the afternoon and still no one has mentioned anything and everything feels completely normal. Probably I am ridiculous for thinking it was more important than it was and forgetting that games are fun and consequences minimal. At least they are at Shadowlands.

I think it might have given me an insight into why shock is such a shit emotion – could it be because it takes the wonder out of the world and scuppers imagination? I'm trying so hard to banish it, but it feels almost indelibly ingrained inside me, so little sparks of it flare along my skin too often. But I don't see how I can hope to be a writer if I continue to feel it. I need to be able to imagine myself in any situation. More than that, I need to be able to think up any situation — however outlandish or disgusting or embarrassing. But there's no hope if I perceive certain things to be wrong. I have to get over myself.

25 June

A car pulled up this afternoon, as I was sitting on the terrace battling away with Thomas Hardy's *Jude* and all his obscure wants. Lying by the pool had proved too hot and Tom had left for an NA meeting forty-five minutes away, so I'd decamped to some shade, but was still wearing my swimsuit, which the heat had dried onto my body, with denim shorts which I made from a pair of jeans.

The car was brand new, which is unusual for a Shadowlands guest, and it intrigued me, so I put down my book. A woman stepped out who reminded me of Delia, although she had a slash of red on her lips and her dress was more fitted than anything Delia would wear. She opened the back door and helped a young girl out, but then she noticed me watching and stopped.

'My God, he hasn't managed to persuade Delia to have another one living here, has he?' Her voice was high, like her breath never went below her chest, and so sharp it reminded me of knives.

I stood and walked towards her. 'I'm sorry, can I help you?'

She took the child's hand and pulled her towards me. 'Who are you?'

'Hope. I'm Rosie's secretary.'

She snorted. 'Still calling it that, is he?'

The little girl was looking at her feet so I could see her scalp was red underneath her blonde hair, which had been pulled into two imperfect plaits.

'Well, if you're his secretary, can you get him?' the woman said dismissively.

I hated her almost violently. 'He's working.'

The woman jutted her weight onto one hip and looked me up and down so blatantly I folded my arms across my stomach. 'Just do as you're told, there's a good girl. Tell him Fiona's here.'

I did as she asked because even though Delia had told me never to disturb Rosie when he's writing, Fiona was impossible to refuse. Rosie groaned loudly when I gave him the message, but at least he stood and followed me outside.

'Fifi,' he exclaimed as soon as we stepped through the front door, 'what a wonderful surprise.'

His face had totally changed from the grimace in the study to a picture of open delight. He marched forward and took Fiona by the shoulders, kissing her on both cheeks, and I momentarily saw her soften. His behaviour annoyed me because I thought his initial reaction meant we agreed on Fiona, yet there he was making her feel like the most welcome person in the world. I wanted to tell him how rude she'd been to me. I wanted him to take my side and tell her to fuck off. For once, I wanted to be sure I was getting his true, authentic self.

'You said you'd call,' Fiona said in an annoyed tone that surprised me because I didn't know people got annoyed with Rosie.

But he didn't seem to mind, shoving a hand into his hair, as if completely exasperated with himself. 'Oh God, I did, didn't I. I've lost all track of time recently, totally consumed by this new book.'

Fiona looked over at me, a sneer on her face. 'I'm sure. Anyway, it's been two months. Your daughter will forget what you look like.'

Shock was a very hard emotion to suppress at that moment, but I forced it away, instead concentrating on how interesting it is, the different ways that people live.

Rosie knelt by the little girl, who pressed herself closer to her mother.

'Darling Tills, it's so lovely to see you. I'm sorry I've been such a dreadful, forgetful daddy.' He stood back up. 'Anyway, let's get you both a drink or some food, maybe. Hope, perhaps . . .'

'Actually, I won't be staying,' Fiona said. 'I need a break.' There was a tremble in her voice and her eyes had teared up.

'Oh, but . . .' Rosie looked at me desperately, making my stomach flip, because at that moment it was definitely him and me against bloody Fiona. 'I mean, we're not really set up for children right now. Why don't we sit down and have a drink and discuss when Tilly can come and stay properly?'

Fiona snorted. 'If you're not set up for children, why do you keep fucking having them?'

I looked between Rosie and Fiona and tried to keep my face still. Mum has always told me to keep my emotions in check, to say I'm fine when people ask how I am, to smile through any pain. But Shadowlands is teaching me that lots of people don't live like that. Lots of people live with their skin flayed open and their nerves exposed. They can be shouting and screaming one minute and laughing the next. It feels like a much more real way of being and makes me think that my life before was full of pedantry and needless embarrassment.

Fiona half pushed Tilly forward and then turned and stalked back to her car. She wound down her window and, as a parting shot, said dramatically, 'I'll be back when I feel like it.' We watched as she reversed into a flower bed, then sped off back down the drive.

'Right,' Rosie said. 'How about a biscuit or something, Tills?' She shrugged, her little shoulders holding up the straps of a sweet pink sundress patterned with white ducks. He looked back up at me, his face contorted like we were speaking a secret language, which again flipped my stomach. 'Could you go and tell Delly what just happened while we find a biscuit?'

My heart was tight beneath my ribs as I crossed the lawn to Delia's studio. I presumed I wasn't literally on my way to tell Delia that Rosie had a daughter, although I couldn't imagine how hurt she'd be at having to interact with her. Because I'd seen their wedding photos in which they both looked like children themselves, which meant they had to have been married for at least twenty years, whereas Tilly couldn't be more than seven or eight. I was passing the French doors and the light was catching on all the silver frames on the piano. So many of those photographs are of children, a thought which set off a strange knocking inside my skull. And then there's everything Tom told me about Sara. I couldn't stop an image of Dexter's wife from assaulting my brain then, her face red and her eyes wide as she called me a slag. One thing I know is that Delia, whatever she thought, would never behave like that.

Delia's studio is a beautiful low clapboard building on the edge of the woods that run along the bottom of the garden.

UNRELIABLE NARRATOR

Rosie told me he had it built after she installed a potter's wheel in a bedroom. It's painted a pale green and has a large fig tree growing across its front that attracts wasps and scents the air like a delicious dessert. We eat the figs often, warm from the tree, so the sweetness fills your whole mouth. And every time Rosie makes the same joke – biting into one lasciviously as he says they remind him of pendulous, swinging old-man balls.

The door was ajar but I still knocked and waited for Delia to call me inside. She was sitting at her wheel, her bare legs stretched out either side and her hands turning some clay, the dogs asleep at her feet. She looked up as I walked in and pushed her hair out of her eyes, leaving a streak of pinkish plaster on her forehead. I decided my best bet would be to fake the nonchalant air with which they dealt with everything.

'Rosie asked me to come and get you because Tilly's been dropped off,' I said.

Delia blinked. 'Oh God, when?'

'Just now.'

'And I suppose her bloody mother didn't say for how long?'

'She said she'd get her when she feels like it.'

'Fuck. Shit, you disturbed Rosie, I take it?'

I felt myself blush. 'I'm sorry, I had to. Her mother was . . . well . . . she insisted, and she wasn't very nice about it.'

Delia sighed. 'That's the fucking understatement of the year. Sorry you had to deal with her, Hope. Just let me get cleaned up.' She walked over to the sink and began washing her hands. 'I almost feel sorry for the girl, with a mother *that* totally nuts.'

I was partly relieved and partly shocked that Delia was taking the news so calmly, like it was totally normal to welcome your husband's child into your home. I was also burning with questions, but they all felt too revealing of my true curiosities, so instead I looked at the rows of pots and sculptures that sat on the wide, rickety shelves spanning one whole wall of Delia's studio. Before that afternoon, I hadn't thought about what Delia does in her studio. It's never talked about and has always felt quite sweet and unimportant, a nice little hobby. But her pots are glorious – fluid shapes which seem almost too natural to have been made by hand, decorated in sweeping bright colours. They tugged at something in my chest and inexplicably made me think of rivers and starlight and joy.

'These are so good,' I said, turning to her.

She made a dismissive noise. 'Well, they keep me busy.'

'No, but they're *really* good.' I hated that I couldn't think of a better word. 'Do you show them somewhere?' That is not a question I would have asked before I came here, but it's the language I hear spoken at all their supper parties. Everyone always has a show, or a book coming out, or is writing the score for a film, or directing or acting in a play.

Delia laughed. 'God, no. That would take way too much time.' (I still can't work out what she meant by that, as she seems to have all the time in the world.)

As I watched Delia drying her hands, I noticed a large painting hanging above the sink. It was obviously another Seigal, and it made me feel nearly as uncomfortable as the one in Rosie's study. A teenage Delia stared defiantly out, dressed in a thick tartan skirt and socks, but naked from the waist up, a window behind revealing a barren landscape, the cold of the room evident in the erectness of her nipples. She followed my gaze up behind her, so I felt I had to say something. 'Rosie told me you were Seigal's muse.'

I expected her to reply with something witty, or proud, but she surprised me by grimacing. 'Well, muse might be pushing it. He was my father's best friend, and he started painting me when I was twelve. Others came along later, though, so it wasn't just me.' Her voice sounded harder than I'd heard it before and I was worried that I'd offended her somehow. But she clapped her hands, which made the dogs stir. 'Come on then, let's deal with Tilly.'

Rosie and Tilly were on the terrace and Rosie was making her laugh. They looked so sweet together, and it was suddenly easy to see she was his daughter in the height of her cheekbones and the length of her legs. Mrs A brought out tea and biscuits and we chatted away, Rosie and Delia asking Tilly lots of questions about school and her friends, what she wanted for her birthday. At one point Rosie drew her onto his lap and kissed the top of her head. I was probably Tilly's age when I last saw my father, and there had been no giggling or head kisses. I felt a sharp pain in my chest, longing for a life in which emotion was easily expressed, the fear of rejection only a dot on the horizon.

After about an hour Rosie had to get back to work and so Delia found a swimsuit for Tilly and asked me to take her to the pool, where we played for ages. Mrs B made an early supper, which Rosie and Delia joined us for. Tom wasn't back from his meeting, but I saw Delia save a plate for him and put it in the fridge. After supper, Tilly and I went upstairs to watch TV and she fell asleep, so I carried her into the bedroom down the hall from mine, where Delia had said she should sleep. When I laid her on the bed, she curled into herself in a way that reminded me of the hornets, so I had a terrible moment of imagining being woken by her screams, coming in to find her smothered by the insects, all injecting their poison into her over and over again. It made me agitated enough to go back to the sitting room and check the cupboard. They were still all dead but, even so, I pushed the chair tighter against the door.

It was still relatively early and I wondered if Tom was back, so went downstairs and into the drawing room, making for the terrace via the French doors. Sure enough he was sitting with Rosie and Delia round the terrace table in the gathering dusk, all of them holding glasses of wine and smoking cigarettes. The sight made me bizarrely shy, as if I might be intruding by joining them. Except that's how we spend every night and no one has ever made me feel like I'm not entirely welcome. I dithered in the doorway and, as I did, the piano started to take up more and more of my peripheral vision, a huge black bulk looming in the corner. I crept over to it, bending over each photograph, until I found Tilly in her frame. There were eight other children on the piano, all of whom could be said to bear a resemblance to Rosie. My chest burned like I had indigestion, and I wanted to march out onto the terrace and demand to know what their arrangement was. As if I had a personal stake in the situation, as if I had somehow been the one slighted. I looked up and, as I did, watched as Delia laughed at something, cupping her hand round the back of Rosie's head. He took it and kissed her palm.

The scene filled me with a hot, inexplicable fear, the whole room closing around me. Delia is such a good person and sometimes I can't understand how she does it, I don't even know if it's right. But is that how to be good? To smile and love and accept without accusation? Except Rosie isn't like that and he's a genius. Oh God, it makes no sense. I left them to it and ran up the stairs, two at time, back to my room where I got into bed, my heart hammering and my mouth dry. At some point in the night Tilly padded through to me, climbing into bed beside me. And because it's so hot I now can't sleep, but also I can't bear to move her, for her to wake up again in a strange bed, scared and disorientated.

26 June

Tilly left this morning, just before Rosie and I were due to start work. Her mother seemed much more contrite this time and her eyes were red-rimmed. I watched Rosie and Delia say goodbye to them from my spot behind the stairs in the hall. They all acted like nothing out of the ordinary had taken place. They kissed each other on the cheeks and Fiona reminded Rosie that she had to get that 'bloody expensive' bridesmaid's dress made for Tilly. To which Delia said, 'Oh, but totally worth it. I, for one, can't wait to see her looking beautiful at the wedding.' Whose wedding I have no idea, and will they all go together? Does everyone in their circle know of the arrangement they have? Genuinely, are none of them ever embarrassed?

Stop thinking like that, Hope!

Tilly looked over her shoulder as her mother led her to their car and I managed to catch her eye and wave, which made her smile. I wish I'd had the courage to say goodbye properly and I hope she doesn't think I don't care, or that I didn't enjoy our time together. Rosie put his arm around Delia as the car drove away, but she shook him off and walked away without saying anything.

Rosie didn't sit down when he came into the study and there

was a strange tension in the air, as if the dead hornets had come to life and were all beating their wings at once.

'What would you like me to do?' I asked, which made him laugh.

He walked over to his desk and leant against it. His trousers were especially creased and the buttons on his shirt were done up the wrong way, so I could see the slant of his collarbone. I became too aware of my body and the heat in the room, the sun beating through the windows he never opens.

'Did you enjoy that game we played the other night?' he said, folding his arms across his chest and jutting out his chin, his voice cool in the steamy temperature. His gaze slinked down towards my lips and I immediately felt his tongue in my mouth again. I don't know what the correct answer to that question would have been, or what I wanted in that moment. I don't know what I would have done if he'd tried to kiss me. Rosie is a man whose sexuality radiates off him like heat, so it's hard not to imagine what it would feel like if he pressed his body against yours. Harder still to imagine saying no to him. And even though I understand that he and Delia must have some sort of open relationship, surely that wouldn't include someone like me. Sara, after all, isn't here any more. Which makes me fearful because I love it here so much and have no intention of having to leave because I've made another stupid decision.

Later –

Tom is in a very surly mood and it's making me paranoid. He barely spoke over supper and didn't look at me once. Have I done something to annoy him? I hate the thought of that. It feels strangely imperative that everyone at Shadowlands not just likes me but values me. My dream would be if everyone has a secret that they felt confident telling only me, and for me to make it all better, imparting a deep, important truth that makes them feel indebted to me.

27 June

Went to the pool after lunch and Tom was there, lying on a lounger. I felt embarrassed so I simply peeled off my dress and dived in. The water was dirtier than usual, a morass of leaves and dead insects swirling along the bottom, my hand constantly brushing against tiny corpses. I wanted to stop and scream, to twirl in the pool pushing all the little lost lives far away, but Tom was watching, and I want to seem coolly fearless and unbothered.

'You have a nice stroke,' Tom said, when I eventually got out.

I stood over him, aware of the effect that the water rushing off my golden-brown body would have. I squeezed the moisture out of my hair, wanting to prolong the moments in which he could take me in, again unsure what I wanted, but drunk on the steadiness of Tom's attention. It's not that I was unaware of my physicality before I came to Shadowlands, but something about this place has heightened my senses, so I find myself often drawn to mirrors, fascinated by my own face. Although sometimes it feels like however hard I look I don't properly see myself. As if there's a gap in my vision or a haze over the image, blurring everything about me, which sends me into a momentary panic that I'm slowly disappearing.

'I'm sorry I was in a bad mood yesterday,' he said. 'Meetings always do that to me.'

I lay on the lounger next to him and turned my head, shielding my eyes from the sun in the same way Delia does. He didn't make any attempt to hide the fact that he was staring, his eyes travelling over me in a way that made me feel like he was touching me.

'Are you okay now?' I asked.

He finally met my gaze. 'Yeah, better. Sorry I've been an arsehole.'

'You weren't that bad.'

He sat up and swung his legs round so he was facing me with his arms resting on his knees and his head bent low between his shoulder blades, a thin gold chain glittering against his dark skin. 'It's just, those meetings are good and all, but they remind me of who I am.'

'Who you *were*.'

He shook his head. 'No, you're always that person. You could be clean fifty years and still be an addict.' I held my breath, desperate to reach out and press my finger into the hollow behind his collarbone. 'Nothing is ever enough when you're in its grip. There's nothing you wouldn't do or say to get a fix. You stop recognizing yourself and your life shrinks down to this one tiny point. And I hate being reminded that I'm that person. That I always will be.'

I wanted to say something meaningful, but was so out of my depth, I didn't know where to begin.

His eyes were almost vibrating, making him look desperate

in a way that chilled me, despite the heat of the day. 'Sometimes I think I have this horrible black hole at my core that sucks all the goodness into it.'

I took his hands in mine and a strange spark shot between us that made us both jump slightly. 'Tom,' I said, 'I haven't known you long, but I promise there is no black hole at your core. You are a good person. I know it.'

He dropped his eyes back to the floor between us and something stretched in my chest, like my heart was aching. It was too easy to see the child in him, which made it obvious that he'd been frightened for so much of his life. I suppose none of us see ourselves clearly, but Tom's vision seems especially clouded. I want to find a way to make him see himself how I do.

28 June

After I turned off my light last night, I found I couldn't sleep. I lay awake in the sticky heat and my mind was filled by that gold chain Tom wears. I imagined it brushing against my face if he lay on top of me, and how I would like to run my hands down his arms and feel that little indentation he has right under his shoulder before the muscle starts. I put my hands on my body and they belonged to him, soft and gentle. Except, when I shut my eyes, it wasn't Tom behind my lids, but Rosie, and he was rougher than Tom, wanting to explore my body in a way that quickened my breathing. And when I eventually fell asleep, I dreamt that Delia was in the bed next to me, and she kissed me so softly I had to draw her into me and then I couldn't stop touching her because she was made of the thickest, silkiest velvet I'd ever felt. Could my brain be helping me out – leading me down unshockable pathways and showing me more interesting ways of being?

3 July

Rosie and Delia are going away for the weekend. Delia told us at lunch today, and I found I couldn't look at Tom as she spoke. A thick tension has been building between us. Often I know instinctively where he is in the house, as if his vibrations can find me through the air. And I don't think I'm alone in the feeling. His gaze rests on me for too long and when I come into a room he flushes.

But I'm here to work and avoid mess. Except I don't think anyone here would be bothered if something happens between us. This is a world of emotion and being true to those feelings. Or, the other option is, we could just keep it secret! Although I'm not unaware either of how a relationship with Tom could cement my position – not that that would be my motivation.

It's not that I lack experience in matters of the body and heart, but I still feel a mixture of fear and exhilaration at the thought of us together. I have a sense that maybe I've never experienced anything particularly real before. Perhaps I've been playing at emotion and never fully understood what it means to truly want someone. Which is also scary because I can't work out how you ever satiate want. What does enough feel like, and can you have too much?

6 July

When we finished work this morning Rosie said, 'Don't have too much fun while I'm gone.'

I was about to leave the study but turned back to him smiling, that lascivious painting of his wife hanging above his head. He reminded me of the wolf in 'Little Red Riding Hood', a book I was fascinated by when I was young. *Not again*, Mum would say every night, but I would force it into her hands and snuggle up tight to her side as she read so I could see the pictures. Even as a kid, I knew that the little girl didn't actually want to pick her grandmother flowers. I knew that, really, she didn't want to follow the path.

'Spare a thought for me while you're living it up,' he said, leaning back in his chair and clasping his hands together behind his head, 'while I'm surrounded by old farts.'

I laughed because I've met too many of their friends. 'Oh, I'm sure you'll manage some adventures as well.' My heart was thumping hard against my ribs, but I made myself leave, having to stop on the other side of the door to take a few deep, steadying breaths.

7 July

Tom and I were strangely coy with each other last night. Mrs A and B have been given the weekend off, so we made sandwiches and took them up to my sitting room with a bottle of wine. We watched a crappy film and our conversation felt stilted, so we were in bed, separately, by ten.

It meant I woke with the dawn this morning and knew immediately that I wouldn't be going back to sleep. The day was alive with a humming possibility, and I was eager to get going, so decided to dissipate some of my energy with an early swim. Except when I reached the next landing, I saw that Rosie and Delia had left their bedroom door open. It was too tempting.

Their room is huge, with a mammoth bed pushed against a large semi-circular window looking out over the garden and down to the river. The sun was streaming through, casting light over the tangled sheets, a cotton slip discarded on the edge of the bed, making the whole scene look like an arthouse photograph. I went to Delia's dressing table and ran a hand along her pearl-inlaid hairbrushes and through the necklaces she hangs off the mirror. A pot of cream was open and I dipped a finger into it, pushing right down until I felt the bottom. A door on the left wall led to a bathroom, the air infused with Delia's unmistakable musky rose scent, and more clothes were strewn across the floor, a wet towel discarded in a corner. I even looked in the toilet, rewarded with a smear of shit on the white porcelain.

Back in the bedroom I opened the wardrobe, revealing rows of beautiful dresses and shirts and trousers. They were so soft against my skin when I held them to my face and I could smell her again, but more faintly this time. The silver dress that she wore to my first dinner party here glinted out at me, so I took it down and held it against my body, pressing into it as I looked in the mirror. Something about it made me feel greedy, and in that moment I felt a level of want that was stronger than I'd ever known, more than I knew was possible. More than the touch of her things or the run of her room. I wanted a moment of actually *being* Delia.

I slipped my nightshirt over my head, standing naked in their bedroom for a beat, before slithering the dress over my head. It fitted me so well I think Delia and I must be the same height and shape, when I've always thought of her as being taller and slimmer. And the mirror revealed that I wore it nearly as well as she did, which gave me a giddy sense of excitement and abandon.

I lay on their bed. It was a silly, reckless thing to do, but it also felt inevitable, as if the act of lying in their sheets and resting my head against their indented pillows would somehow bring me closer to them. The bed smelt musky, like they'd marked their territory, which made me turn onto my stomach. Every nerve in my body was alight, so even the silk against my skin made me groan, softly.

I don't think it's that I desire Rosie or Delia specifically. It's more about their essence. I undoubtedly love them both, but not in a traditional sense. Would I lie between them? Possibly. But I think it's more that I would eat them if I could. Consuming every part of them until they become part of me.

8 July

Time is so strange, isn't it? Sometimes dragging, other times racing. Yesterday, I think it's fair to say, I appreciated every second. Tom slept late and, when he came down, I was in the kitchen making a sandwich for lunch. I had my back to the door, but he said my name and when I turned, his eyes reminded me of Delia's in the painting in Rosie's study. He strode across the kitchen and pushed me against a cupboard, his hands snaking into my hair as he kissed me.

Does it sound pathetic to say I've never been kissed like that before? Is it too much of a cliché to say I lose myself in his kisses? Rosie would describe this better, because it's more than that and I need to find a way to articulate it if I want to be a writer. Okay, how about: when we kiss, I long for the unreachable – those parts of another person that always remain just beyond our grasp. He makes me want complete absorption, nothing about him unknown. When our bodies are together a strange desperation passes between us that both excites and revolts me. He makes me feel powerful and powerless at the same time, as if the possibility of pain is right there, just behind the pleasure. When our flesh is pressed against each other's, I sense a hunger, like neither of us can get enough. As if there's too much to know, and not enough time.

'What did you think the very first moment you saw me,' I said as the sun rose this morning, sleep a mere concept that neither of us will ever need again. We were lying in his bed, our bodies glistening, the sheets in a pile on the floor, the air heavy with heat and sex.

'I thought you were beautiful.'

I rolled onto my side and propped my head on my elbow. 'No, I don't mean that.'

He smiled up at me and we both knew what I was saying. 'I thought you were someone I could like very much. I thought you looked kind and clever and bright.' He rolled me onto my back, following the movement, so he was suspended above me. 'Hello,' he said.

'Hello,' I replied.

'Hello, finally,' he said and my heart felt warm.

'I wish I'd known you all my life,' I said and he laughed.

And yet I'm also looking forward to Rosie and Delia's return. They infuse Shadowlands with an energy that has dissipated with them gone.

Tom wants to tell Rosie and Delia about us, but I'm surprised by how that thought makes me feel like I've drunk tar. I think it's something to do with how I don't want anything to disrupt what I have with Rosie. Not that I want anything like that to happen between us, but I do worry that the idea of me with Tom will upset him. I think Rosie is a bit like me, in that he wants to be everyone's favourite, and that's fine, I can give him that. Because what this weekend has solidified is that I cannot allow anything to jeopardize my time here. I simply can't conceive of leaving.

UNRELIABLE NARRATOR

There is so much I had barely known existed, but now can't imagine living without. How, for example, have I lived without cool stone or warm grass under my feet, soft birdsong in trees, clear water as it rises over my head, sun glinting off tall mirrors, flickering candlelight on warm nights, soaring music through open windows, laughter around tables? Before Shadowlands I never understood that beauty could be tangible. It's not restricted to people and places, but can be found in objects. Delia calls her favourites things 'gems', and she's right, they are precious. Chosen with care, or passed through generations, even the functional here is imbued with stories and money. It's funny, because in a house stuffed with silver and art, I find myself most drawn to the china, a little bowl on a shelf in the drawing room particularly, its interior patterned with a tangle of interconnected roses, complete with their thorny stems. The roses are a colour I've never seen before, a brownish pink that makes me think of love. I pick it up sometimes when I'm alone, holding it up to the light so I can see the sun shining through it, its fragility so absolute I have to resist the urge to hurl it to the floor and watch it shatter around me.

12 July

Rosie and Delia have brought an odd mood back with them. Delia seems down and Rosie extremely up. She drinks more than usual at supper and talks less, in contrast to Rosie's almost manic effervescence. When Delia goes to bed, he begs Tom and me to stay up, so the nights often end in the early hours. I don't think it's about us, more just that we're there and he's always hyper, because I've also noticed that the heat of his attention has shifted from me. He's still funny and charming and mornings in his study are intense and heady, but his eyes don't linger on me any more and often it's easy to tell that his thoughts are elsewhere. I miss the attention in an immature and greedy way, because I'm also consumed with Tom.

Our time together has become almost more delicious now we have to grab private chances; snatched kisses by the pool, hands resting on hot flesh a moment too long, breathy desires whispered as we pass. Nothing excites me more than hearing his low tread on the stairs after the house has quietened, knowing we have hours to spend in my pillowy bed, the night crackling around us.

Delia has started asking Tom to sit with her in the afternoons when she's in the studio and when I pass, I hear them chatting away. It makes me jealous. Not conventionally, I just can't bear that Tom has anything to say to anyone else, or that he doesn't want to spend every second with me. Which is sort of how I feel about Rosie and Delia as well. I want them all to love me best.

Maybe the heat is getting to my brain. The weather has shifted from a hot British summer to something newsworthy. The temperature climbs every day and the radio shrieks about droughts and breaking records, of dogs and babies suffocating in cars. None of us has felt heat like it in England before, the sort that cracks the ground and dries up rivers. Pete spends most of every day watering so the flowers and plants still stand tall, but the grass has turned a brittle yellow, which at least makes the dog shit easier to spot. Mum told me that London is unbearable, and she has to sleep with a cold flannel wrapped around her neck.

'Maybe you could come back for a weekend,' she said when we last spoke, and I made up a bad excuse about being needed every day. I can't think of anything I'd like less than to go home, which is confusing because I love Mum so much, but this life . . . oh, this life.

15 July

A hand-drawn card from Tilly arrived this morning, which Rosie showed to us at lunch. It was clearly a picture of me and her jumping into the pool, but he thought the woman was Delia. Their mistake sent a hot, flaring fear through me. I thought I was assimilating into this life so well, but that can't be true if I'm unidentifiable. I want to be integral to them. I need to find something that makes them understand that they can't do without me.

After lunch I recklessly followed Tom up to his room, not caring if Rosie and Delia noticed. The day was as hot as ever and I lay on his bed, enervated by the heat and my anger. My eye was drawn, as it always is in his room, to the large patch of damp above the window, where the wallpaper is peeling away.

'Are they short on money?' I asked.

Tom was getting something out of the chest of drawers, but he turned to me. 'What are you talking about?'

I gestured at the spot. 'So much of the house is slightly broken. And the dishwasher is mad. And the fridge is probably older than my mum. And the washing machine is always leaking. And their car.'

He started to laugh, a deep guttural sound that twisted inside me. Then he came and lay on his stomach next to me on the bed. 'You are sweet, Hope,' he said in the end.

My irritation was rippling and I hate the way I still don't understand some things. 'What do you mean?'

'It's all just part of their aesthetic.'

'What aesthetic?'

'You know, their too cool to care, bohemian charade.'

'I'm not sure I understand.'

Tom rolled onto his side, supporting his head, so he was looking down at me. 'Okay, so when you have too much of everything, it becomes a choice to deny yourself, right? Like, imagine trying to explain to a starving African why people in the West restrict food to look like they're malnourished. It's the same shit going on inside all these big country houses. Not fixing anything when they could afford to do it ten times over. Scoffing at people who have new things as if it's wicked.'

I laughed but the sound was strangulated. Tom kissed the top of my nose. 'And you know what, Hope, you and I, as authentically poor people, should feel annoyed by it all, but actually we're charmed in exactly the way we're supposed to be. But you mustn't believe everything you see here.'

'What, not trust the evidence of my eyes?' I said sarcastically. 'The final, most essential command of the party.'

'George Orwell knew what he was on about,' Tom said, and when I let my surprise show on my face, he snorted and said, 'You're not the only one Rosie gets a kick out of educating.'

I was worried that I'd offended him, so tried to think of something to let him know I wasn't up myself. 'Mrs A and B hate me.'

Tom sighed. 'Don't be daft.'

'No, really. I've known it for a while, but it gets more obvious every day. When I brought my plate in after lunch today Mrs B was stuffing a chicken and when I said it smelt like heaven, she looked at me like she wouldn't scrape me off her shoe. Then she rammed her fist so far up the bird, it could only be interpreted as an act of violence. And the other day when I told Mrs A that she could leave early to make sure Rosie's letter to his editor made it to the post, which he'd asked me to say to her, she snorted like I'd sworn at her.'

Tom laughed again and the sound irritated me, so I went on. 'To be honest I find them annoying as well. If this was my house, I'd sack them both. I hate the way they just lurk on the outside of life here. Like some sort of feudal crap.' Although writing that down makes me feel strange because when you boil it down, I can't exactly see the difference between me and them. When all is said and done, I too am paid to be here, I don't have any actual claim on anything – a thought which makes my gut ache.

Tom rolled off the bed. 'It's too hot for this, let's go to the pool.' I sat up reluctantly, thick tears stuck in my throat. 'Everyone loves you, Hope,' he said. 'And I'm pretty sure Mrs A and B hate all of us. Which, you know, is probably totally fair.'

17 July

Before this job I presumed writing was a bit like transmutation. Some people born with a gift that meant they just had to wait for their muse and then everything would pour out of them in an artistic rush. (Slight exaggeration, as obviously I also understood that you have to create characters, work out a plot, find a setting etc.) But I didn't realize it was quite so laborious, or that so much of it isn't actual writing. Rosie and his editor have an endless correspondence, fat A4 envelopes leaving and arriving a couple of times a week. Rosie hunches over the pages his editor sends, sighing and exclaiming and then writing away furiously. After he finishes I file them away, intrigued by what I see. So many of Rosie's words are scribbled out and new ones written on top in a spidery writing. The margins are also often covered in detailed notes or sometimes single exclamation points. Today I read the words, *don't put anything on the page that hasn't earnt its place*.

It seems impossible that anyone talks to Rosie like that, as if there are things he doesn't know, or ways he could improve. It makes me feel as embarrassed as if I'd walked in on him on the toilet. It sounds like an obvious thing to say, but I hadn't quite realized how, well, made up all these made-up stories are. And this knowledge is turning life into a succession of scenes. Something happens and I feel eager to capture it, as if words are birds we can trap in cages.

20 July

Rosie thinks nothing of subjecting us all to his inner workings and his moods infect the whole house. When he's happy the atmosphere is giddy and when he's sad it's heavy. I've become sensitive to him in an almost telepathic sense, always trying to pre-emptively guess what he needs and to have it ready before he thinks to ask. But even that hasn't soothed the tetchiness that's enveloped him in the past few days. I know he's having trouble with the book, and not to take it personally, but still, sometimes being in that study feels unregulated, as if he's capable of anything.

This morning he put me to work looking at photographs of Camden, which is where he's decided T (will it be Teresa? – I hope so. Imagine reading the book when it comes out and knowing I named the main character) and the man she's going to fall in love with (definitely called Aiden) are going to meet. But after only a few minutes, he began to pace, circling the room like a tiger. And then he came up behind me, standing so close I could feel the heat of his body. His presence tangled my brain, so my eyes could barely focus on what was in front of me. He leant forward, his chest brushing against the top of my head.

'That one,' he said, tapping his finger on a photograph I'd discarded. 'I can see them there.'

His proximity did something to my breath, so I didn't trust myself to answer.

He straightened up. 'God, Hope, you make me feel old. I'm trying to write about young love and I'm flummoxed.'

I wanted to laugh because Rosie and Delia are brighter and more vibrant than most people half their age, but I kept myself as still and quiet as possible in case he stopped talking.

He put a hand on my shoulder. 'Go on, tell me about love, young person.'

I looked out of the window at the glare shining off the river, but I could barely see straight. Everything felt dangerous, as if my longings had unmoored me, so I spoke words I normally would never have thought. 'I think . . . it's a bit like an illness.'

'Go on.'

I heard the click of Rosie's Dictaphone, so I tried to speak more coherently, but Rosie's hand was moving, running across my shoulder and to my neck, and I couldn't stop myself from shutting my eyes and exposing my neck, a shudder travelling involuntarily through my body. Delia's warnings rattled through my head, but there was no world in which I would have moved away from his touch.

'It consumes you, a bit like a fever. So you're never entirely in the world and your mind is never completely your own. You have that weird thing of feeling stronger than normal, but also weaker.' His hand moved down, onto the top of my chest, and it felt hot and huge, as if it would barely take any effort for him to break my bones and reach inside me. I was only wearing a vest and my whole body strained for him to keep moving, to touch a part of me that was forbidden. 'It's like something else has taken over your body,' I continued, 'and you know you're at its mercy. Which is exciting and amazing, but also, when you really think about it, very scary.'

Rosie took his hand away and stepped backwards, which made my body sway as if he was a magnet. 'Oh yes, scary love is always the best kind.'

He went back to his desk then and began scribbling away, his head bent low, his concentration absolute. I knew the next time he looked up he wouldn't say anything and everything would return to normal. But my heart was pounding and my mouth was dry. Tom rushed to my mind, and I don't know if I should feel guilty or not. I even looked up at the painting of Delia above Rosie's head and felt like she'd witnessed what had just happened. And, as I looked, it was as if her mouth curled into a sneer and her legs opened a little wider. There is an ugliness to the painting I hadn't noticed before, something bleeding through the lines that made me look away.

But, oh God, even now, hours later, I can still feel Rosie's hand on my skin, his fingers tracing my bones. The idea of being desired by Rosie is as intoxicating as it is insane. I want Rosie to want me. Which is different from wanting Rosie. What would I have done if his hand had kept on moving? In a way, I don't think I'd have had a choice, because the idea of refusing him seems impossible. The truth is, I'm not in control, which is exciting but also terrifying. I have this strange sense that the longer I stay here, the more parts of myself I will lose, and I can't work out if that's a good or bad thing.

23 July

I have been very stupid. Or maybe myopic might be a better word. I've even answered the phone to a breathless female voice asking for Rosie and failed to put two and two together. Tom told me this afternoon, after I spent over an hour waiting for him by the pool, oscillating between trying to find it sweet that Delia enjoys Tom's company to terrible annoyance that she monopolizes his time, and then to a clawing desperation that I might not see him 'til supper, which felt like a week away. But just as I'd given up hope, he came through the gate, wearing just his swimming shorts, and dived into the pool. I sat up to watch him, jealous that the water got to touch him before I did.

'I needed that,' he sighed, as he flopped onto the stones by my lounger.

'I'd almost given up on you.' Tom smiled but something hot was bubbling in my stomach. 'Don't you think it's odd that she wants to spend so much time with you?'

Tom rolled onto his side and squinted up at me. 'Do you mean because of our age difference? Or maybe because I'm a man and she's a woman?'

I felt myself blush then, like I'd given too much away. 'Sorry, I don't know why I said that.' Although I did. I knew what was possible behind closed doors.

'Well, if it makes you feel any better, I don't think it's me, it's just that I'm here. She's in a state about the situation.'

'The situation?'

He sat up, crossing his legs at the ankles and leaning back, his muscles contracting at the top of his arms. 'You know, with Rosie and the new woman.'

My heart thumped against my ribs. 'What do you mean?'

He looked over at me. 'Surely you know? Rosie met someone when they went away for the weekend. Apparently, it's upped a gear in last couple of days. He's talking about going to meet her for a couple of nights.'

I instinctively put a hand to my mouth, like a parody of shock. 'Oh God, that's awful.'

Tom laughed. 'It's how they live.'

'Doesn't Delia mind?' I cringed at the judgemental tone of my voice, but deep down, I felt genuine panic at the thought of anything or anyone coming between what the four of us had.

Tom reached for a packet of discarded cigarettes underneath my lounger. He put two in his mouth and lit them, passing one to me. 'I didn't used to think so. She's been pretty cool about everything over the years. But this time she seems much more upset.'

The rush of nicotine combined with the unrelenting sun was making me woozy. 'What do you mean?'

'I don't fully understand it. But I think it boils down to the fact that she can't bear the thought of more children.'

'Is Tilly the youngest?'

'No, there's another – I think she's called Cassie – who's only three or four.'

The light was shining on the pool in a way that had turned it totally opaque, no chance of seeing to the bottom. 'But, I mean . . .' I felt strangely sad, an urge to cry overtaking me so I had to sit up quickly, hugging my knees to my chest.

Tom held out his hand, so I let him pull me off the lounger onto the hot stones next to him. He pulled me into his wet body. 'You're so sweet.'

'I just can't . . .' My feelings felt too big, like they wanted to climb out of me. 'Tom, I would so hate to live like that.' It was the first thing I'd said for ages that felt completely honest, and yet it was also exposing.

He pulled away and for a horrible moment I thought he'd seen me as the pedant I've come to realize lies at the heart of me. But when I dared look into his face I saw it was kind, filled with a beautiful softness. 'So would I.'

I laughed to hide my embarrassment. 'Really?'

He leant forward and kissed me, his lips soft and pliant against my own. I pulled him closer, our bodies meeting, and then his hands were on my face and it was as if I could feel his love like it was physical and able to penetrate my skin.

He broke away, but kept his hands cupped around my face so we could only look into each other's eyes. 'Hope, just because I'm here a lot, doesn't mean I'm part of this world. Rosie and Delia . . . I'm not like them. You and I are the same. All the things I say to you are real.' He laughed. 'And there is no fucking way I'm sharing you with anyone.'

I leant forward and pressed my lips against his, overcome by the feeling that I would never get enough of him.

'Rosie and Delia are great,' he said, 'and I owe them so much, but I also know they're far from perfect. But you, you're a breath of fresh air. I've never met someone like you before, so emotionally open.' I've never thought of myself like that, but the compliment swelled inside me. Criticizing Rosie and Delia felt illicit, but delicious.

He grabbed at my hand with an urgency that surprised me. 'I want to make this work. Hope, I . . .' He glanced down and I could feel embarrassment, or maybe wariness, radiating off him. 'I don't know if this is too early. I mean, I don't want to scare you off. But I'm falling for you.' He laughed. 'No, actually, that's bullshit. I've fallen already. I think I'm done for.'

The moment contracted around us, as if we were the only people in the world. Nothing existed beyond us, even Rosie and Delia melted away. I leant back into him and pressed my mouth to his and then his hands were slipping inside my swimsuit, finding their way to my flesh. He pulled me closer, leaning back until I felt that moment when you've tilted too far and there's nothing you can do but accept you're going to fall. I once watched a programme on sailing and a man said that moment is called the vanishing angle. I wrote it down because it sounded like a good title for a novel. And it is a perfect description because, in that moment, everything vanished as Tom and I were suspended momentarily in mid-air, before we tipped and landed in the water, falling under, tumbling against each other, our senses dulled for one delicious moment. Sinking together, unsure if we would find our way back to the surface.

27 July

I'm not surprised that Rosie is stuck, because how are writers supposed to describe love? Even as I write those words I recognize their absurdity – I've only known Tom about five weeks and we've been together for even less time, but honestly, that must be what I'm feeling.

I only feel completely real in Tom's presence. Without him, it's like my body turns to smoke, wafting through life longing for his gaze or his touch. Sometimes the feeling scares me because it's like trying to describe a colour, impossible to reach into its essence and extract a meaning. Has anyone ever been able to write down words to explain what blue is? It's mad to think that we will never know if the colours we see are the same as anyone else does. And love is the same. You can never be sure that anyone is experiencing anything exactly as you are. Which makes love a contradictory emotion, united yet separate. Essentially it might be just us, our individual atoms multiplying, our eyes seeing, our ears hearing, our hearts beating. Maybe we can only ever make sense to ourselves, and even that seems unlikely.

1 August

We had just started work this morning when we heard heavy footsteps stomping into the house and then a man shouting, 'Ambrose Glencourt. Ambrose Glencourt, come out, you fucking cad.'

The word cad was so old-fashioned I initially giggled, but then I worried the voice could belong a mad fan with a vendetta, or even a knife, and stood, as if I could physically protect Rosie. But he had simply leant back in his chair, smiling while he tapped a finger against his lip, as if suppressing a laugh.

'You could go through the window,' I said. 'Hide down by the river.'

But he snorted. 'I'm not hiding from bloody Sebastian Glover.'

'You know who that is?'

'Of course I do.'

The man's shouting had increased and then we heard Delia saying, 'For God's sake, Seb, what are you doing?'

'Oh, fuck off, Delia,' the man shouted. 'You might think all this is normal and okay, but you've been fucking brainwashed. That husband of yours is a total arsehole and you're a total arsehole for putting up with him.'

Rosie stood at that and strode to the door, throwing it open. 'Don't *ever* speak to my wife like that again,' he shouted.

On seeing him the man let out strange sort of cry and then rushed towards him, hitting him in the chest, so they both half fell into the room, followed closely by Delia. A strong stench of stale alcohol was coming off the man and I could see that his eyes weren't entirely focusing. He jabbed a finger at Rosie. 'Leave her the fuck alone, do you hear me.'

Rosie walked back to the other side of his desk and sat down. 'Or what, Seb?'

'Or I'll knock your fucking block off, you entitled prick.'

'Seb, please, this is ridiculous,' Delia said, trying to take his arm. But he shook her off and stumbled towards the desk.

'You don't even deserve to call yourself a man,' he shouted at Rosie. 'You just take, take, take. Like the world was made for you.' There was a thrill in hearing someone talk like that to Rosie, a strange sense that he could be right, although the thought was almost blasphemous. I was desperate to know who they were talking about, desperate not to just hear half of this story, although the other half was easy to guess at, especially with what Tom told me about Sara, and the children on the piano.

Rosie flicked his hand in the air, like he was dismissing something. Seb growled, then swept his arm across Rosie's desk, sending papers and the vase holding pens crashing to the floor. The whole scene made me think of when Dexter's wife had accosted me in the restaurant, although she hadn't broken anything. I got that same floating sense of unreality as I'd had then.

'If you don't leave, I'm going to call Bea,' Delia said. And again the story floated just out of my grasp, because wouldn't calling the police make more sense? Who was this woman they were fighting over? And why was Delia taking Rosie's side?

The man turned to her. 'Oh, fuck you all,' he shouted. But her words did appear to have an effect on him because he rubbed at his face, then stumbled from the room. After a moment we heard a car start and screech off down the drive. The atmosphere in the room felt feral and I realized I was still standing in the exact same place as I had been when we first heard Seb shout, my heart wild and my blood thrumming.

'Why don't you give us a moment,' Delia said to me.

I ducked gratefully out of the room, not able to look at either of them and intending to find Tom, but almost as soon as I'd gone through the door Rosie and Delia started to laugh. It was such an odd response I stopped.

'What a ghastly man,' Rosie said.

'Terrible,' Delia replied. I could hear the sound of rustling papers and presumed she must be picking them up from the floor. 'Fuck, that vase has had it.'

'I bet he's the sort of creep who sends his food back in restaurants, or never parks on a yellow line, or goes to the back of the queue.'

'Just forget about him, darling.'

'Oh God, don't you just hate most people. More and more I find a stultifying ennui overcome me when almost anyone opens their mouth.'

'Lack of imagination, as you always say.'

'Oh Delly, I do love you. No one else comes close to understanding me like you do. Come here.'

I heard the soft smack and slurp of lips and tongues, which made me walk away. Tom would no doubt be outside somewhere, but I felt a little dizzy and climbed the stairs to my room instead, where I lay very still on my bed, tasting my heartbeat in my throat. I guess you don't have to understand everything.

2 August

Neither Rosie nor Delia have mentioned yesterday. Everything was fine at supper last night and when I went into the study this morning there were no papers on the floor and the pens were in a new vase. Although, I say everything was fine, but in fact Delia drank more than she usually does and she didn't take part much in the conversation, often looking deep in thought. I told Tom about the scene with Seb when he came up to my room last night and he said she'd seemed very low that afternoon.

'Does she ever have her own affairs?' I asked, as we lay in my bed, the moonlight undulating across us.

'I wouldn't have thought so,' he replied. 'Certainly nothing I've witnessed. I don't think she'd want to. And I don't think Rosie would stand for it.'

'But that's not fair.'

'It's weird because he definitely loves her. He'd be totally lost without her.' We were both quiet for a bit, maybe both trying to work out how the two things could be true at the same time. What, I wonder, does love look like for Rosie and Delia? And who's to say they're wrong? There can't just be one way of being that works for every person. Perhaps the ultimate act of love is freedom?

Tom spoke again. 'She once said to me that it wasn't about the women for Rosie, but the children.'

'How so?'

'I suppose, like, he wants to leave a legacy or something.'

'Can Delia not have children then?'

I felt Tom shrug next to me. 'I don't know. I think, though, she hadn't counted on so many.' The whole idea made me feel unsafe and I drew in closer to him, snuggling my head against his chest, so he wrapped an arm around me. It was like being warm in bed when there's a storm outside. Possibly dangerous to admit, but I feel smug at my luck.

4 August

Some afternoons Delia sends me on errands to the village and I've taken to browsing the charity shop. Yesterday I found a beautiful pale blue sundress among the old lady skirts and chain-store T-shirts. It's unlike anything I've owned previously, simple and understated, elegantly loose and yet perfectly fitted to my body. I felt gorgeous in it, but when I stepped onto the terrace in the evening Delia let out a shriek, leaping up and grabbing at the dress.

'Darling, where did you get this?' she said. 'Rosie, do you recognize this dress?'

Both Rosie and Tom of course turned to me which sent waves of heat pulsating through my body. Rosie shook his head, but it was Tom I was watching, as he looked me up and down until our eyes met and he blushed as well.

'The charity shop in the village,' I said.

'Oh, how funny,' Delia said. 'I guessed that was where Mrs A takes them.'

I started to understand what was going on. 'Oh, God, is it yours?'

'Yes. Well, no, not now, obviously.'

I wanted to sink through the stones at my feet. 'I'm so sorry.' But Delia laughed. 'Whatever for? It looks wonderful on you, much better than it ever did on me. And listen, if you like that, I've got bags waiting to be disposed of and Mrs A is dragging her heels. You must have a rummage. Take anything you want.'

Tom and Rosie didn't seem too bothered by the conversation, going back to the discussion they were having on an obscure point of language, and I thought I'd got away with it. But we all drank a little too much at dinner and, as we were going inside afterwards, Tom pulled me back. 'Keep the dress on,' he whispered in my ear. His breath was hot on my neck and it travelled across the length of my skin.

And then today, when I went upstairs after lunch, a black bin bag filled with clothes was waiting at the bottom of the stairs. When I emptied them on my bed, Delia's scent rushed up at me and it felt like all my Christmases had come at once. They're all Delia signatures: beautiful fabrics, pale colours, clean lines. Some of them are brand new, their expensive tags still attached. I want to clear out my drawers and replace every single item with hers, but that would be too revealing, so I've squirrelled them away and plan on introducing them gradually. I hope Delia doesn't comment every time I wear something of hers, but I want to feel her noticing. This can be our own little delicious secret, that her body and mine have been in such close proximity. And, judging by Tom's reaction last night, he'll enjoy it as much as I do.

'From the back,' he said, 'I'd have thought it was Delia.' When he was inside me, I pretended I was Delia. It made me move against him more confidently, made me feel sexier than I ever have, made him gasp against my neck in a way that felt reckless.

6 August

Casper Waites won the Albemarle last night.

'If that's not me next year I'm going to fucking slit my throat,' Rosie shouted as the announcer on the radio read out the name. 'What's the fucking point. I might as well give up now. If that's what the Albemarle want, I don't even want to win it.'

Delia was looking flushed and her voice had started to slur. 'It's a fucking travesty,' she said, but there wasn't much passion behind her words.

Rosie downed his glass. 'I could take it if it was Ben or Jarrold. But fucking Casper. His book had no plot and his sentence structure is appalling.'

I had seen Casper Waites' book on the shelves in the office. The back cover had a quote from Rosie on it: *Filled with verve and humour, a novel for the ages.*

'You'll win next year,' Delia said, pouring out another glass. She hadn't touched her food. In fact, she's lost weight in the past couple of weeks and I felt worried looking at her, a strange twisting in my stomach like there was something waiting for us in the woods it would be better not to know about. 'You have to. It's your destiny.'

'And last year it was that ridiculous woman,' Rosie said. 'With that stupid book about absolutely nothing.'

Delia motioned with her eyes for Tom and I to leave, which I did gratefully as we could all see a mood beginning to settle over Rosie. As we went upstairs, Tom told me Rosie's last book wasn't even shortlisted, and that he'd been in the same Oxford college as Casper Waites.

'He expects too much,' Tom said as we reached my landing. His tone was gruff and when I turned to look at him his jaw was clenched and there were deep shadows round his eyes.

I stood on tiptoes to kiss the side of his mouth, which softened him and he smiled at me. 'What do you mean?' I asked.

Tom drew me into him so my head was resting on his chest and I couldn't see his face when he spoke, although I felt the vibration of his words travel through him. 'They say desperate people are dangerous, but you know, I think people who've never known real desperation are worse. They have no idea what it's like to lose.'

I shivered even though all the hot air of the day had risen upwards, so my floor was stifling. Sometimes I don't even know the questions I'm meant to ask, which makes me feel like I'm missing whole chunks of knowledge here.

And now today the house is dripping with Rosie's despair. We've all been tiptoeing around him like supplicants scared of an omnipotent god, which is easier for everyone who doesn't have to spend hours shut in a room with him.

The sun has burned so relentlessly and for so long it's like it's bleached the sky, which is just a white strip above our heads. When I go to Willerton Banks I see livestock huddled under the shade of trees and the river in the wood has almost dried up. We all constantly glisten with sweat and complain of headaches because no one is sleeping properly. The only place I feel human is the pool, except Tom and I are the only ones who use it regularly, which makes me worried for everyone else, especially Mrs A and B, who are surely too old to be getting this hot.

The words I had to transcribe this morning were almost unintelligible. Lots of swearing and false starts, tiny bits of sentences, sometimes abstract words, all of which made me feel deranged as I sat there typing up Rosie's ravings. It's such an odd thing to do, his words beating straight into my brain so sometimes I can feel their vibration. Sometimes it feels like the most intimate thing you can do for someone.

8 August

A horrendous, strange morning – Rosie was working on a set of pages from his editor, while I attempted to make sense of a series of unconnected words: *shit, shovel, pleasure in pain or should that be pain in pleasure, although what's the use, beauty of the damned, damned words*, when suddenly he threw a paperweight across the room, narrowly missing the window, but taking a chunk out of the wall. I stopped the Dictaphone and took off my headphones.

'Are you okay?' I asked.

He groaned and rubbed his hands across his face. 'Sorry, Hope. I shouldn't have done that.' Rosie only goes outside for minutes at a time in the day, but even he's picked up a faint tan and he looked very handsome, the sunlight catching in his brown eyes. 'It's too hot to work and I'm a miserable git, why don't you go and jump in the pool or something.'

I sensed that he wanted to be alone, but also I got a strange feeling walking out and leaving him with his troubles. Rosie's troubles feel bigger than the rest of ours. He's battling such important things, his brain working in a way the rest of ours don't. I went straight to find Delia, who was reading at the edge of the wood, and told her about the thrown paperweight.

'Oh God,' she said, sitting up. 'Thanks for letting me know, Hope.'

I watched her walk back to the house and through the open French doors, which to my knowledge haven't even been shut, let alone locked, for the past two weeks. It was too hot to be outside and I wanted to find Tom, but when I stepped into the hall from the drawing room I could hear voices from Rosie's study. Of course I should have walked on, but I wanted to know for once exactly what was going on, so crept up to the slightly ajar door.

'It's just not coming,' Rosie was saying.

'You always feel like this,' Delia replied. 'And you always get through it.'

'But what if I can't this time? What if this is it?'

'Of course it isn't, darling. You're a genius, it will never be it.'

'No, this feels different.' His breath shuddered. 'I don't think I can resolve it.'

'Of course you can. We've put so much in place to help you this time.'

'That makes it worse.' He paused. 'I have my heart set on it being this grand passion. You know, totally all-consuming in the way of the young. That's why *Romeo and Juliet* worked, because they were teenagers. Imagine if they'd been in their thirties, it would have been absurd. Adults don't fall in love like that.'

'Ah, but remember,' Delia said, '*Romeo and Juliet* is all a trick. I'm not even sure it's a love story. Don't you think it's more about control?'

'Love and control often go hand in hand.'

'God, that's a depressing statement.'

'Life is fucking depressing.'

I felt Shadowlands encircle me with those words, the absurdity of them there like a joke.

'What's going to change things?'

Rosie sighed dramatically. 'I don't know. I look at Hope and I want to bottle all that youth and passion she has. It almost drips off her and even though it's right in front of me, I can't get it onto the page.'

'Ssh, sweetheart, you're getting all worked up.'

'But, Delly, I can't work it out. The power, the sureness of youth is so strong, I can't figure out what it would take to break that. Look at me, I can't even work out the story, let alone get two half-decent characters on the page.'

I was holding my breath, lost in the idea that Rosie watched me, that he saw something in me worth capturing.

I heard the click of a lighter. 'How can I help?'

'I don't fucking know. If I knew I'd help myself.'

Footsteps walked across the room, towards the window. I was pretty sure they were Delia's.

'Please, Delly, I need you.' Rosie sounded desperate, like he was drowning, and I felt a stab of jealousy that no one has ever spoken to me that way.

'What's the main problem?' Delia said, although her voice sounded more distant, so I suspected she was looking out of the window.

'God, I don't know, all of it.' They were both silent for a moment and then Rosie said, 'I suppose the ending.'

'But we've gone over it so many times.'

There was a silence as I tried to work out what she meant. Then Rosie spoke again. 'I think I might have to witness it.'

'Witness it?' Delia laughed. 'But that's . . . well, that would be pretty hard.'

'But you said you'd help.' Rosie sounded surprisingly childlike, and it made me feel a bit nauseous. 'You know this is my big chance. I have to make this one work.'

'Yes, but . . .'

'Delly, this is so unfair. I'd do anything for you. I'm not even asking for much. It's nothing. These other people, they don't matter.'

I could hear her dragging on her cigarette in the heavy silence. 'Okay,' she said eventually. 'If that's true, then I want something in return.'

'Anything, my darling.'

'It has to stop. And it can't happen again.'

I didn't understand the parameters of the conversation. This world is wonderful, but it's also so hard to navigate. Lives here are lived in a way I've never encountered before and it sometimes feels like they're speaking a different language. 'Those are your terms?' Rosie's tone was cool.

'Those are my terms,' Delia repeated. 'No negotiation.'

'And if I say no?'

'I won't leave. But I won't be part of this any more. And I certainly won't help with your ending.'

A beat of something dangerous vibrated in the air. 'You know I always wanted to have children with you,' Rosie said.

'Don't,' Delia said.

'But . . .'

'No. I would never take that chance. It's way too dangerous for me.'

'But you would be a wonderful mother.'

'Seriously, Rosie, if you go on speaking like that I will leave this house and never come back. I know who I am.'

'Yes, but sometimes *I* don't feel like I know who you are. I wish you'd talk to me about it.'

'There's nothing to say. Except maybe take that thing down.'

I leant into the door so I could see through the crack in the frame. Delia was staring at the painting of herself, tears snaking down her face. Rosie stood and went over to her, wrapping his arms around her. She let him pull her into him and rested her head against his shoulder, but her arms stayed hanging by her side, as if she didn't have the energy to raise them.

He pulled away, so he could look straight at her. 'It's always you, Delly. No one else means anything.' The words landed in my stomach like I was hungry.

'That's not enough any more,' she said.

'Okay.' Rosie spoke in a way that made me think there had never been a decision to be made. 'Okay, I'll ring Bea this evening.'

Delia nodded before turning away abruptly and heading for the door. I rushed up the stairs, my heart thrashing about in my chest like a caged animal. I nearly knocked on the door of Tom's room, but I needed to be alone. And even after writing it all down I can't form a complete picture, although I am consumed by the idea of living a life so totally entwined with another, where you don't have to explain anything, where you hold hands of cards, where power slips and slithers. There's an excitement to that that could be better than peacefully loving someone.

Later –

Rosie and Delia are down by the edge of the wood, their cigarettes lighting up the dark like fireflies. When I came down to supper this evening, they were on the terrace. Rosie was standing behind Delia, pressing into her so tightly there wasn't a millimetre of air between them. One of his hands was cupped around a breast and the other slipped down the front of her skirt. Delia's head was tilted back against his shoulder, her eyes shut and her tongue darting between her lips as she panted in the air. I should have walked away, but the sight was so mesmerizing I hung back in the dusk of the sitting room. Rosie's right: it is always her. The rest of us pale in comparison. Watching them, now and then, I can feel a reverberation deep in my stomach, not so much of jealousy, but desire. It's not that I want to disrupt them, more that I long to be part of it.

10 August

Can't get the conversation I overheard between R & D out of my mind. I rang Mum after work today and asked how it could be dangerous to have a child.

'Medically it could be,' she said.

'No, I don't think it's that.'

'Why do you ask?'

'Oh, just something in Rosie's book that I typed up for him today.' Lies come strangely easy to me here, like they're woven into the fabric of the atmosphere, a world in which stories are made creating a world of stories.

'I suppose then,' Mum paused for a moment, 'I suppose, he could mean how you love your children so much you're suddenly aware that the whole world is dangerous.'

A strange excitement coursed through me. 'Go on, in what way?'

'Well, just, like after I had you I had this period of time where I barely wanted to leave the house. I saw danger everywhere. And not just the obvious stuff like someone stealing you or a car knocking us over. I even saw it in the air, like I was suddenly aware of all the diseases everywhere. Or I'd have to check every plug ten times before I went to sleep to make sure there wasn't a fire while we slept.' She stopped, but I waited, sure there was more. 'And, of course there's all the things you could do to a child. You know, you suddenly realize that you're responsible for a whole life. And not just literally in that you have to feed and clothe and bathe them. But, also, like how they'll turn out, how secure they'll feel. There are a million and one ways you can fuck someone up and often you're just a kid yourself or there's loads you don't understand or no one taught you.' She laughed. 'Sorry, he probably didn't mean any of that.'

I laughed back, although I felt like crying. 'I love you, Mum,' I said.

14 August

Is there some law of physics that states only one couple in close proximity can be happy at a time? Rosie and Delia's love is palpable at the moment, just as Tom seems to be becoming more distant. Sometimes I can't find him anywhere and then, when he appears, he's hardly present, his eyes glassy like he's barely seeing me. Last night he didn't even come to my room, which meant I lay awake until three this morning, turning over and over what I might have done wrong. And earlier, when I was passing Delia's studio, I heard them arguing – not raised voices but the tone was hard and flat. I could see Delia through the window, leaning against the sink under the painting of herself. She was wearing her cut-off dungarees and a tiny vest, one arm across her stomach and the other gesticulating at Tom, who was obscured from my view.

'I just don't want to,' he said. 'It's so fucking mean.'

'You of all people should know that life is mean,' she answered, and something hard dropped through my stomach.

'But even the thought of it makes me feel like shit.' His voice wobbled in a way that made me want to cry, because I should be the person he unburdens himself to. Although, Mum is the person I usually go to when things get hard and Delia has said that she sees Tom as a sort of son. Not that I can talk to Mum about this because I still haven't told her about Tom. Her not knowing about this big important thing in my life makes me feel scared, like a gap is widening between us. I don't want that, but also I don't want to give up even a small part of my life at Shadowlands.

'Well, I'm sorry,' Delia said sarcastically, 'maybe just tap into some gratitude then.'

The dogs came running out of the studio, barking overexcitedly at the sight of me, which meant I had to hurry on because I would have hated having been caught eavesdropping. In an attempt at calmness I went and lay in the spot in the woods Tom and I like by the trickle of the river, my head under the dappled shade of the trees, my body baking in the harsh heat of the sun. I thought he might come and find me, but he didn't. Everything here feels like half a story and it's driving me mad.

16 August

Why has Tom become so hard to reach? There's a constant clawing in the pit of my stomach, fear dancing continually through my veins. When we're in the same space, I long for him to brush my leg or smile so desperately it feels like a physical need. But he never does. When he comes to my bed at night and we fuck (because that's what it is now), I sense him pulling away from me even when he's inside me. Then he leaves in the early morning and I cry into my pillow like a schoolgirl. And it's not just me – he's moody with Rosie and Delia in a childish, daring way. Last night Rosie was talking about some theory to do with how human emotion might be more dictated by tidal currents than circumstances when Tom started laughing, but not in an amused way.

'Christ,' he said, 'only someone who has never been beaten down by circumstance would think that.'

They looked at each other across the table, the candlelight flickering on their faces, and I knew Delia was holding her breath in the same way I was.

'If you're talking about me specifically,' Rosie said eventually, 'then I've had my fair share of bad circumstance.'

Tom snorted, looking up to take in the house. 'I'd say you've been softened.'

'Maybe.' Rosie lit a cigarette. 'But also maybe we've all become too accustomed to letting our emotions show. Or blind-sided by thinking they're important. When really we're just part of a big cosmic fuck-up.'

Delia put her hand to her forehead and shut her eyes for a beat. I couldn't help looking over my shoulder, into the blackness of the garden.

Tom laughed again. 'Cosmic fuck-up? I guess if that's how you see life, then you wouldn't care about individual people.'

'Caring too much about individuals gets you nowhere,' Rosie said, although he reached across and took Delia's hand as he spoke. She flinched at his touch.

Tom drained his wine. 'Life lessons from the great Ambrose Glencourt.'

Rosie smiled at him. 'You don't have to listen to me if you find what I say so offensive. No one is forcing you to stay here and sit round my table drinking my wine, sleeping in our comfortable beds, swimming in the pool.'

Delia stood and started clearing plates. 'Come on, you two, this is boring.'

I was breathing too heavily and sweat had formed at my temples and under my arms. Tom stood abruptly, his chair clattering back against the stones. But he didn't pick it up before he strode into the house. I was desperate to follow him, but felt stuck to my seat, like whatever happened I had been abandoned. Rosie sighed and stood as well, following Delia, who looked like she was about to burst into tears, as she carried the plates round the side to the kitchen. His movement released me, so I was able to stand and dip into the house through the French doors.

I knocked on Tom's door and when he answered he looked like he'd been crying.

'Are you okay?' I asked, wanting to reach out and touch him, but losing my nerve.

'I can't do this tonight, Hope,' he said, shutting the door in my face.

17 August

At least Rosie's dictated notes have become easier to transcribe – whole scenes and sentences in my ears rather than all those disconcerting single words. Yesterday he told me that he's figured out the ending, no mention of Delia, and I'll be hearing bits of it through my headphones soon. But first, he said, we had to backtrack a little because, 'I've introduced a character too early.' He leant back in his chair, tapping his pen against his lip as he spoke. 'I don't know what I was thinking because it's a fundamental rule of writing. Never give away too much too soon.'

I'm worried that I've given away too much of myself to Tom too quickly. No element of surprise, no card left unturned. And no doubt in my constant revelations I've shown him something that's disgusting or boring? I've been trying so hard to fit into life at Shadowlands, but there are still lots of little things I get wrong or don't understand. Tom obviously doesn't come from this world, but he's been part of it for so long and from such a formative age it's seeped into him. Even his background helps here, makes him interesting. Whereas I'm so bloody normal. In fact, I've come to realize that what links everyone who sits around the terrace table is the fact that they've done or are about to do extraordinary things. Extraordinary is the most important commodity in this world and I don't have it at all. What if I never work out how to make myself extraordinary? What if it's beyond me? Can you fake it? Can you steal it?

19 August

Every day I wake with a thumping heart and that constant sense that I've forgotten something important, or that bad news is just around the corner. Supper last night made me feel particularly anxious – the guests were two Oxford dons and their daughter, who hasn't yet left Oxford (of course), but is having her first play produced at the Royal Court theatre in London this autumn. I barely said a word but kept on getting these waves of sadness that made tears actually well in my eyes.

By the time Tom made it up to my room after they'd gone I couldn't hide the fact that I was crying, my eyes red and puffy. He looked genuinely upset at the sight of me, which was the first proper connection we've had for days. But when he asked what was wrong I felt too embarrassed to be completely honest, stammering out something about how inadequate I felt compared to all the brilliant young people who file through Shadowlands.

He snorted and I saw the hardness return to his expression. 'God, Hope, haven't you worked it out yet? Her godfather's the head of the Royal Court.' He cut his hand through the air as if he wanted to hit something. 'This whole world runs on favours for favours and friends of friends. They all bloody know each other. They're either related or went to school together, or both. It's all one incestuous little clump.'

I haven't seen any of the people who come to Shadowlands like that before. They've all just seemed supremely talented and interesting, open and funny and ready to help each other. But what if there is more going on than that? If they're all linked, then they're like a fence, guarding a precious secret. If I stay here long enough will Rosie and Delia start to open doors for me? If I ever do write a book, would Rosie show it to his editor? Is it possible that one day I could be sitting round the terrace table legitimately?

We were lying on my bed and Tom lit a cigarette, blowing the smoke up into the air above our heads. I lifted my arm and ran my hand through the smoke and was struck with the weirdest sensation. I was suddenly completely aware that the smoke had been inside Tom and now would be inside me and that thrilled me. I want him to be able to penetrate my skin, to alter my DNA.

21 August

Rosie asked me this morning if I like the painting of Delia in his study. I didn't know what to say because, truthfully, I don't know what I think. But it didn't matter because as I squinted up at it he said, 'Delly wants me to take it down, but it's such an important work.'

That I could agree with and so nodded, although some sense of injustice or something rose through me and I spoke without thinking properly. 'Yes, but if she doesn't like it.'

He frowned. 'It's not like it's in the drawing room. No one sees it from day to day.'

I looked back down at my fingers, ready to transcribe Rosie's words. Except for you, I wanted to say. You see it all day every day and maybe that's what she cares about. Although I didn't speak because I didn't know if that was right, or exactly why she would care about that.

22 August

The world has tilted again and I am high on life and love and the sheer brilliance of existing on this strange, spinning planet. My God, the relief.

Last night we had a lovely supper, just the four of us, like old times. I don't know what's changed, but everyone was finally in a relaxed good mood. The air stayed hot long after the sky had darkened and the stars came out, as the Beatles sang to us about love through the French doors and the candles dripped down to the top of the candlesticks. We all drank more than usual; I certainly felt a little unsteady on my feet when I climbed the stairs to bed.

I was in that liminal space between sleep and wakefulness when I heard a sharp thwack on the glass of my window. I jumped out of bed and saw Tom standing on the lawn, his arm tensed behind his head, ready to throw another stone. When he saw me he put a finger to his lips and beckoned me down. I didn't need to be asked twice. The stairs only creaked once on my descent and then I slipped out through the drawing-room doors. The remnants of our meal were still on the terrace table, plates smeared with congealed food and stubbed-out cigarette butts, red-stained wine glasses, a bowl with wilted salad at its base. And, even in my excitement, I felt a stab of shame that Mrs A would clear it all up in the morning before any of us came downstairs.

Tom was waiting for me on the lawn, but when he saw me he started to run. I picked up my pace, following him into the woods at the bottom of the garden. He stopped once we were hidden by the trees and pulled me to him, kissing me like he used to, in a way that makes me feel like I'm melting.

'You looked like a ghost in your white nightdress in the window like that,' he said.

I wanted to ask him what had changed and why he'd switched back to being the person I'd first met. *Who are you, really?* I wanted to ask, but the question felt too loaded, and I didn't want to ruin the moment, so I said, 'Did I scare you?'

He laughed. 'I don't think you could. Although I hope you'd haunt me if you died.'

'Tom!' I pushed his chest. 'Don't say that.'

A frown creased his brow. 'Don't you ever think about the people you love dying?'

'What? No.'

He fished a packet of cigarettes out of his back pocket and lit two, handing one over to me. 'I think I've always known that life is fragile. Even as a kid.'

My spine vibrated in a way that Mum once told me meant someone was walking over my grave. *What do you mean?* I'd asked her. *Someone in the future*, she'd said, *is walking over your grave and you're feeling it now.*

Tom leant back against a tree and fixed me with the intensity of his stare. 'We all have to face our fears in the end, Hope. Who's the person you love most in this world?'

'My mum.' The words were automatic, and they are true, but the question made me aware of a time when she will be surpassed. When who, or what, I love best becomes more complicated.

'Okay. And how would you feel if she died, right now? Think about it.'

I don't know if I'm a late developer or incredibly selfish or maybe stupid, but I hadn't thought deeply about that question before. I had the usual childhood worries about Mum, but they never took root. The question felt dangerous.

'I'd be devastated. I think my life would be over.'

'I thought you'd say something like that.'

I tried to read Tom's expression in the moonlight, but it was distorted by his dragging on the cigarette. I reached out involuntarily and traced a finger down the scars on the inside of his arm. 'I couldn't bear it if anything bad happened to you, either.'

He surprised me by grabbing my hand. 'Life can play tricks on us sometimes, Hope.'

I wanted to scream at him to stop talking in riddles like the rest of them, but his mood felt too fragile and I thought of the way Delia picks her moments and plays to her advantage.

Tom rubbed a hand harshly across his face. 'I'm finding this hard. Letting myself fall for you, I mean. I didn't expect it to feel this, well, real.'

'Being loved doesn't have to be scary,' I said, thinking how pathetic Rosie would find that statement.

'Doesn't it?' He looked up at the sky. 'I don't know what to do with it. I'm not used to being cared for.'

Shame smarted through me that I'd been so focused on my own feelings I hadn't stopped to consider his. 'Oh Tom, I'm sorry.'

He shook his head. 'I really don't want to fuck this up, and sometimes that's not in our control.'

'If you don't want to, then you won't.' But I couldn't help thinking of Rosie. Of course, in the end, I would choose Tom, and of course, in the end, Rosie would choose Delia. But still, just the fact of Rosie feels like an absence of choice.

'But I might do something unforgivable?'

His words felt like a monster hiding in the trees. 'I suppose all you can do is try to be your best self.'

He snorted. 'I'm not even sure who that is.'

'You're doing fine as far as I'm concerned.'

He pushed himself off the tree and walked a pace away. 'Maybe you should go home.'

My heart dropped through my body. 'Do you want me to?'

'No.' He ran his hands through his hair and his eyes twitched like he was trying not to cry. 'But I don't think there's any hope for me. I don't think I know how to be good. You should save yourself the pain.'

I could feel the moment, which had felt so full of promise just moments before, spinning away from us, and I couldn't bear it. I stepped towards him and took his face in my hands so he was forced to look in my eyes. 'Tom, I am not going anywhere. Do you hear me? The only pain would be in not being with you, so you can stop this stupid talk right now.'

We stared at each other and I could see a million words behind his eyes, but then he sighed and took my hand, leading us further into the wood, towards the river. It has dried almost completely, so the bottom is just a muddy strip, but still it felt cool when we stepped into it, onto slick mossy stones. We climbed up the opposite bank, releasing the sweet scent of the marjoram which grows right by the edge, and emerged into a field with tall grass. A slight breeze had blessedly blown in and, in the silvery light of the moon, the field looked like it was undulating.

'Like the sea,' I said, which made Tom laugh.

'I love the way you look at the world,' he said, 'like you still believe in magic.'

'Of course I believe in magic,' I said, which is true. Because isn't that what love is? Our bodies and minds firing in ways we can't control, creating something out of nothing. Which, when you think about it, is the same as writing, that strange fragmentary capture of moments which we make real on the page.

We lay down, making an indentation in the landscape, as if our being there was the most natural thing imaginable. The stars sparkled above our heads, the grass was soft against our backs and the crickets sang just for us. I've never been a fan of love songs, but I wanted a soundtrack to that moment. I want to listen to lyrics in the future and say smugly, yes, I know that feeling.

Tom lit us both another cigarette, wrapping his arm around me, so my head was resting against his chest and I could feel his heart thumping out at me.

'Oh, Hope Jenkins,' he said. 'What are you doing to me?'

I stretched my leg against his and thought how I'd like to climb inside him. 'The same thing you're doing to me, Tom Markham.'

'It'll be okay, won't it? Promise me it'll be okay.'

I laughed to hide the fear that I felt at his words. 'Of course. As long as we're together it'll always be okay.'

The moment contracted around us, the words we wanted to

say like a physical presence, and then he was brave enough. 'I love you,' he whispered.

'I love you too,' I whispered back, tightening my grip across his chest.

'Whatever happens, you must remember that,' he said, so again it felt like I was only hearing half the conversation, even though I was there and Tom was speaking to me.

Is it possible that I've found my way inside those pages of the great love stories – can I be Cathy or Juliet or Elizabeth Bennet? Or perhaps I can write a new story with Hope Jenkins as its hero.

25 August

Delia was sitting on the riverbank in the woods this afternoon, with the dogs scattered around next to her. The woods are usually empty when I walk there and the scene looked so picturesque I blurted out a hello as soon as I saw her. But when she turned her eyes were red and swollen and her nose pink. At first she tried to pretend she was fine, but gave up pretty quickly.

'Sorry,' she said, 'just having a bad day.'

I wanted to sit next to her and put my arm around her, pull her against me and smooth her hair. But it all felt impossible, I didn't even know that Delia had bad days, so I hovered a couple of paces away from her. 'Anything I can help with?'

She laughed dryly. 'No, no.'

'Perhaps I can get you something?'

She looked up at me, leaning back on her hands, and I was reminded of the time by the swimming pool when it felt like she was scrutinizing me. 'I've seen the way Tom looks at you,' she said finally. 'It's nice to see him happy.'

I heated immediately. 'Oh well, I hope . . . I mean, I hope it's okay.'

But she waved away my concerns. 'Christ, we all have to take happiness where we find it.' Clem lumbered upwards and then sank back down next to her, his head on her lap, which she stroked absentmindedly. 'Do you like him a lot?'

'I do, yes.' I wrapped my arms around my waist as I spoke, filled with the sense of my vulnerability.

'Well, be careful,' she said. 'Always expect the unexpected when it comes to love.'

I thought of Rosie and his women and children and felt a surge of tenderness for Delia that she didn't have the sort of honest love that Tom and I do. 'Sometimes, I think it just comes down to being kind to each other.'

Delia laughed again, looking back up at me. 'Oh God, Hope, you really are an idealist, aren't you?' It sounded like an insult and I shifted uncomfortably, my feet sore suddenly. 'The truth is, I think it would disgust me if someone was too kind to me. Tragic, I know. But the thing is, we get taught how to love when we're young and then that's it. That's how we feel we should be loved for ever.'

I wasn't enjoying the conversation. It was uprooting the things I'd always believed and I wanted to set it straight. 'But you and Rosie. You love each other?'

'Oh, of course we do.' She pulled herself up to her feet, brushing dirt from her skirt and swaying slightly, so I wondered if she'd been drinking. 'I suppose what I'm saying is that no one else is ever the complete answer. You have to be strong yourself. Protect yourself.'

We looked at each other across the shadowed woodland and I wondered what she was really saying. I'm sick of that feeling, of nothing being fully clear here, and it made tears prick at my eyes. She took a few steps towards me and reached out a hand, as if she was going to say something else, but then thought better of it and shook her head. 'Sorry, don't listen to me. I'm just feeling maudlin.'

She turned and walked away, the dogs trailing after her, and I was reminded of Rosie saying that dangerous love was the best love. Looking at his wife I wasn't sure that was true.

28 August

No sense from Delia that we ever spoke by the river. I haven't told Tom about it because our happiness still feels fragile and what she said was bleak. Anyway, she appears to have returned to her old self, ebullient and funny, beautiful and serene. Rosie and her smile at each other over our heads and she's gone back to saying that everything is 'heaven'. She looks me in the eye when she speaks and there's not a hint of vulnerability or embarrassment. Maybe I imagined it all?

30 August

We meet at night by the river and gasp into the open sky, or Tom creeps up to my room and we feel like we're on top of the world. As he passes me in a crowded room he puts his hand on my arm as if we're just chatting, the heat travelling between us. In the pool, he pushes me into the side, or we swim into each other under water.

'One day,' he said to me this afternoon, 'I'd like to show you where I was brought up. It's not a pretty sight, but I don't think you'll really know me until you see it.'

Maybe he's right. Maybe we can't know anyone fully until we see where they've come from and open the door on all their worst moments. I kissed the inside of Tom's arm, where the scars are raised. 'I want to know everything,' I said.

2 September

Joy is the word I keep coming back to. I haven't been writing in here the past few days, because every second spent away from any of them feels like a waste. This last week has been like a dream, almost as if Tom has become part of me. My lips feel singed and the hairs on my skin constantly raised. Energy passes between us, a current that I can't believe no one else feels. This is what I want for ever. We have become a series of moments, aching desire so sometimes I forget where we both begin and end, my whole body hollows, my throat opens and it's like I will never be full enough, there is always more, for ever and ever. Sometimes when he's inside me he pauses and we lie there, his hand against my forehead, our eyes locked, and time stops and we both smile and laugh because it's crazy we got this lucky.

Imagine if you hadn't seen that advert, he says. And I know my line: Imagine if Mum hadn't brought that magazine home. Because it seems incredible that all these random chances brought us together. We thrill at the possibility of not meeting, in the same way that people tell the story of near misses. If I'd just stepped into the road one second later, if I'd replaced the batteries on my alarm and made that flight.

We are drunk on the possibility of not meeting, because it reinforces our certainty that we were *meant* to meet. We have always been destined to be together. We have been all of history's great lovers. Our love reincarnates time after time because it is us. Always us.

8 September

I keep dreaming about being pregnant. It's not unpleasant. I love the idea of being completely filled by Tom. Of creating something that belongs just to us. Of having something that means we will be bound together for ever. But the dreams make me feel sad for Delia. I understand why she didn't want Rosie to have any more children. It's not the humiliation or the gossip or anything like that, it's because those other women are tied to him in a way she never will be. And yet in that conversation I overheard, it was clear that he would love to have children with her. She said it was too dangerous and I wonder if Mum is right – I wonder if she meant that the danger lies within her? Except I've never seen a mean side to Delia. I can't believe that she has a bad bone in her body.

10 September

The book is finally flying. When I finish a dictation now sometimes a whole page has formed in front of me. Teresa (yes, it's official – he's using *my* name!) and Aiden have a tempestuous relationship. Extremely passionate but also combative. Like they're in a constant competition with each other, a stubbornness to both their characters that wounds. It makes me feel pleased how Tom and I are navigating our way so much better than them. Although I have also become fond of Teresa and her hectoring need to be loved. This morning, after we finished work, I told Rosie how much I like her.

'Ah yes,' he said, 'vulnerable but feisty, a good combination for a heroine. But you might not be so fond of her by the end.'

I asked what she's going to do, but he tapped the side of his nose. 'Now that would be telling. And I don't want to ruin the surprise.' He leant back in his chair, stretching his arms above his head and yawning. 'Shall we call it a morning? I'm knackered.'

The day was as hot as ever and the pool was waiting for me, so I was quick to stand.

'Actually, before you go,' Rosie said, 'can you pass me a new pen? This one's nearly done. They're in the box on the bureau.'

There were two boxes on the bureau, but I didn't want to ask which he meant. I opened the one at the front and saw a sleek silver gun nestled inside, lying on a bank of blue velvet. It was such an unexpected sight I let out a little scream.

Rosie jumped up and was beside me before I'd even shut the lid. 'Shit, sorry, Hope. I didn't think. I didn't mean for you to see that.'

'I . . . I . . .' I tried to think of something to say but nothing came.

'Promise you won't tell Delly. She hates weapons of any kind. I told her I'd got rid of it years ago.' He'd reddened. 'I don't even know why I have the stupid thing.'

It might sound pathetic that I was so affected by the sight of a gun, but unless you've seen one in real life it's hard to understand how it makes you feel. A strange mix of power and terror, a bit like when you stand on a bridge and imagine jumping. It's not that you want to, it's the fear of what's possible. 'Is it loaded?' I managed.

'I presume so. I've never used the damn thing, wouldn't even know how.' He was even more blustery than usual, his hand pretty much wedged in his hair. 'It was my father's. I've only kept it out of some totally misplaced sentimentality.'

I went straight to the kitchen, where Mrs A and B were chatting, although they stopped as soon as I came in, both turning their backs to me. I downed a glass of cold water, but it didn't help, so I went upstairs, only to find Tom's room empty. A strange panic was taking hold of me, weakening my limbs and making it hard to pull air into my lungs. I ran back downstairs and across the lawn to the pool, where Tom was doing lengths. I sank onto a lounger, biting on the side of my nail as I tried to work out why I felt so agitated. His proximity calmed me, and I reasoned that I needed to dial down my worry. Surely there was nothing wrong with keeping your father's gun, especially if you didn't even know how to use it.

'You look like you've seen a ghost,' Tom said, as he flopped onto the stones by my feet.

'Do you know Rosie has a gun in his office?' I tried to keep my tone neutral, but my voice sounded squeaky.

Tom sat up sharply and I saw the shock in his features which made me feel better about my reaction. 'No. Where?'

'In a box on the bureau.'

'How do you know?'

'He asked me to pass him a pen and I opened the wrong box.'

'What did he say?'

'That it was his father's and he keeps it out of sentimentality.' Tom drew his legs up into his chest and I saw that his hands were shaking slightly as he reached for his cigarettes. 'Are you okay?'

He tried to smile but it looked like his muscles wanted to pull in the opposite direction. 'Yeah, no, it's fine. I just wasn't ready.'

'Ready for what?'

He shook his head. 'I just mean, I hate weapons. They remind me too much of my youth.'

And once again I felt ashamed, my life inexperience a palpable weight between us. 'God, sorry, I didn't think.'

'It's fine.' He hauled himself up and held out his hand to me. 'Come on, it's a beautiful day. Let's make the most of it while we can.'

Rosie once told me that sex scenes are the hardest to write. I thought of that as Tom and I lay deep in the woods, marvelling at each other. Give me a good ol' murder any day, Rosie said, much easier to blow a body apart than put it back together again.

12 September

Oh God, but this morning seemed normal. How could I not have known, how could I not have sensed what was coming? But maybe that's because love makes fools out of all of us. We temporarily forget that mankind is capable of terrible cruelties, that wars rage, that men kill, that lies abound, that children go hungry. We forget about our histories, forget that we exist outside of moments.

In my blissful ignorance I sat in the study with Rosie this morning, doing my usual jobs, listening to his funny remarks, no sense of doom on the horizon. Delia poked her head round the door at one point to say she was sending Mrs A and B home because it was far too hot to work and she was worried about their health. We heard Mrs A's car on the drive not long after and my shoulders relaxed knowing that I wouldn't have to face them again that day. We finished work around midday and I went upstairs to put on my swimsuit. I even leant out of my window like I had all the time in the world, looking at the shimmering haze of heat hanging over the garden and hills beyond underneath the bleached, motionless sky.

A heavy silence was coating everything when I got back

downstairs. The terrace stones were hot underfoot and there was a vibration in the air, almost as if the heat was humming. I ran across the grass which felt more like hay underfoot, avoiding a dog shit that had dried like a stone, and diving straight into the pool. The water was deliciously cool and when I emerged I laughed like an idiot. I lay on my back, the water lapping in my ears and my body undulating in the slight ripples I'd created. The moment was perfect. I wanted to smother myself in Shadowlands, rub myself against every surface, inhale every smell, touch every object. I dived back under, swimming a length, enjoying the feeling of my screaming lungs.

I don't know how or why I've just written all of that, apart from that it feels important to record it. As if now the only way I fully understand things is to write them down. Or perhaps I can change it somehow? Perhaps there's a combination of words that will help me see what I need to do.

When I emerged, Tom was sitting on a lounger looking at me. 'Come in,' I said, pedalling myself to the side in what I hoped to be a seductive fashion, already imaging him pushing me up against the tiled wall. But he shook his head and then I noticed how pale he was. 'Are you okay?'

'I need to talk to you, Hope.'

At his tone, a dark sickness immediately took hold of me. I hauled myself out and sat next to him, but he didn't move closer like he should have done, refusing even to meet my eyes.

'What's wrong?' Dread had taken root in my stomach and I wanted to slap my hands over my ears so I didn't have to hear what he was about to say.

'I'm sorry,' he said and, despite the searing heat, I started to shiver.

My mind was racing through scenarios, but also there weren't that many because we never go anywhere – there is so little to disrupt us, apart from terrifying changes of heart.

He fixed me with his gaze. 'Before I tell you, Hope, you have to believe me when I say everything I've ever said to you has been true. We can get through anything together. Remember that. You've got to trust me. Promise you'll trust me, Hope.'

'For God's sake, Tom,' I shouted. 'What the fuck's going on?'

He didn't even have the decency to meet my eye when he said, 'It's Delia.'

'Delia?'

'I love her.'

The world did a strange swoop. 'Well, of course you love her.'

'No. I'm *in* love with her.' He didn't sound like himself, his tone strangely monotone. And then he started to cry, as if he was the one who should be upset.

But of course, even though I would never have guessed that was what he would say, it also made the most sense. I was, I am, never going to be able to compete against Delia. Any fool can see that. 'You just asked me to trust you,' I said, as if that was the worst thing he'd done.

'Oh God,' he said. 'It's so fucking complicated.'

'Are you saying you want this to end?' I asked desperately, as I motioned between us and a spray of water followed my movement, which reminded me I was sitting in my wet swimming costume, my hair plastered to my forehead, my skin dimpling.

Tom dropped his head into his hands. 'I don't want to keep leading you on. It's not fair on you. What I feel for Delia, it's something different, something . . .'

I stood because I couldn't listen to Tom telling me what I

already knew, that Delia is special in a way I never will be. She already has Rosie, and I hate her for that not being enough, because most people would kill for that alone. I ran from the swimming pool as Tom called my name, across the lawn and back through the house, up to my room, where I collapsed on the bed, trying to blot out hectic images of Tom and Delia together, their bodies connected, their breath sharp.

Of course I cried and wept and thrashed. But now I've worn myself out a numbness has coated me like a fog, so I can't work out what I'm feeling. A deep, visceral misery, an acidic betrayal, a hollow bitterness, a lacerating embarrassment, all of the above? Oh God, what if I have to leave Shadowlands? I can't go back to my tiny flat, the litter-speckled streets outside, exhaust fumes trapped by the heat, the barren wasteland of my local park, no water for miles around, the endless suppers Mum and I will eat on our knees, the stale TV shows we'll watch. No late-night music, no bottles of wine, no cigarettes, no flowers in long borders.

And it's all so unfair. I've worked hard to assimilate myself into a life that had been beyond my imagination, and now it's going to be snatched from me, for no fault of my own. Fuck Tom. Fuck him for being too pathetic to understand what we have. He knows what Shadowlands means to me.

My heart feels dangerously stretched, like I'm aware of every beat and the damage flowing through it. Losing Tom is like death, something I will never recover from. He'll just have to tell me he's sorry and it'll be okay, I'll forgive him for anything.

And thinking about it like that, surely there's another way of looking at this. Tom told me that he loves Delia, not that she loves him. Delia can't love him. At least not in that way. And if that's true, then we can work through this silly infatuation together. This can be our trial, like all the great loves have. I can heal him by showing him what real, requited love is. His childhood probably made it impossible for him to distinguish between infatuation and the real thing. Delia rescued him from his addiction and gave him stability – she must seem like a mother to him, a figure he has to have been searching for in some way. Of course he's in love with her.

I need to get over myself. I can help Tom, be the person who makes it all better, and take her place in his mind. Which will make Delia grateful as well. We won't have to leave Shadowlands; we won't have to stop loving each other. We can work through it together and, when he realizes how much I truly love him, he'll understand that I'm right and love me back in the way he said he wanted to. It's going to be okay. Nothing has to change.

October ??

Can I do this again? What's the point in writing anything more when I've destroyed it all? I'd forgotten about this notebook. All the stupid hopeful things it contains. Meaningless nonsense. Ramblings of a naive girl who didn't know who she was. But I know now.

Oh God, oh God, forgive me. I am the worst person in the world.

If only Mum hadn't insisted on unpacking for me last night, because then this journal would have stayed rotting in my bag as it has been for weeks. Maybe I should have just thrown the whole suitcase away. Although I wouldn't know about the bowl then. Can't work out if I wanted to see that or not.

'What's this?' Mum said, unwrapping it from the two T-shirts someone (God, let it have been Rosie) packed it in.

The sight of it made my heart ache so badly I thought I was going to choke. 'A gift,' I managed, because it has to be. After she left I made myself get up and walk shakily over to the bookshelf and picked up the bowl, where Mum had put it next to this notebook. But the sight of those perfect roses in its centre was too much for me and I was crying very quickly, those ugly, heaving sobs that feel like they might break you.

I'm not entirely sure how long I've been in bed. When I was well enough, the first thing I asked Mum was if Rosie or Delia had called. She said Rosie had twice and was very concerned by how sick I was, which sent tremors of longing through me. I said she had to let me speak to him if he called again and she rolled her eyes and said something like, I don't know when you're going to learn, Hope. No idea what she meant, but now I jump every time the phone rings. Because I need to understand exactly what happened. I'm supposing that Rosie must have got rid of the body somehow. He obviously didn't call the police, or they would have arrested me by now. But isn't disposing of a body also a crime? Which means I can't confess until I've spoken to him because none of this is his fault. I deserve to be punished, but to bring Rosie down would be very unfair.

I can't answer the question of why I aimed for Tom's stomach and it plagues me like a hunting dog latched to my leg. Because if I follow that thought all the way through, as I must, I can only remember the feelings of anger and betrayal in the moment I pulled the trigger. I have seen who I truly am, and I hate myself. And then I hate not just myself but the whole world. I blame physics, even. Time has begun to seem ridiculous, impossible not to be able to dip in and out of. Surely, if I try hard enough, I can go back and will my hand downwards so the bullet just grazes his knee.

But what was I supposed to do? When Delia came bursting into my room and said that Tom and Rosie were fighting I had to follow her. And then when I walked into the study and saw Rosie pinned to his desk by Tom, who had his hands round his throat and was shouting about how he didn't deserve to lick the dirt from her feet, I could only have felt a sick betrayal. And also Delia was screaming at me to stop Tom, that he was going to kill Rosie. I did try as well, I tried to reason with Tom, I tried to push him, but he wouldn't even look at me. I saw Rosie was fading, using his last strength to motion with his eyes to the bureau behind him, which reminded me of the gun. When I held it up I wasn't even sure if it was loaded, and I had assumed the safety was on. Aren't all guns stored that way? I certainly hadn't got as far as thinking about firing the stupid thing. But then Tom looked up at me and smiled and it felt like he was taunting me, as if everything about our love had been a lie and it was so mean and senseless, so before I knew it, I'd pulled back on the trigger. And then that sound. My God, I will never not hear that in my dreams. Or see the way Tom lurched off the desk, his hands clutched to his stomach as blood bloomed behind them before he fell forward, almost right to my feet.

The problem is I can't entirely remember how I got into such a bad state afterwards. All my memories are weird snapshots in my head.

I have a hazy memory of being taken into the sitting room and Delia giving me a pill. Then the terror of waking suddenly on the sofa and the memory of what I'd done rushing back to me like a swarm of hornets. All I wanted was to see if Tom was okay, but it was dark and I crashed into the hall table, which toppled the vase of flowers. Everything was in disarray in the study, the contents of Rosie's desk on the floor and a dark patch on the rug that must have been blood. That was when I started screaming and then Rosie and Delia were there, but they weren't answering any of my questions and I ended up running into the garden and down to the woods. But it must have been raining because I was wet very quickly. And the next thing I remember was waking up on my bed, still soaking, but now both boiling hot and shivering.

I have vague memories of Rosie and Delia checking on me, of my head being lifted and water spilling down my front, of pills being coaxed down my throat. But at night, when I was alone and helpless, Tom visited, sitting by the side of my bed as he wept and begged me to forgive him. He looked so real I was sure that I would be able to feel his warm flesh if only I had the strength to move. But mostly I wanted to tell him to be quiet, because I was the one who should be asking for forgiveness.

Then Mum was there and she said we were going home and I couldn't understand what she meant. Someone must have packed my bags because they were waiting in the car, but the house was empty and no one said goodbye to us, which made me howl. I remember asking Mum when I could go back, but she just sighed, keeping her eyes on the road.

The doctor in London said I had pneumonia, but I didn't care one way or another. It was hard to tell if I couldn't breathe because I was ill or because I was having an ongoing panic attack that seemed likely to last for the rest of my life. Mostly Mum has left me alone, apart from bringing me food and water and making sure I take my antibiotics. I've spent the past couple of weeks lying in bed on my back, only able to breathe into a tiny space at the top of my lungs, not really caring if they close up completely.

Rosie just rang. It is 19 October, which I know because Mum's diary was open next to the phone. That means I've been at home for just over a month, which feels both longer and shorter than I thought. I need to write down what we said before I forget.

'I've been so worried about you,' Rosie said.

His voice, or maybe the exertion of standing up, made me dizzy, so I pulled over a kitchen chair to sit on. 'I've been really sick.'

'Your mother said pneumonia?'

'Yes.'

'But you're on the mend now?'

'I feel like I'm going to die.'

He drew in a sharp breath. 'Hope, that's not a useful way to think. Your mother said you should be better very soon, and you'll need to get on with your life.'

I snorted. 'What life?'

'That's a silly thing to say.' His admonition smarted against my raw skin. 'You're young and have everything ahead of you.'

I lowered my voice. 'Are you mad?'

'No, Hope, you can't think like that. Everything just got very out of hand. What happened wasn't your fault.'

I started to cry then because of course Rosie would think I'd fired the gun to protect him. But that was because he didn't know what had been going on between me and Tom, so he couldn't guess at my real, disgusting motive.

'Look,' he said, his voice calmer. 'Please help me out here, like I have you. This is a career-ending scandal.'

'I know.'

'Not to mention that we'd both go to prison if this gets out?'

'Yes.'

'Have you told your mother, or anyone, anything about what happened?'

'No. Of course not.'

He sighed. 'God, what a stupid mess. But you do understand, don't you, that you can never say anything at all about this to anyone ever?' I didn't answer, so he went on. 'Look, you want to be a novelist, don't you? Well, think of this as nothing more than a story.'

'But it's not a story. It's real.'

'Oh God, we'll both get into so much trouble if you say anything. Our lives would be ruined. Please don't do that to me.'

I wanted to tell Rosie that I didn't care about getting into trouble and I wished he hadn't got rid of Tom's body and just rung the police. But that would have been mean because he'd risked so much to protect me, and I had to hang on to that. 'I promise. I won't say anything.'

His tone was much softer when he next spoke. 'Listen, Hope, you're bright and beautiful and brilliant. You'll go on to have a wonderful life. You just need to forget all about this and move on.'

I was crying so hard I couldn't answer.

'I'll think of you often,' he said, sending a last pang of longing through me.

After we'd finished speaking I didn't move for a while, letting the dial tone vibrate through my body.

I want sunsets and first times. I want a wedding dress and to feel our baby pushing against my ribs. I want to hold hands. I want to argue over whose turn it is to take out the bins. I want to vote together. I want to dance. I want to still dance when our knees are tired and our skin is sagging. I want to nurse through illness. I want a favourite mug, or chair, or side of the bed. I want to tell friends he's impossible. I want to look across a room and read a whole life in an expression. I want to throw plates. I want to make up.

But failing all of that, I want a funeral. I want to dress in black and weep and wail. I'd like an open casket. I'd like to feel people watching me. I'd like Delia to put a hand on my arm and tell me that he loved me, that she'd never seen him like that, that I made him happier than she'd dared hope he ever could be. I want to be disgusted by the heavy make-up the undertaker uses. I want to watch his coffin lower into the ground and feel my heart ripping inside me so for whole seconds I consider jumping in after him. I want to be the first person to throw earth onto the coffin, or maybe a rose, yes, that would be better, a single white rose. I think it would be best if I was wearing a veil. I want a grave. I want to be able to go and weep beside it every day for the rest of my life. I want to meet his mother because then there will be at least one person who wants to talk about him and with our words he won't be completely dead.

Halloween

I know it is because children were screaming earlier and when I looked out of the window I saw lots of little ghosts and witches holding their mothers' hands. Trick or treat, they chorused as doors opened. Every day will be Halloween for me now. I will be forever haunted.

But Mum says I'm better and I have to get up, that she's losing patience with my moping. Except I don't know how that's possible. I have ruined the only thing that has ever meant anything to me. I have destroyed everything. I went looking for excitement and instead I found myself. But not in a good way, not like people who come back from travels in India mean. No, I ripped open my soul and found only ugly darkness. And I won't even be punished. This knowledge of who I am is something I will have to live silently with for the rest of my life. Even that term terrifies me: the rest of my life. I can't imagine anything past my bedroom door. I cannot conceive of a future. How am I supposed to carry on? I have seen heaven and I have seen hell and I do not know what life can hold for someone as rotten as me.

Part Two

Chapter One

'I want to report a crime,' the woman said, before she'd even fully sat down.

Nat looked at the piece of paper the desk sergeant had handed her as he'd passed the case over. Just two words written on it: *fruit loop*. She hated how they always found a way to give her the shitty, bottom-of-the-rung cases. The ones that took loads of effort for no results. The ones that meant you would always be passed over for promotion, nothing concrete to show despite years of work.

But she opened her notebook and clicked her pen, setting her face in what she hoped wasn't complete disdain. The woman was looking at her expectantly, her fingers worrying at the sides of her nails, which were bitten to nothing, flakes of skin peeling off. Her hair was lank, her skin dry, and she keep running her top teeth across her chapped bottom lip. A smell was wafting off her that Nat recognized from too many interviews like this one, the stale throb of alcohol leaking from pores and tobacco clinging to fabric.

'Right,' Nat said, 'shall we start with your name?'

'Hope Jenkins.'

It amazed Nat how many parents lacked foresight. How many people must hold their perfect newborn on that first day and give them a bright, optimistic name, not realizing that most people turn out to be a disappointment. At Ben's last birthday she'd been shocked by the number of esoteric names that the kids carrying them had no hope of living up to. When she'd tried to laugh about it with Kira afterwards, her wife had told her that her problem was that she was mean-spirited at heart. Add it to the list, Nat had replied. Thinking about Kira made her glance at the clock: half five, meaning her shift would be over in an hour, but she didn't want to be home in time for bath time.

'So, Miss Jenkins, what crime are you reporting?'

The woman's eyes were skittering, refusing to settle, almost as if she was scared of seeing anything too directly. Nat thought she wasn't as old as she'd first assumed, in fact, they were probably around the same age.

'Someone has written a book about me,' the woman said.

Nat looked up from her pad, now knowing for sure that this was going to be one of those wading-through-mud interviews. 'Without your permission?'

'That's right.'

'And has the book been published?'

Hope Jenkins laughed curtly. 'Oh yes, very much so.'

'What's it called?'

'*The Ruined Girl.*'

Nat stopped writing, wondering for a second if this could be a practical joke. '*The Ruined Girl*, by Ambrose Glencourt?'

'Yes. Have you read it? Or seen the film?'

'No. Neither.' Nat batted away a memory of Kira telling her that she was culturally deficient, another of her problems.

Hope Jenkins nodded. 'Well, up until last week, you and I were probably two of the very few people on the planet who hadn't read that book or seen the film. Which was a massive mistake on my part.'

'Why?'

'I just told you. Because that novel is my story.'

'But isn't it, well, made up? How can it be about you?'

Hope put her hand to her forehead and pressed against her skull in a way that contracted Nat's stomach. She had a bizarre moment of thinking the woman was going to break her skin and bone, that she was going to go on pressing until she'd made it inside, until she'd revealed the very essence of herself, all the grey, meaty sinews that made up her neural pathways. But all she said was, 'It's very complicated.'

What isn't, Nat wanted to say, but settled on: 'Perhaps you could try to explain.'

The woman looked at her like she was stupid. 'I did all the things that he wrote about, in almost the same exact order.'

'As I haven't read the book, you're going to have to tell me what those things are?'

'Well, essentially, I fell in love with a man, who I then killed because he was in love with someone else.'

Nat often thought of cases as having shapes, and this one was starting to feel like a set of tangled fairy lights. She let her pen drop and put her hands flat on the desk in front of her. 'Sorry, have I got this right? You're confessing to a murder?'

Hope dabbed at her brow, a sheen of sweat visible along what had once probably been high cheekbones and a dainty nose, but were now lost under doughy, pallid skin. 'Well, yes, that's part of it. But the point is, Rosie requisitioned my life. When he told me not to say anything.'

'Hang on.' Nat glanced at the piece of folded paper on her desk that contained the words fruit loop. 'This novel's been out for a while. When did this supposed murder take place?'

'September 2016.'

'So, what, ten years ago?'

Hope nodded. 'That's right.'

'Where?'

'At Rosie, Ambrose Glencourt's, house, Shadowlands, in Somerset.'

Nat felt a fresh round of resentment for how they were probably laughing at her right then in the canteen. Getting the psych team involved was always a long and painful process. But, despite herself, Nat could also feel a small spark of excitement coursing through her body. Of course the woman was most likely delusional, but if she was legit this would be *big*. A murder at the home of Ambrose Glencourt. Nat hadn't personally read his novels, but he'd become a household name in recent years. This was the sort of high-profile case that would get her superiors' attention, if she handled it correctly.

'Would you like a cup of tea or coffee, Miss Jenkins?' The woman shook her head and Nat thought she'd have done better offering her a glass of wine. 'Okay, so can you explain what happened as clearly as possible?'

Hope swallowed, her hand going to her throat. 'I went to work for Rosie as his secretary in June 2016, when I was twenty-three, and he was writing *The Ruined Girl*. It was a live-in position because his house, Shadowlands, is in the middle of nowhere. We didn't even have internet or mobile service out there. But I didn't mind because it really is the most beautiful place I've ever seen.' Hope's eyes flickered behind Nat's head and Nat knew she was momentarily back there as her cheeks flushed. 'It was that incredibly hot summer, if you remember?'

'Yes, of course.'

'I think it's still the hottest sustained British summer on record. Although I'm sure climate change will put paid to that soon enough.'

The things the woman said were surprising and Nat attempted a mental recalibration of her initial impression, which was promising in terms of the case.

Hope opened her bag and pulled out a battered-looking notebook. 'Look, this story is impossible to explain. It's all so mixed up and I've never spoken about it. But I wrote down what happened at the time. You need to read my journal.' She slid the notebook across the table.

Normally Nat wouldn't have deigned to touch something as stupid as a journal, only one up in her mind from telling someone your dreams, but the lure of the story and the people who inhabited it made her turn to the first page, where she saw a rounded, girlish hand covering the page.

'Why has it taken you so long to come forward?'

Hope's eyes did fill then, but she pressed her fingers into the bridge of her nose, like she was stemming a tap. 'Because I'm an idiot.'

Nat waited but nothing more came. 'You're going to have to be more specific.'

Hope pulled in a breath, her chest rising dramatically, so Nat momentarily worried she was going to collapse, but then she steadied herself. 'I wanted to protect Rosie. Ambrose Glencourt.'

Nat's blood was moving in a way she'd almost forgotten. 'What were you protecting him from?'

'He must have buried, or somehow got rid of, the body. Which is a crime, right?'

Nat was finding it hard to follow the woman's train of thought. 'Why do you say that?'

'Because Rosie and Delia, his wife, were there when I killed Tom. But when I went back to where it happened, a few hours later, Tom's body was gone. And he asked me not to say anything to anyone ever. Said if I did, we'd both end up in prison, and that didn't seem fair back then.'

Order was needed in the conversation and Nat tried to focus. 'Who was the man you claim to have killed?'

'Tom Markham.'

'How did you kill him?'

'I shot him.'

'And why did you do that?'

Hope's hand grabbed at her throat. 'Tom and I were in a relationship. I thought we were very much in love. But then he told me that he was in love with Delia, Mrs Glencourt, which was devastating.'

The story was becoming more complicated by the second and Nat wasn't sure where to start. 'Can you take me through what happened. Step by step, please.'

Hope drew in a breath to compose herself. 'Okay, so Tom told me that he and Delia were in love. Then he and Rosie had a massive fight over her. Tom physically attacked Rosie. He was strangling him, trying to kill him. I tried to stop him, but I couldn't. I knew Rosie kept a gun in his office, so I thought threatening Tom with that would stop him, but it didn't. I really thought he was going to kill Rosie, and in the end . . . I fired.'

'So it was Ambrose Glencourt's gun?'

'Well, his father's. He didn't even know how to use it. He just kept it out of sentimentality. Something I've thought about a lot over the years is how I only knew it was there by accident.' Her voice hitched. 'If I hadn't been stupid enough to open the wrong box when he asked me for a pen, I wouldn't have shot Tom because I wouldn't have known about the gun.'

Nat was losing track of the story. 'You said Mr Glencourt disposed of the body?'

'Yes. Well, I presume he did.'

Nat rubbed at her tightening forehead. 'What do you mean, presume? You didn't see him do that?'

'No.'

'So, he told you he did?'

'Not in so many words, but it had to have been him or Delia. There was no one else there. And I was sick, so they wouldn't have wanted to upset me by going into details.'

'Sick?' Nat stopped writing for a second.

Hope kept her eyes on Nat's. 'Looking back, I think it was some sort of PTSD, mixed with getting really cold and wet. When I went back to the study and couldn't find Tom's body, I lost it and ended up running into the woods. But it was the night the storm broke the heatwave and I got soaked. I came down with a fever the next morning and it turned into pneumonia.'

There was a lot to take in and Nat gave herself a moment. 'I take it Tom's disappearance wasn't investigated at the time?'

'It couldn't have been, or I'd have been arrested then. And anyway, Tom wasn't someone who would be missed.'

'How come?'

'He was a bit of a loner. The Glencourts had taken him in. He didn't have any contact with his family and I don't think he had many friends.' Hope Jenkins snorted. 'Anyway, people like the Glencourts don't live by the same rules as the rest of us.'

Nat actually agreed with Hope, but she forced herself to say, 'Everyone's equal in the eyes of the law.'

Hope laughed as she pushed some hair out of her face, revealing a large sweat patch under her arm. 'Look, none of that matters anyway. I'm not sure you understand what I'm saying. I shut my life down when I got back from Shadowlands. I wrapped my misery around me like a bloody shroud. I stopped leaving the house. I ignored all my friends. I became so unbearable to live with my mother moved to Spain. And all because Rosie begged me not to say anything, which I thought was the right thing to do because I had shot someone in his home, and he cleaned up the mess to protect me. Or so I thought. But all this time, he'd done the opposite of what he asked of me. He took my story and wrote it into one of the bestselling books of the past ten years. Like it was a work of fucking fiction.'

It was hard not to think about the two words lying on her desk, but Nat told herself that the woman was erudite, even if her story was making less sense by the minute.

'So, you're telling me that even though you were working for Rosie when he wrote *The Ruined Girl*, you didn't read it until recently?'

'That's right.'

'Why not?'

'Because I didn't do *anything* until recently.' Hope's eyes flashed in the sunlight coming through the windows, a glimpse at something inside her she hadn't revealed yet.

'What do you mean, anything? Do you work?'

'Well, yes, obviously I have to work. Not all of us have inherited money like Rosie.'

'But you don't have friends, or a partner?'

Hope leant forward slightly. 'I don't think you're understanding me. After I got back from Shadowlands, I knew the only way I was going to survive was to lock myself up tight. I knew that hearing anything about that life would kill me, so I made sure I didn't, which included not reading Rosie's books. In fact, I stopped reading books altogether. Or listening to music. Or even going to the cinema. So of course I don't have friends or a partner.'

'But why?'

Hope rubbed at her face. 'They all just felt too, I don't know, emotional.'

'So what changed?'

Hope shifted in her seat. 'I saw Rosie on a chat show the other night. He was talking about his new book, a sequel to *The Ruined Girl*. Anyway, he said its central question was asking how you could live with yourself if you'd murdered the person you loved. Which at first made me think, why the fuck is he writing about that. But then I realized that if this book is a sequel, then what the hell is *The Ruined Girl* about. So I read it, and also the journal that I kept when I was working for him.'

Nat thought that any minute she'd be using her training on

how to calm a panic attack. 'Take a deep breath,' she said and Hope did as best she could, but it sounded scratchy.

'When I read *The Ruined Girl*,' Hope said, 'I recognized pretty quickly that I was Teresa. But then I realized that it's the story of the time I spent at Shadowlands as well. I mean, give or take a few minor details, it's exactly what happened.'

'And that made you come here and confess to a murder?'

Nat watched Hope's hands tighten into fists on her lap, her breath so heavy the buttons on her shirt strained. 'It's not about the murder,' Hope said in a way that made Nat want to laugh. Try telling that to the courts, she wanted to say, but instead just nodded so Hope could go on. 'Like I said, I shut down my life for that man. And all this time he'd just thought, oh, I'll take that terrible thing I begged her not to tell anyone about and put it in a book and make lots of money and have a lovely life. He never even bothered to reach out and see how I was getting on. Or to tell me what he'd done.'

Fruit loop. Nat glanced back at the clock. Ten past six. Kira would probably be trying to get some food down Ben while Riley cried. And then there'd be the bath to get through, and reading to Ben, which made Nat want to gouge out her eyes. Plus feeding Riley and getting her into her cot, which was unlikely and Nat could not understand why Kira bothered; it wasn't like their bed was ever used for anything other than sleep.

Hope tapped the notebook. 'It's all in there. And, as you can see, it's dated 2016 and *The Ruined Girl* came out in 2018. It's too much of a coincidence that I could write the same story as the one Rosie published two years later.'

Nat opened the first page again and saw the date right at the top. Although it was in Hope's hand, not an official stamp. But still, if the story was real, then the case would be huge. And if she played her cards right, she might even get to lead it, on the ground at least.

'You have to read it,' Hope said, so Nat looked up at her. Her eyes were darting around and her cheeks were now a deep crimson.

Nat leant forward. 'What do you hope to get out of this, Miss Jenkins?'

'I know I'll have to go to prison.' Hope flicked her gaze to the window and then right back at Nat. 'But that's okay. What you have to understand about me is that I am not a good person. I deserve to be punished.'

The words surprised Nat. Most criminals, most mentally unhinged people in fact, always protested their innocence by virtue of their good character. In all her years on the force she'd only ever arrested two, maybe three people who she believed to be properly bad. Everyone else sat in a grey area, pushed further to one side usually by something almost out of their control. But Hope Jenkins was looking at her with an expression of defiance. This is me, she seemed to be saying. Take it or leave it.

'Listen,' Nat said, 'I'm going to need to make a few phone calls. And have a look through this journal. I'm not arresting you, but I'll get someone to take you to another room and bring you some food and something to drink. Unless you want to leave, of course, and then I'll have to get a warrant to keep you here for twenty-four hours.'

But Hope shook her head sharply. 'Of course I don't want to leave. And I'll tell you what I really want.' She leant forward, so briefly Nat couldn't work out what she was going to do. 'I want Rosie to be punished, too. I've spent all these years keeping still and quiet, not just because I know I'm dangerous, but also because I didn't want to take him down with me. But now I realize he never cared about me at all. The whole thing was one big lie.'

Chapter Two

After Hope was shown into another room, it took all of a few minutes before Tom came and sat on the chair next to her. His presence was hardly surprising. When she'd first started getting out of bed again after Shadowlands she'd seen Tom everywhere, reflected in windows, or turning corners, and she'd heard his laugh bouncing off buildings or in groups of friends. Ten years of emotional vigilance had suppressed this, but reading her journal and *The Ruined Girl* had catapulted her back through time in exactly the way she'd always feared.

The twenty-four hours that it had taken to read both the book and her journal had been a traumatic experience, curled on her sofa, barely eating or sleeping, just reading. The last few pages of *The Ruined Girl* were especially eviscerating, disconcertingly close to how she had actually felt, so she wondered just how all-knowing Rosie was.

When she fired, Rosie had written about Teresa, *it was with intent. It brought a release so pure it felt sexual. And just for a fleeting moment she had never felt better, as if every muscle in her body had learnt how to relax and her mind was free, like the whole world was at her feet.*

Hope had shut the book and waited for the emotional collapse that had been lurking around every corner for so long. But in fact, she was surprised by the rumblings of a dormant anger. It was impossible not to consider how she'd shrunk her life down to its smallest point as Rosie's had expanded, something which she now couldn't be sure had been necessary. Her story had existed in the world for nearly a decade and nothing had imploded. If she'd been a bit less lame and read *The Ruined Girl* when it came out, she could have saved herself the pain of the past ten years, instead of carrying the guilt of what she'd done around with her like a medieval yoke. She could have made an informed decision about whether or not to go to the police. She could have had some bloody control over the narrative.

Her anger led her to Google, something she'd avoided since Shadowlands. But sleep proved elusive and there was a bottle of wine finished and it was so late at night, the darkness outside her window swallowing her resolve. Like she'd predicted, it didn't make anything better. Sure, she'd known that Rosie was rich and famous, but she hadn't realized quite the extent, or how culturally revered he was now. *The Ruined Girl* was the ninth bestselling book of the past decade and the film had won a bloody Oscar.

When she'd woken the next morning she was surprised again to find that, in some respects, she was pleased that she'd finally read the words that had hovered over her head for so long. Beyond the anger and pain, it felt like being reintroduced to an old friend who you hadn't meant to lose touch with. And by that she didn't mean the people, but the very act of writing, the creation of a story. Reading her journal had reminded her how good that felt and the strange rush that came with putting words on a page and using them to build a world.

Except, and here the anger percolated again, Rosie clearly hadn't forgotten anything. Oh no, he'd turned the worst moment of her life into a sodding work of art. Hope couldn't help wondering then if Rosie had begged her not to say anything not just because he didn't want to get into trouble, but also because he knew what a great story she'd created. And the really unfair thing was that he'd known about her ambitions. She'd worked so hard when she lived at Shadowlands to eliminate shock from her repertoire of feelings, but now she wondered if she'd been in shock for the past ten years, too pedestrian to see that what happened was a story begging to be told and that she had always been the best person to tell it. She hated Rosie for not sharing. Hated him for stealing her story and turning it into his own.

Chapter Three

Nat skimmed a few pages of Hope's journal, then flipped to the back where she correctly guessed the alleged murder would appear. Not that it was what she'd call a detailed, or even very coherent, account. She obviously needed to read the whole thing, but first she asked a DC to get Ambrose Glencourt on the phone. It took about twenty minutes, time she spent starting back at the beginning. Nat wasn't a reader, and she especially hated the idea of anywhere where you were forced to record your feelings. It seemed too self-indulgent; one of the many things Nat found difficult about modern life was how everyone thought every single little thing they did needed to be seen and validated. It made Nat want to laugh. The idea of everything having a value was absurd.

Nat had just reached the part where the Glencourts let their dogs shit on the floor because they had staff to clean it up, when her DC said she was going to connect her to Mr Glencourt.

'How can I help you, DI Evans?' a very posh, rounded voice said from the other end, which immediately put Nat's hackles up.

'At the moment, I just wanted a chat,' she said. 'Some allegations have been made that concern you.'

'Me?' Nat couldn't work out if he sounded affronted or incredulous. 'Hang on, I'm going to put you on speaker so my wife can hear this.' The line clicked.

'I wondered if you know a Hope Jenkins?'

'Hope? Yes, well, at least we don't know her any more. She worked as my secretary . . . goodness, ten years ago?'

'She says it was in 2016.'

'Oh yes, the year of the heatwave, that's right. She was here the summer I was writing *The Ruined Girl*. Sorry, it's just I've had quite a few assistants since then. Has something happened to her?'

'No, no.' Although having just spent an hour looking at Hope Jenkins across a table, Nat thought that wasn't entirely true. 'I was also wondering if you know a Tom Markham?'

He coughed. 'Goodness, this is all a blast from the past. Well, yes, again, we did. We last saw him around the time we last saw Hope, actually.'

Nat's heart gave a little surge. 'And did they know each other?'

'Yes. What's this about, DI Evans?'

Nat drew in a breath. The Glencourts lived very far away and there was no way she'd be arresting them without putting these questions to them first, so doing it over the phone didn't matter. Also, if what Hope was saying was true, then they would know why she was calling and she wanted to hear their authentic reaction.

'Miss Jenkins is claiming that she killed Mr Markham during an argument at your house. In fact, she's claiming that your novel, *The Ruined Girl*, is an exact reproduction of what happened.'

There was a beat of silence in which Nat could almost feel the vibrations of shock from the other end.

'Are you serious? So she must be claiming that she shot Tom then?'

'That's right.'

'Oh, really.' Mrs Glencourt's voice was as bad as her husband's. 'That's too ridiculous. Why on earth would she have done that?'

'She says that she was in a relationship with Tom, but he told her that you and he were in love.'

'She what?' Mrs Glencourt said at the same time as Mr Glencourt said, 'But that's preposterous.'

'Did you know she wrote a journal when she was living with you?'

'No.' Mr Glencourt's voice was higher than it had been. 'Have you seen it?'

'Yes. It is very similar to the plot of *The Ruined Girl*.' Nat hoped she wouldn't be asked to quantify that statement.

'But that's . . . I mean, is this journal dated?'

'Yes, 2016.'

There was another pause, which Nat found interesting.

'I suppose she could have written in a diary from any time,' he said eventually.

'Actually, it's not a diary. Miss Jenkins wrote the date in herself.'

He laughed in a way that irritated her. 'Oh, so she could have put any date she liked on it?'

'Well, yes, of course that's a possibility.' Nat tried to recover her advantage. 'You said you last saw Mr Markham around the same time you last saw Miss Jenkins? So, about ten years ago?'

'That's right.'

'And do you know where he is now?'

'Did Hope tell you that Tom was a drug addict?'

Nat cursed internally. 'No.'

Mr Glencourt sighed. 'Delia used to volunteer at a local drug rehabilitation centre. She set up lots of programmes for the younger residents, helped them get back into education, that sort of thing. She met Tom there when he was just fifteen and we took him under our wing. He came to stay here quite a bit until that summer of 2016.'

'How old was he then?'

'Twenty-five. And, by the way, we were under no illusion that he was cured of his habit, but he did seem to be making steady progress.'

'And he was staying when Miss Jenkins came to work for you?'

'That's right.' Mr Glencourt paused. 'We knew that Hope and Tom were sleeping together, and we also knew it was unwise. Tom fell for her, quite hard, and we were very worried as to what that might do to him because she, well, she wasn't the most stable of characters.'

Hope's wild eyes flashed into Nat's mind. 'In what way not stable?'

'She was a complete fantasist,' Mrs Glencourt said. 'She was a bit of a nightmare from day one, actually. We should have asked her to leave, but Rosie was desperate for help with his book, and it had taken ages to find someone prepared to live in.'

'She had a hard time separating fact from fantasy,' Mr Glencourt said.

'And she acted like she'd come to stay, rather than work,' Mrs Glencourt said. 'Our housekeeper and cook couldn't stand her. They said she spoke to them like she was in charge of them.

And she sat in on dinner parties without being invited. She took a bag of my clothes that were meant for charity and wore them, totally brazenly, right in front of me. And she spent every afternoon by the pool.'

'It was very hot,' Mr Glencourt said, his tone slightly more conciliatory than his wife's. 'I mean, it was sometimes too hot to work. But often I found I needed her help after lunch and she was already by the pool.'

'Oh, and we're pretty sure she stole quite an expensive china bowl when she left,' Mrs Glencourt said. 'It's white with a pattern of roses on the inside. If you happen to search her flat, I wouldn't mind it back.'

Nat felt a little winded by the conversation, which was not going the way she'd hoped. A thick headache was opening up behind her eyes and she once again hated her colleagues for dumping this on her. 'Could you explain the circumstances in which Miss Jenkins left?'

'She declared undying love for Rosie,' Mrs Glencourt said.

'Well, I mean, I wouldn't put it that strongly,' Mr Glencourt said, 'but, yes, she told me she'd fallen for me.'

'And when he said the feelings were not reciprocated,' Mrs Glencourt continued, 'she went a bit mad. Screaming and shouting, that sort of thing. Tom and I were in the garden and heard, so we came to find them. It was awful for Tom because he thought she loved him. Anyway, we got her to bed and got a sleeping pill down her.'

'It was the night the heatwave broke,' Mr Glencourt said. 'There was a massive storm and when we came down in the morning she was sitting on the terrace totally soaked. We got her back to bed, but she came down with a fever. We thought we could manage it, but it soon became clear that the problem wasn't just physical.'

'Looking back,' Mrs Glencourt said, 'I think she had a full-on psychotic episode. She stopped making any sense. We had to call her mother, who told us that Hope hadn't had a very easy few years before she came to us.'

'In what way?'

'Not very stable emotionally. Apparently she did well at school, but dropped out of university after just one term with bad anxiety. She hadn't settled in a job since then. And she'd been having an affair with a married man. In fact, her mother said that was one of the reasons she took the job with us, to get out of London. In the end, her mother had to drive down and pick her up because she wasn't capable of getting herself home.'

Nat's headache was stretching across her back. 'Okay. And what about Mr Markham? Why did he leave?'

Mrs Glencourt's voice hitched. 'He did a midnight flit a few days, or maybe a week, after Hope left. Didn't even leave a note.'

'It was terribly sad,' Mr Glencourt said. 'We, Delly especially, had grown very close to him over the years. We looked for him for ages, but no luck. We presume he must have allowed himself to be sucked back into that drug world again.'

'After Hope left, he slipped into a pretty deep depression,' Mrs Glencourt said. 'Which obviously was a real worry with his history. It was a horrific time. I don't have children of my own and I had come to look on him almost as a son. Which makes Hope's claim that we were in some sort of relationship not just preposterous, but also disgusting.'

Nat could hear their anger. 'And he never went back to the centre where you met him?'

'No, none of us ever heard from him again.'

The Glencourts' story did sound more plausible, but Nat wasn't going to let them get away with the convenience of Tom simply disappearing. It was unexpectedly hard to disappear.

'I do feel awful that we didn't check up on Hope,' Mr Glencourt said. 'But we thought it best to let sleeping dogs lie and all that.'

'So neither of you spoke to her after she left your house?'

'No,' Mrs Glencourt said. 'She was young and we presumed she'd go home and pull herself together and get on with her life. She had her mother to take care of her, we knew that. I can't believe she's still thinking about us or that time, to be honest.'

Nat had dealt with too many people to be surprised any more by what people clung on to, or how their brains worked. 'Well, I'm sorry to have disturbed your evening,' she said in her most businesslike voice. 'You've been very helpful.'

'Is that it?' Mr Glencourt said.

'For now, yes. I'll be in touch if we need anything more from you.'

After Nat put the phone down she asked her DC to look into anything concerning a Tom Markham, last seen in Somerset in 2016, aged twenty-five. Family, employers, police record, anything. Then she stood, her back pinching, to go to speak to Hope Jenkins.

Chapter Four

Hope asked the officer who drove her home to drop her at the late-night corner shop, where she bought a packet of cigarettes and a bottle of wine that was too expensive for how yellow and vinegary it was. She sat at her tiny kitchen table, too tired to clear away the filmed-over cup of coffee from that morning, drinking and smoking in an attempt to dial down her anger. It wasn't as if she'd expected Rosie and Delia to admit to what had happened without a fight, but she hadn't been prepared for Rosie to trump her accusation with a better story. She was impressed by his quick thinking, although she supposed she should have expected it after all. He wasn't someone who liked to be outdone in the telling of tales.

DI Evans had said that she would be reading the journal over the next day or so, while following up a few leads. She did however ask Hope about her mother coming to fetch her, which meant Rosie must have told her that and, Hope had to admit, did make it sound like she'd been unhinged rather than just unwell. Although surely they'd be able to check her medical records? She'd countered by pointing out how, in *The Ruined Girl*, Aiden was buried by a river that sounded incredibly similar to the one at Shadowlands, which had to be where they'd buried Tom. Although DI Evans had squinted strangely when she'd said that, like something was in her eye. The annoying thing about the truth was that it so often needed context and that was something Hope felt distinctly lacking from her story.

'Everything I know is in there,' Hope had said as she left the police station, gesturing at the notebook. Although, of course, that wasn't true. She was aware that she'd been pretentious in the construction of her journal, aware of it in the same way Rosie was of his novel. Or, maybe, aware of it because of how Rosie was with his novel. Either way, it wasn't a complete picture, but then again, she wasn't sure if anything ever was.

About three-quarters of the way through the bottle, Hope googled Rosie again. Her screen filled instantly with thousands of results, which gave her a giddy sense of abandon. Rosie had always liked to give his opinion, and she was quickly able to see that the past decade had afforded him ample opportunity to do so. She clicked on articles at random, not able to take anything in properly, too aware of how much information was waiting. If she could have climbed inside the laptop she would have done. She wanted to immerse herself in Rosie's words. She wanted to rub them all over her body.

After she calmed down, she took in a few gems. Never write in the first person, being constantly contactable is the end of a civilized society, avocados taste like dirt. At some point she came across a picture of Rosie with his son, Rory, who had just been cast in a very cool TV show. It made her think of Tilly, who she'd spent that strange day and night with and had to be around eighteen now. She typed her name into the search bar and it went straight to a public Instagram page, showing a pretty young woman, with a mane of expertly highlighted hair, cool clothes and those nails that you had to get done in a salon, often in an exotic location. Both Rory and Tilly had more than a smattering of Rosie in their refined good looks and eyes burning with confidence. She could imagine them both sat around the terrace table, both able to hold court, both never doubting their legitimacy.

Rosie had conducted a few interviews at Shadowlands, accompanied by dangerous photographs that Hope couldn't help enlarging. The wisteria had grown and the woodwork around the windows was now a tasteful pale green. Rosie's study was pretty identical to how she remembered it, messy and book-lined, the lascivious painting of Delia with her legs wide open looking over everything. She used her fingers to enlarge that image until it filled the screen. With ten years' distance, she wasn't even sure it was that good and certainly couldn't understand why anyone would display an image like that of their wife. It felt crude, almost mean, like a taunt.

The most recent interviews were naturally mainly concerned with the sequel. Hope quite wanted to read it. *What does it mean to have murdered someone you love*, Rosie whispered in her ear and she wanted to scream because wasn't it enough that he'd written her worst act for all the world to see? Now he wanted to lay claim to the big question of her life as well? She tried to work out why he'd done something so stupid, so audacious. But of course he would have. This was Rosie and the usual rules didn't apply to him. He'd have no fear of being caught.

Ambrose Glencourt will be signing books at Waterstones on Tottenham Court Road on Wednesday, 27 May, the article concluded. That was two days away. Hope's hand hovered over the green button inviting everyone to add a ticket to their basket. Oh, they were playing a dangerous game, but then again, when hadn't they. She clicked, drunk not just on the empty bottle next to her, but also on the thought that in just forty-eight hours she would once again be in the same room as Rosie.

Chapter Five

Since the kids, Nat found coming home wasn't that different from walking into a crime scene. She was used to it, but still felt her mother's irritation at disorder rippling through her as she stepped through her front door. If she or her sister had left a mess like the one she encountered every evening, they'd have been banished to their rooms, refused supper, probably prayed over. It was insane how she couldn't get the woman out of her head, even after all these years.

Downstairs was deserted, but the TV flickered with a paused cartoon and every light was on, toys strewn across the floor, dirty dishes piled high in the sink, wet washing in the machine, dry washing living on the kitchen table. Nat turned off the TV and a few lights and scooped the toys into the basket that lived next to their sofa. She resented the way Kira let the kids monopolize every corner of their house, so wherever you went you were aware that you would never be alone again. She couldn't face the washing-up, but did at least clear the food off Riley's highchair and transferred the wet washing to the dryer. There was no sign that Kira had eaten, apart from a cold cup of tea and half-eaten plate of toast, which Nat put in the dishwasher, along with Ben's smeared Thomas the Tank Engine plate, which he was surely too old to still be using.

She was that sort of tired where her bones ached and her head was hurting from a mix of too much coffee and deciphering Hope's handwriting. And from the story itself, because she couldn't get a handle on it. The accusation was topsy-turvy, with Hope inexplicably more concerned about the supposed theft of her life story than the actual crime.

Although Nat also hadn't been impressed by the Glencourts. She'd had enough of the smooth talk of people who never doubted their authority, growing up immersed in a religion that wanted to swallow its congregation whole, Pastor Holland's treacly voice overriding every concern. She eyed the kettle, longing for a cup of tea, a takeaway and zoning out in front of some crap TV. But she would be a fool to think Kira was asleep.

Upstairs was mercifully silent, so she crept up the stairs, terrified of waking the kids. The bedroom door was ajar, and a low light was seeping through underneath. She pushed it open to see Kira lying, fully clothed in her customary tracksuit, staring at the ceiling. She raised her head slightly to look at Nat, then let it drop back down again.

'Be quiet,' she hissed. 'I've just got Riley down.'

Nat hated how Kira always played the martyr. She wondered sometimes what her wife thought she did with her time, but all she said was, 'That's late.'

Kira pulled herself up and leant back against the headboard. 'Nice of you to make an appearance.'

'Sorry, I texted.' Nat started to get undressed, feeling the release of undoing buttons and pulling on her own tracksuit.

'Yeah, I got it.'

'This case came in and no one else was available.'

'Right.' Kira had an amazing ability to make words sound like weapons.

'You make it sound like I've been at a party.'

'Guess I wouldn't know if you had.'

Nat sighed. 'Kirri, please. I've just done a sixteen-hour day. Maybe we could save this one.'

'You know if you've done a sixteen-hour day, then I have as well, right? Or do you think I lie around getting the kids to feed me grapes or something.'

Nat looked at her wife and wondered if there would ever again be anything she could say to make it better. Wondered if she would ever again make her laugh, or if they'd even share an easy conversation. 'Has it been a bad day?'

Kira snorted. 'They're all bad days.'

Once Nat asked if there was anything Kira liked about being a mother, which was not a mistake she'd make again. She couldn't remember exactly what had been said, but the gist of it haunted her like a bad dream. Something about how the kids had consumed her, emotionally and physically. How she loved them so much they were now part of her and everything they did was connected to her, which meant it all had to be right, which wasn't possible and so she would never be happy again.

'Have you eaten?' Nat asked.

'Oh, I'm so sorry I don't have dinner waiting for you when you get home. Perhaps I should telepathically intuit when you might be gracing us with your presence every evening and whip up a three-course dinner.'

'Okay, that's not what I meant. I meant do you want me to make you something?'

Kira rubbed her eyes. 'Sorry. Yeah, a cup of tea would be great.'

Nat squeezed her wife's foot, which felt cold even though it had been a warm day. 'It'll get better, babe.'

She walked to the door, but the slight thaw in their exchange made her bold. 'By the way, do you know the secretary at Ben's school?'

'Miss Jenkins? Yeah, why?'

There was no way she was going to tell Kira the truth because she was a terrible worrier, especially concerning the kids. Not that having either a potential murderer or deluded fantasist around their children wasn't a legitimate worry, but Nat wanted a little more time trying to work this out. She'd felt the shock herself when Hope Jenkins had said that she worked at Lady Catherine's, but she'd tucked it away because she'd kick herself if the fact that Ben went to the school where the woman was the secretary jeopardized the case for her. And she'd checked; the woman had been there eight years without incident, which didn't mean she wasn't capable of something bad, but made it more unlikely.

The bottom line was that something had to change for Nat. She couldn't go on feeling this mixture of exhaustion, burn-out and unloved for much longer. And maybe a promotion was what she needed. 'Just something at work today. What's she like?'

Kira was wrapping her hair into a bun and Nat noticed the grey at her hairline, which she thought was new. 'She's not in trouble, is she?'

'No, no. Just related to something minor.'

'She's a bit of a dragon.' Kira leant back again, which made her look pale in the side light. 'None of the parents like her.

You know, she's snappy, even if you're asking a perfectly reasonable question. Makes you feel like you're bothering her just by breathing.'

It wasn't impossible to reconcile that description with the woman Nat had met earlier. 'Sounds delightful. Also, you've read *The Ruined Girl*, haven't you?'

Kira squinted at her. 'These questions are bizarre. Of course I have. And seen the film. Just like everyone else.'

Nat absorbed the slight. She'd googled it at work, but the blurb hadn't given too much away. 'What's it about?'

'Seriously?'

'Humour me.'

It could go either way with Kira at any time and Nat watched the decisions flit across her wife's face. In the end she sighed and said, 'Basically, it's about a young woman called Teresa who meets a young man called Aiden. They fall hard for each other in the way that a straight, white male must find sexy. Then they go and stay at his parents' country house and it turns out that he's, like, an aristocrat or something. Anyway, they're super loaded and Teresa is bowled over and sort of falls for the house as much as him. His dad's this brilliant professor and his step-mum is like this super-hot vixen-type bombshell. It all gets a bit weird and then it turns out Aiden and his step-mum are getting it on. There's a huge fight and Teresa shoots Aiden and, in a totally fucked-up ending, his step-mum persuades his dad to help bury him because she doesn't want any scandal. I mean, it's enough to put you off heterosexuality, even if you are that way inclined.'

'Do we have a copy, do you know?'

'I expect somewhere on the shelves downstairs.' Kira yawned. 'Don't get too excited though. I didn't like it that much.'

Chapter Six

Hope woke the next morning with a sharp pain across her temples and a sickness in her stomach, which wasn't unusual. She needed to get up in order not to be late for work, but a whirling terror, which she had spent many years controlling, was spinning through her. There was momentarily something appealing in letting it do its worst because surely eventually her screams would alert the man downstairs, or the school would wonder why she hadn't been in and someone would have to deal with her. But also it was too far removed from the person she had become to make that sort of fuss.

In desperation she looked around her pitiful bedroom for something comforting, but that made everything worse because the flat wasn't really hers, at least not in the sense that she'd chosen it. In all the time she'd lived there she hadn't added to the space in any way. Everything in it was essentially her mother's; she'd just taken on the rent and furnishings when the woman had moved to Spain about a year before Covid. Hope missed Covid. It had been cosy to know that everyone else was as trapped as she was. And much easier for her and her mother to not have to explain why they weren't desperate to see each other. Then when the restrictions had been relaxed, it wasn't like either of them had jumped on a plane, instead simply giving up their Zoom calls and making do with the odd awkward phone call. And her job was no better. It had only been meant to be temporary, but could you call something temporary when you'd been doing it for eight years and gone back after a pandemic?

She wished then for something she had taught herself not to need, a friend. But there wasn't one human being she could call. She'd known she was lonely, but that morning solidified just how isolated she had become. Her life was completely threadbare. But not in the way of a teddy bear loved too hard, or a well-worn jumper washed too many times. No, hers was the cheap kind, the sweat-shop version, material so lacking in quality or substance that it frays on the first wear and is consigned to the back of the wardrobe.

Hope grabbed her phone off the bedside table without a real reason beyond the simple desperation to connect with something outside of herself. She still felt gorged from all her googling of Rosie the night before, but there was always Delia. Her name didn't produce nearly as many results as Rosie's, mainly a few old shots of her with him at *The Ruined Girl* film premiere, but they weren't satisfying. Hope skimmed through a couple of lifestyle pieces in which Rosie mentioned Delia, and then began on an article about the artist Robert Seigal. It was about a campaign to get his work removed from galleries around the world, after his daughter's revelations that he'd abused her from the age of twelve, followed by two more women coming forward and saying much the same. Delia was mentioned in the article as his long-time muse, the subject of more of his paintings than anyone else. *The daughter of renowned historian Antony Wallis,*

UNRELIABLE NARRATOR

Delia has always refused to comment on the many hours she spent alone with Seigal, the journalist had written, *although after her marriage to the novelist Ambrose Glencourt, she ceased all contact with her parents.*

A buzz started in Hope's head as she found herself experiencing a strange kind of pity for Delia, which felt very wrong, because Delia was a woman she'd never imagined feeling anything other than admiration for. Surely Delia couldn't have been a victim? That wasn't who she was. She saw Delia again by the river, her face blotchy, and she wanted to scream away the memory. The bed was starting to feel spongy, like she might sink through it, or perhaps the floor was going to tilt away from her and upend everything.

Chapter Seven

Nat went into work early because she wanted to read Hope's journal before she made her next move. Riley had woken them at five anyway and her afternoon was going to be taken up by an old case that had finally made it to court. She made herself coffee and sat at her desk with a sense of excitement because, even though Hope's story sounded outlandish, Nat couldn't think of a reason why she would have made it up, unless she was crazy, which was a definite possibility, but one Nat wasn't totally convinced of yet. On the other hand, she could definitely think of quite a few reasons why Ambrose Glencourt would deny everything.

The story Nat read was compelling, and there were times when she was almost surprised to look up and see her messy office and the grey streets outside her window, instead of Shadowlands' sumptuous grounds. But the narrative, if that wasn't too poncy a way of putting it, didn't run clear, and she couldn't get a complete handle on who Hope had been more in love with, Rosie or Tom. Sometimes she even wondered if it had been Delia. Her infatuation dripped off the page, almost as if Nat could hear Hope's heartbeat in the words.

In fact, the more Nat read, the more uncomfortable it made her feel, like some sort of weird grooming had been going on. Had Hope and Rosie kissed during that fucked-up wine passing game? What the hell was he doing touching her in his office when he'd asked her about love? And how the fuck did Delia smile at all his infidelities? Or walk past that horrible painting every day? It had all happened just before #MeToo, but Nat was sure women's rights hadn't been quite that lacklustre a decade before.

And then those last entries when Hope got back home were so . . . visceral. Nat didn't see how the woman could have made them up unless she was a bloody novelist herself. And, whatever the Glencourts said about her, they couldn't produce Tom or give any proof that he was still alive. In fact, they couldn't even say they'd seen him since just after the time that Hope claimed to have shot him. A tingling started in the tips of Nat's fingers. She needed to read *The Ruined Girl* and see just how close the two stories were because, if they were as identical as Hope was claiming, then surely that had to mean something.

Just as she was leaving for court her DC came over with a printout, which she put on Nat's desk.

'I've found an investigation into the disappearance of Tom Markham in September 2016,' she said, shifting her weight as she spoke. 'Also, he was fully in the system as a kid. You know, social services, police record, the lot. And he was definitely a sometime resident at Ridgeview in Somerset. But the trail goes completely cold from the time of this investigation.' The DC tapped the papers on the desk. 'I mean, there's nothing. Nada. No social media, no bank account, no passport, no social security. He really did vanish.'

Nat's stomach turned a little somersault. 'Thanks,' she said, her mind already working overtime. But she needed to leave right that second if she was going to make it to court in time, so she had to make do with folding the papers in half and putting them into her bag.

Chapter Eight

The school's office was just inside the main doors and, over the years, Hope had come to think of herself as a sitting target. There were six different grades at Lady Catherine's, as well as Nursery and Reception, and at least five parents per class who were certifiably insane. She could spot them on their first day. The ones who smiled too brightly and listened too intently, but whose eyes danced with anxiety. If male, they were likely dressed in jaunty T-shirts and baggy jeans, often carrying a laptop as if they had somewhere else to be. Female, and they were more likely to be in gym gear, with a Thermos of coffee and overly polite manner. At Christmas they would obsequiously hand over bath salts and a card that Alfie or Iris had made themselves, which Hope genuinely thought they expected her to frame, but always went straight in the bin.

Miss Jenkins, they started every conversation, how are you? As if any of them cared. She had learnt to set her face hard when they asked their silly questions and to pretend to finish things on her computer before she deigned to pull back the Plexiglass partition that separated her from them. She knew they all hated her and talked about her; sometimes she'd watch one of the yummy mummies go back to her group of friends in the playground after speaking to her and they'd all laugh as they flicked their highlighted hair.

At ten past twelve a knock on the door told her Charlie had arrived. The situation with him was becoming untenable and yet she couldn't work out how to end it. When she opened the door he was looking up at her with worried eyes, his hands obscured by his sleeves.

'Hello, Charlie,' Hope said, as brightly as she could manage.

He slipped past, to the chair he always sat on, just behind the door, so no one could see him if they came to the window, scratching at his arm, which made his eczema look livid, red and raw with a few grazes, then sniffed loudly, which worried Hope because it was too warm for colds.

She pulled a Tupperware box of sandwiches out of her bag. 'I've got cheese and pickle today. How about you?'

He slowly unzipped his lunch box, imprinted all over with zooming spacemen. 'Hummus and carrot,' he said, taking out one half and proceeding with thoughtful bites, which he chewed meticulously. Whoever made Charlie's lunches was keen on variety and nutrition, but Charlie never seemed to notice what he ate. The other kids complained about their lunches daily, their list of dislikes longer than most people's patience. But Charlie never expressed any opinion on food. He simply ate whatever was provided and stopped when there was nothing left. That day he had the other half of his sandwich, a squeezy yoghurt, a small KitKat and an apple. Hope had taken to buying similar products, for reasons she couldn't entirely place. Although she weirdly enjoyed the nursery food – it was quite comforting to suck yoghurt out of a pouch.

It had started a few months before when Charlie was sent to the office with a stomach ache. Hope rang his mother, but she didn't answer, so then tried his father, who said it was impossible for him to get out of work. She told Charlie to sit still while she kept trying his mum, or maybe it would get better. Stomach aches were something lots of children used to get sent home, and often they gave themselves away when told to sit still. But Charlie was clearly in genuine pain, leaning over his stomach and trying not to cry. Hope was eating a jam sandwich, pretty much all she could be bothered to make in those days and, after a while, realized he was watching the transfer of sandwich to mouth intently. She asked if he was hungry and he nodded, so she handed it over, then the banana that had been in her bag for three days. He was well enough to go back outside ten minutes later.

Charlie turned up with a stomach ache the next day and the next. Stupidly, Hope started packing a little extra of whatever she was eating because, at first, she thought maybe he wasn't being sent in with food. But when she checked his peg a perfectly nutritious lunch was waiting for him in a clean lunch box. So then she watched him at break and saw how he hung around at the edges of the playground, never interacting with any other child and looking constantly on the verge of tears. The next time he came to the office door she suggested, like an idiot, that he bring his lunch with him. Hope hadn't been impetuous for many years, but the recognition of a fellow loner in the boy made her speak without first checking herself. She also thought that he'd get bored of sitting in a bland office pretty quickly, although they were now two and a half terms into the arrangement and he wasn't showing any signs of moving on.

'What lessons have you got this afternoon?' Hope asked.

Charlie pulled his bony shoulders up to his ears. 'Don't know. But I hope art.'

'Oh yes. Who's your favourite painter?'

Most children would be dumbfounded by such a question, but Hope knew Charlie better than that. 'Picasso,' he said without missing a beat.

'Have you ever seen one of his paintings in real life?'

He nodded. 'Mummy takes me to galleries in the holidays. Although my favourite is museums. I like the Royal History the best.'

She smiled at his mistake. 'The big dinosaurs?'

'They have one that moves.' He scratched at his arm as he spoke, which made it bleed.

'Let me put something on that,' Hope said, reaching for the first aid box.

Charlie hurriedly pulled down his sleeve. 'It's okay.'

'Oh, come on.' She popped open the tub of antiseptic cream. With children she'd noticed often the intention was more important than the action. He held out his arm, so she pushed his shirt up which revealed, just above his elbow, a sprawling dark bruise, grey at its centre and fading out to a purplish yellow. They both flinched slightly.

'How did you get that?' she asked as casually as possible, while rubbing the thick cream onto his flaky skin.

'Fell off my bike.'

'Did it hurt?'

He shrugged. 'Dad says I'm clumsy.'

After Charlie left, Hope felt unduly agitated, which she tried at first to put down to her worry for him. But she was too intelligent to fool herself like that. Her agitation was being brought on by something far more dangerous than a troubled kid. The truth was, it was beginning to feel like the past ten years of abstinence had never happened, and she could feel Shadowlands starting to rise, almost as if the honeyed bricks were stacking themselves neatly one on top of the other in her mind.

The feelings worsened when she got home to her cloyingly quiet apartment. She turned the television on for company, but it was her worst show, a couple looking for a house in the sun. It reminded her too much of her mother and how there hadn't even been six months between her meeting Gary and moving out to Spain. How she'd longed to be asked to go with them, or even been enough of a reason for her mother to stay. But by then they were long past such things, the closeness of the first twenty-three years of Hope's life vanished. And really she couldn't blame her mother because Hope knew she'd been intolerable after she got back from Shadowlands. Although still, she wished her mother hadn't been so irritated by her. It was painful to remember how much she'd longed for a hug and a question about what was going on. Because, even though Hope had made Rosie the promise never to reveal what had happened at Shadowlands, she couldn't be sure that she wouldn't have broken it in that circumstance.

Hope took the bottle of wine and family pack of Doritos she'd bought on the way home into the kitchen. The wine wasn't particularly cold, but she poured out a glass and took a long sip that turned into half a glass. Except it didn't have its usual soothing effect and her nerves refused to receive the message that they could artificially relax for the next few hours. Rosie's words, as told to her by DI Evans, kept repeating in her brain, making a fog of unreality settle over her, filling her with the sense that she needed something tangible to prove her existence.

The only thing she could think of was something else she'd avoided for a decade – her mother's photograph albums. She hadn't looked at them once since she'd got home from Shadowlands and why would she have? Because why would she want to be reminded of a time when she'd thought of herself as a basically decent person? Except, desperate times and all that. Hope took the wine and went to the room she still thought of as her mother's, completely unchanged since the woman had moved out, the bed stripped, with the duvet and pillows neatly folded across the mattress. Dust had settled on every surface and there was still a hair caught in her mother's discarded brush. But she refused to linger on such things and went straight to her mother's bedside table, hauling the albums out and onto the bed.

The majority of the photos were of her as a baby and child and they weren't too bad because they were removed enough from who she was now. The teenage ones were harder, so she had to steel herself as she turned the thick, plastic-covered pages, revealing more and more images of a beautiful, bright young woman always laughing or reaching for something, gesticulating with her arms as if her opinions counted. Christ, she felt sorry that the woman on the page had had to become who she was now.

The post-Shadowlands section was tiny, just one or two pages that revealed the same, and yet totally different, young woman, now with grey skin and blank eyes. The last photograph was easy to date because the television was on in the background, fireworks exploding behind the London Eye, which was emblazoned with a giant 2017. Her mother was holding a glass up to the camera, but her eyes were trained on Hope, who was looking down at the hands clasped in her lap. Hope knew no one had been behind the camera, knew they'd set it up on a timer, so she could almost hear the click and then watch herself stand and shuffle off to bed, not even bothering to wish her mother a happy new year.

Hope put her hand on her chest in an attempt to calm the rattle of her desperate heart. She'd read somewhere that women are born with all their eggs fully formed inside. Which meant, in a small sense, she had been born at the same time as her mother, that they were part of each other before either of them was able to think. She was struck then by how her mother must have felt watching her daughter disintegrate before her eyes. It would have been as bad as suffering herself. Although maybe it was worse. Maybe the person who comes from you is more important than the person you are? It was one of the many things Hope would probably never know. She couldn't let herself love anyone, more pertinently, couldn't let anyone love her. Besides, you needed to have sex to become a mother and that wasn't something that had been on her agenda since Tom.

Not to mention all the things you could do to a child just by being their mother. She remembered listening to Delia in Rosie's study, saying that it was too dangerous for her to have children and knew, finally, exactly what she meant. If Hope had a child, there was a strong chance that her badness, or whatever you wanted to call it, would pass down through her DNA. She had to remember that it was a good thing that their genetic line would be stopping with her and not long for impossible things.

Except she couldn't look away from the photos, which her mother had not just taken, but had developed and then placed in an album, as if there was something worth preserving about her daughter. A seam opened in Hope's stomach, as something ripped through her internal organs, lacerating the very essence of herself. She poured out the last of the wine as a burning indigestion began behind her breastbone. At least she would be seeing Rosie the next night. Maybe she should take the albums with her and force him to look at the evidence. She would look him in the eyes and see if he could deny everything to her face.

Chapter Nine

Nat's afternoon at court had been so busy, she still hadn't read the papers her DC had given her by the time she got home, too late to help put the kids to bed. The house was quiet, so she crept upstairs. Kira and Riley were sprawled in the bed, both asleep, the light still on. She turned it off and covered them over with a blanket, as Riley sucked furiously on her dummy in her sleep. Then she crossed the hall to Ben's room and peeked through his open door. He'd kicked off his duvet, and his little body, so tiny and vulnerable, curled into itself, caught in her throat. She wanted to smooth the hair off his sweaty face, but she didn't dare in case it woke him. Her feelings about Ben often surprised her, as if they were constantly waiting for her around corners, always ready to leap out and attack. He was much harder to read than Riley, who was a mass of energy and need, calmer and quieter in a way that worried Nat because she knew it made the world so much harder to navigate.

She went back downstairs to the messy kitchen where she ate the remains of a spaghetti bolognaise from the pot, not even bothering to heat it up. Then she opened a beer and took it to the sitting room, where she took off her boots and curled into the sofa. She was exhausted, but she wanted to know what was in the papers her DC had given her and really she should make a start on *The Ruined Girl*.

The papers concerned a report filed by Mrs Glencourt concerning the disappearance of Tom Markham on 22 September 2016. The first thought Nat had was that you wouldn't report someone missing if you'd disposed of the body, but then something else struck her. The fact that there'd been any investigation at all was odd. A twenty-five-year-old man with as erratic a past as Tom's would hardly be cause for concern. Certainly weeks, if not months, would normally pass between a person like him being reported missing and something actually happening. And yet, within days, both the Glencourts had been interviewed, Tom's mother, the manager of Ridgeview and a few of the residents. Nat read the Glencourts' statements carefully, only realizing when she got to the end that neither of them even mentioned Hope Jenkins. Which seemed pretty bizarre, especially considering that Mr Glencourt had said they thought Tom left because he'd been so upset by Hope's betrayal of his feelings. There was also a note that a photograph had been removed from the file, annoyingly with no reference to what it was of, and which Nat would very much like to see.

And then the case had been closed on 12 October. Nat leant her head back when she'd finished; there was nothing obviously wrong with what she'd read, but also something about it nagged at her. But she was tired and she had another busy day to look forward to that would start in only a few hours' time. She pulled the blanket off the back of the sofa and slid down against the lumpy cushions, still dressed in her clothes.

Except sleep eluded her, her brain whirring in the way it did when she got overly tired, phrases and conversations refusing to leave her alone. She longed for Hope's story to be true, and she worried that was blinding her judgement. It was just it was one of those cases that could change things and she needed that. Nat had been filled with that itching sense of things always being just outside her grasp since she was a teenager. Sometimes she worried that she'd used up all her bravery in loving Kira and now she was being left behind.

Except she also had to tread carefully because all the things that made the case exciting also made it dangerous. Powerful men always knew other powerful men and Hope wasn't a totally credible witness. But also it was hard to explain Tom Markham's disappearance into thin air. Almost everyone left traces, however faint, in modern life and the only people who didn't were usually dead. Of course that didn't mean that Hope had killed him because a drug addict was always capable of doing that for themselves, but it did mean that Nat wasn't being ridiculous investigating. She just needed to keep her head and progress slowly, not jumping to conclusions or getting angry and alienating people. She cringed at the memory of her last review: *sometimes, her boss had said, you really need to take a breath. The world isn't out to get you.* Which, in her experience, wasn't necessarily true.

Chapter Ten

Hope got through the next day, which was as much as could be said about so many of the days of her life. Charlie came at lunch and told her that his mother was taking him to a pet shop at the weekend. 'Oh, what are you getting,' she asked, stupidly, desperate for some good news, but he'd winced. 'Nothing,' he replied, 'Daddy says I'm not responsible enough to have a pet. And he's right, I do get a lot of things wrong. But I like to look.' After he went back to class Hope tried to erase the conversation from her mind, which made it take up more space. She didn't want to worry about Charlie. She needed to focus instead on finding a way to stop him visiting. But nothing came to her all through the long afternoon, until finally it was the end of the working day and for once she had somewhere to go. There was no time to go home first and the Tube was hot and she had too many bags, which meant she could smell the sweat that had leaked into her cheap nylon top by the time she arrived at the book shop.

The queue was already long, filled mainly with excited women in groups, chatting animatedly. The sight of them made Hope long for a glass of wine as a familiar tightening began to build across her shoulders and up her neck, an early indicator of a sharp, mean pain that would soon be squeezing itself ever tighter through her head. The book shop had set up a special table just for Rosie's books, a large poster hanging above it depicting his four novels. In an egalitarian way they had all been given equal billing, although Hope was sure that everyone's eyes were trained, like hers, on book number three, *The Ruined Girl*. And now there was the just-released sequel to add to the pain, titled *Teresa's Ruin*, which felt like a personal dig – like he wanted Hope to know that she'd ruined her life.

It took a while to get to a place in the queue where Hope could even see Rosie and when she did a small bomb exploded in her chest. Since letting herself loose on Google she'd fallen down a few Rosie rabbit holes, but still the sight of him was more than she'd been prepared for. Age had improved him and it reminded her of how he'd once said that we should all take a lesson from wine, understanding that maturity is delicious. He ruffled his hair as he absorbed whatever the blushing woman in front of him was saying and Hope thought one of the reasons he looked so good was because he looked his age, which had to be late fifties now, and how well that age sat on him.

She was about twenty people away when she heard his voice, loud and clear and tipped with glass, his words sounded out by individual letters, his speech fast but measured, as if everything he said had value. 'I'm not sure truth has much place in fiction,' he was saying to a blonde woman leaning too far over the signing table, making her giggle in a way that made Hope want to hit her.

But the rest of his sentence was drowned out by the women in front, who started up a loud conversation about the film adaptation of *The Ruined Girl* and how it wasn't nearly as good as the book. Hope had watched the film after reading the book, almost expecting to see herself on the screen. But the actor who played Teresa was a goddess who didn't look anything like she had at twenty-three. But then again, nor had the actors who played Tom or Rosie or Delia. Or at least the characters who stood for them.

'I'm still inexplicably attached to my Dictaphone,' Rosie said from a few people away. The words hurtled Hope back to the study at Shadowlands, sat her up at the desk, put a typewriter under her fingers, as Rosie's voice lodged in her ears, his words making their way through her onto the paper at the clack of the keys.

She was close enough now to watch the expanse of pleasure spread across Rosie's features as he absorbed praise from the people who had travelled and queued just for a second of his time. It was an expression she'd seen many times at countless supper parties, when guests had laughed at his jokes and agreed with his thoughts and told him how much they loved his books. But she also remembered how mean Rosie had been about them afterwards and how she'd laughed along with him, thinking cruelty was his right because he was a genius.

Hope was only one person away and her breath was sticking around her diaphragm, which made her worry about being sick. But she dug her copy of *The Ruined Girl* out of her bag and focused on the cover, a moonlit tree washed red, which she'd never allowed herself to analyse. Rosie's name and the title were given equal prominence in a blocky greeny-yellow. According to Casper Waites it was 'a masterpiece' and the *New York Times* called it 'iconic'.

'Who shall I make it out to?' Rosie said and Hope realized there was no one between them. She slid her book across the table to him. He'd barely raised his eyes and his tone sounded tired.

'Hope.'

He looked up and she watched his smile falter. 'My God, is that really . . . ?'

'Yes,' she said. And all the anger she'd felt leached pathetically from her as she looked into his eyes again.

He stood shakily, turning behind him as if someone might be there. 'What are you doing here?'

'I thought we should talk.'

But he took a step backwards. 'I don't have anything to say to you.'

A young woman appeared next to him. 'Everything alright?'

'Could you get my wife?' Rosie said, which made something hard drop through Hope's stomach.

As the young woman scurried off, Hope could feel the irritation from the line of people behind her, so leant towards Rosie and lowered her voice. 'I can't believe you wrote about what happened.'

Rosie's eyes narrowed. 'Hope, you need help. The allegations you made to the police are insane.'

'Do you think you can get away with everything?'

He jammed a hand into his hair, glancing apologetically at the people left in the queue. But he too lowered his voice when he answered. 'There's nothing to get away with. *The Ruined Girl* is a work of fiction. You were there when I was making it up.'

'I suppose the sequel is about me as well.' Rosie's eyes darted behind her again. 'I can't believe that you begged me not to say anything and then wrote it yourself. You stole my story.'

His mouth tightened into a sharp line. 'Hope, I simply don't believe that you didn't read *The Ruined Girl* when it was published. You were so invested in the story, you were so looking forward to typing up the finished draft.'

Hope's anger was rising, hot and livid. 'Of course I didn't bloody read it. After everything that happened it was impossible.' She could feel her breath hitching. 'I thought you cared about me.'

'Hope.' She pulled her attention away from Rosie to see that Delia had arrived. She of course looked even better than she had in the photographs Hope had seen, embracing a perfect refinement. She was still slim and dressed in a classy pale blue linen trouser suit. Her hair had been tamed into a bouncy blonde bob and she was even wearing subtle but effective make-up. Hope adjusted her cheap denim skirt against her thickened waist and wished she smelt better. Delia reached for her arm. 'Why don't you come with me. Rosie needs to finish his signing and then we can all have a drink and chat together.'

Hope looked between them and saw that old connection pulsing, which made her want to be sick because they'd taken that possibility away from her. 'You can't do this,' she managed. 'It's so unfair. You have to tell the truth.'

Delia's grip on her arm tightened. 'I think we all know what the real truth is, don't we, Hope?'

Chapter Eleven

Nat had unusually spent much of the day reading. The plot of *The Ruined Girl* was definitely unfolding in a very similar way to Hope's journal, but Nat was finding it hard to buy into her claim that the character of Teresa was based on her, because the person on the page was beautiful and funny and flirtatious, none of which were adjectives she'd use to describe Hope. But before she could get back to the book, she helped Kira get the kids down, cooked them a basic supper from the freezer and then followed her wife to bed, where she was now close to finishing. Her phone rang and she'd forgotten to turn down the volume of her ringer, which had to be loud in the station or you never heard it. Riley started to scream from the other room and Kira sat bolt upright, even though she'd been deeply asleep seconds before.

'I'll go,' Nat said.

But Kira was already out of bed. 'No, I'll have more luck.'

'Maybe if you let me try . . .' But Kira was out of the door before she finished her sentence, so Nat reached for her phone. The number wasn't one she recognized and it was half past ten, but being in the police had made her never miss a call if she could help it.

'Is that DI Evans?' The voice was confident and brusque and Nat couldn't quite place it.

'Yes, speaking.'

'This is Ambrose Glencourt. We spoke a couple of days ago about allegations made about me by Hope Jenkins.'

Nat looked at the book lying face down on the bed, her brain taking a moment to catch up. 'Yes, of course. How can I help?'

'Well, I was going to call Peter, but Delly said I should try you first.'

'Peter?'

'Lambert.' He sounded exasperated, but Nat didn't see how the hell she'd been meant to know he was talking about the actual Commissioner.

'Oh yes, I don't think there's any need to involve Sir Peter at this stage.'

'He's a very good friend.' Ambrose let the statement hang in the air as Nat's chest tightened.

'Has something happened?' Riley's cries were rising so Nat got up and closed the bedroom door, feeling like a traitor as she did so.

'Well, yes, actually. I did a signing this evening and Hope turned up. She made a bit of a scene in the queue.'

Nat suppressed an expletive. If this man knew Peter Lambert and she'd missed referring Hope to psych, this case could do the opposite of what she'd hoped for her career. 'What did she do?'

'Well, we got her into another room, so it wasn't too bad. But honestly, I think we need some sort of restraining order or something.'

'What did she say?'

'She was extremely angry. It all seems to be centred around

her allegation that The Ruined Girl is a true story, based on her killing of Tom Markham. She's claiming that I asked her to stay quiet but then wrote about everything that happened in the novel. Which, I am sure you'll agree, stretches the bounds of credulity.'

'I'm very sorry, Mr Glencourt.' Nat had just left Teresa rushing through the house after finding Aiden in bed with his stepmother and it was hard to remember which story they were talking about. 'Did she physically threaten you in any way?'

'No, no.' He sounded exasperated. 'But God knows what she's capable of. Delia and I tried to make her see sense by reminding her of what actually happened that night, but I don't think it worked.'

Nat wished her notebook wasn't downstairs, but she was as sure as she could be that when she'd spoken to the Glencourts they'd denied all Hope's allegations and questioned her powers of reason, but they hadn't said anything specific happened. 'Sorry, what do you mean, what actually happened?'

Ambrose sighed. 'We probably should have told you this when you rang, but, well, it's all a bit sordid and embarrassing. And also I don't have a licence for the bloody gun.'

Nat's hope sparked. 'That's not an issue. But I would like to know if there's anything you're not telling me.'

He paused. 'Well, there was a big argument, and Hope did have a gun, but not in the way she told it.' Something rustled on the other end and Nat had the sense she'd been put on speaker again, because when he next spoke, he sounded further away.

'It was mainly like we said: Hope told me that she was in love with me and when I told her nothing could happen between us she started screaming and shouting. Delly and Tom heard and came rushing in, but she was wild by then. Tom tried to calm her down, but she picked up this old gun of my father's that I stupidly kept in the study. She was waving it around and we were all totally terrified. Tom tried to get it off her, but she bloody tried to fire the thing. Just like that, right in his face. She looked completely mad, like she wanted to kill him. But thank God it wasn't loaded and so we were able to overpower her.'

Nat's confusion was building because now there was another story to add to the one she'd already been told and the one she was reading. 'And what happened after that?'

'She totally lost it. It was awful. Eventually we got a sleeping pill down her and put her to bed. But in the morning we found her outside, soaking wet, like I said before.'

'And that made her sick?'

'That's right. She was delirious and said some odd things, but neither of us recall her ever saying that she thought she'd killed Tom.'

'And then her mother came to fetch her? And Mr Markham left a few days later?'

Mr Glencourt sighed audibly. 'Yes. Tom had a very violent childhood, which caused a debilitating phobia of guns. Also, he had deep-seated trust and abandonment issues. He thought Hope liked him as much as he did her. The two things sent him spiralling. We're sure he went straight to his dealer when he left Shadowlands. Tragically, I expect the one thing Hope is right about is that he's dead. And, also, in a way, she is partly responsible for that.'

Nat let everything she'd just heard sink in before she asked her next question. 'Sorry, if I'm understanding you correctly, it sounds like you did use some of what happened as inspiration for *The Ruined Girl?*'

'Well, yes.' He sounded sheepish. 'Although I'd had the idea for the book, in fact I was well into the writing of it, before Hope arrived. And I never start writing a book without knowing the ending, so I'd already decided that Teresa was going to kill Aiden. But, yes, it would be fair to say that after everything had calmed down, I did think what I'd witnessed, had the gun been loaded, would make for a more dramatic death than the one I'd planned. And, I suppose, in rewrites, Teresa and Aiden did become a bit more like Hope and Tom.' He sighed. 'But, you know, that's what writers do. We use the things we see and hear to make a story. There's no crime in that.'

'No, no, of course not.' Riley was screaming from the other room and Nat had to keep reminding herself that it wasn't an actual soundtrack to the story she was hearing. She needed to get a proper handle on the situation before Ambrose Glencourt went over her head and she got into trouble. 'I think the best thing would be if I came to see you, at Shadowlands.'

'Well, yes, I suppose so.' Ambrose paused. 'You know I've had them before, these stalker types, I think you'd call them. One used to hang around on the lane outside our house. But none of them have ever gone this far before.'

He sounded like a politician and Nat hated them. 'Is it okay if I come up tomorrow?'

'Yes, we're being driven home now.'

Of course he had a driver. 'Well, I'll set off first thing then.'

'Yes, yes. The sooner the better. We want to get this situation sorted.'

Nat went straight downstairs after the call with her copy of *The Ruined Girl*. She only had eight pages left and it was important she found out how it ended, even though she knew she really should relieve Kira. Except her wife probably wouldn't let her take over anyway because she didn't trust Nat's judgement, especially where the kids were concerned. Even the thought of that settled Nat's guilt because how could she be expected to be a good mother when she wasn't allowed to try? She decided she'd say that to Kira if she came downstairs spoiling for a fight. But Riley's cries had subsided and there were no footsteps on the stairs. Nat set the kettle to boil, as she turned to the page she'd been at before Ambrose Glencourt called.

The book culminated in Teresa shooting Aiden during the argument that followed after she walked in on him fucking his stepmother. According to Hope's journal, she'd never walked in on Tom and Mrs Glencourt. She'd only found out about their affair because Tom had told her. But Nat supposed the way Ambrose Glencourt had written it was more dramatic.

She also found herself agreeing with Kira about the ending; even considering Aiden's stepmother's obvious charms, it seemed incredible that Aiden's dad would quietly bury his son to prevent a scandal. But Nat was more interested in where they buried Aiden. Like Hope had told her, his makeshift grave was next to a river at the bottom of their garden, which obviously didn't mean that was where the Glencourts had buried Tom, if he was dead, but still it was worth checking out.

It was close to midnight and she had a long drive to Somerset in the morning, which would piss Kira off as she'd have to be on the road by seven. But it was quiet upstairs, so she fetched her notebook because writing things down helped when she felt confused, and she wanted to see all the stories on the page in black and white.

Ambrose Glencourt: Hope & Tom sleeping together, Hope declares undying love to Ambrose, rejected, there's a fight, fires a gun at Tom but it's not loaded, goes mad, found outside in rain next morning, so ill mother has to fetch her, Tom disappears because feels scared/rejected, presumption that he got back into drugs, possibly died.

Hope Jenkins: Tom & Hope fall in love, he tells her he's in love with Delia, fight between Tom & Ambrose, in trying to save Ambrose Hope kills Tom, body vanishes, spends night in rain, ill so mother has to fetch her, Ambrose begs her not to say anything so she doesn't to protect him, finally reads The Ruined Girl *and sees it's her story, now out for vengeance.*

The Ruined Girl: Teresa and Aiden fall in love, Teresa finds out Aiden sleeping with his stepmother, massive fight, she shoots him because she's so angry and hurt, stepmother persuades father to bury the body to avoid scandal, Teresa runs off into the night.

It was undeniably strange how similar and yet different all the different versions were. It was also undeniable that they must have all influenced each other in some way. Nat just had to work out which one had come first, what was reality and what just inspiration.

Chapter Twelve

As Hope walked to school the next morning she tried to calm her hectic thoughts. The night before, Rosie and Delia had been resolute in their version of events, as if they'd even convinced themselves of their veracity. And there were parts of their story she couldn't deny. She had loved Rosie. But she'd also loved Tom, even Delia and Shadowlands itself. Naturally, they would also be denying her version of the story because concealing a crime and burying a body was a criminal act. Plus, and probably most importantly, Rosie was a consummate storyteller. It wouldn't be hard for him to think up a new plot line.

Charlie came as usual at lunch – ham sandwich for him, cheese for Hope, matching squeezy yoghurts and crisps for both of them. The more she got to know him the more obvious it became that he wasn't a happy boy. But she was the last person qualified to help. And not just because she wasn't a guidance counsellor, or even his teacher, but because she had proved just how bad she was at understanding relationships and controlling her own emotions. It was becoming imperative that she found a way to stop him visiting.

Charlie's eyes welled. 'Mummy hurt her arm last night.'

A crisp scraped the side of Hope's throat. 'How?'

'She fell down the stairs.'

Hope had never seen or met Charlie's father. It was always his mother waiting timidly at the top of the playground, but still the man, or at least a generic man, flashed into her head. It was impossible to tell if she was right to think like that, or if it was just how women had learnt to think. Because Charlie's mother looked like the nervous type, which would make her clumsy, which was also possibly just stereotypical thinking on Hope's part. It was impossible to work out what was right without knowing the full story. 'How did she do that?'

Charlie started scratching the inside of his arm. 'I was in bed. But I heard. Daddy said she tripped on the washing basket.'

The room contracted around them. 'Was your daddy there? Or did you have to help her on your own?'

'No, Daddy was there.' Charlie swallowed. 'He said she didn't need an ambulance. But this morning it was hurting badly, and she said she's going to the doctor today.' A single tear escaped. 'What if they send her to the hospital and she can't pick me up this afternoon?'

Hope wanted to pull Charlie onto her lap and stroke his hair the way she'd been able to do with Tilly. Although it wasn't like she'd tangibly helped her in any way. 'Oh, Charlie, I'm sure that won't happen. And if she does need to go to hospital, she'll ring the school, so we'll know.'

Charlie's lip had started to wobble. 'But . . . but . . .'

She leant forward. 'What is it, Charlie?'

His arm was bright red, the skin about to break. 'Would I have to stay with Daddy? On my own?'

It occurred to Hope that she probably needed to tell someone about the conversation, but that would mean becoming involved in something messy and emotional that, frankly, she didn't have the stomach for. Besides, she couldn't rely on her judgement – it had been proved fatally flawed so many times before.

'I tell you what,' she said brightly. 'I can see the playground from my window and today I'm going to look out at going-home time. If I don't see your mummy, then I'll come and find you and Miss Graham and we'll have a talk.' Of course his father could just turn up, but Charlie didn't seem to have worked that out and Hope didn't have a solution if that happened, so let him believe her false optimism.

Sure enough, his face brightened. 'Maybe I could stay with you?'

And despite herself her heart loosened in a dangerous way. 'Well, I don't know about that.'

His little face fell again. 'And it's Thursday.'

Every child who came to the office spoke in riddles, their thoughts often impossible to keep up with. 'Why does the day matter, Charlie?'

'Because it's my favourite day of the week. Daddy plays football on Thursday and Mummy and I eat supper in front of the telly and I'm in bed when he gets home. But if Mummy's in hospital we won't be able to. And he won't be able to play, will he?'

Hope's brain felt like it was vibrating, but she had to find another room to shut away what he was saying. 'I tell you what,' she said, her voice sounding so falsely jolly she couldn't believe Charlie hadn't noticed. 'If your mummy rings this afternoon to say she's going to be late I will come myself to deliver the message. So you don't have to sit there worrying. If you haven't seen me, then she hasn't rung, which means she will definitely be here at three o'clock.'

He nodded in a heartbreaking way, as if even he was now having to force himself to believe what she was saying. The bell rang, surprising both of them, and he jumped up.

'Charlie,' Hope said, as he reached the door, so he turned and the worry on his face made her want to cry. 'It'll be okay, I promise.' It was a totally idiotic thing to say. Because the truth was, humans were so rarely able to keep their promises, even when they meant them.

Chapter Thirteen

It was a perfect English spring day and, after Nat got off the motorway, it was a little like driving through a painting: verdant green hills, cattle in fields, bright blue skies, scudding clouds. She was aware that most people would find it charming. She was also aware, as she drove through the smart gates onto a well-maintained gravel drive bordered by woods, that most people would be wowed at the grandeur and beauty of Shadowlands. All it did for her was set off a low-level irritation in the pit of her stomach. It wasn't envy so much as a deep sense of unfairness. Nat hated extreme inherited wealth in the same way she hated prejudice. It struck her as deeply wrong that a few people got so much for doing nothing. She saw too much deprivation in her line of work, and she knew too much about being denied things, for privilege to ever sit comfortably with her. She rounded a corner and a huge house loomed into view, like a parody of wealth. Sure, she could objectively see it was beautiful, but it left a sour taste in her mouth that anyone should have that much.

Mr and Mrs Glencourt stepped out of the already-open front door as she came to a stop. Their voices suited them, and they weren't far from what she'd imagined. Mrs Glencourt was much better preserved than her husband, and Nat could see what she must have looked like when Hope had raved about her in her journal, but she didn't think she was movie-star gorgeous. She would describe her as a handsome woman, which Nat suspected was primarily due to money. She thought of Kira and her tracksuits and unkempt hair, and a shot of anger washed through her.

Nat composed her face as she stepped out of the car, smiling her best smile, as she adjusted the waistband of her trousers and smoothed down her shirt.

'How was the drive?' Mr Glencourt asked. 'Not too ghastly, I trust.'

'Not at all. It was fine, thank you.' Nat resisted the urge to compliment the house. The Glencourts no doubt received enough of those.

'Shall we sit on the terrace?' he said. 'Tabitha is going to bring us out some coffee. Unless you'd prefer tea, or water, or anything else?'

'No, no, coffee's great.' Nat was always amazed at how rich people skirted over subjects. Did they really think they were fooling anyone by calling the staff by their names, as if they were friends? But she let herself be led round the side of the house, up a couple of steps and onto a wide stone terrace that spanned the entire back of the house. They sat at a large stone table positioned in front of three huge sets of French doors, all wide open.

'It's very good of you to drive all this way,' Mr Glencourt said, and Nat quite wanted to laugh, because they all knew it was her job and, honestly, she couldn't stand that fake self-deprecation the British upper classes specialized in.

A young woman emerged from the other end of the house, carrying a wooden tray on which there was a cafetiere and three pretty mugs, artfully designed with splatters of pale paint.

'Thank you, Tabitha, I'll pour,' Mrs Glencourt said, as she stood. 'How do you take it, Detective Evans?'

'Oh, please call me Natalie.' Nat waited for the Glencourts to tell her to do the same but they didn't. 'Black, please.'

They covered a lot of the ground that they'd already spoken about, the Glencourts at pains to labour the point of how deluded Hope had always been and how drug-addled Tom. Nat thought they became more so with every telling, which set off some internal alarm bells. She didn't like the way they spoke with such authority, as if it would be preposterous to doubt what they said. Which made her desperate to think of a question that would trip them, or expose some flaw in their story, but it rolled out between them like a red carpet.

'Perhaps I could take a look at the study, where Miss Jenkins claims to have shot Mr Markham?' she said after the tale had come to an end.

'Of course,' Ambrose said, standing up. Mrs Glencourt stood as well, and they led her through the French doors into a huge room. The sun had been bright outside and it took almost the whole walk across the room for Nat's eyes to adjust, but when they did, she was overwhelmed by the amount of stuff it contained. The walls were crammed with paintings, there were massive pieces of china on every surface and more sofas than they could possibly sit on. The whole effect gave off a nasty whiff of greed.

They went through a door into a large hallway lorded over by a massive staircase that disappeared up into the house in a way that made Nat feel dizzy. Delia's shoes clicked on the stones as they crossed over to another heavy wooden door, which Rosie opened and walked through into a long, book-lined room. Nat was immediately struck by the large abstract painting hanging somehow within the bookshelves; she was no artist, but it was obviously meant to make the viewer uncomfortable. It was, after all, a view directly up a woman's vagina. She blushed, but Rosie and Delia didn't appear to notice her embarrassment, or to feel any themselves.

'I think I might have a photo of Tom,' Rosie was saying, as he went to his desk. 'And maybe even Hope as well.' He pulled a file off a shelf and rooted through it for a moment, exclaiming as he held up some photographs.

Nat stepped across the floor and took them from him. They all featured a striking young man, tall and dark, with a confidence to his movements that she could see even in the static images. In one of them he was sitting next to a gorgeous young woman at the table outside where they'd just been sitting. It was clearly evening as a candle was flickering between them, the light catching on their dazzling faces, their gazes aimed squarely at each other. 'Sorry, is this Hope Jenkins?'

Rosie half laughed. 'Yes. I know. I was quite shocked when I saw her the other night.'

Nat handed the photographs back. They made her feel sad because they highlighted how much Hope had lost and she didn't like the way Ambrose Glencourt had laughed.

'I presume you'd like to see the gun,' he said, taking charge in an irritating way.

'Yes please.'

He went over to a dark wooden chest by the window and opened a silver box, taking from it a small silver handgun. He opened the barrel and handed it over to Nat. 'No bullets. Never been any, to my knowledge.'

Nat snapped the barrel shut and handed it back. There was obviously no point in getting it forensically tested after all this time, and bullets were easy to remove, so it proved nothing.

'Would it be alright if I had a look around the garden? Miss Jenkins mentioned there's a river in the woods?'

Ambrose Glencourt glanced at his wife. 'Well, yes, of course.'

The day was even warmer when they got back outside, and Nat felt too hot in her close-fitting clothes. They set off across the lawn, which Nat thought was maybe slightly larger than the park Kira had to spend most of her days in. A wood ran along the bottom of the garden and a low white clapboard building covered in a sprawling apricot rose nestled at its borders.

'My studio,' Mrs Glencourt said, when she saw Nat looking.

'Oh, are you an artist?'

She shook her head. 'I wouldn't go that far. I make pots. But I'm in there most days.'

It was much cooler in the woods, the light on the ground dappled by the branches. Cow parsley and a tall plant with lots of tiny pink flowers grew between the trees, so they had to follow what was clearly a well-trodden path. Nat tried not to be too impressed by the magical beauty of the place, or to imagine what her kids would do with this as their back garden. After about five minutes' walking they came to a river, the water crystal clear, bright weeds undulating in the current.

'Are you looking for something specific?' Mr Glencourt asked.

As Nat looked around she saw it was undeniable that Ambrose Glencourt had the inspiration for where he'd buried Aiden in *The Ruined Girl* right in his back garden.

'Miss Jenkins claims you disposed of Mr Markham's body.'

Nat watched her words land in the slight contraction of his features. But then he laughed again, more heartily this time. 'My goodness, I'm almost flattered she thinks I had that in me.' He waved an expansive hand around them. 'But I do think this is just further sign of her confusion. This is the setting I used when I wrote Aiden's burial scene, which she would of course have recognized, having lived here.'

Nat nodded. 'Yes, I can see the similarities. I've read the book.'

'You're very welcome to dig if you want to.' He laughed at the absurdity of what he'd said, pushing at his hair in an affected way Nat thought was meant to be charming.

Nat tried to formulate her thoughts. Speaking to the Glencourts in any way that wasn't completely acquiescent made her feel like she was transgressing, but she held her nerve. 'The problem is, we can't find any trace of Tom Markham anywhere. No bank account, no up-to-date passport, no National Insurance contributions, no tax paid, not registered anywhere for rent or a doctor or any benefits. Absolutely nothing since September 2016, when you reported him missing.'

A cow mooed somewhere in the distance. 'But surely that proves we're telling the truth?' Mr Glencourt said. He was beginning to sound exasperated. 'I mean, why would we have reported Tom missing if we'd actually watched him being shot and then disposed of his body?'

Nat ploughed on. 'Also, in the interview you gave the police at the time, neither of you mentioned Hope Jenkins, which seems strange considering you told me she was the reason Tom left.'

Ambrose Glencourt's mouth twitched. 'That probably was an

oversight on our behalf. But, to be honest, we couldn't bear the thought of getting her involved after everything that happened. And it wasn't like she could have helped find him. I mean, knowing her, she was likely to send the police on some wild goose chase.' He sighed and nodded at Nat. 'Completely legitimate worries, as it's turned out.'

'Rosie, we should . . .' Nat turned to Mrs Glencourt as she spoke. She was standing in a patch of shade, which made it look as if dark circles had sprouted beneath her eyes. Her teeth were worrying her lip and her hands were clasped so tightly in front of her they had turned almost entirely white. 'Don't you think? I mean, hasn't this gone far enough?'

Ambrose Glencourt stepped between Nat and his wife, putting a protective arm around her shoulders. 'No, Delly's right. We do have something else to show you. We didn't want to because, well, it proves that Hope's a very unwell woman and we'd rather not stir the hornet's nest, so to speak, because God knows what she's capable of. But, yes, you'd better come back to the house.'

Chapter Fourteen

Hope kept her promise and stood by the window at pick-up time. Charlie's mother was in her usual place. She looked pale and her arm was in a sling, but she smiled when Charlie came out. She was making a big deal of her injury, as if it was a funny story. He turned and looked at the office window just before they left and Hope waved, although she wasn't sure if the glare of the sun obscured her or not.

DI Natalie Evans rang while she was walking home. 'Miss Jenkins,' she shouted through the fuzzy line. 'I wondered if you'd be able to come to the station tomorrow?'

Hope turned onto a side street and blocked her other ear with her finger so she could hear properly. It wasn't a call she'd been expecting. 'Have you got some news?'

'I'd rather have this conversation face to face.'

'But has something happened?'

'I'm on my way back from Shadowlands, and I'd rather talk to you about it in person.'

The news landed heavily in Hope's stomach. She didn't like the thought of Natalie Evans being there. No doubt Rosie and Delia would have been on their best behaviour; they would have spoken to her as if she was the most interesting person they'd ever met and acted like nothing was too much trouble. But Hope had seen behind the curtain of their life and knew what they'd really make of DI Evans with chain-store clothes and her habit of dropping gs at the end of words. She knew how they'd be laughing at her the second her back was turned, how they'd have no doubt they could outsmart her. But Natalie Evans had probably already been too charmed by them to be objective. And of course, in many ways Natalie was right to be charmed. Shadowlands was a seductive place and Rosie and Delia were seductive people. It was hard to believe that bad things could happen in those sorts of places, or to people like the Glencourts. Even harder to believe that they could be the cause of the bad things. It was much easier to believe in a young assistant's fallibility; at times it was even easier for Hope. But she pulled back from that thought because it only led in one direction.

'I can come after work, around four thirty.'

'Perfect,' Natalie said and this time it sounded like she was eating something.

Processed foods are the opium of the masses, Rosie said in Hope's ear, and she wondered if she was ever going to be able to shut him up.

'Tom died,' she said out loud after the call ended. 'I killed him.' Except the words didn't sound as absolute in the open as they had in her head. She tried to focus on specifics, on the feeling of pulling the trigger, the look in Tom's eyes as he fell, the exact timbre of Delia's scream. But everything felt fuzzy, almost like she'd let too much time pass without looking directly at the memory, and now it had faded.

Hope looked desperately up and down the street. Two men

who looked like they'd come from a construction site were walking on the other side of the road, laughing at something. And a young woman was pushing a buggy, a toddler wailing against her leg. Hope experienced a weird disassociation, like she couldn't remember who she was. For a decade her purpose had been to hold a terrible secret inside, to carry her badness safely through the world like some women did a baby. Rosie and Delia had to let her own that. They couldn't expect to steal her story, and also reinvent her whole self-image.

When she got home she went straight to her copy of The Ruined Girl. It fell open at the passage she had read over and over since that first read. *Teresa opened the door and saw Aiden's pale, bony back hunched between a pair of long, smooth legs. It was like she was looking at one being, a fluidity to the movement that made sense of everything. Aiden turned, his expression twisted in a moment of ecstasy. When he saw her he leapt away, exposing the whole of Leila, lying there, lying under him. His stepmother raised herself up on her elbows, her gaze steady, her dark hair wild about her face. She kept her legs open, like a dare, the most intimate part of her glistening in the moonlight. In those fleeting seconds Teresa learnt something: there is an animal inside us all. Society is simply a way to hide that fucking, snarling, fighting, shitting beast. We have only taught our bodies to move gracefully and our voices to speak pleasantly. It is not really us.*

Hope knew she'd never walked in on Delia and Tom, but since reading that scene, it felt like she had, taking the moment from a hazy imagining to a vivid memory. The words and the deadening, sickening anger they evoked were her biggest reminder of why she'd pulled the trigger. There had always been so much she didn't understand about that world and top of the list was how free Rosie and Delia were with each other. How Rosie openly had children with other women, how they flirted their way through parties, how relaxed they were with their bodies. But even with all Hope knew about them, it still seemed incredible that he'd been able to calmly describe Delia fucking Tom, which had to have been the inspiration for that paragraph.

She remembered then how Rosie had told her that if you want to write you have to be a burglar of life. He had a quick and brilliant mind and she wondered if, even as he'd held her to his chest as Tom lay dead on the floor, he'd thought, this is exactly what the book needs. Except, of course, he wouldn't have been able to put the scene in the book if there had actually been a murder at his home, which was another good reason for him to have disposed of the body and told her to keep quiet. Maybe it hadn't really ever been about avoiding a scandal, but about the book. When Hope had confronted them after the signing, Delia said that Rosie wouldn't have been stupid enough to write about a murder they wanted to hide for all the world to see. But Hope knew that was a lie. In fact, the only thing she knew to be definitely true was that Rosie would do anything for his art.

Chapter Fifteen

As Nat opened the door to the interview room she was hit by a strange smell, like the morning after a party, spilt beer and full ashtrays left out overnight. Hope was sitting at the table and looking at her expectantly, her eyes wide and her greasy hair pulled inexpertly into a bun at the nape of her neck, which accentuated her double chin and made it look like she was storing boiled sweets in her jaw line.

'So what's going on?' she asked as soon as Nat sat down.

Nat had planned a soft approach, but sitting opposite her, she didn't think Hope would appreciate that. 'Mr Glencourt called me two nights ago. He said you went to one of his signings?'

'That's right.'

'And that you caused a bit of a scene.'

A livid blush was creeping up Hope's neck. 'I'd hardly call it a scene. I just want him to tell the truth.'

'He's very upset by your allegations. I went to Shadowlands to speak to him about everything.'

Hope leant forward. 'And?'

The day was warm and Nat was hot in her jacket, so she

shucked it off. 'I had a look around, even down by the river where you think they might have buried Mr Markham.'

'I bet you could get a warrant to dig there.'

'We wouldn't need one. The Glencourts gave us permission. They even suggested it.' Hope blinked and Nat felt a twist of pity for what she was about to hear. 'But we won't be digging because I believe that Mr Markham left Shadowlands on the twenty-second of September 2016, and took a train to London.'

Hope shook her head so definitely it almost looked dangerous. 'That's impossible. He'd been dead for about ten days by then.'

Nat had to look away from Hope's desperation. Her journal was a testament to what Shadowlands meant to her and, now that Nat had seen the place, she understood how that would be true for most people who went there, especially an impressionable twenty-three-year-old. But there was too much evidence against what Hope was saying for her to continue with the case. Especially after what the Glencourts had shown her the day before.

'Miss Jenkins,' she said, as gently as she could. 'Mr and Mrs Glencourt did actually report Tom Markham missing in September 2016. There was quite a thorough investigation into his disappearance and nothing suspicious was found.'

'But the police wouldn't have suspected them,' Hope said, her voice full of indignation. 'I mean, that's really clever, when you think about it. Like hiding in plain sight. They probably only did it to cover their tracks in case I decided to go to the police.'

Nat agreed with what Hope was saying, and also about the convenience of the Glencourts' story, but sometimes things just were what they appeared to be. She opened her file and slipped out the final nail in the coffin of the case. 'Also, the police found Tom on the CCTV at Willerton Banks station.'

Nat slid the paper across the table to Hope, watching how her body stiffened as she looked at the grainy printout. It showed the back of a young man standing on the platform and was time-stamped 9:03 a.m. 22/09/16.

'That can't be Tom,' Hope said, a complete defiance in her voice. And a tiny part of Nat agreed. When they'd gone back to the house after standing by the river, the Glencourts had shown her the printout and said the police had given it to them just before they closed the case. The time on the CCTV corresponded with the London train, and they were as convinced as the police had been that Tom had boarded it, and possibly succumbed to his addiction there. Nat had nodded along with their explanation, which sounded totally feasible. She was still confused as to why the printout had been removed from the official police file and amazed that it had been given to the Glencourts, although run-of-the-mill shoddy police work was always a possibility.

'The Glencourts are adamant that it is,' Nat said. 'Also, they showed me some photographs of Tom and this man definitely has the right height and build.'

Hope pushed the paper away as if it disgusted her. 'Lots of young men look like that.'

'Willerton Banks is hardly a bustling metropolis. There aren't lots of anyone. Two young men who looked like Tom being there at the same time seems a fairly unlikely coincidence.'

Hope put a hand to her forehead and rubbed her temple. 'Well, then, they must have manufactured this somehow. It's not real.'

Nat was careful to keep her voice steady. 'Miss Jenkins, Mr Glencourt also told me that part of your job was to type up his dictated notes about his book. Is that right?'

Hope nodded. 'Yes.'

'So, you were privy to much of The Ruined Girl before it was published?'

'Well, parts, yes.' Nat watched Hope understand where they were going. 'But it was all very disjointed. Often it would just be single words. Sometimes sentences. And, if you're suggesting what I think you are, he hadn't finished it by the time I left. Not even close. He had an endless correspondence with his editor, so I know you'll be able to check that. In fact, I wrote about in my journal.'

'You did. You recorded how the ending was troubling him, but you also said that he figured something out near to the end of your time with him. And Mr Glencourt told me that he never starts writing without knowing how a book is going to end.' Nat paused, but Hope didn't speak, a deep frown creasing her forehead. 'He said that many of his dictated notes would have been about the ending, which you would have transcribed. Do you think there's a possibility that, with everything that happened, it's all become confused in your mind?'

'No.' Hope's voice was firm. 'Absolutely not.' Nat found it terrifying how absolutely people held on to their stories. Sometimes when she sat in interviews like this, she was reminded of the one time she went back home and begged her mother to accept her. Not literally, but to all intents and purposes, she had begged for her mother's love. But the woman had turned away, saying she couldn't love a daughter who lived a life of sin, that men must not lie with men and women must not lie with women.

You're headed for hell, she'd whispered, a genuine terror in her voice. There had been a second when Nat had wondered if she could learn not to be the person her mother hated, before she'd understood that it was impossible. Hope clearly found something about her story impossible to let go of, but Nat knew that didn't make it true.

She softened her voice when she next spoke. 'But there were so many strong emotions involved. Whatever actually happened, you all admit that there was a lot of falling in and out of love. Lots of opportunity for hurt and rejection.' That can make you feel like you're going mad, Nat wanted to add.

'It wasn't like that,' Hope said, an edge of anger now in her voice.

Nat had been struck by another thought on her drive back from Shadowlands the day before. 'I have another question about your journal. You recorded a lot of conversations in it.'

'That's right.'

'Well, I wondered how you did that. I mean, I'm a police officer, it's my job to record and remember, but still, I'd find it hard to remember a conversation word for word without my notes or a recording.'

Hope's cheeks washed red. 'I have a very good memory.'

'So you're saying every word in this journal is one hundred per cent true?'

Hope shifted in her seat. 'Well, I expect not literally every word. But the gist certainly is.'

'That's quite different.' Nat tapped the notebook. 'That means you knowingly made things up in here.'

'No, that's not what I meant, and you know it.' Hope turned her head towards the window. The sun was streaming into the room, and the light was slanted so she was surrounded by dust motes that, to Nat, looked like little thoughts jostling around her.

'I've seen your medical notes, Miss Jenkins. You were prescribed anti-depressants for a year after you returned home from Shadowlands. It's possible you might still be experiencing a form of PTSD. I can help you access the care you need.'

Hope looked back, her gaze steady. 'Just tell me what's going to happen now?'

Nat made herself sound definite. 'The case is closed as far as we're concerned. But you're not in any trouble.' Hope snorted and Nat knew what she meant. She wanted to tell her that she wasn't one of them, she'd so wanted this case to be real and not just because she needed a leg up in her career. She'd love to see someone like Ambrose Glencourt cut down to size. And she'd have liked to help Hope, who she felt a pull towards, a fellow outsider. She softened her tone when she next spoke. 'Miss Jenkins, you have to drop this. If you go on harassing the Glencourts, they've made it very clear that they'll press charges.'

But Hope held her gaze like a challenge. 'You're making a terrible mistake.'

'Miss Jenkins, please . . .'

Hope held up a hand that silenced Nat. 'No, DI Evans. I told you I killed Tom ten years ago, and Rosie and Delia covered it up. And the crazy thing is you have two documents that prove I'm telling the truth and you still won't believe me.' She laughed. 'But I suppose I shouldn't have expected anything else. I guess, if you won't help me, then I'll just have to do it myself.'

Nat's shoulders had tensed into thick slabs and her neck was stiff. She now not only didn't have a big case, she also had a woman as good as making threats against arguably the most famous novelist in the country. Hope stood and so Nat copied her, trying to take charge of the situation.

'Miss Jenkins. I really don't want to have to arrest you, but that is what will happen if you make contact with the Glencourts again.'

Hope smiled in a way that made Nat feel sick. 'I know the most convenient thing would be for all of us to agree that I'm mad,' she said. 'But, unfortunately for you, I've given up being convenient.'

Chapter Sixteen

The weekend had passed in a blur that Hope couldn't entirely remember, and it was a herculean physical and emotional effort to drag herself to school on Monday morning. Her head was throbbing and her body was sore. In the shower she noticed that two large bruises had bloomed on the top of her thighs at some point over the last couple of days, which she couldn't find an explanation for, and her brain felt like it was filled with broken glass. Since getting back from the station on Friday night she'd found wine the only way to dial down her anxiety and she'd lost count of how many times she'd filled up a glass over the weekend. It was clearly going to be up to her to be brave if she wanted any recompense for what Rosie had done, but that seemed impossible when she'd spent the past decade keeping herself as still and quiet as possible.

Charlie was late to school and, unusually, brought in by a man who Hope presumed to be his father. Charlie looked slightly ruffled and didn't even glance in her direction, keeping his eyes on the ground in a way that felt like an effort. Hope called to the man to tell him that he needed to sign the late register, which made him huff loudly as he pushed at Charlie's shoulder, saying, 'Go on then, get to class.'

The man wasn't who Hope had imagined as Charlie's dad. He was good-looking, tall and slim and dressed in a smart suit. His phone was in his hand as he approached her partition and he kept his eyes down as he jabbed at his screen like he wanted to break it. As she waited, she caught her reflection in the light bouncing against the Plexiglass. Even through its distortion she could see that her hair was greasy, her eyes dark and sunken, and her clothes dull and ill-fitting, clinging to all the wrong parts. Once, she would have been the sort of woman this man would have noticed and, even though she wouldn't have chosen someone like him, the invisibility of who she was now smarted, despite it confusingly also being what she'd wanted.

Sure enough, when he finished with his phone the look he gave her was nothing more than a cursory glance. But still Hope saw the disdain in the flick of his eyes, so she knew she was nothing more than an amorphous blob to him, an unattractive woman who existed, if at all, under the label of school secretary.

'If that's all,' he said, in an accent that wouldn't have sounded out of place at Shadowlands. But then his phone rang and so he left without waiting to hear what her response might be.

Charlie was very pale, with dark circles around his eyes, when he arrived at lunchtime.

'How's Mummy?' Hope asked, as brightly as she could.

'Her arm hurts but it isn't broken.' He unzipped his lunch box and stuck his hand in but faltered. 'I don't like it when she cries.'

'It's horrible when anyone cries,' Hope agreed, trying not to focus on another woman buckling under the weight of her existence. 'But I'm sure you make her very happy.'

'That's what she says.' Charlie pulled his sandwich out of his lunch box and, as he did, a small piece of folded paper fell to the floor and landed by his feet. Charlie hadn't noticed, too busy unwrapping his sandwich, so she didn't say anything. But her eyes were drawn to it all through lunch, as she steered the conversation onto more benign matters.

As soon as he left Hope retrieved the paper from where it had ended up, just under the chair he'd been sitting on. She unfolded it and was met with the words: *Bad boy. Everybody hates an eavesdropper. No treat for you today.* The soreness that had coated her body all day amplified and the tinny throb in her head pushed a sickness into her stomach. An image came uninvited of Charlie standing outside a door as his parents shouted behind it, and her heart stretched a little further towards the point at which it was going to snap. But she made herself stand and take the late register down from its shelf so she could compare the handwriting in the note to Dominic Cunningham's signature. There was no doubt it was the same.

Hope's brain was running on overdrive, but she tried to be reasonable. What if the note was nothing more than a misjudged punishment from an over-zealous father? What if Charlie's bruises and his mother's arm were simple coincidences? *Lazy writing*, Rosie said in her mind.

The obvious thing would be to take the note and all the things she already knew about Charlie to the head, Mrs Alperton, but Hope folded it back up and put it in her bag. It wasn't only that she didn't want to get involved in any more messy emotional traumas, but also the past few days had shaken her belief in her ability to affect, or even understand, anything. The possibility still existed that she was reading the situation wrong. What if she was responsible for Charlie being taken away from his parents when he didn't want to be?

The day wound its sticky way on as Hope failed to focus properly on any task. She shouted at two boys who were kicking a football against the wall outside the office and snapped at a parent too imbecilic to understand simple instructions. Then it was time to go home, and a clawing sense of desperation began to creep over her as she thought about her empty flat, *The Ruined Girl* read, Rosie unpunished. And on top of it, all the stupid accusations that had been made about her sitting heavily in her brain.

She was gathering her things when Alice Alperton poked her head round the office door and asked if she could have a word, her smile too tight on her face. Hope followed her into her office, but as soon as she sat down, she wanted to jump up and run a lap of the room. Alice clasped her hands together as she leant forward over her desk. 'I just wanted to check in, Miss Jenkins. Find out how you're feeling?'

The question was so unexpected tears pathetically gathered at the corner of Hope's eyes, but she responded automatically. 'I'm fine, thank you.'

A sticky silence ballooned around them. 'I was thinking maybe you could do with a couple of days off.'

No one took holiday in term time unless it was an emergency. 'I don't . . . I mean, thank you, but no, I'm fine.'

Alice shifted in her seat. 'It's just, I've noticed that you seem a bit, well, distracted lately. And that you're letting things slip a little.'

'I'm sorry?'

A blush was extending up Alice's neck in mean red blotches. She motioned to Hope's clothes and when she looked down, she saw a large yellow tea stain she hadn't noticed on her dress, just above her left breast. She brushed at it ineffectually. 'Goodness, I'm sorry, I didn't realize.'

'Yes, but it's not just dirty clothes, is it, Miss Jenkins?' Alice was looking at her intently, like she wanted to be put out of this misery, but Hope genuinely didn't know what she meant. 'You've worked here for eight years now. And you are such a valued member of staff. But there's no shame in admitting when you need help.'

The sun was beating down on the concrete playground through the window behind Alice, shimmering the world away. 'I really don't know what you're talking about. Have I done something wrong?'

Alice rubbed at a spot on her temple as if it was hurting. 'If I'm honest, I'm wondering if you have a problem with alcohol.'

Hope spluttered, but it felt unreal, the memory of waking fully clothed on top of her covers just that morning, her head cracked in half, two dark circles on her thighs. 'I like a glass of wine, but no more than the next person.'

Alice shook her head. 'No one else comes to school smelling of alcohol, Miss Jenkins.'

It was very strange because as soon as Alice said the words, it was like something opened in Hope's brain and she was able to catch the wafts of acidic stench coming off her body, almost as if she'd dumped a rotting animal between them. 'I . . . I do have a few personal issues going on at the moment, but nothing insurmountable. I don't need time off.' A large part of Hope wanted to beg for a job she'd always thought she hated, but she swallowed it down along with everything else.

Alice smiled in a way that made Hope want to scream. 'Perhaps you need to talk to someone about these problems.' Hope couldn't think of anything worse than that, but Alice was still speaking. 'There are lots of organizations that can help. I don't want to overstep, but my mother had a problem with drinking, and AA worked brilliantly for her. I'd be more than happy to talk to you about it, if you ever wanted to.'

All Hope wanted was to leave the room. 'Thank you,' she managed to stammer, 'but I'm fine. Really.'

'The thing is, a school is really not the best environment for you to be working these things out.' Alice looked down at her hands. 'A few of the parents have complained.'

Hope snorted before she could check herself, which wasn't the best response, but honestly those people were so fucking entitled. Or maybe stupid. Believing they could shield their little darlings from the shit of life.

'What I was thinking,' Alice continued, as if she was too embarrassed to stop, 'is that I'll sign you off for two weeks – on full pay, of course. Then we can revisit. This is absolutely not a disciplinary suspension. It's just to give you a bit of time to work through a few things.'

Hope stood because there was nothing else to do. It seemed suddenly obvious that Alice had probably wanted to get rid of her for years. Hope cringed with embarrassment at the meetings they must have had about her, because of course it was absurd to think that she should be employed in a school. These problems, as Alice so sweetly put it, were simply a good, but necessary, excuse. Alice stood as well, almost reaching towards

Hope, which made her take a step backwards and her leg banged sharply into the chair behind.

'I meant what I said, Miss Jenkins. I am here if you ever want to talk.'

There was nothing more to say. Would there ever again be anything worth saying? Hope blundered out of the room, her vision blurring with her unshed tears. Her body appeared to have almost solidified, so simple movements like bending to pick up her bag were hard. But she forced herself onwards and out of the building. In the open, on the lonely streets where no one knew her, the desperation wrapped itself tighter, threatening suffocation as she made her weary way home. Her life since Shadowlands had been one long lesson in the fact that we're not really in control of anything and ordinary lives are arbitrary, yet it was something she didn't appear to have learnt. Her hangover was intense, but she still stopped at the corner shop, wine seeming like the only answer.

Her head and neck were so tight when she got home that she ran a hot bath and popped two mega-strength ibuprofen with a glug of wine from the bottle. Not that either thing worked, so by the time she got out all she'd managed was to make herself feel sick and dizzy on top of the pain. She put on pyjamas and sat on the sofa, pouring out another glass of wine, surprised to see that the bottle was nearly finished. Which obviously proved something.

It felt like the situation had reached a critical mass that was threatening to crush her. What Natalie Evans had said the day before was festering, like an infected wound. The truth was, Hope couldn't, hand on heart, remember every single thing she'd transcribed for Rosie. Often she would go into an almost dream-like trance as Rosie's voice vibrated through her body in a sensuous, hypnotic fashion, and she had to admit that it wasn't impossible that those dictations could have detailed more of the plot than she remembered. It couldn't be totally impossible that she'd somehow subconsciously absorbed them into her memory, like a faulty glitch in a computer system. And it wasn't like she'd recorded every single thing that had happened or, as DI Evans said, even completely correctly recorded everything. But did that mean the rest of Rosie's story was true? The sharp sting of rejection flooded her again, the soreness of unrequited love, the acidity of betrayal.

Hope stood sharply to try to rid herself of the feelings, but it didn't work, so she strode into the hall, then came back to the lounge. Her breath was sticking in her chest, making her light-headed, so she squeezed shut her eyes, which made coloured swirls spin in the darkness. But when she opened them again, nothing was as it should be. Rosie's desk was sitting squarely where her sofa should have been and the bookcases had wrapped around the walls, her windows erasing her grey street and revealing the dreamy view from Rosie's study. And then Tom and Rosie were there, writhing on the desk, so she remembered how, when she'd first followed Delia into the room, she'd thought for a sickening second that they were themselves fucking. Except Tom's hands were still around Rosie's neck and Delia was still screaming. She saw her own hand grab the gun from the silver box, even though she wasn't moving. And somehow Tom was there, right in front of her face, smirking like she was a joke. Delia was by the door now, Rosie on the desk, or was he up by then? Her hands were shaking and her finger was tight against the trigger, those seconds between knowing she was going to do it and firing multiplying around her until the moment suspended and she felt herself fall through the vortex. Someone was screaming and they sounded so sad she wanted to help, but how can you help anyone when you can't help yourself?

It took a minute for Hope to understand that she was the one making the sound, not entirely able to catch her breath. And why was she on the floor of her lounge? Oh God, she was so sure she'd pulled that trigger, but what if it hadn't happened? Rosie had told her to be a burglar of life, not words. But what if she'd misinterpreted him? What if, in her desperation to be extraordinary, she'd taken his words and fabricated them into her truth, which was actually a lie?

Hope's confusion was so absolute it felt almost manufactured. She couldn't even pinpoint which part she was crying for, although it was probably an ugly amalgamation of her mother, Tom, Charlie, herself. It also felt dangerous, like she'd reached the bottom of somewhere and there was nowhere left to go. She hauled herself to her feet with the vague idea of getting a glass of water, but found she was unsteady, so had to put a hand against the back of the sofa to stop herself from falling. And then she became convinced that she was dissolving, parts of her floating up into the ether so she didn't stand a chance of finding them again. Her headache was so bad she wondered if she should try to get to hospital, and she was hot enough to be running a temperature. So much had been taken from her and now she was going to have to relinquish her memory? Soon there would be nothing left, just an empty shell with no purpose, no reason to get up and go into another and another day.

Life stretched before her, flabby and bilious, like a fat man who's eaten too much. She couldn't think of anything that would make it better, which was terrifying because it meant there was no discernible end. Whatever the truth, she could at least recognize that she was a mess of a person.

The light was hurting her eyes, so she went to draw the curtains. The corner of the bay stuck out and she reached for it for support, but the sharp line felt like something definite. The first time she banged her head was just to stop the spinning, but she was surprised by how good it felt, how comforting the shudder was through her body, and so she banged it again, and then once more. The pain made her fall to her knees, a drop of bright blood landing on the carpet in front of her.

Chapter Seventeen

Since her final interview with Hope, Nat had made a vow that she would stop working late when she didn't absolutely have to, that, when she could, she'd make it home in time for the kids' bath and bed time, that she would be engaged and present. Hope's loneliness practically vibrated off her, and it scared Nat. Hope was two years younger than she was, but she could have been ten older. And it wasn't just how she looked, but how she held herself, like she was so uncomfortable, she'd turn herself inside out if she could.

Loneliness did that to a person, and Nat knew that without Kira and the kids she could so easily succumb. Because, the truth was, there wasn't anyone else. Her family hadn't spoken to her since she came out, and she'd always been wary of people who wanted to be friends, as if they must be desperate themselves to have resorted to her. It was a miracle that she'd waited for Kira to wake up the morning after she'd first gone home with her, and not sneaked out at dawn as usual. Maybe even more of a miracle that she'd agreed to breakfast, that the morning had slipped into afternoon and then evening, that she'd allowed days to follow on from one another, until she was in too deep to commit her usual acts of self-sabotage.

But Nat still found it hard to fully believe in the life she'd created for herself. Her family often seemed like an audacious trick. There were times that she found being with them so hard she worried that her mother had been right and what she was doing was unnatural. That simply wanting the things she wanted made her a bad person. She lived in a world in which her choices were largely considered normal and yet, sometimes, when she touched Kira, all she could hear was her mother screaming. Sometimes it felt like the kindest thing would be to remove herself, to spare her family from the pain of being loved by someone so flawed.

The house was its usual mess, but she tried not to let it irritate her as she walked through the front door. All the sound was coming from upstairs, so she resisted the urge to make a cup of tea and immediately climbed the stairs. Ben was in the bath and Riley had clearly just been taken out because Kira was wrestling her into a nappy on the floor.

'Mumma,' Ben shouted when he saw her, which at least stopped Riley's tears.

'Hey,' she said, 'bath time.'

Kira turned to Nat and closed her eyes for a second. She looked like she'd been in a fight. Her T-shirt was covered in dried bits of food and her jeans were wet. Her hair was so messy it was hard to believe it had ever been brushed and her skin was dry and patchy. Out of the two of them, Kira had always been the one who cared more about her appearance, always in fact the one who looked better. The first time Nat had seen her, dancing in a crowd with little stars shimmering on her cheekbones, Nat had felt cold air rip through her chest. Whereas now, as she looked at her wife kneeling on the bathroom floor, she was reminded horribly of Hope Jenkins.

'Let's get you out then, kiddo,' Nat said, pulling a damp towel off the rail and scooping her son out of the bath.

After that everything was a blur. It felt like hours and hours before she was walking back down the stairs, Ben four stories down and Riley miraculously asleep in her cot. She was aware that she didn't do enough coal-face parenting and yet she still felt assaulted, like the children had physically taken something from her. As if they'd wanted more than her love and attention, but an actual pound of flesh. A smear of irritation was needling her as well, because she couldn't shake the feeling that they were pandering to the kids, that when Kira sung to them or lay in the dark until they fell asleep, it was weakening them somehow. Even at Christmas and birthdays, Nat shrank from the presents and the glee. It all seemed wasteful and sinful, which were her mother's words that she didn't even believe in and yet, there they were, scratching against her skin.

Kira was sitting on the sofa with an open bottle of red and a half-drunk glass. There was even a glass for Nat, which she took as a kind of peace offering. If a peace offering was needed. She couldn't remember how they'd left it that morning, or had it been last night? Their arguments were so never-ending and convoluted she couldn't remember where one ended and another began.

'What are you watching at the moment?' Nat asked as she took the first delicious sip and felt it spread through her chest.

'Christ,' Kira laughed. 'I can't believe that's my life now. Kids or Netflix.'

'It'll get easier. It has to.'

'Shall we get a takeaway? If I try to cook, I think I'll burn the house down.'

Nat knew she should offer but it felt beyond her as well, so she reached for her phone. The moment felt refreshingly normal, so she could almost see outside of herself and witness them as a proper couple, choosing food from a bright menu like lots of people did after a hard day.

Kira poured them both another glass. 'Guess what, rumour is that Miss Jenkins was fired today.'

Nat was surprised by how sad the news made her feel. 'How do you know?'

'Sam knows the head of the PTA.'

'Shit, that seems a bit harsh.'

'Ah, she can be a bitch. And quite a few of us have smelt alcohol on her.'

Nat didn't like the casual way Kira dismissed Hope, even if she was unfit. 'I feel sorry for her.'

'You don't know her.'

'No, but you know, being fired. Did Sam say why?'

'I think some of the parents complained about her attitude. Which is shit.'

Nat hated the thought that Kira might have added to a chorus against her. 'Bloody hell. Fired over a bit of playground gossip.' She knew she'd said the wrong thing as soon as the words left her mouth. The atmosphere chilled and Kira drew her legs up underneath her.

'Yes, because that's all we're good for, us mums. Total airheads. Gossiping away over our washing lines.'

'You know that's not what I meant.' Nat reached for Kira's foot, but it was pulled tighter under her body.

She was expecting a tirade, which she couldn't work out if she deserved or not, but Kira's voice was soft when she spoke. 'Or maybe that is all I'm good for. I don't really know who I am any more.'

It felt hard to even turn her head towards her wife. Nat wanted to help, but she also felt scared. Their experiences had diverged so significantly since Ben, she often felt like they were existing in different universes. Although, the truth was, they had always come from different worlds, which made communication hard. Often when Kira got annoyed over what Nat saw as small slights, she wanted to tell her that it was a privilege to even notice such things. But also she felt a rush of love for her wife as she looked across at her, pulled so tightly together on the sofa, as if she might crumble if she let go. Nat didn't understand why sharing a life with someone had to be so hard, but knew enough to understand that she had to try to meet Kira where she was if she wanted things to get better. 'What do you mean?'

Kira motioned up and down her body. 'Literally that. Who am I? Like, sometimes I watch you go out into the world and I think, that used to me. But my life is here now, this house and the park and the school are the extent of my existence.'

From where they were sitting, Nat could see their whole ground floor, with their table pushed up against the wall in the kitchen because it was too narrow a room for them to sit on both sides. The grandeur of Shadowlands flashed through her mind like a punchline. 'But it's what you wanted,' she said lamely.

'Of course it's what I want. That makes it even more confusing.' They both gulped on their wine. 'You should have had Riley. It's what we always agreed.'

Nat nodded, although her mind was losing focus, the conversation reminding her of standing with the Glencourts as they'd shown her the photocopy of the CCTV of Tom Markham at the train station. *He's like a son to me*, Mrs Glencourt had said as they looked at it. *I wish I could have made things right for him, but it's too easy to let down the people you love.* In her mind, Mr Glencourt put his hand over his wife's. *Delia finds this all very distressing*, he'd said, in a way that made it clear Nat needed to leave. Which made her wonder again if Hope could be right and they could have faked the photo? Anything was possible nowadays, especially if you had money and connections.

'Are you even listening to me?' Kira said.

'Of course I am,' Nat lied.

'But do you agree? We have to make peace with being good enough?'

Nat snorted. 'Good enough? What do you mean? You're always perfect.'

'You say that like it's a bad thing.'

'No, but . . .' Nat searched for what she meant. But the Glencourts were too prominent in her mind. Were they good? Was she? Was anyone?

'Do you even love me any more?' Kira asked, a catch in her voice.

The question was as terrifying as it had ever been. Her mother had often told her that she only punished her because she loved her, that anything easy wasn't worth having, that God loved the world so much he sacrificed his only son. Except to Nat's mind all that was the opposite of love, it was violent and distressing. But it was hard to shake the idea that she was wrong and that love had to be hard won or it was meaningless.

'Your silence is very loud,' Kira said, her eyes wobbling with tears.

'I don't know . . .' Nat tried. 'I do, of course, yes. Of course I love you. But, also, I'm not sure I really know what love is.'

Kira's tears fell then. 'I think, ultimately, it might be letting someone else in.'

'Making yourself vulnerable,' Nat said, before she'd even properly formulated the argument in her mind.

But Kira nodded. 'Well, yes. That's true. But that doesn't have to be scary.'

Nat felt her own tears building. Except she never cried and she pushed them down, into the pool of unshed tears she sometimes thought of as existing deep in her stomach, ready to drown her if she ever let them. Scary love was the only kind she knew and it didn't feel good.

Chapter Eighteen

The world beyond Hope's eyelids was too bright, which made it feel like she was surfacing from somewhere far away, deep down. She rolled onto her back, causing pain to shoot up her spine into her shoulders and head. Her tongue was huge in her mouth and her whole body felt dry and clammy. She opened her eyes, and the world exploded around her in pops of too-bright colour. Sitting up, her brain lunged against her skull, a sharp, stabbing agony beating behind her eyes. But she went with the momentum of movement, hauling herself upright, every joint aching, her feet tender, and limped to the kitchen where she gulped down glasses of water with three mega-strength ibuprofens. A sense of bad things hovering took her back to the lounge. From the doorway it looked dangerous: a line of blood on the wall, all the furniture in the wrong place, an empty whisky bottle sideways on the carpet.

The sight of the blood released a memory which made Hope raise a hand to her forehead where a hard lump had formed. It no doubt needed attention, but everything felt too difficult. Her tastebuds scarily prickled towards alcohol, but if she was someone who started drinking in the morning, then it had to be a short road to becoming one of the people who existed under the flyover, their bodies shaking and their eyes dead. A cold fear knotted in her stomach, but she had no one to call and now no job to go to. Just a hangover that felt deadly. For a brief moment she thought of reaching out to her mother, but everything about making that call felt too difficult. Except, she had to do something, because the day could not slink past until it was time for another drink.

The Ruined Girl was lying on the floor, open to its most incriminating page. It was a story so entangled with her own she could barely remember any more where her memories ended and the book began. She reached for it, flicking her fingers against the pages and, as she did, a thought began to tickle against her brain. Maybe the answer literally lay in the pages beneath her fingers. Maybe it wasn't about the story, but the construction. Rosie spent so long on the building of the story and not the writing, which meant that had to be the most important thing. A tiny spark of excitement flickered in Hope's chest for a second, like the strike of a last match, because, if that were true, then surely the fact that she'd seen Rosie's systems meant she was the best person to work it out.

What she was thinking was mad, but she had to remember that she'd never before doubted her version of the story, or her memory. She didn't have to give up just because Rosie said she was wrong. Hope searched the trashed room until she found her phone under the sofa, the screen a mass of cracks. But it still worked enough for Google to reveal three rental-car places within a thirty-minute walk of her flat. After that it was just a question of sobering up enough to drive.

She showered before looking in the mirror. A large purple

lump had formed above her left eye, and there was an ugly cut across the top of her eyebrow, with a tip of crusted blood. It felt tender to the touch and like it might split apart if pressed too hard. Her mother had always kept a first aid kit in the flat, which she felt both thankful for and depressed by as she retrieved it from under the sink. It seemed unlikely that going forward she would remember to replace its contents and, at some point in the future, imagined herself opening it to nothing. Although, it was best not to look too hard at a time when she would regularly need things like first aid kits because it revealed a world in which she lay alone on the floor, limbs twisted and heart breaking, no one on their way to help. She bathed her cut in stinging iodine, then attached two long sterile strips which were raised by the lump. The finished effect was quite shocking, but there wasn't time to worry about it. After that she felt more human but still popped another ibuprofen and drank an entire pot of coffee before leaving.

Chapter Nineteen

'Sorry,' Nat's DC said as she approached her desk, 'I've got Tom Markham's mother on the phone, and she's insisting on speaking to whoever's in charge.'

Nat had forgotten to tell her DC that they were closing the investigation and now she felt embarrassed that she'd wasted the woman's time. 'It's fine, put her through.'

'DI Evans,' she said as she picked up her phone. 'How can I help, Mrs Markham?'

'Are you the person in charge of finding my son?' A woman with a West Country accent said on the other end.

Nat looked out of the window, at the greyly dirty sky, where two pigeons were fighting. 'Well, not exactly. The investigation into your son's disappearance was closed ten years ago. I'm, I mean, I was, investigating a claim made by someone that they killed your son.'

The woman drew in a sharp breath. 'Yes, that's what the policewoman I just spoke to said. But what do you mean? Who said that?'

There was a tightness in Nat's throat. 'I'm afraid I can't tell you that. But I can assure you that we've investigated her claims and dismissed them.'

'Like last time.'

'What do you mean?'

Mrs Markham sniffed. 'Like that posh twat last time, who asked me a load of smarmy questions and didn't listen to my answers.'

Nat opened a drawer and pulled out the copy of the investigation into Tom Markham's disappearance she'd already read. 'Can you remember the name of the officer you spoke to?'

'Andrew something,' the woman said. 'But I tell you what, he'd made up his mind that Tom was a useless drug addict who'd gone back to his addiction before I opened my mouth.'

Nat didn't doubt that was true. 'When did you last see your son?'

'Oh God, about thirteen years ago.'

'And to your knowledge, was he involved with drugs?'

The woman laughed. 'Yeah, you could put it like that. He was a right little shit. Always stealing, always lying, always had the law banging on my door. I had to kick him out in the end, it was too disruptive for my other two. But he'd made such good progress at Ridgeview. I'd spoken to him a few times while he was there, and I was hoping to see him again soon. We spoke just before he went to that place for the summer . . .'

'Do you mean Shadowlands?'

'Yeah, with that do-gooder woman, Delia.' Nat heard the sneer in Tom's mother's voice.

'You didn't like her?'

'I never met her. Tom loved her though. Said she'd saved him.' Nat reassessed the sneer in her mind, realizing it was jealousy. 'Anyway, he said he was spending the summer there. But then he rang while he was there, totally out of the blue, and said he'd met someone, and he was going to bring her to meet me and his brothers.'

Excitement trickled down Nat's spine. 'Can you remember when that was?'

'The thirtieth of August, which I know 'cos my youngest's birthday is the twenty-ninth and I remember being pissed off that Tom didn't mention it when he rang. I remember saying to him, if you'd just rung yesterday, you could have said happy birthday to Paul, and he was all like shit, I'm so sorry, and he sounded genuinely sad about it, which surprised me.'

'Did he say who he'd met?'

'No. But he said I'd love her.'

Nat leant forward over her desk so far it cut into her stomach. 'Mrs Markham, did you ever get the impression that your son and Delia Glencourt were in a relationship?'

There was a shocked silence on the other end. 'Isn't she much older than him?'

'About twenty years.'

The woman snorted. 'I tell you what, no way would Tom have said I was going to love her if he was planning on bringing that posh bird here.'

Nat pressed two fingers into the corners of her eyes. If Tom had been talking about Hope, then it actually made the Glencourts' story more plausible, because surely it would make it less likely he was sleeping with Delia, and more likely that he'd have run off when Hope said she loved Ambrose. Although, it also matched up with what Hope had said about her and Tom being in love. But if that was true and he'd told his mother about her, why the hell would he have said he loved Delia?'

'And that was the last time you spoke with him?'

'Yeah. But listen, I know my boy, I know he wouldn't of just run off like they said he did. I told that policeman where to look in Bristol and who his mates were, but I know they never bothered. I went round all those lads' houses back then and no one had spoken to them. Not that it mattered, 'cos they hadn't seen Tom.'

Nat knew she could just be listening to a mother who felt guilty and missed her son and was saying the things she wished were true. But also so much about the investigation didn't make sense. There shouldn't have even been one, but as there had been, she couldn't understand why it wasn't done properly. 'The police think he went from Shadowlands to London. Did he know people there?'

Nat heard the click of a lighter down the phone and Mrs Markham drawing on a cigarette. 'No way. He didn't know nobody there. He'd have come back to Bristol if he'd wanted to get drugs. Or even if he didn't.' In the pause Nat heard canned laughter from a television in the background. 'You know what, I think . . . I think something happened to him at that big house and those people didn't want to get into trouble so they covered it up.'

Nat was surprised by how similar Mrs Markham's assessment was to Hope's. But of course that didn't make it true. 'I can assure you, Mrs Markham, that we've fully investigated—'

'Oh, don't give me that tosh,' the woman said. 'If you're going to fuck us over at least have the decency to admit to it.'

The line went dead and Nat felt the slight. She replaced the receiver and rubbed her hands across her face, but it didn't release the building tension that would become a headache. She pulled Hope's journal out of the drawer and put it in her bag. It wouldn't hurt to look at it one more time.

Chapter Twenty

Willerton Banks wasn't much changed, although the butcher, where Delia had sent Hope many times, had been given a snazzy refit with lots of signs in the window shouting out its organic credentials. And there was some sort of gift slash coffee place where the old tea shop had been. The pub had also undergone a makeover, so she could imagine people coming from London and not being disappointed. They had a room, which the woman on reception seemed almost reluctant to relinquish, her eyes darting to Hope's forehead. It was small but very pretty, with white walls and a gingham bedspread with a view over the village green. In another life it would have been the perfect place for a romantic weekend.

Hope's headache was so bad she slept for a few hours and, when she woke, at least some of the pain had shifted. There was no point in arriving at Shadowlands while everyone was still awake, so she took herself to the gift-cum-coffee place where a bright young woman, who made Hope feel bad about every aspect of herself, served her an unsatisfying bowl of quinoa and roasted vegetables. At least they had Coke in a can, which she chased with two more ibuprofen.

After that she killed a couple of sober hours in the pub before setting off for Shadowlands at eleven, which meant she arrived just before half past. She parked on the lane outside the gate, not wanting the gravel to announce her arrival, and set off on foot, cutting up through the woods at the bottom of the drive and walking along the very edge of the garden by the wall which separated it from the road. The old coach house loomed into view, and she noticed a light on in an upstairs window. From there she turned up towards the house, through the woods, until she was right by Delia's studio on the edge of the lawn.

The moon was full, which meant the house and garden were bathed in an ethereal silver light, all the colours washed away like it was under water. The sight stopped Hope in her tracks. It was like seeing a lover again after a long time, so bittersweet you almost wished you'd stayed away. Time had blurred the edges of her memory but having the solid flesh of Shadowlands, almost unchanged, in front of her was too much to process. Fear rose like mist from the ground, blurring the image, so it became hard to believe in its reality. She had longed for the moment of return for so many years and yet, lurking in the shadows, the idea of going backwards seemed suddenly terrifying.

No lights were on behind any of the windows and the curtains of Delia and Rosie's bedroom were drawn. Hope was sure they must have a housekeeper or secretary who would no doubt be in her old rooms, at the far end of the house, invisible from the garden. She skirted up the side of the lawn by sticking to the swimming-pool hedge, which she couldn't help peeking through. Dark water lapped quietly against the sides, so for a heart-stopping moment she saw herself in the corner, pressed up against the tiles by Tom. The woman was still weeping at the far end, although a diving board had been added in front of her, as if she was about to walk the plank. And the loungers were the same but with newer, not-stiffened towels hanging off them.

From there she made it to the back end of the house and the kitchen, cupping a hand round her face to look through the windows at the neatly wiped-down surfaces. The material that had acted as makeshift cupboard doors had gone, replaced by tasteful wooden doors, and a coffee machine that would rival the ones in most coffee shops sparkled by the sink. The door was locked, which made Hope's heart set up a steady thump as she tried to imagine what would happen if she was caught, if they'd installed a fancy alarm system, or even if they'd started locking the French doors. But she forced herself on round to the terrace.

Three wine glasses were on the table, red sediment in their base, along with a pair of candlesticks heavy with wax. The three chairs at the top of the table were pushed out, as if the people had just stood up, and she wondered, with a pang of envy, if their housekeeper or secretary or whoever she was usually ate dinner with them.

The French doors looked exactly the same, which made her hopeful that they hadn't been replaced. Hope chose the middle ones and pushed down on the black iron handle. It gave, opening with a little sigh that made her want to cry with relief.

Not much had changed in the sitting room. The sofas had been refurbished, the leather armchairs by the fireplace were new and the cushions looked decidedly less worn, but all the pictures and china had a refreshing familiarity about them and the rugs on the floor had to be the same, albeit a little more threadbare. The piano was still in the far corner and Hope couldn't resist inspecting the photographs, which had been added to. A lot of them now showed teenagers; a young man in a graduation gown, a teenage girl holding what looked like a sporting trophy, Rosie and his eldest son, Rory, at what looked like a film premiere. She found Tilly, sat at the terrace table with a frown on her face, as if she was listening to something she disagreed with.

As Hope stepped into the hall she held her breath, listening before she made any moves. Everything was very dark and still. She tiptoed across the cool stones to Rosie's study door which was, as usual, shut. The handle clicked, which halted her progress, but the house kept its counsel, so she stepped across the threshold into the room bathed in moonlight, long oblong streaks lying across the floor and desk. The world made a dangerous swoop, so there was an overwhelming moment in which Hope thought she would faint. Time spun down a hole and spat out Tom, lying on the floor with Delia screaming over him as Rosie hauled himself off the desk. Hope was still there too, shaking over by the window. She glanced under the desk where the gun had skidded, but it was gone, so she forced herself past the ghosts to the bureau and, when she opened the box, her heart buckled at the sight of it back nestled on its blue velvet.

Rosie's desk was still the same mess as when she'd worked for him, although the typewriter had been replaced by a computer. Hope sat in his chair and saw her bulky outline reflected in the dark monitor. The shelf by his desk now held four large box files, the titles of each of his novels along the spine, the one closest to her ominously labelled *Teresa's Ruin*. She was there to look at the file which contained all the notes on *The Ruined Girl*, but couldn't resist pulling out *Teresa's Ruin* first. Perhaps she would be able to find out what was going to happen to her.

She didn't dare turn on a light, so had to use the torch on her phone, which meant the box was cast in harsh shadows. But she could see a notebook at the top, which she pulled out and laid flat on the desk. Rosie's wild handwriting had scrawled *Ruined 2* across the front, which started a churning that felt very like longing in Hope's stomach. The first page contained a series of questions: *If Teresa has got away with it for all these years, how is she feeling? Where is she living? Does she have a partner/kids/friends? What is she doing? How does she live? Where does she work? What is it to be a murderer when you're not a killer? Who is Aiden to her now? A ghost? A memory? Does she still love him?*

Rosie was asking her defining questions again, as if he still knew her better than she knew herself, but she forced herself to keep reading. Over the next few pages, a plot began to take shape. The book was set in the present, Teresa now in her mid-thirties, living a lonely life, no partner, children or friends, working on reception at a builders' merchants. Aiden's disappearance had been put down to the disposition of an oversensitive young man. *But somehow*, Rosie had written, *she has to face the past because what are we without our history?*

There were smaller bits of writing next to the establishing scenes, tiny scrawled notes that reminded Hope of the hours she'd spent transcribing Rosie's scattered thinking. Near the start of his plot points he'd written along the edge of the page: *lonely, this is a woman bereft, her days like a desert, mean winds always on the horizon*, and then a little further down, *need to work in the danger of admitting who we are to ourselves*. She turned another page: *physical deterioration is shocking – traces of her beauty flicker sometimes, which is almost worse, reflection of mental damage?* Then a few lines down: *D's idea interesting – what is memory? How reliable is it? Impossible that any of us remember the same thing.*

Hope reached back into the box and felt the shiny surface of photographs, which she pulled onto the desk. At first she couldn't work out what she was looking at, couldn't in fact work out where she began or ended. Because the photos were of her. She flicked through them quickly, seeing herself morph and change. They went back years, from not long after she'd left Shadowlands to just a couple of months before the present day. In one of them she was wearing the same jeans she had on at that moment. They were all either of her coming out of school, her flat, or the corner shop, which, after all, were the only places she went. She was scowling in most of them, hunched in on herself, a bottle of wine usually outlined against the plastic bags in her hands. And even through the shock, Hope's disgust surfaced, as she understood that all the ugliness at her core was visible to the world.

Acidic bile burned up her throat and a fine sweat broke out across her body. Something was building that was going to crash through her and there was nothing she could do to stop it. She lay her hands flat over Rosie's words, as if they might convey some meaning up through her body into her brain, but all it did was reveal the quickness of her pulse in her fingertips. Rosie had witnessed the nothingness of her days; he had seen her so alone and ugly and unloved. A dark fear thumped around her and she glanced at the door, frightened suddenly for her actual safety.

Little fragments of understanding settled on Hope for brief moments before being blown away, until slowly a possible explanation began to take shape. *The Ruined Girl* had given Rosie a success that most people could only dream of, but it was also true that before the sequel he hadn't published a novel since. He must have been somehow paralysed by the success, desperate for his next book to be as good, or better, even. She knew how vain he was at his heart and how much being stuck would have hurt, even though he'd had a dream of a life by any standard. But Rosie had started from a point most people would never reach, which meant his expectations were higher than most people would ever consider. His hatred of clocks gave him away and she could imagine how now, in his late fifties, he would be yearning after that big prize which had always eluded him to solidify his legacy. Revisiting one of the most successful novels of the past decade must have started to feel like his only option. And once he'd accepted that was what he was going to do, mining her life all over again wouldn't have given him any sleepless nights, as he'd done it once already. Hope looked down at all the photos of her and nearly laughed. What had he called Antonia's sequels – the pathetic fallback of a washed-up novelist? God, he'd have hated to sink to that level . . . but also the photos had to be the proof that she'd been right – she had been the inspiration for Teresa, and the plot was hers.

Hope's belly felt hot, like lava was about to bubble up her throat and out of her mouth. She imagined Rosie coming in the next morning and finding her on his desk, her insides spilt out. He would probably sort through them for anything useful and then get someone to clear the rest away. She understood then that she and Tom had been totally disposable, both of them secondary to the inspiration they provided. She had been a fool all these years, letting the fantasy of Shadowlands outweigh the reality. And it wasn't even as if the clues hadn't always been there. Rosie and Delia were mean at their hearts;

they laughed at people and used them, ultimately only concerned with maintaining a way of life that had always been theirs. People did things for them and were fascinated by them. They would never fear punishment from a system they controlled. They would have covered their tracks since the very beginning, which maybe explained how Rosie had so effortlessly come up with the story of her being in love with him when Natalie Evans had contacted him.

A cog creaked slowly round in Hope's brain. Maybe there had been nothing effortless about it? Being back in the study reminded Hope how hard Rosie found it to get his books right, and how much outside help he needed. My God, had she really been that stupid? Rosie probably had that story ready for years, because of course there would have been no way he could have predicted when she would read *The Ruined Girl*. Hope remembered then how exasperated her mother had been with her when she got back from Shadowlands, at a time when she'd expected care and understanding. Was it possible that all those years ago Rosie had explained her illness by spinning her mother the exact same story of her being sent mad by love for him?

A bird screeched hopelessly outside, a sound Hope had grown accustomed to when living at Shadowlands, some poor unfortunate creature losing its life in the darkness of the night. A door banged open upstairs and footsteps creaked on the boards above.

'Hello?' Delia shouted from the top of the stairs, and then, 'Tabitha, is that you?'

Hope's heart migrated out of her body, clattering around in the darkness of the room. In a panic, she shoved everything back in the file and replaced it on the shelf. Leaving through the sitting room was too risky, so she crossed over to the window where she could see the bloody river shimmering beatifically in the moonlight. On the other side of the river was the field with long grass where she'd lain with Tom the first time he'd told her he loved her. Time collapsed in on itself so she wasn't sure which version of herself was standing there, couldn't be sure that they weren't ping-ponging back and forth between realities. It felt like if she ran, she could catch up with her younger self, that she could rest her head against Tom's chest, that she could choose to not pick up the gun. She eased the window open and climbed out, her body ungainly in such a manoeuvre, so her T-shirt ripped under the arm. But all she wanted was to escape, which was not a feeling Hope would have ever imagined associating with Shadowlands.

Chapter Twenty-One

Nat had one of those headaches that had burrowed into her shoulders and neck and hurt so badly she worried about meningitis. But being at work was better than being at home, which meant she'd already broken her vow to leave on time. Since their conversation about love, their home had felt weighed down with sadness and Nat could feel Kira pulling away, as if she'd given up on her. Which she wouldn't blame her for – Kira deserved better – but Nat wasn't good at being left and every nerve in her body told her to run before that happened. Her mother had taken up residency in her mind, slamming doors in her face, which she didn't think had even happened literally, but was still dangerous because if enough doors are shut on you eventually you can't find your way out.

She timed leaving work to miss bath and bed time, trying to calculate as she trotted down the station steps if she could afford to rent somewhere for herself and keep paying the mortgage. What would it be like for Ben and Riley if she wasn't there? She suspected not much different, but she worried at what their relationship might look like in ten years' time if she had to make a concerted effort to see them. She couldn't bear the thought of history repeating itself with her own children, but that was the thing about history, it so often did, and she didn't know how to stop that.

As Nat stepped onto the pavement, her head full of her own personal transgressions, someone called her name. She turned, only seeing Hope Jenkins when she was already halfway across the road, waving at her to stop, breathing heavily. A large lump gleamed on her forehead, red at the centre and grey round the edges.

'Are you alright?' Nat asked before she could stop herself, dreading hearing what had caused the injury. But Hope raised her hand to the lump in a way that made Nat think she'd forgotten about it.

'Oh yes, that's nothing.' She took a step closer, bringing with her a cocktail of stale sweat and tobacco that made Nat want to gag. 'I need to speak to you.'

Nat looked pointlessly down the road. 'Have you been waiting for me?'

Hope nodded like there was nothing strange in that. 'I didn't think you'd see me if I came in and asked for you.'

'But how long?' Nat checked her watch and saw it was approaching eight on Wednesday night. It was tragic that neither of them had anywhere better to be.

'A couple of hours.' Hope took another step closer, so Nat took one back. 'I've found out something important.'

Nat liked the sound of something important, but she had to be realistic. 'What's that?'

'I went to Shadowlands yesterday.'

At first Nat wondered if she'd misheard, but Hope's face was triumphant. 'Mr and Mrs Glencourt asked you to their home?'

But Hope shook her head impatiently. 'No, they'd never do that.'

'Then why . . . ?'

'They never lock their doors.'

Nat's whole body heated. 'You broke in?'

'I don't think it's breaking in if you just have to open a door.'

'Of course it is.' Nat had a vision of calls from the Commissioner, but part of her still felt for Hope. 'Did they see you?'

'No.'

'What were you doing there?'

Hope tucked some hair behind her ears. She was sweating despite the fact the sun had set and dusk was creeping in. 'I know you think I've made this whole thing up, but I promise you I've been telling the truth. I did shoot Tom Markham at Shadowlands. Rosie and Delia did somehow get rid of the body. And Rosie did use the whole thing as the plot for *The Ruined Girl*.'

Nat had a terrible image of Hope digging up the Glencourts' land. 'Miss Jenkins, this has gone far enough, and I did warn you . . .'

'No, listen.' Hope scraped at her scabby lip with her teeth. 'It's all connected to *The Ruined Girl*. And I know you think I somehow absorbed the plot of that book when I was working there and have made it into my life, but you're wrong.'

Hope's eyes were sparkling, like she could see something Nat couldn't. She looked like the people they got in shouting about the dangers of 5G or crop circles. 'But what did you hope to find at Shadowlands?'

Hope smiled, which had the opposite effect to softening her. 'Rosie keeps notes on all his books. He's obsessed with making sure nothing gets lost, like he thinks every single thing he thinks or does is important. So I thought I should look in *The Ruined Girl*'s file and see what I could find.'

'And?' Even Nat was intrigued.

'Well, I got distracted. I looked at the *Teresa's Ruin* file first, because it has to be about me as well.'

Nat was starting to feel confused. 'Why?'

'Because it's a sequel, about Teresa. And I'm Teresa. I told you this.'

Since seeing the photographs of a young Hope, Nat found that easier to believe. 'Okay.'

'Anyway, I found all these photographs of me in that file. From just after I left Shadowlands to now. And he's written notes that can only be about me.'

Nat's vision was starting to blur at the edges, which usually meant she had to lie very still in a darkened room, not that that would be possible at home. 'Taken without your permission, I take it?'

'Of course.'

Nat tried to organize her thoughts. 'What exactly are you saying?'

'Well, it's proof, isn't it?' Hope waited expectantly, but Nat couldn't connect the dots. 'He can only have those photos of me because he based Teresa on me for the first book. He must have been watching me to see how killing Tom has affected me. Working out a new story.'

The pain was making Nat's thinking slow. 'I'm sorry, but I don't see how that proves anything. Even if he did base Teresa on you, that's only a character, not what she did.'

'No, you don't understand.' Hope looked exasperated. 'We

only care about what happens in stories because we care about who's doing it. My plot and my character are interconnected.'

Nat wasn't about to debate semantics; she liked to deal in facts. 'Do you have the photographs?'

'No, I got scared and left them there.'

'Right.' Nat put a hand to her forehead in a move that felt clichéd. 'So, you've come here to tell me that you broke into the Glencourts' home, when I specifically told you to stay away, where you supposedly found some photographs of yourself that you didn't take?'

Hope's eyes welled and she put a hand to her throat. 'Oh God, I know this all sounds unlikely, but you have to believe me.'

Nat thought of Ambrose Glencourt in his fancy house. She wouldn't put it past him to have used someone like Hope as a template, she supposed. He'd already admitted to being inspired by witnessing Hope pull the gun on Tom in the fight they all had, but also, he was right, that wasn't a crime. 'Look, even if he did base a fictional character on you, he hasn't committed a criminal act.'

Hope rubbed a hand across her face, red blotches flaring where she pressed her skin. 'No, but murder and disposing of a body are.'

Nat rubbed at the tension in her neck. Mrs Markham was sharp in her brain. *See*, the woman was shouting, *what did I tell you*. 'There's no evidence that a murder took place.'

'Apart from the fact that I'm telling you it did.'

Nat cringed because Hope was right, it should have been enough that she was saying something had happened for there to be a proper investigation. But, also, Nat knew how the system worked and that it wasn't enough, so she made herself say what she had to.

'And Mr and Mrs Glencourt are saying that it didn't. Plus there's the CCTV to take into consideration. And Mr Markham's erratic personal history.'

Nat watched Hope's shoulders round slightly. 'So you're telling me there's nothing I can do? Rosie's just going to get away with it all? He's going to write his new book and everyone's going to say he's a genius and he'll lap up the praise and probably win a prize.'

'We've been over this. I'm not sure there is anything for him to get away with. It has never made sense that he would have written about a murder he wanted to conceal.'

'Not to us it doesn't. But someone like Rosie doesn't have to worry about things like being punished. That's just not how it works in his world.'

Nat pushed away thoughts of the Commissioner. 'No one's above the law.'

Hope looked to the floor, but when she looked back up her expression lodged itself uncomfortably in Nat's chest. 'So you're not going to help me.'

'I've offered you help.'

'I don't mean in that way.'

The bottom line was, there was no gain to Nat believing Hope, even though she could see the very real desperation in her eyes, and even though the woman's journal was sitting next to her bed, half re-read the night before, because she wanted to believe her. Ambrose Glencourt knew too many people and his book was so beloved. Maybe Teresa was based on Hope, maybe he had spied on her, or maybe the photographs didn't even exist. It didn't really matter, because even though those were the things that mattered to Hope, they didn't matter to anyone else. A case against someone like Ambrose Glencourt would have to be completely watertight to stand even the smallest chance. And not only was this case full of holes, there was no body and no chance of obtaining any forensic evidence. The CPS would tell her she'd gone mad herself because all she really had was a drug addict who had disappeared and the allegations of a lonely woman with an obsession.

Nat forced herself to sound definite when she next spoke. 'Miss Jenkins, I could arrest you right now for breaking and entering, but I'm not going to do that.' She paused, praying that Hope wouldn't want to be arrested, that she wouldn't really have to explain to the Commissioner why she'd let it get to this. 'What I'm going to do is advise you in the strongest possible terms to never again contact the Glencourts or go near their house. This absolutely has to stop. It really is your final warning.'

Nat had the sense that Hope's energy was pooling between them, as if she'd shot her and she was bleeding out. 'Everything's designed for them, isn't it,' Hope said in the end and Nat found her breath catching in her throat. 'There's no hope for people like me, is there?'

'There is help available if you . . .'

But Nat stopped speaking because Hope had turned and was walking away. She hitched her bag onto her shoulder as she made her way down the street, the outline of her bra digging into the skin underneath her T-shirt and her skirt too tight against her waist. The sight pulled at something in Nat because Hope was right, whatever had really happened, it clearly hadn't been good, and the deck was stacked against her.

Chapter Twenty-Two

Hope hadn't made it far down the road when she stopped, the utter predictability of feeling so lost and hopeless flooring her for a moment. Natalie Evans had made her excitement at the photographs sound stupid. On the drive back from Shadowlands it had all seemed obvious, but now she couldn't pull together the threads of the story. Her confidence deflated like something dying, leaving a pocket of stale air under her breastbone. A couple jostled her as they passed, laughing at something, a floral scent trailing in their wake, hearts and flowers imprinted in their footsteps. It was Wednesday night, mid-week, and people had places to go, friends to meet, lovers to encounter, lives to be lived. Hope thought of her stuffy flat, her mother's forever-shut door, the bottles of wine waiting, and a constricting despair nearly smothered her.

She could still see Natalie Evans at the end of the road and she walked quickly to catch up with her. She hadn't explained herself well and she couldn't expect the woman to understand how the world of literature worked. Although, as she got closer, she slowed down, because she could also imagine the look on Natalie's face if she accosted her on the street again. Except, if she didn't, then what was there? Because Hope also couldn't make herself turn back towards home. It was much easier to keep walking behind Natalie Evans, matching her pace from just far enough back, than it was to make any other decision. It was a lovely evening, warmth still in the air and a tenuous beauty in the dying light. The action of walking soon became hypnotic, the turning of corners, the relinquishing of responsibility, the blind trust that a destination would be reached.

Hope felt disappointed when they turned onto a road and Natalie began fumbling in her bag in the way Hope did when she was looking for her keys. There had to be something ethically wrong in following someone, a police officer especially, to their front door, but they lived in a supposedly free country, there was no law against knowing where someone lived. And then Natalie Evans was turning up a path and putting her key into a bright yellow front door and what was the point in not seeing now.

The lights were on inside the house and the curtains were open, which created a cinematic view of a small messy sitting room, filled with children's toys. Hope watched Natalie walk in and sigh as she began an attempt at creating a bit of order. A tired-looking woman came through from a room at the back and leant against the door frame. She said something which made Natalie stop what she was doing and look up. It was a peaceful domestic scene, and Hope was filled with a deep envy. It was too unfair that the woman who was saying no to her came home to a house filled with love and mess and people. No wonder she didn't understand what all of this meant to Hope; she had a full life and the cases she took on were just her work, which she probably forgot about as soon as she walked through her front door.

Hope turned away, her belly tight and her shoulders stiff, and headed back the way she had come. She had to find something for herself, she had to, or she would die.

Chapter Twenty-Three

'You're late,' Kira said.

Nat avoided looking at her wife by keeping her eyes bent to the toys she was shoving into baskets. 'Sorry, manic day.'

'When isn't it?'

'I know, right.'

'We both need a bloody assistant,' Kira said, as she went back to the kitchen.

Nat looked up, the words still vibrating on the air. Oh God, she was an idiot.

She dropped the small wooden trains she was holding and rushed upstairs, where she grabbed Hope's journal from her bedside table. Her hands were shaking slightly as she flicked through it until she came to the place where Rosie had called Hope by the name of his old assistant, Sara. And then a few pages on Tom saying how Sara had left suddenly, possibly because of an affair with Rosie. Nat's mouth dried. It was shoddy that she hadn't connected the dots before now.

She went back downstairs, pulling her mobile out of her back pocket as she went, and dialled the Shadowlands number.

A female voice she didn't recognize answered and so she asked to speak to Mrs Glencourt, which seemed like the safest bet.

'I saved you some supper,' Kira shouted, so Nat stayed in the hall, her head too full of the things she might be about to find out to answer.

'Detective Evans,' Mrs Glencourt said in her ear. 'I didn't expect to hear from you again.'

Nat turned to the wall, hoping to muffle the call from the kids sleeping upstairs. 'Sorry to call so late. I'm just following up a few leads and I wondered if you had a number for Mr Glencourt's assistant before Hope Jenkins. I believe her name was Sara.'

There was a pause on the other end, then, 'I thought the case was closed.'

Nat's heart clenched. What she was doing was stupid, especially considering they were good friends with the Commissioner. 'It is. But if something new comes to light we do have to investigate.'

'I see.' Mrs Glencourt's tone was clipped. Nat could feel the tension through the phone.

'Why did Sara leave, if you don't mind me asking?'

Mrs Glencourt sighed. 'She became rather infatuated with Rosie.'

'Like Hope?'

'I think you'll find they were not the only two, Detective Evans. My husband was, in fact still is, infinitely attractive to young women.'

Nat quite wanted to laugh. 'I've read that he has children outside of your marriage.'

'That's right. But I can assure you that was never going to be the case with Sara.' Her tone had hardened so it reminded Nat of stone walls. 'You might find the way we live unconventional, but it suits us and that's all that matters.'

'Can I ask how it suits you?' Specifically you, Nat wanted to say, but didn't dare.

Mrs Glencourt huffed. 'I don't see how that's relevant.' Nat let the pause linger; she had learnt that most people liked to justify their life choices. 'I never wanted children,' Mrs Glencourt said. 'And Rosie did. I was hardly going to deny him that, was I. And besides, it would be criminal to let Rosie's genes die with him.'

Nat couldn't help looking up the stairs towards her kids' bedrooms. It sounded dangerous to think of life that way, like there was a pre-ordained order. 'If you have Sara's number, I would be most grateful.'

'I don't.'

'Well then, her surname and where she was from?'

Mrs Glencourt hesitated again. 'Clarke, with an E. And Halifax.'

'And what age was she when she worked for you?'

'Early twenties. Now, if that's all, I really must go.'

Nat gave an involuntary fist pump as she ended the call, but when she turned Kira was watching her from just inside the sitting room. 'Glad to see something can make you happy,' she said. 'I take it that was work.'

'Sorry.' Nat put her phone back in her pocket. 'I'd forgotten something.'

Kira raised her eyebrows. 'What, like your family?'

Chapter Twenty-Four

Hope found it very hard to keep track of her thoughts the next morning, when she woke into the emptiness of her life. Being suspended from her job meant that every day had become a weekend, which she'd hated for a long time. Although the holidays were even worse as they felt like being swallowed whole by a giant whale. Brightness was leaking in from the sides of her blinds which made her want to cry. She much preferred winter and cold, rainy days in which everyone looked miserable and hurried back inside. Sunny days lured people to parks and picnics and gardens and friends. And all those things and connections she had taught herself not to want were pushing to the surface again.

She sat up and her brain wobbled in her skull, adrift from too much alcohol the night before and general misery. The light was peaking around her blinds and it reminded her of something. Today was an inset day. And then a fleeting possibility presented itself. Because, one of the strange things she'd learnt about life was that it is much easier to repeat an action, even a bad one. And she had taken action the night before. Following Natalie

Evans home might not have been right, but it had been something.

Charlie lived on a very nice street, which Hope was pleased her memory led her to from having looked up his address only a handful of times. It was lined with handsome houses with rounded bay windows, neat front gardens and pristine paintwork. It was a road that wore its credentials proudly, advertising the industriousness and affluence of its inhabitants. Charlie's house was near the end and she stood on the opposite side of the road looking up at the generous expanse of it, the sunlight highlighting the sandy colour of the brickwork. The windows sparkled, but the glass was opaque behind the sun's glare.

It reminded her of the first time she'd seen Shadowlands and how clearly she'd imagined the richness of the world behind the windows. Had it really taken her that long to understand that beauty could hide ugliness? That for all of us, our own truth and fiction are muddled?

After a while, the front door opened and Charlie and his mother came out, so Hope fell into line behind them. At the top of the road, where they turned onto a semi-high street, Charlie's mum took his hand. They looked in the window of a posh bakery, Charlie pointing at something, then turned off as the nicer, knick-knacky shops gave way to Poundlands. Hope kept telling herself to turn back, but she had become connected to them, which wasn't an unusual feeling. Over the years she had often found herself on a bus, or walking down a street, and suddenly someone would pass who seemed so fully formed it was as if she knew everything about them, almost as if she could become them if she tried hard enough. The imaginary solidness of Charlie's hand pressed into hers and, with each step they took, she became more and more aware of a place where she had a little person trotting next to her, Tom waiting at home, somewhere to go, people to meet.

At the top of the next road, they turned left. Hope recognized where they were, a road away from a trendy part of the area, speckled by bars and restaurants, expensive interiors shops and boutiques for women with money and time. But about halfway up the road Charlie and his mother turned left again, disappearing from the street in a way that made Hope's chest tighten. They appeared to have been swallowed by the buildings and she wondered if what she'd seen was real, or if her mind was playing tricks. She quickened her pace and saw a space where a house had been that she couldn't make sense of. Her brain juddered with the possibility of a break so bad as to cause hallucinations. But she forced herself to focus and then saw a green rectangle behind the houses, surrounded by clumps of bushes and tasteful planting. The sight calmed her because of course the unexpected could still be real.

A meagre playground was in the far left-hand corner of the mini park that Hope stepped into, keeping to just inside the gate. Charlie was gamely crawling through a red tube while his mother watched from a bench. It should have been a happy scene, but there was something desolate about it and Hope couldn't work out if that was because of the tall houses shrouding the playground, or the way Charlie and his mum both held themselves, as if everything could collapse at any moment. Another person might not have noticed that was how they were feeling, but Hope knew all the signs of the fellow shrinker and that terrible desire to turn inwards to stop others noticing the pain at your centre.

The sight made her feel too sad, which hadn't been what she'd hoped to get from the day, so she walked on, her feet simply propelling her with no destination in mind. A strange sense of being off-balance overtook her, so she found herself walking closer to the wall, as if it might prop her up. The next road was peppered with cafes and she sat at a table outside one because she couldn't remember when she'd last had a proper meal. Usually she didn't treat herself to nice things. It felt stupid and frivolous, especially when the sandwich you bought cost the same as what you earnt in an hour. But she was feeling lightheaded and life was refusing to lay itself clearly in her mind, like a veil drawn between her and the world.

After eating, she felt slightly better, well enough to at least get home. The little playground was empty and she couldn't help slowing as she passed Charlie's house. He and his mum were in the front room, curled into each other, their eyes focused on the TV, which was playing a manic-looking cartoon. Rosie started up in Hope's head, opining about how people who let children watch television should be done for child abuse. He'd said that after Tilly's visit, lamenting about how she'd talked about cartoon characters as if they were her friends. His point had seemed so valid at the time, but now Hope wondered at the reality of entertaining a child all day every day, without gardens to run in and a swimming pool to jump in.

Even though she was on the other side of the glass, Hope felt the atmosphere shift and looked up in unison with Charlie and his mum. Dominic Cunningham had come into the room. He wasn't shouting, but his stance radiated anger, his mouth contorting as he spoke. He crossed to where they were sitting, towering over them both. His eyes were locked on his wife, the tension pulsating through the glass. He leant down and took her jaw between his thumb and forefinger, a red spot forming under both with the pressure. There was no telling what he was going to do and Hope imagined her jaw bone cracking, a quick spin of her head to break her neck, spit in her face. But in the end he just let go, smirking as he turned away. Charlie had shrunk behind his mother, burrowing into her back like an animal. And one thing Hope didn't doubt about herself was her ability to recognize fear. She knew it in the same way that a dog can sense its owner in a crowd of people.

Chapter Twenty-Five

Nat had never before lied about being called in, and the guilt gnawed at her as she shut her front door. She had at least waited until after the kids' nightly routine was completed, even though her whole body had itched with the desire to run. As she walked down the road she glanced into lit windows and saw families sitting happily round TVs together. She wondered if her mother was right, and she did have a missing or faulty gene. It wasn't that she didn't love Ben and Riley, but also she found it easier not to be with them. She watched Kira with them and could clearly see that the children were essential to the very fabric of her being. And yet, also, the thought of not having them scratched at Nat's soul and when Ben had snuggled into her that evening a warmth had spread through her that felt like a hug.

Sara Clarke hadn't been at all hard to track down when you had a police database at your fingertips. But then again, even without that, it wouldn't have taken long. Nat dialled her number as she walked and it was answered quickly by a high-pitched voice, the sound of a television in the background.

'Is that Sara Clarke?'

'Yes, speaking.'

'Hello, my name is DI Natalie Evans.'

'Yes?' Sara's tone was immediately worried, as always happened when Nat called someone out of the blue.

'Nothing to worry about. I just wanted to ask you a couple of questions.'

A baby started to cry in the background and Sara Clarke said, 'Oh shit,' and then, 'yeah, could you. Sorry,' she said back into the phone, 'that's my son, he's teething. But my husband's taken him upstairs.'

Nat tried to refocus. 'I'm calling in relation to an ongoing investigation. I wanted to ask about the time you worked for Ambrose Glencourt.' Sara didn't reply and a coldness filled the silence. 'I'm looking into the disappearance of a Tom Markham, last seen at his house, Shadowlands, in September 2016. I wondered if you knew him?'

'How did you get my number?' Sara's tone had quietened.

'Just routine police work. We're trying to speak to anyone who might have known Tom around that time.'

'Well, I didn't,' Sara said. 'And I left Shadowlands in May 2016, so.'

'You never met him?'

'Well, yes, once, maybe twice. But I didn't know him.'

'And how did he seem when you met him?'

'How did he seem?' Sara paused. 'You know he was a heroin addict, right?'

'Yes, we do.'

'Well, that's what he seemed like. Surly. Spent most of the time in his room.'

'Right. And can I ask why you left that job?' Sara was silent again, so Nat went on. 'We've been told that you became infatuated with Mr Glencourt?'

Sara snorted. 'By Delia, no doubt?'

'I'm afraid I can't say.'

'You know what.' Sara was whispering now. 'It was a really horrible time that I'd rather not talk about.' Nat stopped walking, looking up over the houses at the setting sun. Nothing Sara was saying was damning and yet, when you put it all together with everything else, it left a nasty taste in the mouth. 'Look, I have to go,' Sara said. 'There's no story here and I don't know anything about Tom.'

The pub that they sometimes met friends at on a Sunday was just across the road and Nat couldn't bear the thought of going home. She felt like a loser as she pushed through the door, but sitting in the same room as Kira would end in a row. She'd give it a couple of hours then go home, hopefully Kira would be asleep and in the morning she'd try harder. Maybe she'd agree to the therapy Kira was always begging her to try. But for now it was mercifully quiet in the pub, so Nat sat at the bar and ordered a pint, getting out her phone more as a way to occupy her hands than anything else. Someone sat on the stool right next to her which made her look up from her scrolling. Hope Jenkins smiled.

Nat turned to look at the nearly empty pub. 'What are you doing here?'

Hope waved at the barman. 'A glass of white wine, please.' She turned back to Nat. 'Nice pub.'

A strange panic was building in Nat's stomach. 'What's going on? Are you following me?'

Hope accepted her drink and touched her card to the reader. 'No, of course not. Let's just call this a lucky coincidence.'

Nat felt like she was losing control. The phone call to Sara Clarke had been stupid and now this. 'Following a police officer is very inadvisable. I've told you that the case is closed and I'll organize the return of your journal on Monday morning. There's nothing more to discuss.'

But Hope waved a hand in front of her face. 'I haven't come about that.'

Nat took a long gulp of her beer but felt like she probably needed something stronger. 'I'm off duty. You'd do better taking whatever this is to the station.'

'And we know how seriously they take me there.' Hope leant forward and Nat wondered when she'd last showered. 'Listen, I know you think I'm crazy, but I'm really not.'

'I don't think you're crazy.' Although probably when you had to tell people you weren't crazy, you were halfway there. Nat took another long sip and her head lightened in a pleasing way.

'There's a boy at Lady Catherine's, Charlie Cunningham. I want to talk to you about his father, Dominic Cunningham.' Hope paused and Nat felt herself nod, even though she didn't want to know whatever it was that Hope had now decided to care about. 'Charlie has sat with me at lunch break for coming up to a year now. He's a shy, timid boy and he hasn't got any friends, so I didn't really see the harm in it.' Hope took a sip of her wine and Nat got a strange sense of seeing something beyond the surface, an essence of an inner life. At their first meeting Hope had been at such pains to tell her what a bad person she was, and yet this wasn't the concern of someone without good feelings. The passion vibrating off her reminded Nat of how she spoke about Tom Markham. One thing Nat didn't doubt was that Hope had been in love at Shadowlands, she just still wasn't entirely sure who with and what that could have made her do.

'I'm starting to wonder if his nervousness could be something different, something more sinister,' Hope was saying. 'He has bruises on his body. And recently he told me that his mother had fallen down the stairs and he was very worried about the idea of spending a night alone with his father. Then, the other day, his dad brought him to school and he'd written a cruel note in his lunch box.'

Hope actually had a strong sense of morality, which Nat hadn't appreciated before. And, now she was thinking about it, it was the same in her journal. Hope felt wrongs keenly and she wanted to put them right. All that stuff she'd written about trying not to be shocked had never rung true because there was something shocking in the way the Glencourts behaved and Hope had seen through it. 'Have you spoken to the school about this?'

'No. In fact, I'm not there at the moment. I'm having a couple of weeks off.'

Nat tried to look surprised. 'Perhaps you'd be better off taking that time for yourself.'

Hope sighed. 'No, I've been doing that for too long. Some might say I've been negligent. Let too many people get away with too much shit.'

'But still, you'd need to address this with the school. If anything is going on, and that's a big if, it sounds like a social services issue.'

Hope narrowed her eyes. 'Why did you become a police officer?'

The question felt intimate and Nat faltered. 'I . . . I mean . . . I guess I wanted to do good.'

'And do you feel like that's what you do?'

'I hope so.' But her words sounded lame.

'One more question,' Hope said before tipping the last of her wine into her mouth. 'What are you doing here, alone in a pub, on a Thursday night, when your wife and kids are at home?' And there it was again, that sense of morality running through so many of the things Hope said that Nat couldn't believe she hadn't noticed before and left her unable to answer. Hope hitched her bag onto her shoulder as if she was getting ready to leave. 'There are so many bad parents, in fact bad people, out there.'

Nat snorted. 'You don't have to tell me that.' An image of Kira with their kids flashed into her mind and she couldn't stop the intense spark of anger that followed. But sometimes it was hard not to feel angry with her wife for loving Ben and Riley in a way she didn't recognize, which she knew was the wrong way round. It was just hard sometimes to switch from right to wrong. And maybe that was also true the other way around. Nat looked at Hope sitting so uncomfortably on her stool, her face red, and wondered at the things she'd written and said about herself. She believed herself to be bad, when her concerns were good. And surely the only reason for that was because she'd done something she considered irredeemable.

'When I was working for Rosie one of his kids came to stay,' Hope said, 'and I thought he was the best father. I actually imagined a life in which I wouldn't have to leave, in which I'd be sort of adopted by them. But that's such bullshit. He has nine children by God knows how many women and he's never lived with any of them. Which, by the way, should make you wonder about his moral compass.'

'Nine?' Nat was thorough and that didn't sound right from

the things she'd read. She picked her phone off the bar and typed her request into Google. 'No, look, he's only got four.' She held out the phone to Hope, who took it and squinted at the screen. 'Two by one woman and then two others. And his wife knew all about it.'

When Hope looked up from the phone she had paled and her mouth had turned down in a way that made Nat want to say something comforting. But Hope slipped off the stool. 'I have to go,' she said, her voice much quieter than it had been. She crossed her bag over her body, her shoulders hunching forward and her head dipping downwards. The Glencourts were so keen to cast Hope as over-emotional, lovesick, highly strung and by far the most believable explanation would be to agree with them. And yet, Nat knew what it was like to be told that the way you felt was not normal. Her mother had spent a lot of time praying for her, her lips moving even when she was cooking or cleaning, so Nat would know what was going on. The Lord will help you see the right path, she'd say, and Nat had wondered who this Lord of everything was. Not in a literal sense obviously, but metaphysically. *It's just a story*, she said to her mother once, as a Bible was pushed into her face. *Who says it's real? Why do you think these words hold so much power?* She raised her hand to her cheek, her skin still smarting with the sting of her mother's slap.

As Hope left, Nat snatched her phone off the bar and typed 'Dominic Cunningham' into an ever-open Google, ready and waiting to deliver a billion stories to whoever wanted them. It wasn't hard to find him when she added Lady Catherine's and Charlie: an open Facebook page showing a fit, smiling man who worked in the City and liked football and craft ale and music. He occasionally even posted shots of his son, who looked like a scrawny, nerdy kid, but that was hardly grounds for calling in social services. The most logical explanation was that Hope liked to put herself at the centre of stories, which sometimes happened with lonely people. It was something Nat herself had done in her youth, reading *Time Out* under her covers late at night and getting over-excited by other people's lives. Although that came with a tendency to make two and two equal five, like when she'd first gone to a gay bar in Soho and been shocked that it wasn't filled with women standing around earnestly discussing politics, but was in reality a sticky-floored, house-pumping, light-flashing sweat box. Except that thought didn't sit right, because it had also been the place that showed her how she wanted to live wasn't a sin.

Hope should have been completely implausible, and yet there was something about her that made sense. Like smoke you can't find the source of, but that still tells you something has to be burning.

Chapter Twenty-Six

Hope had gone to Natalie Evans with her concerns about Charlie because there was no one else and she simply couldn't remain passive any longer. After witnessing Charlie's dad's behaviour, she had at first wondered at the coincidence of looking in their window just at the moment his aggression rose to the surface. But then she remembered how Rosie had said coincidence was lazy writing, and it made her realize it was more likely that was how he behaved all the time. She'd gone to Natalie's house with some half-formed idea about knocking on her front door. But, as she'd been building up the courage, Natalie had emerged and headed off down the road, her face contorted in a scowl as she made a phone call.

Hope bought a bottle of wine on the way back to her flat and went straight to her computer. It didn't take long to confirm that Natalie Evans was right, and Rosie did only have four children. She tried to remember why she'd been so convinced that he had nine. It was the photos on the piano in the drawing room, she guessed. Lots of pictures of young children, which she'd found Tilly among, and then counted eight others. No one had ever told her they were all Rosie's children. She'd simply connected the strands of a story together and turned an assumption into a fact.

Hope shakily poured herself another glass of wine. Never once in the past decade had she doubted her story. She'd gone to the police assuming that Rosie and Delia weren't going to admit to Tom's killing, but she'd envisioned their gardens being dug up and their house searched. That it would simply be a matter of waiting for proof. She hadn't imagined them countering with all these other stories. Stories that were, when all was said and done, more plausible than her own. A thought that had been circling since her first meeting with Natalie Evans finally landed: what if everything she'd written in her journal had in fact been nothing more than assumptions, pure guesses at what people were thinking and feeling? What if, in her attempt to become a writer, she had become confused by fact and fiction and her journal, her memory even, was no more real than Rosie's novel?

A rush of heat spread through Hope, burning from the inside until she was sweating. She lit an ill-advised cigarette, the nicotine spinning her head in a way that made her think she needed to eat. But the idea of preparing food felt ludicrous so she simply poured out another glass of wine. She scanned down the list of results on her computer again, settling on Tilly's Instagram. In one click her screen filled with Tilly on a beach, on a boat, in the sea, skiing, climbing a mountain, posing next to ruins, sitting on the back of a horse, in a rickshaw, on an aeroplane, in a school shirt covered with graffiti, getting ready for a party, at a party, pressing her face next to a series of equally pretty girls. The images were dizzying, like a roll call of all the things that money and privilege bought you. Except Hope also remembered the little girl who'd been dumped by her mother and climbed into her bed in the middle of the night.

And, when she thought of that, she realized those twenty-four hours were a tangible memory. It was something that had, or maybe had not, happened at Shadowlands. If Tilly remembered their time together in the same way that she did, then there was the possibility that she hadn't misremembered everything else. If Tilly didn't, then, well, that was a bridge she'd have to cross if she needed to. Hope tried to enlarge an image with the thought of maybe leaving a comment, but Instagram told her that she would need an account to go any further. She had deleted hers years before and she didn't want a new one that would suggest people she used to know, dangling their lives in front of her. But also, she had no other choice, so she took a pathetic photo of her front room as her first post. And, actually, she could use that – maybe it would work in her favour.

The message she sent took nearly forty-five minutes to compose, although Hope remembered how those people all spoke and prayed that what she'd written sounded like a quick, spur-of-the-moment missive.

> Hi, Tilly, I'm new to Instagram and it's suggesting friends for me and you came up and it made me wonder how you're getting on. I don't know if you remember me, but I worked for your dad about ten years ago. You came to stay for a day and night at Shadowlands and I looked after you. Anyway, looks like life has been treating you well. I'm so pleased. Much love, Hope Jenkins

When she pressed send it felt like her whole body whooshed away with the message and a deep fear washed through her. But, as with many things in life, there was no going back.

Chapter Twenty-Seven

Friday was meant to be her precious day off, but Nat was itching to get to work, so she lied again and said that she'd been called in because something from the night before still wasn't resolved. Kira looked so distraught she nearly recanted, but the conversation with Sara Clarke was heavy in her head and she couldn't shake the memory of the way Hope had looked when she'd left the pub. She had to exhaust all avenues before she gave up on the case, and she knew she was missing something.

'But it's Leon's party after school this afternoon,' Kira said, as the kids screeched around their feet. 'You know, Ben's friend from school. You said you'd come and meet some of the parents.'

'Oh God,' Nat said, 'what time is it again?'

'Three-thirty. In the park.'

'I'll try to get back for it. I promise.' And she told herself she really would, although Kira just shrugged as she kissed her goodbye.

Once at her desk, Nat laid her copy of *The Ruined Girl* next to Hope's journal and scanned through them both again, marking off the similarities. Hope wrote in the journal about a conversation she'd had with Rosie in which she'd said love felt like an illness, which was repeated almost word for word on page 98 of the book. Her discombobulation at a strange drinking game also featured in the novel, except in *The Ruined Girl*, Teresa had to watch Aiden transfer the wine from his mouth to his stepmother's, when in the journal it had been Rosie transferring the wine to Hope. And there was the passage: *There was a bowl on a high shelf which Teresa especially coveted and, when she thought no one was looking, she would take it down and run the porcelain between her fingers, holding it up to the light to marvel at its translucency. There were times that she considered taking it upstairs and wrapping it in her clothes, shoving it deep in her bag. It wasn't that she wanted to steal from Aiden's parents, but also they had so much, she doubted they'd even miss it. And there was no way they could love it like she did. The petals painted so delicately on its surface had wound their way into her heart and grew there now like an admonition of all the things she wasn't.* The Glencourts had accused Hope of stealing a bowl and Hope had said it was gift. Either way, it was a physical object that appeared in both their tellings. And of course, most importantly, in both accounts a young man was shot by a young woman who thought he loved her after sleeping with an older woman who was married to another man.

But the problem was none of it amounted to more than circumstantial evidence. Each version of the story Nat had been told was plausible. She believed that the Glencourts were capable of deceit and bad behaviour, but that equally they could be the victims of an angry hoax by a deluded former employee. She also believed that Hope thought she was telling the truth and that she was capable of murder in the right circumstances, or she could have been suffering from a complex psychological delusion all this time. She believed in the power that places like Shadowlands held over people and, even though she hated the thought, knew it could probably send someone mad with longing. Nat sat back, her back pinching from too much time hunched over her desk. It was one thirty and, if she left now, she would make it home in time for the party.

Nat stood but, as she did, another thought struck her. All this time she'd felt angered by the privilege and connections in the case, but she hadn't followed that thought through. It was a feeling that she was sure she'd just had reflected back to her in her re-read of the journal. She bent back over her desk and began to flick through the pages. And then she came to it, a conversation between Hope and Tom about the unfairness of that world. *Don't you understand,* she read Tom saying, *this world works on favours for favours and friends of friends.* A little thrill ran through Nat. It wasn't enough to simply register how unfair life was, how stacked against the Hopes of the world. No, in situations like this, you had to look beyond the obvious, beyond what was handed out to keep the normal people quiet.

Chapter Twenty-Eight

Friday morning was a slog, all the markers of Hope's day imprinted in some sort of internal time memory, so she constantly found herself thinking, it's assembly, it's morning register drop-off, it's break. But the real desperation set in around lunchtime when she imagined Charlie turning up at the door to her office and being met by some strange substitute who wouldn't know who he was, wouldn't be able to tell him where she was or when she was coming back. She imagined him slinking away to sit on his own in the playground, probably too anxious to eat, feeling abandoned again. She feared no one else would notice that something was wrong and he'd sink into that well of loneliness and confusion that was so hard to climb out of. She washed down a couple of painkillers with a cold glass of water, although she wasn't sure what or where hurt most. Then she made herself eat, although the only things she could face were coffee and toast which she had to force into her mouth, where she felt herself chew and swallow, but nothing felt real. And when that was done there were still hours and hours to get through, then days and days and weeks and weeks and months and months and years and years.

The past couple of weeks had weakened the barriers that Hope had enclosed herself behind and she found herself longing for her mother before she could stop the feelings. She had visited her in Spain once and she wished then that she hadn't, that she couldn't picture the patterned tiles on the balcony and the pink flowers that tumbled from the window boxes. But, in fact, thinking about the woman reminded her that she had a legitimate reason to contact her. She could ask her outright what explanation Rosie and Delia had given when she'd fallen so ill she'd had to be fetched away from Shadowlands like a delinquent child.

Her mother answered in just a couple of rings, which made Hope feel pathetically better. They exchanged a few awkward pleasantries about the weather and a fiesta coming to the village before Hope said, 'Can I ask you something, Mum?'

A drum was beating in the background of wherever her mother was, probably at a cafe in the square, Gary raising his eyebrows at her. 'Yes, of course.'

'When I got back from Shadowlands, what did Rosie and Delia tell you about why I was sick?'

In the pause Hope knew she'd been right. 'God, do you really want to go over all that. Can't you just forget about those people.'

Hope's stomach twisted. 'Please, Mum. It's important to me.'

Her mother sighed. 'Well, they told me what had been going on.'

'With what?'

'Oh, for God's sake, Hope, you know with what.'

'I don't. Really.'

The drumming picked up, so her mother had to raise her voice. 'With you becoming obsessed with Mr Glencourt. And him having to let you down and you refusing to take no for an answer and then causing a massive scene.' Hope laughed, which made her mother suck in her breath. 'I'm glad you find it funny. God, I was so embarrassed when that Mrs Glencourt rang me. She was so nice and understanding, but I felt like such an idiot when I got there and saw you in that state. Like I'd been a terrible mother and hadn't taught you how to behave properly.'

They were both quiet for a moment; a trumpet had now been added to the drumming. 'None of that happened,' Hope said. 'I wasn't in love with Rosie, but a man called Tom.'

'Hope, please.' Her mother sounded close to tears. 'You've always done this. You were always making up stories when you were young and saying you wanted to be a writer. It was why I showed you the advert for that bloody job in the first place. Well, that and because you needed to get away from that awful situation with that awful man, Dexter. But, God, I should have put a stop to all of it. I think I got everything very wrong. I mean, look at you now. Whatever it is that's going on inside your head is more real to you than anything else. And it's so sad.' Her voice hitched, the tears now audible. 'I wanted so much for you and you're just rotting away in that flat, pining for someone who is never going to love you. Not able to see what's bloody . . .' She paused for a moment. '. . . well, what's bloody real.'

There was something so terrible about seeing herself through her mother's eyes, knowing that the things she was saying were true, but not necessarily right.

'I'm sorry,' her mother said into the silence. 'I love you, Hope, but I don't know what to do with you.'

She started to say something else, but Hope ended the call

because there was only so much more she could hear about herself before she gave up. Besides, her stomach was contracting, rushing her breakfast back up her gullet, so she had to cup a hand over her mouth and run to the bathroom. Her throat felt like it was on fire as she gagged, the taste of fermented alcohol unmistakable with the half-digested lumps of toast, little specks of blood on the white porcelain. She was shaking and wet with sweat by the time the heaving stopped and fell backwards onto the bathroom floor. The bottom of the toilet seat was dirty and there were balls of hair and dust in the corners of the room, the side of the bath buckling so she could see a cold blackness beyond. Nothing made sense. Nothing had ever made sense. She couldn't just go on and on through life without looking directly at herself. She remembered the words she'd read in Rosie's notebook: *she has to face her past*. Oh yes, he still knew her so well. Shadowlands was calling her back and maybe that was the only answer. Maybe there had never been anything else.

Chapter Twenty-Nine

Nat had made it past the main doors of the station when her mobile rang. There was no caller ID on her screen, but she still answered. And she was very pleased that she had because it was Sara Clarke's high-pitched voice on the other end.

Nat stopped on the steps of the station, the sun bright against the pavement. 'How can I help you?'

'I just . . .' Sara had a hitch in her voice, like she'd been crying. 'Look, my husband said I should call you. I really don't know anything about Tom, and I did only meet him once or twice. But, well . . .' Nat was holding her breath, not wanting anything to derail Sara in any way. 'That whole place is fucked.'

A quickening started behind Nat's eyes. 'Can you elaborate?'

'Like, the way they live is so weird. You know Rosie has children with other women and Delia, like, doesn't mind?'

'Yes, I did know that.' Nat checked her watch and saw it was two, still time to get to the park. 'Did something happen when you were there?'

'It's hard to explain. I thought Rosie and I were in love.' The words reminded Nat of Hope when she'd first sat opposite her, except she'd been talking about Tom. 'But, well, I don't know exactly what the truth is now. You know, I was twenty-two and he was forty-seven and, looking back, I don't even know how consensual it all was.'

'Are you saying he forced you?'

'No, not really. I mean, he didn't hold me down or anything. But he made it impossible to refuse. And, you know, at the time I would have said that it was absolutely what I wanted. But, now, I mean, you know now I'm a bit older, I'm not so sure.'

Nat touched a hand to her forehead as if the movement could stop the spinning in her mind. 'Are you calling because you want to press charges?'

'No, no.' Sara drew in a breath that almost sounded painful. 'I mean, I don't think there's anything you could even charge him with. I just, I just wanted you to know that nothing about that time, or place, was right. It was so fucked up. Rosie and I were sleeping with each other and at first Delia didn't seem to mind, not that we ever had a conversation about it, but Rosie said she was cool. But then after a few weeks she started freaking out. I could hear them screaming at each other when I went to bed and Rosie said she was going mad. And it was so confusing, because I thought they had some sort of open marriage. But the atmosphere became unbearable. Like, she wouldn't be in the same room as me and she was always crying. And Rosie was in a total state, one minute saying we had to stop and the next saying he couldn't let me go. We even talked about him leaving her.'

Nat sat on the steps, feeling suddenly very tired. 'But you said you're not sure it was consensual.'

Sara sighed. 'I don't even know if that's the right word. I guess what I mean is, Rosie decided he was going to sleep with me almost as soon as I got there, and I don't think there was anything I could have done to stop him. He has this way of making everything he thinks sound like the only option. And, you know, I was in his house and they both made me feel like I was part of their life. Like we'd all be together for ever. After a couple of weeks he started coming up to my room in the afternoons when he was meant to be writing, just to chat at first. But soon he started telling me how beautiful I was. How he'd never wanted anyone as much as me before. And he was always touching me, like a hand on my arm or making sure our bodies connected whenever he walked past me. It sounds pathetic, but it really didn't feel like I had a choice.'

Nat remembered something that Hope had written about everything about Rosie feeling like an absence of choice. 'So how did it end?'

'Delia told me about Annie.'

'Annie?' A car horn beeped and Nat jumped.

'She was his assistant before me. I didn't know anything about her, but one day Delia came and found me by the pool and told me that I was nothing special. That Rosie would never leave her and I should do the decent thing and go home. When I said that Rosie loved me, she laughed and said, just like Annie. I felt like such a fool then. I found Annie's number in Rosie's things and she told me to get away as quickly as I could. We're still friends now actually, and you know, I think she had a worse time of it than me.'

Nat let out a long breath. 'What do you mean, worse time?'

'It's not my story to tell.'

'Do you think Annie would speak to me?'

'Maybe. I can ask her.'

'Please do. Give her my number, tell her to call any time.'

'Look, there's nothing you can do about any of it,' Sara said, but it sounded more like a question than a statement.

'Not unless you wanted to press charges.'

'But what charges? He didn't force either of us physically.'

Nat rubbed at her forehead. Hope had said so many of the same things to her and she'd tried to find reasons not to take her seriously. 'If anything criminal's gone on then I will help you in any way I can.'

Sara's baby started to cry in the background. 'Listen, I have to go. And sorry if I've just wasted your time. But it felt wrong how we left it last time. And Jason, that's my husband, he's all about closure. He said I needed to at least tell you what happened because, you know, I really wouldn't put anything past Rosie and Delia. And Tom was sweet. A mess, but sweet.'

Nat stood again and her legs felt stiff. 'You haven't wasted my time at all. Thank you for calling. I know it must have taken a lot of courage.'

It was now quarter past two, she could still make it to the party if she went straight to the park, but she hesitated. It wasn't just that she could feel a breakthrough about to appear, but also the thought of the party chilled her. She wasn't sure she could watch happy families, or that she could pretend to be part of one. Was it time to face the truth that she was the person preventing this, and that Kira, Ben and Riley would be happier without her?

Nat turned back inside and hurried to her desk, where she read again through all the statements. It was still odd that an investigation had happened at all, still odd that the Glencourts hadn't mentioned Hope when they were questioned and still odd that the CCTV evidence had been removed without being copied. But everything else was above board and standard and none of it was enough. Nat sat back, frustrated with herself, because she had to be missing something. Her phone buzzed with a message from Kira: *you coming?* She glanced up at the clock and saw it was now twenty to three, which made even getting to the park on time impossible. She bashed out a quick reply: *still at work, where will you be? I'll come and find you.* It was too easy to imagine Kira's face as she read the message, but her reply was straightforward: *by the bandstand.*

Nat pulled her chair up to the desk again and held her finger against the side of the pages like a kid, making sure she didn't miss a word. And it was worth it, because she had missed the important thing, which didn't come until right at the end of the file. The person who had authorized the removal of the photograph and closed the case was the Chief Constable of Somerset, who under no circumstances would be involved in a minor missing person's case. More damning still however was the man's name: Andrew Lambert. *Posh twat, Andrew something,* Tom's mother said in her head. Nat did a quick Google search and yes, Andrew had indeed been the younger brother of Peter Lambert, the current Commissioner. A shining, bright young man inevitably tipped for the top, who'd died in a skiing accident in 2018. He was buried at the family estate in Somerset which, on another quick Google search, proved to be only a thirty-minute drive from Shadowlands.

Chapter Thirty

Hope was all too used to feeling like a failure, the gap between who she wanted to be and who she was like a chasm, but waking on Saturday morning felt like emerging into a void. She scrabbled desperately around in her mind for something, anything. And then, like a saviour, a promise emerged: the drunken message she'd sent Tilly. She navigated quickly to her Instagram page where there was a bright red 1 next to an arrow. Like magic, Tilly had replied.

> Hope! How lovely to hear from you. I'm good thanks, just about to go on a gap year before uni!! Of course I remember you. You were a high point at a difficult time. Mum and Dad have had a fractious – lol – relationship all my life and that was a pretty low point. In fact, and sorry if this sounds creepy, but Mum bought me a new doll when she came to get me that time and I called it Hope. Carried it around with me for years! Trust all is good with you too xxxxx

Something thumped in Hope's chest. It was too delicious to imagine herself as a doll, loved and carried around, a thing with meaning that gave comfort. Perhaps she could ask Tilly for a photo of the doll, or even to meet for a cup of tea, perhaps a drink. But, even as the thoughts were forming, they also died. Those fantasies of casual meetings and new friends didn't belong to her any more. She tried instead to concentrate on the positive fact that Tilly had remembered their time together in the same way she had. But the relief she'd expected to feel refused to come. And then it began to seem like a ridiculous conceit to imagine it meant anything. So what if she had definitely been kind to a little girl ten years before? It didn't blot out what she'd done only a few weeks after that day, or suddenly turn her into a good person. And, if Tom wasn't enough evidence of her badness, then the fact that Charlie had sat with her for nearly a year, his distress like a red light above his head, and she hadn't done anything to help, was surely definitive proof.

Hope put her hands either side of her forehead and pushed slightly but firmly, a trick she'd learnt when she'd first come back from Shadowlands and often felt like she was in danger of floating away. The action helped a little because it made her realize that surely it was too much of a coincidence for those twenty-four hours with Tilly to be the only ones she'd remembered and recorded correctly. The sun was beating down outside and the sweetly cloying scent of weed wafted in through the open windows. Someone across the street put on music, a low, steady thump which took up a beat with the pain in her head.

Except, the truth was that nothing, beyond definite proof, was going to alter the fact that Rosie was still getting away with everything, and neither of them were going to be punished for what they'd done. Hope doubted very much that proof existed, unless they really did dig up Tom's body, which seemed pretty unlikely to say the least. But that didn't mean that Rosie should be allowed to get away with casually publishing a sequel that was once again based on her and the murder. She couldn't allow Rosie to mine the worst moment in her life and the end of Tom's life as if it was make-believe and meant nothing. No, he had to be stopped and, as she'd told Natalie Evans already, if no one was going to help her, then she would have to do it for herself.

Chapter Thirty-One

Usually Nat hated working weekends, but not this one. She was still smarting from the row she'd had with Kira the night before, after she'd failed to make any appearance at the party at all. Her wife had naturally waited until the kids were in bed and the words she'd spoken had been hushed, but filled with disappointment. Nat hadn't been able to answer why she so consistently let them down, why she always put work first, why she was seemingly incapable of love. It had instead been easier to argue back. She'd told Kira she was controlling and uptight, that her expectations were too high, that her neediness was smothering. And then, almost the moment she'd arrived at work, a man had taken his ex-partner and their baby hostage. It was nearly eight when she got back to the station and Nat knew she should go home.

Except she found herself googling Andrew Lambert again. Posh people, she'd noticed, often had lots of things recorded about them, as if they couldn't simply disappear like everyone else, as if they had to be accounted for and remembered. But in this case it was useful, as she was able to read lots of mini biographies about the man. More than once the various writers mentioned how Andrew Lambert was always known as Drew.

After the fourth time of reading that something clicked in Nat's memory. She pulled Hope's journal out of her drawer and flicked through it, manically searching for something half-remembered. But she was right. On 22 June she found Drew at the party which had shaken Hope so much, when they'd passed wine to each other through their mouths. In fact, he was the man who had initiated the whole game.

Nat's heart was beating too fast and a slick of sweat tingled on her skin. These powerful men always looked out for each other and of course Ambrose Glencourt would have wanted the scandal of a drug addict being shot at his house to be covered up, especially if he had disposed of the body. Hope could even be right about him hiding the crime in plain sight by reporting it to the police as a missing persons case – something which he'd have felt pretty confident in doing considering he was friends with the local chief of police, who also liked to get into compromising positions at parties. If she could just prove that the Drew in Hope's journal was Andrew Lambert, they might have enough to investigate further. It was a long shot, but there was a chance that Hope might be able to describe him and the description might match one of the many photographs she'd seen of the man.

'How did you know I was here?' Hope said when she answered.

'Sorry?' Nat said. 'What do you mean?'

Hope laughed. 'Oh, sorry, I thought you'd tracked me or something.'

Fear brushed along Nat's skin. 'Where are you, Miss Jenkins?'

'Shadowlands. Or, at least, I've just pulled up outside the gate. I'm going to walk up the drive. I don't want them to know that I'm coming.'

Nat stood, looking around the station in desperation, not sure what to do. 'Miss Jenkins, I told you not to go back there. You must turn around now.'

But Hope laughed again. 'I don't want to do that, I'm afraid.'

'I believe you,' Nat tried, although it felt a little like things were happening too fast and she wasn't entirely sure what she believed.

Hope snorted in a way that curdled on the air. 'It's a bit late for that.'

'No, listen, that's why I was calling. If you wait, we can go through the proper channels. Get this done correctly. I might have another angle into this thing.'

'Oh no, I'm done with waiting. Ten bloody years I've spent.' Hope sounded like she'd started walking, which made Nat want to scream. 'I've read about cases like mine. I would have been charged with manslaughter and probably got less time.'

'We can dig,' Nat said desperately, promising something she knew she wouldn't be able to make happen. 'We might find bones.' It felt like she was bargaining with Ben, her absurd offerings worth the price of a few more minutes in bed or, in this case, avoiding the total destruction of her career.

But Hope wasn't a child. 'And we might not. We have no idea if they actually did bury Tom by the river. No. I'm doing it my way.'

'What are you going to do?'

Hope didn't answer for a minute, her breath heavy. And when she did Nat wished she'd stayed silent. 'I told you I was bad,' she said, before the phone went dead.

'Fuck,' Nat shouted into the dial tone. A few people looked at her, but it wasn't that strange for an officer to lose it now and again. She forced herself to sit, her heart thumping into her fingertips and ears. Fuck, she'd screwed up. Hope was right, she *had* told her everything. That she'd shot someone, that Ambrose Glencourt had disposed of the body, and that yes, she was a bad person. And, whether or not any of that was actually true, and Nat was leaning towards thinking that it was, Hope Jenkins clearly believed it all and sometimes that was all that mattered. Hope had been let down, time and again, no one listening to what she said, and now she was on her way to do God knew what to a bloody beloved National Treasure, who was also the Commissioner's good friend.

Nat pulled up Ambrose Glencourt's number on her phone but didn't go as far as calling because she couldn't be seen to admit to liability. And there was still a chance that Hope wouldn't go through with whatever she had planned, or that she could be stopped. Nat grabbed her car keys and sprinted out to the parking lot. If she put her foot down she could probably make it to Shadowlands in three hours.

Chapter Thirty-Two

Hope walked through to the woods that ran up the drive on the opposite side of the house. Dusk had fallen and the light was in that strange in-between state where it looked like there was a mist covering everything. She hadn't formed a complete plan for what she wanted to achieve, but she knew that things couldn't carry on the way they had been. Her bad character had made her shoot Tom, but Rosie had to take responsibility for what he'd done since. For not including her or looking out for her. In her wildest fantasy the sight of her so broken would be enough for him to admit everything, to promise to pulp *Teresa's Ruin*, to ask her to live with them at Shadowlands. And, if he did that, she would forgive him everything, because the sweetness of being loved by them was still one of her best memories. Except, she knew that really she was probably going to have to get the gun and threaten him. That, if it came to it, she would pull the trigger again. That one way or another she'd stop him.

When she reached a position where she was still hidden but could see the edge of the terrace and through the front door, she stopped. It was a beautiful evening, the sky a deep pink on the horizon. She edged forward, coming right to the boundary of the wood, just before the moment she would be seen.

'It's a spurious argument,' she heard Rosie say.

'Well, not entirely,' Delia replied.

Hope moved slightly to the right and then she was able to see them sitting at the table on the terrace, the French doors open behind them, both with tall glasses in their hands, their faces turned to the dying light. Music was coming from the drawing room, a soaring aria that sounded a little like a scream.

'But is that really what he said?' another voice said, from inside.

And then it felt like Hope had given birth to her heart and everything she'd planned became meaningless.

'It is,' Delia said, turning as he stepped out onto the terrace.

He stepped. Him.

Hope's internal organs followed her heart, plummeting through her body. She pressed herself against a tree, trying to catch her breath, trying to catch anything that returned her to reality. But it was as if she'd been launched into space and she was freefalling, stars whizzing past her eyes, the oxygen levels dipping. She shut her eyes, too scared to face this most unbelievable of realities.

'I wonder if we'll realize,' he said. And once again her body emptied. Because it was a voice which had existed inside her head for so long and yet there it was, so present and complete she wanted to scream.

She forced herself to look then and she wasn't going mad, or maybe she was, because Tom was standing on the terrace, a glass in one hand and a cigarette in the other. At least, a version of Tom was. He had aged too much for ten years, so he looked at least a decade older than he was, scrawny, with knocked knees and unkempt hair that now also sprouted on his face. But it was unmistakably him. Not that it was entirely possible to believe in what she was seeing. Even with the evidence right in front of her it felt like a trick, an impossibility that she couldn't quite allow to be real.

Time stood very still and it also raced. For a few minutes Hope didn't think she would ever move again as every aspect of her life shattered into a million discordant pieces. *Tom* was alive. Tom *was* alive. Tom was *alive*. However she said the words, they didn't make sense. Her brain whirred as it tried to reassemble the story of her life. Rosie and Delia had been telling the truth. She hadn't killed Tom. She wasn't a murderer. Every single thing she'd built her pitiful life on was false. Which meant she must be crazy. She held a hand up to her face to check her physical reality, but the gloom and the wood was making everything feel like a malignant fairy tale.

Tom turned in her direction, a smile on his face from something he'd been saying and, for a second, it felt like their eyes locked. Hope saw the contraction in his features, the beginnings of a frown, the glitch in the system. But then he turned back and drained his glass, as Delia pointed at something behind him. It was enough to break the spell and so she ran, in a way she hadn't for years, tripping over roots and creeping ground flowers. Hope made it to the car, where she fell onto the back seat. The tears came like a monster wave, big and heavy, their power shocking, wrenching out of her from a very deep and dangerous place. She curled onto her side, pulled her knees into her chest and wrapped her arms around her head. This was the proof she'd been searching for since she read *The Ruined Girl*, except it had never been her broken mind that she'd expected to find.

Chapter Thirty-Three

The traffic was snarled up on the M25, which made Nat bang on the steering wheel and swear into the air. She kept her police radio on, dreading hearing about personnel being called to Shadowlands. And then she started to wonder if Hope had really even been at Shadowlands when she'd called her, if she was capable of murder, or if she'd got everything wrong again. *You do not think correctly*, Pastor Holland would say to her after three-hour-long prayer sessions, with her mother hovering. Nat wanted to dig her fingers into her eyes and scrub out the people who had made her life such a misery growing up, but it was so fucking hard.

Riley won't go down and I'm drowning here, Kira had said when Nat called to say she had no idea when she'd be back. And, just for a second, Nat wanted to give up and lie down on the back seat because she too had been drowning for so long she wasn't sure she could save anyone else. *Two wrongs don't make a right*, Pastor Holland said in her head. No, she answered him silently, two wrongs make things doubly worse.

But then her phone rang, another number she didn't recognize flashing across her dashboard. She answered thinking that it was probably Sir Peter bloody Lambert, calling to fire her, maybe even to charge her with something. But in fact, it was a woman's voice, a woman who said her name was Annie Metcalf and she was calling to speak about Ambrose Glencourt.

At one point in the call Nat pulled onto the hard shoulder because she was shaking, her foot wobbling against the brake pedal.

'He'd been flirty for weeks,' Annie said, 'and, if I'm honest, I was flirty back. But you know he was over double my age, not much younger than my dad actually, so I didn't take it very seriously. But then I woke up one night to find him leaning over my bed, with his hand on my breast. And it's not like I said no, or pushed him off, or anything like that, but it didn't feel entirely . . . well, good, I suppose. But he said all the right things afterwards and after a while I thought he loved me and, I don't know, it sort of became a thing. Until, I guess, he must have got tired of me and one day Delia told me it was time to leave and, when I did, I couldn't really understand what had happened. Or why I'd let it happen.'

'I didn't have a good time for a quite a few years afterwards,' she said later in the call. 'It was the humiliation. You know, before that I'd never really understood the concept of shame. I mean, I had intellectually, of course, but I hadn't appreciated what a disgusting emotion it is. Like, it was all I could think about. Not the actual act of sleeping with Rosie, but the fact that I'd let it happen. How I'd just sort of accepted it, like I was this totally pathetic kid. If I'd said absolutely no that first night I'm sure he wouldn't have raped me or anything. And then I could have said no after as well. Or I could have asked him what the deal was with him and Delia and me all in the same house.

But I didn't. I just sort of let him get away with whatever he wanted, as if I had no other choice. And I hate myself for that. Even now, even after a lot of therapy, I still sometimes wake in the morning and I can feel the shame on my skin. Like this extra layer of filth that lets me know I'm not a totally proper person. I'm not sure I'll ever be able to completely trust myself again.'

Chapter Thirty-Four

After a while Hope simply wore herself out, the panic and fear which had existed inside her for so long reaching some sort of climax. She was lying on the back seat of the car, her heavy breath steaming the windows as the world darkened, trying to work out where it had all snapped, at what moment she'd allowed a fantasy to overtake reality. But something was also wrong with that question, which stopped her from fully falling into this new version of herself. Because there were anomalies in Rosie and Delia's story that begun to surface as she calmed. Why, for instance, had they said they hadn't seen Tom for ten years? And why, when Natalie Evans came to Shadowlands, didn't they just produce him?

The clock on the dashboard said it was ten when she climbed back out of the car and once again walked through the pillars of Shadowlands and into the woods. It was hard to see exactly where she was going, but she wasn't scared, there was after all nothing more terrifying than what was going on in her mind. The lights were on again in the coach house and Hope wondered why she'd so easily walked past it before. But, she thought, perhaps the truth is everyone misses the clues that make up their lives. We don't solve the puzzle of ourselves until it becomes imperative.

Hope knocked loudly and Tom answered quickly. He frowned at first, but then recognition dawned and he took a step backwards, both of them staring silently at each other. He was even more changed close up. His skin was loose on his bones, grooved by lines and pitted by spots that looked like bruises, his eyes were yellow and bloodshot and his hair was limp and greasy, thin streaks of grey already among the black. But still the years cascaded between them.

'Hope,' he whispered finally, 'is that really you?'

She nodded, not trusting herself to speak. He lunged then, wrapping her in his arms, so she could feel his bones through his clothes. His reaction was so far from what she'd expected she was too shocked to move, her arms staying limp by her sides, too much concentration needed to keep herself upright. Eventually he pulled back but held on to her shoulders as he studied her face. 'What happened to you?'

At first she took him literally and withered at the thought of him comparing the Hope in front of him to the Hope of before, but then she realized he was looking at the lump on her forehead. She raised her hand and pressed the soft, still-tender flesh. 'Nothing, walked into a wall.'

He stood back as he opened the door wider. 'You always were a bad liar.'

The room he led her into was a mini version of Shadowlands, the same sagging, comfortable furniture covered over in the same faded floral linens. The same low wooden tables and kilim rugs, paintings that must have been taken from the walls of the main house, tall lamps with wonky shades giving off a warm glow, even an age-spotted mirror above the wood burner. It smelt of Tom, a musky scent that did something funny to the back of Hope's neck.

Tom was scratching at his chest and swaying slightly, his pupils like pin pricks. His shirt looked like one of Rosie's. Maybe it was a cast-off, as it had clearly been worn many times. The buttons were done up wrong and Hope could see a triangle of his flesh, the skin red and inflamed. He walked over to a small oval table on which there was a silver tray filled with bottles of spirits. 'Would you like a drink?'

She could have cried with relief. 'Yes please.'

He handed her a glass of clear liquid, then sat in a battered-looking chair by the wood burner and motioned for her to sit in the one opposite. Hope gulped at the drink, which burned the back of her throat. Despite Tom's deterioration he still took her breath away. Maybe not with his beauty any more, but simply with his presence. She wondered if that was what happened to couples who remained married for decades, if they stopped seeing each other physically because too much had changed. If the human brain ends up being considerate to the ravages of time.

Where to start at first seemed impossible, but in the end obvious. 'I thought you were dead.'

Tom reached for a pack of cigarettes on the table next to him which made his shirt rise so Hope could see fresh track marks on the soft skin of his inner arm. He shook two out, offering one to her which she accepted. His hand was shaking when he lit it.

'My God,' he said. 'I can't believe it's you. After all this time.'

A shifting started deep in Hope's bones. 'Didn't I shoot you, Tom? Or have I imagined the whole thing?'

He pushed some hair out of his eyes so she could see the deep lines across his forehead. 'I never thought you'd fire.'

Her breath stuck in her throat, which made speaking hard. 'But what happened? You didn't die?'

He stood and refilled their glasses, downing his in one. It strangely seemed to bring him back to the moment. 'Not in a literal sense, no.'

'But I saw you on the floor. There was blood. I thought . . . I don't understand.'

'The bullets were fake. So was the blood.' He poured more liquid into his own glass and sat back down. 'Oh God, Hope. I'm so sorry.'

'No,' she said, holding a hand out to him. 'You don't get to say sorry. You have to tell me what happened.'

He swallowed so harshly she was filled with the sense that he was arming himself in some way. But he leant forward and cradled his drink between his knees. 'Rosie was very stuck with his writing, you remember that?'

'Of course.'

'He wanted to write this modern-day *Romeo and Juliet* and he came up with the idea of watching two young people fall in love right in front of him.' Tom glanced up at her.

It took Hope a moment to compute what he'd said, but then she felt sick. 'Sorry, you're saying the whole thing was a set-up? From the beginning?'

He looked back down at his glass and nodded. 'When they asked if I'd do it, I thought it would be a bit of fun. A good way to spend the summer. I didn't realize I would actually fall for you.'

'Fall for me?' The words sounded grotesque. 'But you told me you loved Delia.'

Tom gave a little moan. 'No, that was part of it. They wanted to see how far you'd go if you thought the worst had happened, like when Romeo thinks Juliet is dead, but really she's faked it.'

'But she fakes her death to get out of marrying Paris, because she loves Romeo so much.'

Tom shuddered. 'I was doing it for us as well. Giving Rosie what he wanted to shut him up and leave us alone. I thought you'd understand.'

The chair rocked under Hope, so she had to hold on to the arms. 'How could you agree to something that cruel?'

But Tom shook his head. 'No, that's not how it was. And I agreed to it all before I met you, and they never said we were going to take it that far. It was only after we'd been seeing each other for a couple of months that Delia said Rosie wanted to see the ending, or some shit like that. It was messed up.'

Hope remembered the conversation she'd eavesdropped on in the study when Rosie had said just that. The terrible thing was that she'd had so much more of the story than she'd ever realized, but not enough to put it all together. 'Oh God,' she said as another realization hit her. 'When he asked me for a pen, he did that so I'd see the gun.'

Tom nodded. 'He told me that was the sign for it all to happen, that when you told me you'd seen the gun I'd know it was time.'

Hope had to put a hand against her head to steady her thoughts. 'But why didn't you tell me, afterwards?'

'You were so ill, there was no getting through to you.'

'You saw me?'

'Oh God, the way you cried.' Tom squeezed the top of his nose and the movement passed through Hope like time. If she'd reached out and touched him, like she'd wanted to when she'd been sick in bed, his flesh would have been warm and he'd have spoken to her. Another throw of the dice and everything would have been different.

'I sat with you every night, but you weren't making any sense,' Tom said. 'You were delirious. In the end Rosie and Delia said you needed to go to hospital and asked me to pack your bags. It was only after you'd gone that they told me they'd called your mother and you weren't coming back. I begged them to tell me where you lived, but they refused. Rosie said it had all got out of hand and was too dangerous. That you could ruin his career and we had to forget about you. But I came anyway.'

The CCTV footage of Tom boarding the train. He had been in the same city when she'd thought she was dying. 'But what did you do?'

He shrugged. 'It was useless, obviously. I had a few lost weeks there, and then came back to Shadowlands because I didn't know what else to do.'

'And you've been here ever since?'

He nodded, but she didn't press the point because he'd told her before what addicts were like, willing to do anything for their next fix. When someone tells you who they are you should always believe them. She felt Rosie's hand on her shoulder; tell me about love, young person, he'd said.

Tom started to cry. 'I think you would have understood if I'd been able to tell you. I know I shouldn't have done it, but I owed them so much, they're so good to me . . .'

'But I thought I killed you.'

'In a way you did.' He paused, but then obviously decided not to spare her. 'Hope, I was there, remember? I looked in your eyes when you pulled that trigger. I tried to smile at you, to let you know it wasn't real. Do you remember that?'

Hope had to look away from his gaze. She did remember, she remembered that his smile had been what had finally made her fire, the thought that he was laughing at her, but she didn't know how to tell him that.

'I know you wanted to hurt me,' he said and she could hear the pain in his voice.

She tried to push away his words, flailing around for some sense of who they'd both been. 'Do you remember that night we snuck out?'

He frowned. 'What night?'

A spinning started in the pit of her stomach. 'Just after we got together. You threw a stone at my window and we went and lay in that field on the other side of the river.'

'I don't know,' he said. 'I try not to remember too much any more.'

He had forgotten one of the most important, most fulfilling moments of her life. Perhaps the only truly fulfilling moment she'd ever had.

'Everything's a story,' he said into the silence and Hope felt a weird sense of shame at not understanding life, like when he'd laughed at her by the pool for not knowing what Shadowlands meant.

'But nothing I thought was true is real. I've lived the past ten years based on a lie.'

'Hope,' he said, his voice desperate, 'I think the truth is, we're all made up.'

Hope understood then that she had failed to look closely at anything, failed to stop and think. She had once wanted to be a writer and yet she hadn't asked herself such basic questions. The atmosphere was closing in and she needed fresh air or she was going to faint. She hauled herself out of the chair and stumbled out of the coach house, where she dropped her hands to her knees, gulping at the cool air.

Tom followed her into the darkness of the night. 'Do you still have the bowl?'

'The bowl? It was you who put it in my case?'

He nodded. 'I knew you loved it. I wanted you to have something you loved from here to remind you that so much had been good. That we were good.'

His words tore at her like thorns dragging through her skin, all the waste and the scum and the pain. She took a step towards him, unsure whether to kiss or kill him, as time collapsed and collided once again. But the glowing coach house was framing him and the sight made her realize that she didn't feel any jealousy that he'd stayed at Shadowlands all this time; instead it gave her a terrible sense of constriction. A strange disgust leached through her, Tom morphing before her eyes into a person she pitied. She couldn't even stand to look at him, so turned her back and walked up through the wood towards the house.

The disgust curdled in her stomach, pushing into her veins and pumping through her body with a feeling that she couldn't quite place, almost as if someone had put her in a pan of boiling water. And then slowly she began to recognize the emotion, the burning stretch of tension at her core. This was anger and she'd forgotten how powerful it could be. It reminded her of how she'd felt when she pulled the trigger, which also made her realize that both Tom and Rosie were right. She had been angry when she'd fired; she had wanted to hurt him, maybe even kill him, which meant the act wasn't the important thing, but the intention. She'd known herself all along. She was a bad person, if she'd killed Tom or not.

Hope didn't bother to creep or hide this time, simply walking onto the lawn and across the terrace to the French doors. They were unlocked as usual so she walked through the sitting room, into the hall and straight across to the study. This time she kept her eyes up, away from the floor where Tom had never died, which meant the painting of Delia was directly in her eye line, as it would be for anyone who came into that room, so public and unabashed. She went right up to it, pulled her phone out of her pocket and opened the torch so she could see it clearly. She concentrated on every brushstroke as she worked her way up the body, to the face. Hope held Delia's gaze and saw in her eyes the terror she had missed before. But of course she'd missed it, distracted by the acclaim the painter enjoyed. Now, standing in front of the grotesque image, she wasn't sure that Rosie was any better than Robert Seigal. Because who displayed an image of their wife with their legs open to the man who must have taken so much from her? She remembered then standing outside the study door and hearing Delia asking Rosie to take it down. But here it was, ten years later, still dominating. Some things, Hope realized, really were shocking and she had been right to have recoiled from this painting when she first saw it all those years ago.

Hope went then to the bureau and opened the silver box. Of course the gun was waiting patiently for her in its nest of blue velvet and when she picked it up the metal was cold and hard. She opened the barrel and saw two bullets in the cylinder, which heartened her because she wouldn't have known where to buy those. If she shot Rosie, Delia might thank her, might even pull back the covers on their huge bed and let Hope lie next to her for a while before she called the police. There would be such pleasure in holding the gun to his head, in watching him squirm and plead. She wanted him to beg for his fucking life and she wasn't sure that she'd spare it. Because what he'd done to her wasn't just mean or misguided, it was cruel. Everyone thought he was this wonderful genius, when really he was a psychopath hiding in plain sight. Except somehow, as she'd always known, the usual rules didn't apply to him.

Hope pulled in a deep breath. She had to calm herself. Acting in anger was what had got her into trouble in the first place and she needed to think clearly. It was strange, but as she stood composing herself in the study, Rosie's gun in her hand, violent thoughts in her head, it was Charlie who came to mind. There were lots of bad people in the world, lots of people who used others, who hurt and damaged, who inflicted pain and suffering. Maybe her own personal retribution wasn't what mattered any more. She had the chance to do one good thing with her badness. If the past few weeks had taught her anything, it was that she'd spent too long hiding and cowering. It was time to at least live up to herself.

Chapter Thirty-Five

Nat was so tired and worried by the time she turned through the gates at Shadowlands, she felt almost high. It was just past midnight and the moon was new, which meant the darkness felt impenetrable. She slowed as her wheels crunched onto the gravel, her headlights only managing to carve out a small space in front of her car. But she hadn't gone more than a few metres before a dark figure veered into the light and Nat skidded to a stop, momentarily convinced she was seeing a ghost. Fear poured onto her skin but she made herself kill the engine, leaning forward over the steering wheel, trying to work out who or what was there as her heart skidded in her chest. The figure laughed, which meant she knew it was Hope before she came and leant into Nat's open window. Nat stepped out of the car and was immediately enveloped in the manic energy radiating off the woman.

'What are you doing here?' Hope said.

'Coming to find you.'

'You're a bit late for that.'

Nat couldn't see any signs of a fight on Hope, no blood or torn clothes. 'Please tell me you haven't done anything stupid.'

'Oh God, I've done lots of stupid things.'

Hope looked so broken, Nat closed the gap between them and put a hand on her arm. 'What is it? What's happened?'

Hope made a strange guttural sound. 'They were telling the truth. I didn't kill Tom. He's been living here all this time.'

Nat looked behind her into the swimming darkness of the gardens, ready for a ghost to really walk out of the shadows. 'Sorry? I don't understand, what . . . ?'

'But I was telling you the truth as well,' Hope said. 'I did shoot him. Except, I didn't kill him because it was all fake.'

'What do you mean, fake?' A mean pain was thumping through Nat's head.

'They set it all up for Rosie's book. I guess so he didn't have to imagine anything. They engineered the whole thing.'

'For a book?' Nat looked into the impenetrable darkness again, but it gave nothing away. 'But how do you know all this?'

Hope made a sound that could have been a laugh. 'I've just spent an hour with Tom in his nicely renovated coach house.' She rubbed a hand across her face. 'I can't get over how mean it was. Letting me think I'd killed a person I loved for all these years.'

Nat thought of *The Ruined Girl* and how it ended, Teresa as abandoned by Rosie as Hope had been. Kira was right, it was a shit ending. 'But why didn't they tell you afterwards? I mean, once you'd shot him, I guess Ambrose must have got what he needed?'

Hope pushed two fingers either side of her nose, into the corners of her eyes. 'Tom said it was because I got so sick. That really scared them. Rosie was desperate to avoid a scandal that would have derailed his career. Which must be why he rang me after I got back home. Not because he cared, but to make sure

I wasn't going to say anything. And, no doubt, why he's been watching me all this time.'

'Shit.' Nat took a step back and blew into the air. It was bizarre that this, the most outlandish version of the story she'd heard so far, sounded the most plausible. A wave of intense anger flooded her. 'Come on, let's go and talk to them.'

But Hope shook her head. 'There's no point. Legally they haven't done anything wrong, have they?'

'No, but . . .' Nat wondered why Hope's moral code was faltering at this final hurdle. The conversations she'd had with Annie and Sara were vibrating inside her, but the moment was volatile and so much damage had been done already she couldn't think straight.

'I'm tired,' Hope said, 'I just want to go home.' She shook Nat off her arm. 'You were right, there is nothing you can do to help me.'

'No, that's not . . .' But Nat's words died as Hope stepped out of the beam of lights into the darkness. 'Wait,' Nat shouted after her. But the darkness swallowed her, and Nat let her go because she was of course right, the Glencourts hadn't done anything legally wrong.

But also, Nat couldn't just walk away. She got back into her car and drove on up to the house. The lights were all on downstairs and the central French doors which led onto the terrace were open, so she stopped the car and walked across the lawn. She could see the Glencourts and a crumpled-looking man sitting on the sofas in the lounge. Nat stepped up onto the terrace and walked across to the doors, where she knocked lightly, which made them all jump.

Ambrose Glencourt stood when he saw her. 'My God, Detective Evans, what are you doing here?'

She crossed the threshold into the bright room. 'I know Hope Jenkins has just been here.'

The other man, who had to be Tom Markham, groaned. He didn't look particularly well, too thin and pallid. Mrs Glencourt rubbed his back.

'That bloody woman,' Mr Glencourt said.

But Nat wasn't going to let him get away with his act again. 'Do you want to explain what's going on? I presume this is Tom Markham?'

Ambrose Glencourt sighed as if she were bothering him. 'Yes. That's right.'

'But we launched an investigation into his disappearance. I came here and you didn't bother to tell me he was living in your coach house? I could charge you with wasting police time.' Although the words sounded hollow, because they all knew that wasn't going to happen.

'We're very sorry,' Mrs Glencourt said from the sofa. 'We didn't say anything because Tom is very vulnerable.' She reached over for his hand as she spoke. 'We didn't want to expose him to all this. Especially not Hope knowing he was alive, because we knew she'd cause a massive fuss, just like she has done.'

Nat spluttered. 'But you made her think she'd killed him.'

Ambrose Glencourt took a step towards her, so she could feel his anger vibrating off him. 'No, Detective Evans. Hope made herself think that. Her accusations are absurd. Everything that we told you is true. Tom and Hope were in a relationship, she declared her love for me, I rejected her, there was an argument in which she threatened us with a gun, she had some sort of psychotic breakdown. The only part we lied about is that Tom came back here after he disappeared. We had two weeks of hell, not knowing where he was, and then he returned. He was deeply traumatized by the whole thing and we've kept him safe ever since. Because, like we've said all along, he is like a son to us both, Delly especially.'

The room pulsated with the story. Nat was aware that she was right back in the same place. Both Hope's and the Glencourts' versions sounded plausible. 'Is that true, Mr Markham?' she tried.

He didn't look at her and Nat saw Mrs Glencourt squeeze his hand. He moved his head in what looked like a nod, but Nat couldn't be sure.

'But Hope just told me that you told her the whole thing was a trick. Information-gathering for Mr Glencourt's book.'

Tom started to cry.

'DI Evans, please,' Ambrose Glencourt said. 'This is why we lied about Tom living here. His mind is completely addled by drugs. Even if he did say that to Hope, even if he actually thinks it happened, I can assure you he's mistaken. Christ, he often doesn't know what day of the bloody week it is, let alone what happened over a decade ago.'

'Mr Markham,' Nat said, 'is that possible?'

Mrs Glencourt moved across the sofa and pulled Tom into her. He turned his head against her shoulder as his body shook. 'Please,' she said, looking at her husband.

'Or, you know what,' Ambrose Glencourt said, so forcefully Nat had to look back at him. 'Hope could be bloody lying about the conversation. I mean, it would hardly be the first time, would it. I told you from the beginning. That woman is deluded.'

'I don't think . . .'

But Ambrose Glencourt cut her off with a raised hand. 'Look, we won't be pressing charges. None of us wants anything more to do with Hope Jenkins. And right now, our concern is for Tom and what this will have done to him, so I am going to have to ask you to leave.' He narrowed his eyes at her. 'I mean, there's no point in getting Peter involved, is there?'

They stared at each other for a beat, both calculating their next move, even if a move was needed. The conversations she'd had with Sara and Annie were vibrating inside her, but it was also true that the law wouldn't help any of them, that power always rested with the same people, that often what you saw wasn't real, that reality could be dismissed as fakery, that sometimes the only truth you could fully trust was your own. Nat understood then what Hope had meant when she'd said she would have to sort it out herself. She turned to leave, and it was good to step back into the night. Even the long drive ahead seemed preferable to staying at Shadowlands.

Chapter Thirty-Six

Hope had begun to wonder if maybe the point of humans was to work out the plot. Their own personal plots, the ones that made up their lives. Why else do we remember some things and not others? Wasn't that proof of an internal editor guiding us in the right direction? She'd had hundreds of conversations with Charlie and yet the one she remembered most clearly was the one in which he'd told her that his father played football every Thursday. *Don't put anything on the page that hasn't earnt its place*, Rosie's editor had written on the manuscript of The Ruined Girl. Hope had thought that only applied to fiction, but in fact it was true of life as well.

The following Thursday, Hope followed Charlie's dad to his football game, then on to the pub, then on his route back to his house. She was looking for her moment and she found it when he turned onto the road with the break in the houses that concealed the little park where she'd watched Charlie and his mum. People always posed those questions about going back in time and killing Hitler if you could, but she didn't see why it should only apply to him. If someone had gone back in time and killed Rosie before they met she'd have been eternally grateful and she wanted to do the same for Charlie. Morality was generally shabby and, in the end, you could only count on your own.

Hope pulled a scarf out of her bag and wrapped it tightly around her head and across her face, leaving just her eyes clear. The street was deserted, only a few lights on behind drawn curtains, a murky, heavy sky above their heads. Dominic Cunningham was swaying slightly as he walked, his pace ponderous. She fitted her hand around Rosie's gun in her pocket and quickened her pace, coming level with Dominic as they reached the entrance to the park. He turned at the exact moment she pushed him, a half-smile on his face that flickered a moment longer than it should have. The element of surprise combined with the alcohol he'd consumed meant it was quite easy to get him through the gates and onto the grass.

'What the hell,' he shouted.

Hope raised the gun, using two hands to hide her shakes. He stumbled backwards, lifting his own hands up above his shoulders.

'I've got money. A phone. You can have anything.' His voice was high-pitched, like a squeal.

But she ignored him, waving the gun to make him back towards a small clump of trees on the far side of the little park. Sparks of adrenaline were shooting through her so she worried she might trip, but she kept him in her sights and concentrated on the fact that she'd done this before, that she'd already had the courage to pull the trigger.

When they reached the bushes, Hope waved the gun at him. 'Kneel down and put your hands behind your head.'

He made a strange hitching noise as he thumped to the ground. 'Listen, I've got lots of money. Not just what's on me. I can get you anything you want.'

Hope took a step towards him and aimed the gun at the top of his head. It felt strangely erotic. She'd never come close to that much power before and it was intoxicating, like a strong perfume and fine wine all rolled into one. It was appalling to admit, but in that moment, she almost understood Rosie. Dominic was snivelling, a trail of glistening snot running into his mouth.

'You're a piece of shit,' she said.

He was trying to make her out in the darkness, scanning her body, but she saw the blankness in his expression. He'd stood a few inches away from her, his kid had eaten lunch with her every day for nearly a year, but he'd never noticed her. 'Is that you, Susie?' he said finally. 'I didn't mean . . . We were both drunk and . . .'

'Shut up.' Hope's finger squeezed against the trigger, but her brain felt tight, like it wanted to break free from her skull. The scene was refusing to stay still, like it wasn't real, but happening in a film. And then it shifted again and it wasn't Dominic kneeling in front of her, but Rosie. Even more confusingly, she couldn't tell if there was a difference between them. People like them believed they were in charge and everyone else was only there to make life work for them.

'Are you going to kill me?' Dominic spluttered, crying openly now.

In *The Ruined Girl*, Rosie wrote about the ecstasy Teresa felt when she fired, everything releasing, all her anger and pain contained within a single glorious moment. Hope knew the joy of the feeling and she tried to make herself want it again. But also could she really kill everyone who did bad things? Wouldn't that make her no better than them? And Hope wanted to be better, she'd always wanted that.

Dominic was snivelling in front her in the very same position that she'd fantasized for Rosie. And was that really what this was about? Was he really going to dictate the terms of the next ten years of her life as well? Was she really going to condemn herself to living in his warped version of reality? The next few seconds and minutes stretched out in front of Hope, all the possibilities colliding together so for tiny moments she lived them all. And yet of course they wouldn't exist on their own. As with every second it would bleed into the next and on and on until it made up a life.

'Please,' Dominic gasped. 'Please don't do this.'

The sympathy that she should have felt for Tom flooded her then. Which made her realize something. She couldn't be all bad because a truly bad person wouldn't have felt a remorse so deep it had ruined the past ten years of her life. Humans are changeable and we all make terrible mistakes. The thing is, ultimately, the ending of every story could go in so many different directions. And she had been given a lifeline – an ending she had never seen coming, an ending that wasn't even an end. All this time she had believed herself to be bad, when the truth suddenly seemed so much more complicated. She had already lived with the consequence of taking all those waiting seconds from someone and it was huge, never-ending, destroying. Why would she do that to herself again? It was surely time to try something different.

'Here's what's going to happen,' she said, her voice shaky because she was making it up as she went along. 'You are going to leave your wife and son alone. No more notes in lunch boxes and fists in soft flesh when no one's looking. Do you understand?'

Dominic nodded dramatically. 'I'm sorry, I didn't mean . . . They just push my buttons and I . . .'

'Shut up,' Hope said again. She took a step closer to him. 'I'm your worst nightmare, Dominic. I am someone with absolutely nothing to lose. I've pulled this trigger before, and I'll happily pull it again. This is your only warning. I'll be watching you and if you don't get out of that house and leave your wife and son alone, I swear I will make it my mission to hold this gun to your head and *use it*.'

'Who are you?' he said again.

'All you need to know is that it's all about the story, Dominic.' She let her voice relax in a way that made her realize the shake had gone from her limbs. 'Who tells it better. Which version is the most credible. We've got to learn that it belongs to us as much as it does to you. It's funny, but I've only just worked out that there are lots of stories out there and lots of ways to tell them.'

He was looking past her desperately, in a way that showed he thought she was completely mad. 'Up,' she said, waving the gun at him. He scrambled to his feet. 'Okay, we're going to walk out of here now and you're going to go home. And in the morning, you're going to ask your wife for a divorce. You need to leave her and Charlie alone.'

At the entrance to the park Hope couldn't resist digging him in the back with the gun, feeling the hard metal against his flesh before she waved the gun in the direction of the street. He didn't need telling twice, running so fast he was out of sight in seconds.

All the air left her body in a rush, so she had to drop forward and lean her hands on her knees as she pulled off the scarf, gulping at the night like it was water. But she didn't stay like that for long because she had to get away in case Dominic called the police. The shake in her legs made walking hard and she started to worry that she wasn't going to make it home, that she was going to collapse on the street and have to be carted off in an ambulance. Maybe what she'd just done meant she was mad? Maybe everyone had been right all along? She had to lean against a wall, where she made herself take some deep breaths. And, as her heart rate stabilized, so her thoughts settled. In her agitation she'd forgotten that she'd switched narratives. She wasn't the cowering, pathetic, beaten woman any more, she was someone with agency and strength. It was enough to get her off the wall and back home.

Chapter Thirty-Seven

Nat hadn't been in work long when an alert came through about a woman, average height, slightly overweight, wearing a denim skirt and black T-shirt, who had pulled a gun on a thirty-six-year-old male on Stanford Road at approximately 11.30 the night before. She pulled up the details of the case on her phone, her heart leaping as she read the victim's name: Dominic Cunningham. *Fuck*, she whispered silently to herself, because Hope had fooled her again. When they'd stood on the dark Shadowlands drive Nat had wondered why she was so easily letting the Glencourts get away with they'd done. But of course it was just because she'd moved on. Hope liked to right wrongs, and Nat had to start really listening to the things she said. She got straight up from her desk and hurriedly left the police station.

It was not what she should be doing. In fact, not immediately telling someone that she was pretty sure she knew who had held a gun to Dominic Cunningham's head was enough to get her sacked. But Hope had touched something in Nat that she'd kept closed for a very long time and it was making her feel dangerous. The way she'd looked on the driveway at Shadowlands, illuminated by the headlights, had refused to leave Nat alone. She couldn't quite pinpoint the emotion it roused in her, but it felt like a mixture of sadness and fear and vulnerability. And all the while that time ran out on the case, she was aware of it also running out with Kira, because her wife needed something from her that she didn't think she could give. Nat had had a disdain for need since she'd left home at eighteen and had to learn to fend for herself. Need made you vulnerable and without it you were the strong one who was fine alone.

'I am not responsible for your happiness,' she'd said to Kira, just the night before.

But Kira had shaken her head. 'What a sad thing to say. Of course you are. Just like I should be for you. Not totally, obviously. But if you love someone, part of the job is making them happy.'

Nat was sweating by the time she rang Hope's buzzer and her body felt jittery, a feeling that intensified when Hope didn't seem particularly surprised to see her. The flat that Hope led her into had clearly lost its personality many years before, almost as if it had been furnished in another era. They went into the kitchen, which was small and tatty, cupboard doors not entirely aligned, permanent stains on the countertop, a mouldy apple sat next to the kettle, five empty wine bottles lined up next to the bin and a saucer heavy with cigarette butts on the tiny table in the way some people would display flowers.

'Would you like some coffee?' Hope asked. 'I was just about to make some.'

Nat nodded, surprised to see that Hope made coffee in the European way, as Nat thought of it. One of those silver pots that you pressed real coffee into and boiled on the stove. The air almost immediately smelt of the water percolating the rich grounds, which cancelled out the staleness. Hope turned as she waited for the coffee, leaning back against the sink, a frown gorging out lines on her forehead, the lump now a distant yellowed bruise.

Nat waited until Hope was sitting opposite her before she said, 'Dominic Cunningham was attacked last night.'

Hope raised an eyebrow. 'That's a shame. What happened?'

'I'm not sure I need to tell you.' She paused but Hope just sipped at her coffee, so Nat gestured at Hope's denim skirt and black T-shirt. 'He's reported that a woman wearing a denim skirt and black T-shirt held a gun to his head.'

Hope snorted. 'Hardly an unusual outfit.'

'Your clothes don't look fresh on today.'

'Did he say why he was attacked?'

'No. He claims to have no idea of the motive, and nothing was stolen from him.' Hope nodded, but didn't lower her gaze. 'Where were you at around eleven o'clock last night, Miss Jenkins?'

'Here.'

'Can anyone corroborate that?'

'What do you think?' But then Hope sighed. 'This is silly, DI Evans. We both know nothing I say now means anything. You haven't arrested me or read me my rights. You're sitting in my kitchen drinking coffee. Why are you actually here?'

Nat looked round the kitchen again and it suddenly felt like looking into her future. It was as if she'd sleepwalked her way there, except she was awake, and it was all real. And why *was* she there? The question felt larger than it needed to be and in her mind Kira shook her head again. Nat scrabbled for her disdain, but it was hard to pinpoint, and that terrified her because who was she without it? Dangerous tears gathered in the corners of her eyes and then they fell, in thick, ugly rivulets that she couldn't stop, however hard she hit them away as they touched her cheeks.

'It's okay,' Hope said. 'There's a certain bravery in letting go.'

No there isn't, Nat wanted to scream, because what the fuck happens then? But all the words were stuck in her chest. Hope stirred sugar into Nat's coffee, waiting patiently for her to pull herself together.

'I'm sorry,' Nat hiccupped. 'For not believing you.' She hadn't even known she was going to say that.

Hope shrugged. 'I'm not very believable. And it turns out I wasn't telling the truth anyway.'

Nat pulled in a ragged breath, full suddenly with that strange purity that comes after crying. 'No, but as good as. If people like us don't believe each other, then nothing changes.' People like us? She sounded like a greeting card and yet she meant it.

Nat pulled her bag onto her lap and took out Hope's journal, which she slid across the table to her. 'Sorry for hanging on to this. Also . . .' She hesitated, but if she didn't show Hope she'd be as bad as the rest of them, so she slid another piece of paper across the table as well. On it were two names, Annie Metcalf and Sara Clarke, along with their mobile numbers. Hope looked at her inquisitively. 'You weren't alone. I mean, the same thing that happened to you didn't happen to anyone else. But, those women, they have a lot to say about Ambrose Glencourt.'

'Oh God,' Hope said.

'I'm sorry,' Nat said again, 'I have a habit of letting people down.' The sound of traffic from the main road was blowing in with the breeze through the window. 'My mother hated me and now my wife does too.' She didn't know what she was doing, but the words were falling out of her. Which was maybe why you shouldn't let yourself go, why you should hang on to the disdain, why you should build a wall . . .

'Why?' Hope asked, and it was such a stupidly simple question that Nat couldn't work out why she'd never thought to ask that before.

But the strangest thing was, words were there again, when she hadn't known she thought them. 'I think, maybe, it's like you said. I'm not believable. Or, at least, I can't quite believe in myself and so I'm not a completely real person.'

'Who is?' Hope said, but her tone was soft.

'My mother always told me I was bad.' Nat clasped her hands together on the table in front of her. 'But I don't want my wife to think the same.'

'Can't you tell her that?'

And there it was again, that simplicity that she hadn't known was possible. 'I don't know.'

Hope sighed, her gaze flickering in a way that clenched Nat's stomach. 'You know, I don't think we have to believe the bad things people say about us. In the end, we're all made of stories, and we just have to decide what's the best one and go with it.'

The sentiment sounded dangerous. 'What do you mean?'

Hope looked back at Nat. 'I guess, just, that none of us ever knows the right words. We all wish we'd said something better sometimes. We all believe we could have changed things if we'd spoken differently. But I don't know if that's true. Everyone has their own narratives inside their heads that might totally contradict our own.' She rubbed at something invisible on her cheek.

'Someone I know once told me that everything's a story, and he's right, but I think he got it slightly wrong. I think we're all scrabbling around trying to convince ourselves that our story is the right one.'

Nat felt hollow, like she hadn't eaten for a while. If what Hope was saying was true then the world would be bursting with stories, and there'd be no chance of ever finding the right one. 'But then how do we ever know the truth?'

Hope shrugged. 'Maybe there isn't one. Maybe you just have to go with the best version and make it real.'

And Nat supposed that was what she'd done with Hope's story, in the end deciding which version she found easiest to believe in. It made her think of her mother in the house they'd grown up in. She'd contacted her sister when Pastor Holland had been convicted of fraud, her mother's life savings squandered along with those of so many others. *All Mum does is sit in a chair in the lounge now*, her sister had said, *like she isn't there any more*. Nat guessed that must be what it felt like to realize that you'd believed in the wrong story your whole life. It made her long for Kira like a physical ache.

'What I really want to tell my wife is that I'm scared.' Nat looked up and Hope was smiling kindly at her.

'Do it then. What have you got to lose?'

Nat tried to laugh. 'Everything.'

But Hope shook her head. 'No, I didn't realize this before, but I think you only lose by not doing or saying or whatever it is you need to.'

Nat stood, but then she hesitated. Hope was probably right, and the mistake was in the not saying. 'Also, my son is at Lady Catherine's. Ben Ashe-Evans in Reception.'

Nat watched Hope absorb the news, first surprise then delight. She stood as well, putting her hand to her forehead. 'Oh my goodness, I was wondering where the coincidence was hiding. I love it that you're mine.'

Nat laughed. Hope really was the strangest person.

Chapter Thirty-Eight

Hope watched Natalie Evans jog down the stairs, her jaunty pony-tail bobbing behind her like a lie. She hoped she was on her way home, or that she would at least make it there soon. But she couldn't let her mind linger on another story for too long, because she had her own to deal with. She went back to the kitchen, taking in the space as Natalie Evans might have done. Nobody had visited the flat for so many years she wasn't used to seeing it through a stranger's eyes. She saw now that it was a depressing space, too revealing of who she was, or at least who she had become.

The panic nearly overtook her, but Hope shut her eyes and forced her breath to steady. It was still hard to work out exactly who she was and sometimes, when she thought about everything that had happened, she couldn't work out what was real, or who had been telling the truth. Because in a way they all had and hadn't been. But, just like she'd said to Natalie Evans, it was time to choose the best story. And, in the end, surely everyone would go for the one that saved them.

Hope sat back down and let herself think about Shadowlands. It came to her in the way it had done all those years ago, the first time Delia had driven her up through the gates. She let the feelings of wonder and excitement flood her again and, in that moment, saw clearly how the place had given her life a narration she'd been so desperate for. That house was filled with history and Rosie and Delia knew it all. They could see thousands of meals around the dining table, trace the origin of all the heirlooms, remember trees being planted. By comparison it had made her feel rootless, her home a rented flat in a long line of rented flats, the only things passed down ugly and worthless. In comparison to Shadowlands her beginnings had felt like they came from concrete and rubbish, and she'd wanted something more substantial, something that gave her a place in the world. But what she understood as she sat at her tiny kitchen table was that Shadowlands was an illusion because it wasn't just her life that had been stolen. She was reminded of a project the Year 6s had done the year before on the dissolution of the monasteries. All that land and wealth and art and money taken and distributed among a group of men who happened to be in the right place at the right time, and since then passed it on down through generations. But the problem with a stolen history was that it cast a long shadow. Whereas her history was her own. Everything she did from now on belonged to her and only her.

She thought then about Tom, so diminished and broken, just like she had been. They had both done a terrible thing, but they had also both been trapped and caught up in something so much bigger than themselves. If she could sit opposite him again and summon the lines she needed at the time, rather than after the event, she would say that the whole of human history is based on lies and theft and sometimes the only way we can live with ourselves is to pretend that nothing is real, that life is fiction.

But the mistake is in thinking that fictions are unimportant. History itself is only the telling of stories. And who could claim to have ever told a perfect story? Who has a perfect memory or a totally unbiased view? Whoever told an absolute truth, even when they meant to? By its nature history is imperfect, which means it must be impossible to ever arrive at a complete, perfect truth.

Hope stood and pinned the numbers Natalie Evans had given her to the fridge with a magnet of anchovies in a can that her mother had brought with her the one and only time she'd come back from Spain. She would ring both Annie and Sara, but not yet. First, she went into the sitting room where her laptop was lying on the sofa in a patch of sun. She had wanted to be tied to Rosie, Delia and Tom for ever and, in a way, that's exactly what had happened. Their shared story had done that. Her fault had been in thinking there was only one way to tell a story, an absolute truth to be arrived at. And what she had to remember was that the right instinct was surprisingly already within her. When she'd stood over Dominic Cunningham in that dark park, she'd behaved like a proper writer, looking past all the words she'd always told herself about herself to find a truer story. One that suited her better. Now she just had to repeat the trick, and where better to do that than in a completely different place, somewhere new and exciting, somewhere that made her forget who she was.

'Mum,' she said, when the woman answered. 'Can I come and stay for a bit? I have something I need to do.'

Part Three

Chapter Thirty-Nine

Delia had to lie to Rosie about where she was going, but she didn't feel that bad about it. He barely even registered what she said anyway; he and Tom were building an ineffectual bridge across the stream in the wood, an enterprise that Delia didn't completely understand. Over the past couple of years Tom's addictions had worsened worryingly and the only thing that calmed him was walking in the field on the other side of the river. The winter before, when the river had swollen, he hadn't been able to reach it, which had agitated him horrifically, so Rosie had suggested the bridge. Delia suspected what they were constructing wouldn't support a man's weight, but she didn't care, because the project was taking all Rosie's time and attention. She worried about what would happen when it was finished and hoped he wouldn't go back to bed.

It had seemed a waste to buy a day ticket, when she had no intention of staying for the day, only interested in the one panel that she arrived with just enough time to attend. The venue wasn't far from Shadowlands, which was why she'd chosen it, in the grounds of a slightly depressing hotel. The smiling young woman on reception directed her over to a large marquee on the lawn and, as she walked towards it, she was filled with fear that she might see someone from their past life. Inside the marquee was already busy, groups of mainly women chatting excitedly, a general buzz of anticipation in the air. She chose a seat near the back, unsurprised at the quickness of her heartbeat. Rosie's old agent and editor passed along the central aisle thankfully without noticing her, choosing seats together much nearer the front.

Hope's face hadn't enlarged particularly well on the screen at the back of the stage. She had clearly pulled herself together since their last meeting, or else the photographer had been a genius, but still it looked slightly grotesque hanging so large like that. Next to her face was the cover of her book. Delia was impressed by the design, an ill-defined pencil outline of a woman lying on her side, just a few strokes really, but still telling you all you needed to know. *The Muse* was written confidently across the top in a bright blue with Hope Jenkins smaller along the bottom. Glowing quotes ran along both sides. Delia smiled at Casper Waites' 'A brave and tender novel'. God, he'd have loved that. She was very pleased that Rosie had banned any mention of the book from their home.

A woman walked onto the stage and stood at the front. 'Welcome,' she said, as the crowd hushed. 'My name is Carol Yates and I am very excited to be speaking to Hope Jenkins, writer of *The Muse*.' She turned to the side of the stage. 'Welcome, Hope.'

Delia was impressed by how confidently Hope walked onto the stage, and by what she was wearing. A loose linen trouser suit in a dusky pink, with a white T-shirt and trainers. Her blow-dried hair hung in highlighted waves around her face and her make-up was subtle, but good, on skin that lay flat against her bones, all that terrible puffiness gone. She looked disconcertingly familiar and, momentarily, Delia's throat tightened.

'Well,' Carol said, as they sat in two rounded blue chairs either side of a low table. 'Firstly, congratulations on the success of *The Muse*.'

Hope smiled. 'Thank you.'

'You must be thrilled. Not many debuts get such an amazing reception. Or such good sales.'

Hope looked down as if she was embarrassed. 'It's certainly beyond what I expected. I think I got lucky. It caught the zeitgeist.'

'Absolutely,' Carol said. 'It certainly did that. Was that something you were aware of when you were writing?'

Delia watched Hope compose her face. 'Well, in a way, yes. When all the allegations came out about Robert Seigal I remember thinking, bloody hell, another one. Another person who we all thought was pretty cool and who we, you know, listened to and respected. And then it occurred to me that maybe it's not a coincidence. That maybe the wrong people have been telling our stories all this time and that can, well, give a false picture of how things should be.'

Carol nodded. 'And of course, there was that rush of allegations against cultural figures after Robert Seigal. Men we really didn't expect to be involved in things like that.'

Hope sighed dramatically. 'No, it's all very sad. I suppose the past few years have taught us that lots of the so-called great men weren't, in fact, that great.'

The crowd laughed appreciatively as something cold dripped down Delia's spine.

Carol leant forward slightly. 'And, of course, you worked for Ambrose Glencourt?'

Hope nodded, setting her expression tight as if the memory was painful, which made Delia roll her eyes. 'Yes, but a long time ago. Nearly fourteen years in fact, when I was only twenty-three.'

'You've always maintained nothing happened between you. He never behaved inappropriately with you?'

'No, not literally. But as soon as Annie and Sara came forward, I recognized patterns of behaviour that had always made me uncomfortable. And then, of course, the way he treated the mothers of his children. I'm certainly not defending him just because he didn't physically assault me.' Delia shivered, as if a cold wind had passed through her.

'And, in a strange coincidence, his wife was Robert Seigal's muse?'

Hope laughed. 'Oh, I'm not sure there are many coincidences in life. More like patterns of behaviour. And, just to be clear, the painting in my book is not real. I know there's been so much speculation, but Ambrose Glencourt isn't Seb, and Delia Glencourt isn't Bea.'

Delia shut her eyes. But Hope was behind them as well, in so many different incarnations. The manuscript had arrived about six months after all the terrible stuff in the news, at a time when she'd felt simply raw. Rosie was still fighting it then, still sometimes going on right-wing radio shows and saying that it was impossible to be a man nowadays and that the woke agenda had dulled our minds. She took to not listening and saying she had because he didn't really care what she thought anyway and not agreeing with him would have meant a whole new life choice she wasn't prepared for.

'No,' Hope was saying as Delia tuned back in, 'I don't think we can separate the art from the artist. And I use the term art loosely, to include film and books and music, any form of creation really.'

'I think that's going to count out a lot of great works,' Carol said.

'Well, then we just have to create new ones.' The audience murmured their appreciation of that sentiment. 'You know, when I was researching this book,' Hope continued, 'I spent a lot of time in galleries, and I was struck by just how many naked women there are in them. And not just naked, but flagrantly so. I mean, there are a lot of vaginas on walls out there.' The audience laughed. 'And I thought, how many men do you see in paintings on those walls lying around naked with their legs open and their, well, penis exposed for everyone to gawp at?'

Carol laughed. 'You're so right.'

Hope beamed. 'It made me think maybe we've let the wrong people get away with too much for too long and it's dulled our sense of shock at things we *should* be bothered by.'

Delia looked over Hope's head at her book. Her own sense of shock had been violently reawakened by *The Muse*, but maybe that would only be true for her. No one else would have recognized themselves so absolutely on the pages and wondered how someone had been able to see into their soul. Which at first had infuriated her and then terrified her and finally saddened her. Hope's novel was the story of a woman called Bea, married to a man called Seb. They lived in a grand country house in which hung a huge painting by a very famous artist, depicting Bea lying on a bed *with her legs splayed so you could see her pubic hair and the intricate redness of her vagina,* as Hope had written. Bea hated the painting and periodically asked Seb to take it down, but he never did, always saying it was a work of genius. And then it emerged that the artist had been a serial abuser of women and Bea admitted to Seb that he had raped her, numerous times, over many years. But still Seb refused to take it down, until eventually Bea couldn't decide who was more real, her or the woman in the frame.

The first time Delia read Hope's novel she cried, but after the second time she went into Rosie's study and took down the painting of herself with her legs open. She took it back to her studio where she covered it in clay, forming peaks and troughs, moulding and shaping. By time she'd finished it looked like a series of hills, or maybe the bodies of many women lying together. She added colour and patterns, letting her brush move however it wanted. In the end even she could see it looked beautiful, when usually she hated her own work. She rehung it back in its old place and Rosie had never mentioned it.

A smattering of applause echoed round the marquee, which made Delia concentrate again.

'And you still work at the school where you've been for over ten years?'

Hope nodded. 'Oh yes, I couldn't leave. I love the community and how there's always new children to get to know.'

Carol nodded. 'So what are you working on now then?'

Hope glanced at the audience and laughed. 'My agent and editor are here, so I'd better not promise too much. But I'm thinking about a story about a woman who thinks she's someone she's not, you know, a really bad person, maybe even a killer. I think we all tell ourselves stories about ourselves and they can become a bit stuck. I'm very interested in exploring what makes us who we are.'

'Intriguing.' Carol looked out over the audience. 'And I'm sure we all can't wait to read it. But for now, Hope Jenkins, thank you so much.'

Delia waited in her chair as the applause died down. She watched Hope being led to a table at the back of the marquee, where a queue started to form. Rosie's, or actually not Rosie's any more, agent and editor both said something to her before hurrying off. Delia however hung back, only joining the queue when she was certain she was the last person in it. As it inched slowly forward, Delia watched Hope receiving praise, holding her smile, signing her name. She had adopted the same self-deprecation Delia had always hated in Rosie.

Hope only noticed Delia when she was standing right in front of her. A bright blush washed instantly across her face and she stood, leaning forward almost as if she was going to hug her, but then thought better of it.

'Congratulations,' Delia said.

Hope looked behind her, checking probably to see if Rosie was there. 'I didn't know you were here.'

Delia opened her empty hands. 'I didn't bring my book for you to sign.'

'Well, you don't need to, do you?'

To D, it said on the inside page, a dedication Delia had been surprisingly moved by.

'But I did bring you this.' She opened her bag and drew out a Dictaphone, which she passed across to Hope. The tape waiting patiently in its spool had lived inside the box file of *The Ruined Girl* for many years and Delia doubted Rosie would miss it. If he did, she would tell him that there were some things he had to accept didn't belong to him any more.

Hope laughed as she picked it up. 'Are you trying to turn me into Rosie?'

Delia shook her head. 'Listen to the tape inside it. I think you'll want to hear it.'

Hope frowned. 'Thank you.'

'No,' Delia said. 'Thank you.' She hoped it was enough. She couldn't go into all the sorrys, and there wasn't an explanation, so really, what else was there? 'Well, anyway, I'd better get on. Rosie will be wondering where I am. Nice suit, by the way.'

Hope looked down at herself, her hand running over the material. 'I did learn from the best,' she said, and Delia was struck by the brightness in her eyes when she looked back up, so momentarily they seemed to whizz back through time, dropping the years behind them and she felt like she did actually need to say something real. 'I like the sound of your new book.'

'Oh, do you?' Hope tucked some hair behind her ears. 'It's in the early stages still, but I'm really interested in the idea that we're not always who we think we are.'

Delia nodded, but then she knew she was going to cry, her mouth turning downwards involuntarily. 'He told me I was bad,' she said, speaking words she'd never uttered before, feeling their weight as they left her body. 'He said he could see I wanted it. That anyone who looked at the paintings would see it too. That everyone would know how bad I am.'

Hope stretched out her hand and touched Delia's arm, which made her wince, in the way physical contact so often did. 'I hope you know that's not true.'

Delia met Hope's gaze. 'I'm not at all sure that I know what's true.' She tried to laugh, but the sound that emerged was strangulated. 'We're all such bloody unreliable narrators.'

Hope frowned, but then made a sound that was much more like a laugh. 'I hadn't thought of it like that, but yes, you're right, we are.' She took her hand away from Delia's arm, although the warmth remained. 'Be careful, I might steal that.'

'Fair enough,' Delia said with a confidence she didn't entirely feel. 'I hope you know . . .' The ground shifted beneath her feet. 'Well, I hope you know, I feel ashamed.' And only as she said the words did she realize how true they were.

Hope leant across the table, lowering her voice. 'I don't blame you. Not any more.'

Delia's tears were hot against her skin. 'Why didn't you say anything to the press? When Sara and Annie . . . ?' Her heart still ached with that time when she'd expected Hope to reveal all the things she'd accused them of. Still sometimes now she woke in a panic, instantly reaching for her phone so she could scour for the story.

Hope's face glistened with a sheen of sweat. 'It didn't seem fair on Tom. And, in the end, it didn't matter. I found a way to tell my story.'

Delia looked down at the books on the table. 'Except it's not your story, is it?'

'Oh well,' Hope said, her eyes narrowing. 'I'm not sure that any story belongs to just one person.'

Delia thought she knew what Hope meant, but she wasn't going to agree with her. There had been times over the past four years in which she'd thought she was a liar, then deranged, then opportunistic, until she'd realized that Hope believed fully in her own version of events, as if there were no other points of view. Still, the same applied to herself, as she'd realized when she read the testimonies of all those women accusing Rosie of such horrible, careless things.

There was nothing more left to say and so Delia nodded once, before turning and walking towards the entrance of the marquee. It had started raining and the sky had darkened, but it wasn't far back to the car park and then Shadowlands, where Rosie would be waiting, hopefully exhausted from a physical day. Lots of things felt like lasts at the moment, but Delia hoped that was an illusion. No, she told herself as she stepped into the rain, there was surely plenty more to come.

Chapter Forty

Hope was tired and her head hurt by the time she got back to her hotel room after dinner with her agent and editor. She shucked off her jacket and pulled off her trainers, then took the Dictaphone Delia had given her out of her bag. She was both desperate and terrified to listen to it. The whole encounter had felt very much like an ending, and she wasn't ready for that. The desire for a cold glass of wine ambushed her, but she was good at dismissing those temptations. Her sponsor had told her that she'd crave alcohol for ever, but that it didn't make her special. Everyone has cravings, he said, so choose a memory that makes you feel happy and think of that every time you want a drink. Hope liked to think of when she'd held the gun to Dominic's head and not pulled the trigger. It made her feel both strong and good.

Her phone buzzed and so she pulled it out of her bag gratefully. There was a good luck message already there from her mother, along with a photo of her cat basking in the sunshine in a spot Hope now knew well. The new message was from Annie: *Looking forward to seeing you tomorrow. Sara can make it as well now.* Hope sent back a thumbs-up emoji and then the screen switched to her screen saver of the card Charlie had given her on his last day at Lady Catherine's. It was a picture of him and his mum in their flat with their new cat. It was likely that she'd never see him again, a thought which made her chest tighten, but also she had to let him go. Charlie had no idea of the part she'd played in his story and that had to be okay, because sometimes you have to be loud and sometimes quiet. And, besides, she still had years of seeing Nat and Kira in the playground, watching the way they became ever easier with each other, and the little smiles Nat gave whenever she passed by the office window.

Hope wanted more than anything to be at home then. The decorators had only left the week before and thinking about the flat was soothing. She hadn't realized until it was finished how much like Shadowlands it felt. Subconsciously, she'd gone for the same muted off-whites that Delia favoured, teamed with the same blowsy floral fabrics and tasselled cushions. The walls were filled with old paintings picked up in charity shops, as well as photographs of Hope and her mother which she'd liberated from behind their plastic sleeves. Books, which she read, were piled on little round tables, and she planned to always have fresh flowers in earthenware vases, but not the ones you buy in supermarkets. But the change she was most pleased with was one that neither Rosie nor Delia would have thought of. She'd had the bowl which Tom put in her suitcase framed. The man in the framers had done a lovely job, positioning it against a very pale pink background, which accentuated the deep pink of the roses, the bowl itself tipped forward to reveal all the interconnected thorny stems in the bottom, which had always been Hope's favourite thing about it. She'd had the mirror in the bathroom taken away and the bowl hung in its place. Which meant, when she showered, she could look at that rather than herself. Although, in a funny way, she thought it was almost the same thing.

It was time. Hope took the Dictaphone over to the bed and sat on the edge. Her finger hovered over the play button, but in the end, what was the point in hiding. Surely that was a lesson she'd learnt. She depressed the button and first Rosie's and then Tom's voices leapt out at her, filling the room so completely she had to shut her eyes.

You seem happy today.
It's freaky. I didn't know you could feel this sort of, I don't know, contentment. Is that the right word?
I don't know, it's your feeling.
I'm not used to feeling safe. Is that normal, do you think?
What, feeling safe?
No, I mean, not ever feeling safe.
No, I think most people feel safe more often than not.
Like, I don't think she'd fuck me over.
No, I don't think she would either.
I love the way she looks at the world. I keep thinking of this night we lay in that field on the other side of the river . . .
Oh yes.
She said the grass looked like the sea. Don't you think that's clever?
It's nice, yes. Go on then, tell me about love, young person.
Oh shit, right. I don't know. It's like . . . sort of you feel full? No, hang on, like you can feel it in your blood. All these little electric particles shooting through you.
That's how you feel when you're with her?

Even when I'm not. Just talking about her now I'm getting these corny tingles. I think about our future sometimes. I've never thought about the future before.

Mmmhmm, go on.

I guess with her, it's like I want to be my best self. Like, you know, there's a point to all this shit.

It's funny, isn't it, how the person we most love is also often the person we most hurt.

She's not going to hurt me.

Well, maybe not. But also, who we choose to love isn't an accident, Tom. It's either someone who will help us forget who we are, or who will make us confront it.

Maybe she's going to do both.

Maybe. But what you have to remember is that humans are endlessly surprising. Sometimes in good ways, sometimes bad. We can't control people, however much we'd like to, or however much we try. Every single thing any of us does is, in the end, of our own making.

The voices stopped, but their presence filled the room so entirely there was very little air left. Hope's hand was against her heart, which was beating out at her like it wanted to break her ribs. A spiralling panic began to wind its way up through her body, contracting her head. She wondered if she might start screaming. Because she couldn't even work out in what spirit Delia had given her the tape. She felt suddenly very cold and crawled under the covers, not capable of taking off her clothes first, pulling them up to her throat instead. It felt like things could go lots of different ways in the next few minutes. There was a version in which she stripped naked and ran screaming around the hotel. A version in which she got in her car and drove to Shadowlands and shot Rosie. Or maybe fucked him. Or didn't bother with the main house and went to Tom and either shot or fucked him. A version in which she laughed at what she'd heard and left the tape by mistake in the hotel because she cared so little. A version where she took it with her and played it to Annie and Sara the next day and they all laughed. But the problem was nothing felt like the right reaction. Nothing felt particularly real.

Hope lay still and made herself breathe deeply, counting and holding her breaths until the throbbing calmed in her ears. And, as her body relaxed, her mind retreated kindly into her favourite fantasy. It was the one she liked to play with when she woke clear-headed into an early morning and it seemed as likely an ending as any, so she went with it.

I, Hope Jenkins, am a good writer, and I manage to write another book that outsells *The Muse*. And not just because I want to go on being paid to make up stories, but also because that will mean I earn enough money to make Rosie and Delia an offer on Shadowlands they can't refuse. They'll need to sell it by then because Rosie obviously will never be published again, and sales of *The Ruined Girl* and *Teresa's Ruin* will fall off a cliff after people begin to move away from those types of stories told by those types of people. In the summer I will carry on Delia's tradition and open the doors of Shadowlands to underprivileged children and let them roam through the space. No one will disturb Tom in the coach house and, tentatively, over time, we'll become friends again. Charlie and his mum, Nat and her family, my own mother, and Sara and Annie will all come to stay all the time. On hot summer days, when I finish writing and step onto the terrace into a dusky, scent-filled evening, I will hear children shouting in the pool, their voices lifting upwards. And in that moment I will be reminded that I might be unreliable and life might be a fiction, but that's okay. Because those are the two things you need if you want to tell a good story. Which is exactly what I plan to do, for ever and ever, happily ever after, the end.

Acknowledgements

At its heart this is a novel about story-telling. I am a storyteller and my biggest thanks, as ever, go to the amazing women who make my stories infinitely better: Lizzy Kremer, Francesca Pathak, Daphne Durham and Brianna Fairman. Thanks also to everyone at DHA, most especially Nicky Lund and Sylvie Rabineau, who take my books and help turn them into insanely exciting film and TV projects. Also thank you to Emma Pidsley for the beautiful cover design. Thank you to all the vital people behind the scenes, all the marketing and sales and publicity (special thanks to Laura Sherlock) departments in Macmillan and Putnam, without whom this book would never be talked about or available in any shops! Thank you to all the bloggers and reviewers who take so much time creating beautiful posts and crafting thoughtful words. And thank you to all the readers – in a world of instant gratification, I am so cheered that so many of us still enjoy the slow, building pleasure of a good book. Finally, thank you to my parents for always telling me stories and opening up the world of books. And to Jamie, Oscar, Violet & Edie, for letting me tell them stories and being my most reliably perfect narrative.

About the Author

Araminta Hall has worked as a writer, journalist and teacher. *Unreliable Narrator* is her seventh novel. Two of her books, *Everything & Nothing* and *One of the Good Guys*, have been Richard & Judy picks. Her novel *Imperfect Women* has been made into an Apple TV series starring Elisabeth Moss, Kerry Washington and Kate Mara. Four of her other novels, *Everything & Nothing*, *Our Kind of Cruelty*, *One of the Good Guys* and *Unreliable Narrator*, are under option and in various stages of production.

She lives in Brighton with her husband and alternating variations of her three grown-up children.

For more information follow her on Instagram @aramintahall or visit her website aramintahall.com

ONE OF THE GOOD GUYS
ARAMINTA HALL

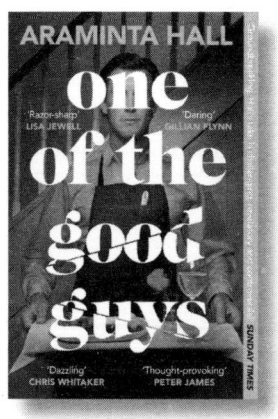

'Razor-sharp, spine-tinglingly convincing and unputdownable' – Lisa Jewell

Cole is the perfect husband: a romantic, supportive of his wife, Mel's, career, keen to be a hands-on dad, not a big drinker. A good guy.

So when Mel leaves him, he's floored. She was lucky to be with a man like him.

Craving solitude, he accepts a job on the coast and quickly settles into his new life where he meets reclusive artist Lennie.

Lennie has made the same move for similar reasons. She is living in a crumbling cottage on the edge of a nearby cliff. It's an undeniably scary location, but sometimes you have to face your fears to get past them.

As their relationship develops, two young women go missing while on a walk protesting gendered violence, right by where Cole and Lennie live. Finding themselves at the heart of a police investigation and media frenzy, it soon becomes clear that they don't know each other very well at all.

This is what happens when women have had enough.